THE BELIAL WARRIOR
A BELIAL SERIES NOVEL

R.D. BRADY

SCOTTISH SEOUL PUBLISHING, LLC

Copyright © 2016 by R.D. Brady

The Belial Warrior

Published by Scottish Seoul Publishing, LLC, Dewitt, NY

All Rights Reserved. No part of this book may be reproduced or transmitted in any form or by any means, electronic or mechanical, including photocopying, recording, or by any information storage and retrieval system without the written permission of the author, except where permitted by law.

Printed in the United States of America.

❦ Created with Vellum

BOOKS BY R.D. BRADY

The Belial Series (in order)
The Belial Stone
The Belial Library
The Belial Ring
Recruit: A Belial Series Novella
The Belial Children
The Belial Origins
The Belial Search
The Belial Guard
The Belial Warrior
The Belial Plan
The Belial Witches
The Belial War
The Belial Fall
The Belial Sacrifice

Stand-Alone Books
Runs Deep
Hominid

The A.L.I.V.E. Series
B.E.G.I.N.
A.L.I.V.E.
D.E.A.D.

The Unwelcome Series

Protect

Seek

Proxy

Be sure to sign up for R.D.'s mailing list to be the first to hear when she has a new release!

CAST OF CHARACTERS

Sparta and Mycenae
    Helen—Queen of Sparta, ring bearer
    Menelaus—husband of Helen
    Hermione—daughter of Helen and Menelaus
    Davos—son of Helen and Menelaus
    Theron—son of Helen and Menelaus
    Castor—Helen's brother, Pollux's twin
    Pollux—Helen's brother, Castor's twin
    Achilles—hero of the Trojan War
    Clytemnestra—Helen's twin sister
    Leda— Queen of Sparta, mother of Helen
    Tyndareus—King of Sparta, father of Helen
    Proteus—King of Pharos, Egypt, father of Barnabus, close friend of Leda
    Barnabus—illegitimate son of Proteus, friend of the Spartan royal family
    Agamemnon—King of Mycenae, Menelaus's brother, Clytemnestra's husband
    Iphigenia—daughter of Clytemnestra and Agamemnon
    Morcant—loyal servant of Clytemnestra

Adorna—loyal servant of Helen
Cergen—Agamemnon's servant from Mycenae
Faenus—Zeus's agent who scoured the globe for him
Claudius - Agamemnon's spy

Troy
Paris—Prince of Troy, scum of the earth
Priam—King of Troy, father of Paris, Cassandra, and Hector
Hecuba—Queen of Troy, mother of Paris, Cassandra, and Hector
Cassandra—sister of Hector and Paris, daughter of Priam and Hecuba
Patroclus—best friend of Achilles
Briseis—spoil of war given to Achilles
Chrysies—spoil of war given to Agamemnon
Hector—brother of Paris, son of Priam and Hecuba
Dugal—Myrmidon, one of Achilles's closest friends
Agaro—Paris's servant

Crete
Minos—King of Crete
Orestes—young boy from Minos's palace
Gaelous—successor to Minos

For the sake of reader understanding, modern geographic names are often used rather than historical ones.

"Indeed, she was proud to have inflamed leaders, to have torn apart the world in war, and to have gained an infamous reputation for her shameful beauty."
—*Joseph of Exeter, Trojan War (AD 1180)*

"Well-behaved women seldom make history."
—*Pulitzer Prize-winning historian Laurel Thatcher Ulrich*

CHAPTER 1

THE CHANDLER SCHOOL FOR CHILDREN, BALTIMORE, MARYLAND SIX MONTHS BEFORE THE WORLD TURNED AGAINST DELANEY MCPHEARSON

The sea of teenage faces looked up at Father Patrick Delaney as he stood in front of the classroom. Most were engaged, although more than a few glanced toward the clock, counting down the last few minutes of the class.

Patrick ignored the clock-checkers and focused on the engaged instead. "The city of Troy and the Trojan War were long believed to be a legend, until the 1870 discovery of Troy in Turkey by Heinrich Schliemann."

A girl with long, dark, wavy hair and bright eyes shot her hand into the air.

"Lou?" Patrick asked.

"But I was reading that Schliemann actually stole the site from a guy named Calvert."

Patrick smiled. Lou Thomas, age sixteen and a Fallen, had taken to history like a duck to water. She was always looking for more reading above and beyond what he assigned in class.

"That's true," he said. "Originally, Schliemann wasn't even interested in Troy. It wasn't until after touring the world that he met up with Frank Calvert and developed an interest in the ancient city. At the time, there were three potential spots in Turkey where Troy was believed to be located: Bunarbashi, Hisarlik, and Alexandria Trois. The third was believed by many to be a long shot. The first, Bunarbashi, was believed to be the most likely. But Frank Calvert, he was digging at Hisarlik. In fact, by the time Schliemann arrived, Calvert had been digging at Hisarlik for seven years. He had dug three trenches and found enough to convince him he was at the correct site."

"So how did Schliemann get the credit?" asked Rolly Escabi, who was sitting next to Lou.

"Well, Calvert told Schliemann all about his finds and beliefs. Within a year, Schliemann was digging at Hisarlik under Calvert's permit and with Calvert's men. When he struck pay dirt, he gave Calvert absolutely no recognition."

"Jerk," Lou muttered.

Patrick smiled. "Yes, I would have to agree."

A hand shot up in the back. Patrick called on Chris Santos.

"So," said Chris, "if they found Troy, does that mean everything that Homer said about the Trojan War was right? Gods, a ten-year war, and cheating Helen?"

A few students chuckled at Chris's last words, and Patrick tried not to cringe. Ever since he had learned that his niece, Delaney McPhearson, had been Helen of Troy in a previous life, he had been researching the historical figure to try and figure out the truth about who she was. And while it was proving a difficult endeavor, he could at least say that history seemed equally clueless when it came to the famous queen.

"Well, that's the question, isn't it?" Patrick said. "But you have to remember that the Spartans never wrote down their own history—the facts were handed down by oral tradition only. And Homer's tale was written five hundred years *after* the Trojan War, so it—like any tale handed down by oral tradition, or like any game of 'telephone'—undeniably changed in that time, no doubt making it more exciting, and less accurate."

Theresa Schneider, who usually sat quietly in the first row, spoke up, her voice shaky. "But the gods—they were *us*, weren't they?"

Now Patrick had the attention of everyone in the classroom. Every set of eyes looked at him, as everyone wanted an answer to that question. Because the Chandler School for Children was no ordinary school. All the students here were either Fallen, or they were nephilim—the child of a human and a Fallen angel. And all of them knew that this was not the first lifetime they had lived—although none could remember those past lives. Now like Patrick, they wondered which moments of history they had been a part of.

The idea of past lives wasn't an easy thing to accept—especially for Patrick, a Roman Catholic priest. But when he was preparing for this lecture, he knew this question was going to come up. He took a breath, sitting on the edge of his desk. "I think it's possible, yes. The gods had incredible abilities—speed, strength—but also some that were supernatural, like the ability to control the weather or move the sun across the sky. I think the stories of the gods, like the tale of the Trojan War, are based in fact but diluted by exaggeration."

The bell sounded, and everyone looked up. "Okay, read chapters seventeen through nineteen by Friday. There will be a quiz."

A groan sounded across the room, making Patrick smile. He gathered his papers and pushed them into his briefcase as the students filed out.

"Father Patrick?"

He looked up. "Lou. What can I do for you?"

"The Bronze Age, it was also called the Age of Heroes, right?"

Patrick nodded. "Yes."

"But there were no women. All the heroes—they were men.

The women were all supporting players. Cassandra, Leda, Hecuba, even Helen—and the whole war's about her."

"That's how it's written, yes."

Lou shot a quick glance behind her, and Patrick had the impression she was checking to make sure everyone was gone before speaking. "Do you think that's true? That the women had nothing to do with the war besides Helen being the catalyst? That it was only the men that were the heroes? I mean, do you really think Helen of Troy was nothing more than the adulteress history has made her out to be?"

As Patrick looked into Lou's eyes, he knew this question was more than just an academic one. All the students knew Laney was the ring bearer, and they looked up to her; Laney was a superhero come to life. Lou felt the same way. But what Lou knew that the others didn't was that Laney had once been Helen of Troy.

"What I said in class was true," Patrick said. "*The Iliad* was written at least five hundred years after the Trojan War. And that was a time when women were viewed as little more than property; a strong woman in any capacity would have been viewed unkindly. And history was written by men. I think Helen is another case of history being particularly judgmental, if not downright inaccurate, about women."

"So you think she was more than an empty-headed woman controlled by her passions?"

Patrick smiled. "Helen is called Helen of Troy but remember, Helen was the Queen of Sparta. Spartan women were not easily fooled, nor did they suffer fools easily, which is what Paris appears to have been. She was known around the world well before *The Iliad* was written. For hundreds of years after her death, there were cults dedicated to her across the Mediterranean. So no, I don't think she was simply a pretty face who launched a thousand ships. I think history has been very unfair to her."

"What do you think the real story is?"

"I don't know. And I don't think we ever will."

Lou grinned. "But it's probably a good story."

Patrick pictured his niece. Time and time again she had faced every challenge presented her, at great cost to herself. And she had kept her morality and her priorities correct through it all —*protect as many as you can and do the right thing, no matter how hard it may be.*

"Yes," said Patrick. "I think whatever the true tale is, it's probably amazing."

CHAPTER 2

SPARTA, GREECE 1450 BC

The sword arced toward her head. Thirteen-year-old Helen of Sparta, heir to the Spartan throne, ducked. She stepped under Lucia's outstretched arm, grabbed it, and slammed her elbow into it, breaking it.

Lucia cried out, and Helen twisted the woman's wrist, stripping the sword from her hand.

Helen let Lucia drop as she scanned the courtyard for more opponents. Not one of the muscular women dressed in leather tunics now stood to face her. A few women held their sides. Blood dotted more than a few faces and bodies. It was Helen who was responsible for their injuries but she felt no guilt.

And none of the women held any resentment at her for being the creator of those injuries. A few even smiled as she scanned across them. Finally her gaze came to rest on the woman in charge of all female training for more than fifteen years. Boudica's body was pure, sculpted muscle. She stepped forward with a rare grin. "Well done, Helen."

Helen straightened, feeling a sense of accomplishment. This

was the annual test of strength: all the women in Sparta without children fought for the honor of top warrior. And for the first time, Helen had won—and she had done so at a younger age than any woman in the rite's history.

A chuckle came from behind her. "Yes. Nicely done, sister."

Helen glanced back. Two eighteen-year-old men—identical from their blond hair, deep violet blue eyes, and muscular builds down to the matching smirks on their faces—lounged against the stable wall.

"What are you doing here?" Helen asked.

Castor and Pollux strode toward her. Helen noticed more than one woman straighten her posture as they approached, and she stifled a sigh. Her brothers could turn fierce warriors into giggling schoolgirls with one look.

Pollux beckoned her toward them. "Come with us."

Helen frowned, but she nodded at her sisters-in-arms and followed her brothers out of the courtyard.

The boys set a quick pace through the busy training grounds. Helen felt proud as she witnessed the Spartan warriors competing in archery, wrestling, hand-to-hand combat, swords, and staffs. These were her people, and they were the greatest fighting force in the world.

The boys turned away from the main house and instead cut through a side gate that led to the hills north of the citadel.

Helen frowned. "Where are we going?"

Castor glanced back. "You'll see."

With a grin, the twins began to race for the top of the hill. Helen sprinted after them. Pollux blurred, and in seconds he was at the top, waving down at them.

"Cheater," Castor yelled, but Helen just dug in and sprinted past her brother with a grin.

"Hey!" Castor yelped, picking up the pace. They reached the summit side by side, both panting.

Even without the sprint, the view would have taken Helen's

breath away. Almost all of Sparta lay spread out before her. The river valley was bounded by Mount Taygetus to the west and Mount Parnon to the east, and behind her, hills reaching thousands of meters high added to the natural boundaries that had kept Sparta from ever being sacked. The Eurotas River itself ran right through Sparta, sparkling in the sun, and providing fresh water to the city.

Castor and Pollux headed to the plateau used for competition, and Helen followed. Ruts in the dirt showed where the chariot races had been held, and the benches were still in place for the crowds. Helen loved watching the competitions. Of course, she would have preferred to compete herself, but her mother never let her. Some nonsense about her being female and it being unfair to the other male competitors. Sparta might know the true value of a woman, but the rest of the world was still outdated in its views.

Her brothers stopped five feet ahead of her and turned their feet braced apart. Helen came up short, glancing between the two of them. Castor threw a sword at her feet.

Keeping her gaze on them, Helen crouched down to pick up the sword. "Okay. So what exactly are we doing?"

"Pollux and I have decided that you need to learn how to fight."

Helen laughed. "Did you guys miss the big announcement? I've just beaten every woman in Sparta."

Castor smiled. "And now we'll teach you to beat every man." He lunged.

CHAPTER 3

HALFWAY BETWEEN PRUDHOE BAY AND BARROW, ALASKA PRESENT DAY

A small man with a large hammer was trying to pound his way out of Delaney McPhearson's skull. Even with the pain, she clung to the memory of the dream. Helen's life played out behind her eyes, and she felt the lingering warmth of her friendship with her brothers, Castor and Pollux. The three of them had formed the triad—just like Laney, Jake, and Henry did today.

It had been a long time since she'd had a dream of one of her past lives, and she had thought she was done with them. Why had those dreams returned now?

A chill ran through her. Pulling her legs to her chest, she curled her arms around them. *Because now it's time for me to fight my own war.* Just the thought of it made the man in her head pound harder.

She groaned, keeping her eyes closed as if somehow she could will herself back into the darkness.

"Ah, you're awake. Lovely."

The voice—educated, amused, and snarky—brought back a recollection of what had happened prior to her blackout. She had been hiding out in Colorado for a month, only to be found by the police. They had surrounded her cabin and opened fire. She would have died—if not for the man who flew in the cabin's back door and covered her body with his own as the bullets flew. That man had saved her life.

Her eyes flew open. She was on a soft leather couch in what looked like a small cottage. A blue blanket lay crumpled beside the couch on an ivory wool rug, and a fire roared cheerily in a stone fireplace to her left. Windows surrounded the place, showing her a lake rimmed in snow on one side and a forest of green on the other. The room opened to a sleek, modern kitchen of white and silver that took up half the space. At the back of the open kitchen were French doors through which Laney could see a light dusting of snow. And Drake—Las Vegas entertainer, consummate egoist, and sabbatical-taking archangel—sat across the room.

She sat up quickly. "You—" A wave of nausea rolled through her. She grabbed her stomach and leaned forward.

"Careful. I'm told that drug packs quite a wallop."

"You *drugged* me. After you knocked me out and kidnapped me," she said, gritting her teeth against the pain in her head and the anger in her chest.

"You say kidnap, I say save. You say drugged and knocked out, I say forced relaxation."

"Drake…" Laney warned. She imagined herself pummeling the archangel. She could not simply order him to do what she wanted like she could with fallen angels. But she was pretty sure a shower of lightning bolts would remove some of his ego.

"There's some water and aspirin on the coffee table," he said.

Laney started to shake her head—but thought better of the idea when pain lanced through her brain. She spied the pills and pulled them to her. She inspected them, noting that they bore the logo of a well-known aspirin.

"Where's the trust?" Drake groused.

Drake stood over by the kitchen counter now sipping from a coffee mug. She hadn't heard him move. "Why are you all the way over there?" she asked.

Drake raised his coffee cup in salute. "Merely staying out of striking range until I assess your mood. I have no interest in marring this beautiful face."

Laney ignored the remark as she swallowed the pills, followed by the water and she said a quick prayer that they worked quickly. She closed her eyes, wishing she could fall back asleep and stay asleep until her head stopped pounding. Better yet, she wished she could wake up to learn that Drake's appearance—and everything about the last few weeks—had all been just a bad dream.

She opened her eyes to Drake's amused grin. *No such luck.* "Is there any coffee for me?"

"Why, of course." Drake poured her a cup.

"How long have I been out?" she asked.

"Almost twelve hours."

"*Twelve* hours?"

Drake shrugged. "The dosage is a little tricky. I may have given you more than recommended."

Laney bit back an angry retort. "Where are we?"

Drake brought over her coffee, placing it on the coffee table. "My cabin," he said.

Laney looked around again. The cabin had some expensive pieces, but it was comfortable, understated. "I expected more mirrors."

Drake laughed and Laney took her first good look at him. Gone were the leather pants and unbuttoned silk shirts he usually wore. In their place were a navy blue wool sweater and sage green corduroys with brown boots. He looked like he had stepped out of a Ralph Lauren photo shoot. His blue eyes were as observant as ever, and his cheekbones just as sharp, but his outfit softened his appearance, making him... attractive. Laney took a sip of her coffee. *There must have been more than painkiller in those pills.*

"And where exactly is this cabin?" she asked.

"Alaska."

Laney jolted. She had been planning on heading to Alaska to hide out.

"See?" Drake said, as if reading her mind. "You and I are not that different after all."

"Did you rent this place?"

Drake shook his head. "It's mine. I've had it for, oh, a hundred years or so."

"Will someone be able to trace it to you?"

"Tsk, tsk. Not born yesterday, remember? Not even born in the last few centuries. The deed to this place is well buried."

"Still, I can't stay here. They'll be looking for me. I need to go." Laney started to stand.

Drake placed his hand on her arm. "Laney, you're safe here. I won't let anyone harm you."

Laney looked into his eyes. At that moment, she saw none of the flashy Vegas entertainer. Instead she saw the man who had come to fetch her in China after Victoria's death, at a time when she had been unable to think clearly. And now the man who had appeared from nowhere in Colorado, saving her life.

Then Drake dropped his hand, and the moment was gone. "Besides, I don't often bring women back to my place. You should feel honored." He wiggled his eyebrows at her.

And… he's back. Laney leaned back against the couch. "It's nice."

Drake gave her a smile. "I'm glad you like it. Now, through that door over there, you will find a bedroom. I took the liberty of picking you up some clothes. And there's an attached bath for you as well."

"What am I doing here, Drake? In the plane you said I needed to learn about my past life. What did you mean by that?"

"All in due time. Now, I think you'll probably feel better after a shower and change of clothes."

Laney wanted to press him, but to be honest her head still felt fuzzy, and a shower sounded heavenly. "Okay. But then we talk."

He tipped his head toward her, a smile playing at his lips. "Whatever you wish, ring bearer."

CHAPTER 4

The shower was glorious. Laney closed her eyes and stood under the scalding spray, trying to wash off the last month. Memories assailed her—memories of how the media had twisted her actions and made her public enemy number one.

But not on their own, she thought with resentment. Samyaza had directed them behind the scenes, guiding how each event should be viewed. Samyaza had also led Laney along and she hadn't realized it until it was too late and Samyaza had managed to turn the whole world against her.

She pictured Elisabeta sitting demurely with Mike Wallace on *The Sunday Report* set, destroying her world and heard her words again. "She's not who the media has portrayed her to be. The world knows she's powerful, but they don't know that she's cruel. She's dangerous."

Laney tightened her eyes against the feeling of betrayal. *All the time I spent risking my life to save people, and Samyaza turned it all around in an instant.*

Ever since that broadcast, Laney had been under siege. Dozens of law enforcement agencies, both at home and abroad, were looking into her, and a warrant had been issued for her arrest. *Warrants*, she corrected herself.

She'd managed to stay ahead of law enforcement for a while, but then she stuck her neck out to save a girl from two perverts, and the Feds managed to track her down. She should have moved on. But she had hated the idea of leaving Drew's cabin.

An image of Patrick, Henry, and Jake sitting at the table in Henry's kitchen floated through her mind. They were the reason she had run. She had wanted to protect them from the danger that was stalking her. She missed them all so much. But nothing had changed. In fact, the events in Colorado had only reinforced the rightness of her decision. It was a miracle she was still alive. If any of them had been with her…

She shook her head as she turned off the shower and grabbed a fluffy white towel. No. Leaving them was the right choice. The safe choice—at least for them.

After drying off, she slipped into the leggings and long sweater that Drake had left for her. She couldn't contain her surprise at his choice. She'd been expecting something a lot tighter, shorter, and flashier, but like the cottage, the clothes he'd chosen were expensive yet understated.

As she dried her hair, she looked around the room. The walls were wood, and pale lacy curtains hung at the sides of the room's only window. A king sleigh bed with an ivory comforter and pale blue sheets stood in one corner, with a trunk at its foot, and a standing mirror occupied another corner. Laney just couldn't reconcile this cozy, quaint place with the flashy Drake.

But what she really couldn't figure out was how he had ended up in Colorado—and why. Twice now he'd shown up when she needed someone. How had he known? And why had he helped her? She knew there was more than flash under the man's skin, despite the image he projected to the world, but he had risked discovery intervening in Colorado. And he'd taken more than a few bullets for her. What was his end game? Was she some sort of archangel mission?

Laney brushed through her red hair and stared at her reflection, as if somehow the woman in the mirror could answer her questions. But her reflection wasn't talking. Which left only one other person.

She laid the brush back on the dresser and headed to the living room. *Time to chat with an archangel.*

CHAPTER 5

Drake heard the hairdryer going in the other room. He headed to the stove and put on the kettle. And he noticed his hands shaking. *I'm nervous. I can't believe I'm nervous.*

He grabbed some mugs from the cupboard and placed them on the counter. He pulled out some lemon biscuits, changed his mind and put them away again, then pulled them out again. *Oh, for God's sake, man, pull it together.* The kettle whistled, and after placing a teabag in one of the mugs, he poured in the water.

The door to the bedroom opened behind him, and he turned, his smirk back on his face. "About time. I thought you were going to use up all the water."

Laney stepped into the room. The deep purple of her sweater brought out the green in her eyes and accentuated the highlights in her hair. But Drake pretended not to notice.

"Any chance I could get a cup?" she asked.

Drake shrugged. "Sure. Help yourself." He walked over to the couch and took a seat.

Laney shook her head as she walked to the kitchen. "You're a real gentleman, Drake."

He said nothing as he took a sip, just watching her move around the kitchen. Something about her being here gave him a sense of contentment he hadn't felt in… Actually, he couldn't even remember the last time he'd felt this content.

CHAPTER 6

As Laney fixed herself a cup of tea and took a sip, she felt a pang of homesickness for her uncle. He always loved a good cup of tea. She turned to Drake, who sat on the couch staring into the fire with a brooding expression. "Drake?"

The brooding look disappeared from his face. "Yes?"

She gestured around the cabin. "You said you'd tell me what this is all about."

He nodded. "Before you woke, you were tossing about. Bad dream?"

"It—I was Helen. Castor and Pollux were going to teach me how to fight better than any man."

"That they did," he said softly.

Laney narrowed her eyes. "What?"

He grinned. "I've read quite a bit of history, ring bearer. Your brothers were very dedicated to their duties."

"Why do you do that?"

"What?"

"Call me ring bearer. That's not my name, yet that's what you always call me. Why?"

Drake looked away.

"Why?" Laney demanded. Something told her the answer was important.

Drake shrugged. "It puts a distance between us. It reminds me who you are and what your job is. It reminds me of the stakes."

He spoke with no hesitation, but Laney knew he hadn't given her the full answer. "I don't understand."

"No, I suppose you don't." He gave her a small smile. "But you will. You just need to remember. Remember who you were and what you're capable of."

"Remember what? Which lifetime?"

"Helen. Helen is the key."

"The key to what?"

"Everything that's happening now."

Exasperation ran through her. "How can the life of a woman who has been dead for thousands of years be related to what's happening now? Samyaza is going to strike. You know that. How could some Bronze Age information help with that? I mean, what I saw earlier—that was just my brothers and I. There was nothing important in it. No key to fighting the Fallen."

"I think you've learned that history is more than your textbooks have explained," Drake said. "Powers have been gained and lost over the millennia, and some of the weapons of old are more powerful than anything you have today."

"Well, if you were around back then, why can't you just tell me whatever it is I need to know?"

"Because I don't know. Only Helen does. It's why you need to remember."

Laney placed her mug on the counter. "I don't think I can. This dream I had just now—it's the first dream I've had about my past lives since… since Mom."

"Ah, but it's not by chance that you had that dream," said Drake.

Laney narrowed her eyes. "Wait—the drug you gave me? It was a hallucinogen?"

"Not exactly. Let's just say it 'opens the gates'—and once they're open, you do the rest."

Laney sighed. "I don't know what you expect of me."

"I expect a great deal. As does the world."

The weight of Laney's responsibility pushed down on her. She turned away.

She felt Drake move to stand behind her. "You've done this before," he said. "You can do it again."

"I don't remember that life. And I can't possibly have had the odds stacked against me like they are now."

Gently he turned her around. "You'd be surprised."

"I can't remember, Drake. I just can't."

"That's where I come in." He smiled at her, and before she could move he plunged a needle into her arm.

"Damn it." Laney shoved him away. She blinked, her vision darkening at the edges, her legs growing weak. "Drake?"

Strong arms wrapped around her. "I've got you. Now sleep. I won't let anything happen to you."

And for some reason Laney couldn't fathom, she believed him. So she stopped fighting the darkness and let it take her away.

"They called me Helen. Let me tell you all the truth of what has happened to me."
 —Euripides, *Helen*

CHAPTER 7

SPARTA, GREECE

Helen's eyes flew open as the heavy drapes in her room were yanked back. Early morning light shone across the room, highlighting the fresco in the floor and the pale salmon of the walls.

Adorna, Helen's servant since she was born, bustled around the room collecting her clothes. "What time did you get in last night? And what were you doing? These clothes are filthy. Is that blood?"

Helen remembered the race through the countryside with her brothers. They had received word that a village had been attacked. But they had been too late to do anything but help the survivors, few that there were.

Helen rolled over and watched Adorna. "We went to the village of Minochus, outside Plataea. They were attacked by the Followers of Zeus."

Adorna stopped and looked at Helen. "Were there any survivors?"

"Not enough," Helen said quietly.

The Followers of Zeus claimed that their attacks were made at the behest of the king of the gods. And as more and more of these attacks were reported throughout Greece, the people responded by increasing their offerings to Zeus at his temples. The number of temples was increasing as well—all in a bid to placate him. But Helen knew that only men, not gods, were responsible for the attacks.

Adorna bowed her head, some of her light brown hair falling forward as she offered a prayer to the gods. Helen didn't. She'd learned long ago that the "gods" were no more than mortals with incredible abilities. Some used those powers for good, but some used them to destroy and take. Not for the first time, Helen wished she had the power to fight them. Yet even with all her lethal skills, she was no match for the Fallen.

"Your father and mother want to speak with you," Adorna said.

Helen sat up in bed. She felt like she'd barely crawled into it before Adorna had woken her. "Now?"

"They've already eaten. They'll be waiting for you in the courtyard when you're done."

Helen grumbled. *Right—father will patiently wait while I eat.*

She hurriedly put on her tunic, relieved that she didn't have to bother with those ridiculous dresses she'd seen the women in Athens wear. But a glance in the mirror brought her up short. There was nothing surprising about her reflection—short blond hair, bright blue eyes, skin turned golden from the sun—but she reached a hand to her cheek, suddenly recalling the face of a woman with red hair and green eyes and pale skin. *Such a strange dream.*

Her hand moved from her cheek to her short hair. The women in Athens have one freedom though that she envied—they were allowed to keep their hair long. All unmarried females in Sparta kept their hair short, and she would not mind, when she was married, being allowed to grow hers out.

"You're going to skip breakfast, aren't you?" Adorna said.

Helen grinned. "You know what father is like if he waits too long."

Adorna fished a peach from her pocket. "Here." She tossed it to Helen, who caught it with one hand.

"You're the best," Helen said, taking a bite.

Adorna snorted, but Helen caught the smile she was trying to hide.

Then Helen was sprinting out of the room and down the hall. In other kingdoms, the sight of the heir to the throne running full out down the marble halls might have been a spectacle, but in Sparta, no one even blinked.

The citadel of Sparta was a square building with long halls that surrounded a large courtyard. The halls were unadorned—in Sparta, money was not wasted on artwork; instead it was put into fortifications and crops—but Helen loved every single stone. As she reached the entrance to the courtyard, she vaulted over a basket left unattended and landed with a smile. The courtyard with its groves of fruit trees and large untouched green spaces always made her smile.

"Helen."

She turned toward her parents. Her mother's red hair shone even brighter in the morning light, and her violet eyes, which Helen's brothers shared, twinkled. Helen's father stood straight and tall, still strong due to his regular sparring matches with his men, all of whom he still could beat—except for her brothers. His hair was dark, as were his skin and eyes. As she had done many times before, Helen wondered how she had come to bear so little resemblance to him.

As she jogged over to them, King Tyndareus said, "We need to speak with you."

"So I hear," Helen planted a kiss on her mother's cheek.

"Good morning, my dear." Leda's smile didn't quite reach her eyes.

Uh-oh.

"Yes, well," Tyndareus huffed, not meeting Helen's gaze. "I have bestowed upon you a great honor."

Helen glanced back and forth between her parents. "And what honor might that be?"

Tyndareus kept his gaze above Helen's head. "You are reaching a marriageable age. In fact, at sixteen, you are older than most married women. That is your mother's doing. If it had been up to me, I would have had you married off years ago. Your sister has been wed for two years now."

Helen's lips tightened at the mention of her sister's marriage.

"Dear," Leda said quietly.

Tyndareus looked at her, then at Helen. "Right. Well, be that as it may, it is now time for you to marry. Your husband will be the king of Sparta—the greatest country to ever exist. No mere man can take that role."

Helen nodded. "I have thought about that. And I believe Achilles will make an excellent king."

Tyndareus frowned. "Achilles? He brings no men, no kingdom, no power to the match. Besides—he is just a boy." He shook his head. "No. I will choose your husband."

Helen's mouth fell open. "*You* will choose?"

Tyndareus nodded. "Yes. I am going to hold a tournament. The leaders of all the greatest kingdoms will attend. They will pay handsomely for the ability to marry you."

"But—"

"Helen, marriage is about politics, not love."

"But—"

"No." Tyndareus glared down at her, his face turning red. Her father always hated whenever anyone disagreed with him. And it only made him dig his heels in more. "This is your duty. If you disobey me on this, you will be cast out. No family, no home, no Sparta."

Leda's eyes grew wide. "Tyndareus, no."

"Yes," he barked, before turning once again to Helen. "You have received much independence, daughter. But in this, you have no choice. It is your duty to Sparta. And you will do your duty. The tournament will commence in six months' time."

With that, Tyndareus strode from the courtyard.

Helen whirled on her mother. "He can't be serious."

"He is, my dear. And there is something else we need to speak about."

Helen backed away, shaking her head. "How could you allow this?"

Leda reached out her hand. "There is a great deal at stake right now. Not just for you, but all of Sparta. I have put off telling you this to give you a chance at a life unencumbered, but now—"

"I don't want to hear this." A vision of her life ruled by someone else flashing through Helen's mind. A husband chosen through a competition? Like she was some sort of prize! She felt ill.

"Helen, you must listen to me."

Helen shook her head at her mother. Here was the woman who had told her to honor strength and compassion above all things. The woman who told her she was the warden of her own future.

The woman who was now selling her off to the highest bidder.

"No, I think I've heard enough," Helen said.

CHAPTER 8

Helen ran out of the courtyard, through the busy kitchens, and out into the horse training area. A few people called out to her but she only gave them a quick nod before hurrying on. And she just wished everyone would disappear and leave her alone.

She felt betrayed, adrift. Why had they raised her to be independent if for one of the most important decisions of her life they were going to allow her no say? They couldn't actually think she'd go along with marrying someone she did not know, someone she did not choose. Then she pictured her father's face and knew he would do exactly that. But how could she allow it? Especially when she already knew who she was going to spend her life with.

She pulled open the stable door. The long path between the twenty stalls lay open, with only three horses in view. The rest were out being trained, and her hopes dimmed, realizing he might be out as well. "Achilles?" she called, her heart pounding in her chest.

Achilles appeared at the end of the long line of stalls, a rake in his hand. Helen's whole body thrilled at the sight of him. Already taller than anyone else in the kingdom, Achilles placed the rake against a stall and strode toward her. He was wearing only a leather skirt, and his well-defined chest was sweaty from raking the stalls. His blue eyes searched her for injury, and she could tell the moment he knew she was physically unharmed. He reached for her, his hand running over her short hair. "Helen? What's wrong?"

She threw her arms around him, not caring who saw. "My father—he's going to arrange my marriage."

"What? To who?"

Helen looked up at him, her heart aching at the sight of the face that haunted her every moment. "I don't know. It's to be a contest. The winner will be my husband."

He smiled then, the cockiness she loved returning to his face. "Then I will win. Helen, the only man who stands a chance of beating me is Pollux, and I'm pretty sure he won't be competing."

Helen shook her head. "You cannot compete. You do not have a kingdom."

"What does that matter?"

Tears trailed down Helen's cheeks. "My father is looking to strengthen our kingdom. He will not let me marry you."

"I will speak—"

"I already have." Helen remembered her father's rage when she had said she wanted to marry Achilles. "He said he—he would disown me. That I would be banished, never to see my family again, never to see Sparta again."

Achilles looked down at her. "He would never do that."

"He would. I am the heir. For ages, Spartan heirs have married rulers of other kingdoms. I have known since I was a child that this was my role. I thought I had accepted it. But now that it is here, now that I have you, I cannot—" She broke off, tears choking her voice.

"Helen of Sparta, no matter what happens, you are mine and I am yours. Do you hear me? You are mine and I am yours."

Helen looked up at him and knew the truth in his words. Ever since she had met Achilles, she had been more alive than she had ever been before. The world had more color, more emotion, and it was all because of him. He was the other half of her soul. Nothing would change that. Nothing could.

She reached up and touched his cheek. "You are mine and I am yours."

Achilles stared into her eyes before lowering his mouth to hers. The kiss started off tender, aching with emotion, but soon it turned heated. Helen placed her hands on his warm flesh. His stomach muscles twitched at her touch as he pushed her back against the wall of the stables.

"Achilles," she moaned.

He trailed kisses down her neck. "You are mine, Helen."

"Always and forever," she murmured, her whole body alive. She slipped her hands lower, and he stilled.

"Helen?"

"You are my all, Achilles," she whispered.

He groaned and pulled her closer. "And you are mine."

CHAPTER 9

Helen lay with her head upon Achilles's bare chest, content to listen to the beating of his heart. They had moved into a stall, where Achilles had laid a blanket over the hay and found another to cover them. Helen would have been happy to stay here forever. He was hers and she was his. That would not change. Their bond was unbreakable.

Achilles leaned down and kissed her on the forehead. "How are you?"

She smiled, snuggling in deeper, loving the feel of him next to her. "Perfect."

"Yes, you are."

Outside the stall, footsteps approached. Achilles and Helen went still.

"When will they arrive?" a voice asked.

"Within the hour," a second voice replied. "The entire town was destroyed. There are precious few left, mostly children."

"Damn the gods. What did Hefgih ever do to them?"

"It must have been a grave insult to rain such destruction."

The voices faded as the footsteps passed by.

Helen looked at Achilles, not needing to say a word. Another town had been destroyed by the "gods." And right on the heels of the attack on Minochus. *Damn them. What I wouldn't give for a way to make them pay.*

Helen sat up. "I need to go. They will need my help with the refugees."

Achilles reached up, cupped the back of her head, and pulled her back to him for a long kiss. Helen wanted nothing more than to turn her back on her duty and stay with him. But the refugees came first.

"I will speak with your father," Achilles said.

Helen shook her head. "No. We will do it together, once the refugees have been settled."

Achilles searched her face. "You're sure?"

Helen nodded. There was nothing she wanted more in this world than Achilles. She would just have to make her father see that he was the one she needed to rule Sparta. Her father would understand. He would have to.

"Together," she promised.

CHAPTER 10

MYCENAE, GREECE

Agamemnon, king of Mycenae, stood on the royal dais. The throne room was a tribute to his power. Trophies from his hunts lined the walls, and the treasures he'd gathered on his many trips around the world were displayed for all to see.

A man of my greatness should not have to deal with a man of no consequence. He stared down at the sniveling coward of a man before him. *Disgusting.* He nodded to the guards. "Take him. Then find his family."

The man flung himself to the floor. "No, King Agamemnon, I am loyal to you and only you. Please. I only took the bread because my son was hungry."

"Then you should be pleased. When he is dead, he will no longer want for food."

Agamemnon's guards yanked the man up by his shoulders.

"No. Please," the man begged as he was dragged off.

Agamemnon dismissed the man from his mind before his cries had even died away.

Menelaus entered the room from the small doorway behind the throne. He nodded down the hall to where the man had been dragged. "What was with all the yelling?"

"Nothing," replied Agamemnon. "A small household matter."

Menelaus' concerned gaze shifted to the hallway,

"It is nothing brother," Agamemnon assured him. "Now, I have news."

"I have news as well. But you first."

The king studied his brother, amazed again at the differences between the two of them. Menelaus was tall and muscular, with hazel eyes, dark hair, and skin constantly bronzed by the sun. His arms were well toned from training and war. Agamemnon's skin, by contrast, had an olive tone, and he had put on some weight in the last few years, resulting in a double chin. But the king knew he was the greatest fighter to have ever lived; he didn't need to prove it on a regular basis, like Menelaus. Besides, Agamemnon's intelligence far outweighed any of his other attributes. And that intelligence had just led him to a plan that would guarantee that the rest of the world would recognize his brilliance for what it was: godliness.

"Have you heard the news from Sparta?" asked the king.

Menelaus frowned. "Sparta? No, I've been in the yard training all day."

Of course you have. Agamemnon smiled. "Well, it is good news. Tyndareus has decided it is time for Helen to marry. In six months' time, he will be holding a competition to find her mate."

Menelaus raised an eyebrow. "Tyndareus is letting a competition determine Helen's husband? What I wouldn't give to have seen how she took *that* news."

Agamemnon frowned. "Why should that matter?"

"Do you *remember* Helen?"

Agamemnon and Menelaus had spent a year in Sparta—a year during which Agamemnon's uncle and cousin had stolen his kingdom from him. Tyndareus had helped Agamemnon wrestle back control. It was then that Agamemnon observed the strength of the Spartans' fighting force—they were as fearsome a group of warriors as any he had seen. Even their women. And Agamemnon knew he needed the Spartan force under his rule.

But Helen… she had done nothing but rub him the wrong way. She was an uppity brat. Agamemnon had seen nothing in the young queen to love, save her status. *That* he had wanted—and had requested.

But Tyndareus had not agreed to his request, and Agamemnon still boiled at Tyndareus's response. He had suggested Helen and Agamemnon's personalities would not suit, as if the personality of a woman was a concern. Then Tyndareus had offered Clytemnestra instead.

Agamemnon had swallowed his anger and accepted the offer. It was important to maintain the link to Sparta. But if Menelaus were to marry Helen, that would bring Sparta under his control—including its powerful army.

"I'm sure she has changed," Agamemnon said. "After all, look at Clytemnestra." Agamemnon and Clytemnestra had now been married for two years, and she had already borne him two sons. It had taken a little time to beat the Sparta out of her, but now she jumped whenever he spoke. She could not do enough to please him.

Menelaus frowned. "Helen and Clytemnestra may be twins, but they were never very much alike. Clytemnestra was always the softer of the two."

Frustration welled up in Agamemnon. Why were they wasting time talking about women's personalities? A woman's personality was the least critical factor in a wife. "Regardless, Helen is now on the marriage mart. And she would be an excellent bride for you."

Menelaus shook his head slowly. "She loves Achilles. She won't agree to marry anyone else."

"She's a woman. She doesn't get a choice."

"You've never really understood her," said Menelaus. "Helen is not like other women. She does what she wants, not what men tell her to do. And Achilles is the man in her heart. He has been for years. She will not agree to marry someone else, not while there is a chance she could marry him."

Agamemnon studied his brother. There was something in Menelaus's voice when he spoke about Helen. And Agamemnon remembered catching his brother staring after Helen on more than one occasion when they were in Sparta. "You love her."

Menelaus shook his head again, but the truth was plain for anyone to see. "No. I barely know her."

Agamemnon snorted. "Brother, if she is the one you desire, I will throw all my power into making sure that a match is made."

Hope sprang across Menelaus's face, but then his face fell. "I do not know if I can attend. An uprising is imminent in Thrace, and I expect to be leaving in a few weeks' time. I have promised my support. It is what I was coming to tell you. I expect it will not be easily settled."

Agamemnon threw an arm around Menelaus's shoulder. "Have no fear, brother. I will go to Sparta in your stead. And I promise, Helen will be your wife. Along with all she brings with her."

"Thank you, brother. You always look out for me."

Agamemnon smiled. "Of course. That's what family is for, isn't it? Now go bathe. Your smell rivals a pig's."

Menelaus laughed. "You've smelled worse."

"Not today." He pushed Menelaus toward the door. "Go."

"All right, all right. I'll just stop in first and see if Clytemnestra is all right."

"Why wouldn't she be?"

"The birth was particularly tough on her this time. She's barely eating."

Agamemnon waved him away. "Fine. I'll see you at dinner."

As Menelaus disappeared down the hall, Agamemnon frowned. He had forgotten about the relationship between Achilles and Helen. That could be a stumbling block to his plans.

And plans he had. Because he was not about to let the might of the Spartan army fall under the banner of any other house but his own.

An idea began to take root in the back of his mind. Achilles was more than he seemed; even Achilles didn't know all that was within him. But that power of his, while useful in a fight, could also be danger to those around him. If Agamemnon could make sure that King Tyndareus saw that…

He turned to his guard. "Find me Claudius."

CHAPTER 11

At the north end of the citadel, the preparations for the refugees were well under way. Helen had jumped into the chaos, helping erect tents and create bedding. She organized the food area and added extra guards to make the refugees feel safe.

A cry went up. "They're coming!"

Pollux and Castor appeared at Helen's side. "Let's go, sis." The three siblings ran to the front gates, which opened just as they arrived.

Ten members of her father's guard entered, and Helen felt the pride she always felt at the sight of them. Strong and tall, they were the best fighters in the world. They were Sparta. But the sight behind them tore at her heart. Children, most with burns and wounds, stumbled along in shock. Some had to be pulled along in carts.

"Damn the gods," Castor whispered.

"We'll damn them later," Helen said angrily. "Right now, we help."

The next hours were a blur of pain and cries. There were dozens of refugees, primarily women and children. Most were injured physically, all of them were psychologically wounded. Some just stared off into space. Other cried, unable to be consoled.

Some of the refugees spoke of the attack. They said that the men who had destroyed their village had claimed to be fighting on behalf of Zeus—and that some of the attackers had the power of the gods themselves.

Helen crushed her fist into her hand. *The Followers of Zeus must pay. This cannot continue.*

One little girl took to following Helen. Her name was Chrythos, and her face had been badly burned. Eventually, Helen got Adorna to take her away and promise to care for her.

When the refugees were largely situated, Helen, needing to get away from the pain and misery, went to stand on one of the balconies overlooking the back hill. It hadn't been hard physical work taking care of the refugees, yet somehow it had made her more tired than a day full of training. She closed her eyes, searching for a few moments of peace, a few moments to shed some of the horror that now coated her like a second skin.

Darius, the head servant, found her too soon. He bowed low as he came to stand in front of her.

Helen sighed. "What is it, Darius?"

"Your mother. She wishes to speak with you."

"Now?"

"Yes. She is on the northern slope."

Helen closed her eyes and blew out a breath. The conversation with her mother from this morning came back to her. That stupid tournament. She did not want to speak with her mother. She did not want to hear all the reasons why she should do as she was told. But there was no point postponing it. "I'll be right there."

Darius nodded. "Yes, my lady."

Helen looked back out at the hill. She wanted to be out there. No, she wanted to be here, but with Achilles's arms around her. Soon. She would go to him soon.

She made her way to the northern slope. She wasn't surprised at her mother's choice of meeting places—Leda preferred to be outside the confines of the wall when at all possible. *Apparently I'm not the only female in the family who doesn't like restrictions.*

Helen found her mother sitting on a rock, watching two hawks soar high above her.

"You took time off for bird watching? That is not like you," Helen said.

Leda turned and smiled. "If only that were all we had to do."

Helen sat down next to her. "I'm sorry I ran off this morning. It's just I can't believe Father is doing this."

"I know how much you care for Achilles. But your father is right—he is not ready to be a king."

Helen turned away. "I do not agree."

Leda sighed. "That is not the reason I asked you to meet with me. Could we put that aside for a moment?"

Helen nodded stiffly. She expected her mother to start talking right away, but instead, she just looked out over the hills. Finally, her mother began. "I have kept much from you, to protect you, to let you live. And at the same time, I have been hard on you. No unkindness has gone unchecked, no vulnerability allowed to go unguarded. I want you to know: there *has* been a reason for it all. And yet now that the time of revelation has arrived, I find myself wanting to give you a little more time."

Leda opened a satchel she held in her hand. "But most of all, I have put off giving this to you." She emptied a ring into the palm of her hand. It was made of a dark metal. Its square face was adorned with two intertwined triangles and set with a jewel in each corner.

Helen wanted to reach for the ring, but something made her clasp her hands behind her back instead. Throughout Helen's life, her mother had told her she had a destiny that would reveal itself in time. She had taught her about all corners of the world and its rich history. She had explained how the gods were not gods, but people with extraordinary abilities. And although her mother had never said it, Helen knew her destiny was somehow entwined with the Fallen.

But there was no joy or even anticipation in her mother's voice—there never had been about this topic. Whenever her mother had spoken of her destiny, there had always been a sadness to her voice, a resignation—as if she wanted to spare Helen what was coming. Helen now had the feeling that once she touched that ring, her whole world would change, and she wasn't sure she wanted it to. "You said you wanted to give me a chance to live. I won't have that when I take the ring?"

"Oh, you will live. You will live more than most. But this ring—it is a promise, a pledge to commit your life to your duty."

"You're not talking about being the Queen of Sparta."

"No. The job of ruling Sparta pales in comparison to the greater duty that you must shoulder." Leda took a breath. "There is more to this world than you realize. There is a power struggle that has been raging unseen for thousands of years. And now, with this latest attack, I fear it is about to spill out into the light. You, my beautiful daughter, are not merely the future queen of Sparta. You are the ring bearer. With this ring, you will have the ability to change the tide of the war to come. You will be the general of the army of the good—if that becomes necessary. And you will lead the fight against our most dangerous foes."

Helen didn't know what to make of her mother's words. "Will I be like Pollux?"

"No. With this ring, you will be able to control the Fallen, the nephilim, the animals of the land, even the weather itself. You will be the most powerful being in the world."

Helen shook her head. The idea of being able to control all of that terrified her. "That is too much power for one person."

Leda smiled. "Which is why it is given to one who understands that. And it is why you were given two people to aid you. Come!"

Castor and Pollux jogged down the hill toward them. Castor grinned at her. "So, you learned the big bad family secret?"

Pollux shook his head. "Ignore him, Helen."

"Your brothers will always be by your side," Leda said. "Together the three of you will accomplish a great deal of good in this world." She eyed her daughter and apparently read the skepticism on her face. "If you accept your destiny."

"Is there someone else who can do this? Who can wield this power?" Helen asked.

Leda shook her head. "No. You are the only one. And you will save a lot of lives, my child. You will fight back the evil forces."

"I'm not sure I'm worthy of this."

Leda took her daughter's hand. "Then trust that I know you well enough to say that you are *more* than worthy. I know what you are capable of. You can do this."

Helen pictured the face of Chrythos, the little girl who had been burned. Someone had done that to her. Someone had decided that that child did not deserve a chance at a good life. Someone claiming to be doing the bidding of Zeus.

"Why are they attacking the villages?" Helen asked.

"They are going after the Fallen," Leda said quietly. "They pursue the ones who are quietly living their lives, drawing no attention to themselves."

Helen knew of the Fallen. She knew certain people were born with exceptional gifts. But she had met only a few who were good, like Pollux, and most she saw only through the destruction they left behind. The idea that some lived their lives without causing harm, it was shocking.

"Why are they targeting the quiet ones?" Helen asked.

"We don't know," Pollux said. "But more Fallen will continue to engage in acts just as cruel."

"Unless someone does something about it," Castor said.

"We have identified the direction in which these latest attackers fled," Leda said. "Their trail is easy to follow. They are heading toward Plataea. All attackers seem to come from that region."

Pollux nodded toward Castor. "We're going after them. We could use some help."

Helen stared at the ring her mother held out to her. *This will continue. More children will be scarred like Chrythos. Unless I do something about it.*

She reached out and curled her hand around the ring. "I accept."

CHAPTER 12

Her brothers had horses waiting at the top of the hill. Helen didn't even have time to stop back at the citadel and tell Achilles where she was going but her mother promised to speak with him.

Helen and her brothers pushed the horses as much as they dared and reached the destroyed village at dusk. They picked up the trail and continued as long as the light allowed them. They had hoped they would overtake them before they reached Plataea but that did not happen. Instead, they followed the trail for a week without any sight of them.

The whole trip Helen's mind replayed what her mother told her about the ring. It allowed the wearer to control the weather, animals, and the Fallen themselves.

It seemed incredible. But on the long journey, Helen had slowly been testing the ring. And she could touch the edges of power. She focused on the tendrils of power and at one point, even sent a lighting bolt to the path directly in front of her brothers. All the horses had reared back and her brothers glared back at her.

Helen put up her hands. "Sorry, sorry. Just seeing what I could do."

"Well, try not to get us killed in the process," Castor grumbled.

Helen smiled weakly at them. But the fact that she had called down the lightning amazed her. She remembered wishing she had the power to fight the Fallen and now she did.

Now, Helen and Castor crouched behind rocks overlooking the attackers' camp. Helen had felt the tingles as they had approached—the same tingle she felt near Castor. Fallen were there—at least two. It was good that Pollux had stayed back, not wanting the men to sense him.

"So, little sister," Castor whispered with a grin. "You ready to try out your fancy little ring?"

While they had been spying on the camp, the men around the campfire had been laughing about their attack on the village—mimicking the cries of the villagers and exalting in their abuse of the women. Helen ran a finger over the ring. "More than ready."

"Let's go." Castor slipped from behind the rocks, his bow at the ready. He let off two arrows, each finding its mark.

Helen stood as well. Her gaze was focused on the men, but her mind was calling on the skies. Lightning bolts blasted down on either side of the camp. *Damn it.* She had been aiming for the two Fallen—who were now sprinting right for her.

Pollux appeared from the shadows, tackling one of the Fallen. But the other Fallen moved so fast, Helen didn't even see him until he was suddenly in front of her. He grabbed her by the throat and picked her up off the ground. Her feet kicked uselessly.

"Release me," she rasped.

The man's eyes grew wide, but he lowered her to the ground and released his hold.

Helen swallowed. "On your knees."

The man knelt.

Helen's anger simmered. This was one of the men who had

laughed around the fire. She had heard him speak gleefully of having taken the innocence of a child—and then having taken that child's life.

Helen pulled her sword from her scabbard, aimed for the man's neck, and swung.

CHAPTER 13

Helen stood back with her brothers, her mind still reeling. She had struck the Fallen in the neck, but he had not died. Instead, he had healed. So she had commanded the two Fallen to stay on the ground, immobile, while she helped her brothers finished off the others.

When only the two Fallen were left, Helen questioned them. Unfortunately, although she could command them to answer her questions, they did not seem to know much. Zeus had visited them originally and recruited them into his ranks. From that point on, he sent notes to Plataea via falcon with the next target.

"Who is Zeus?" Pollux demanded.

"The—the king of the gods," the Fallen answered.

"No, who is he *really*?" Helen asked. But it was obvious the man didn't understand the question.

Pollux shook his head. "He doesn't know anything."

Helen knew her brother was right. "Fine. So how do we kill them?"

Pollux grimaced. "They must be taken apart."

Helen's gaze flew to her brother's face. "What?"

Castor shrugged, not meeting her gaze and she could feel his distaste at the task to come. "We have found no other way. Burning does not work, nor does any wound. Dismemberment is the only way to assure they die." Seeing the look on Helen's face, he added, "We have this part, sister. No need for you to be part of this."

Helen was not squeamish, but she didn't relish the idea of dismembering her enemies. She looked at the Fallen. "If we let you go, will you still follow Zeus's bidding?"

"Yes," the man said defiantly.

"I could order him not to speak," Helen offered.

Pollux shook his head. "We don't know if he would obey that command indefinitely. We cannot take the chance."

Helen pictured all the refugees she had seen over the last year. She remembered the men's violent boast as they sat around the fire. Then she nodded at Pollux. "Do it."

CHAPTER 14

SPARTA, ATHEN

Achilles walked down the long stable. After Helen had left, Queen Leda had found him and explained that Helen, along with Castor and Pollux, would be away for some time. Then she had asked him to join her for a walk. To Achilles's surprise, they had walked and talked for hours. Achilles didn't know how it had happened; he rarely spoke of himself to anyone, yet he had found himself speaking to the queen of things he'd shared with very few. There was just something so very familiar about her. And when he had walked her back to the front gates, she had gotten him to promise that he would come talk to her if he had any problems. Achilles had taken it as a good sign. Perhaps the queen was in support of him marrying Helen.

But now it was two weeks later, Helen was still gone, and Achilles was unsettled.

He knew he was being ridiculous. Helen had responsibilities. But couldn't he have gone along? There was nothing tying him here. And he knew they were mixing it up. He longed for a good fight. It had been ages. Truth was, he was going stir crazy.

"Now there's a man who looks like he could use a good drink."

Claudius grinned at Achilles from the doorway of the stable. He was much shorter than Achilles, which made him seem much younger, even though the two men were about the same age. Claudius had only been working at the stables for a week now, but he had spent the entire time chatting, telling Achilles of his adventures around the world and pestering Achilles to share his own. So far, Achilles had stayed silent, turning down all the man's offers for friendship—but right now, the idea of losing himself in a few drinks sounded just about perfect.

He clapped the small man on the shoulder. "You know what, Claudius? For the first time, you might be right."

CHAPTER 15

It was a long, grueling trip back to Sparta. A storm swept in from nowhere, forcing Helen, Castor, and Pollux to take refuge in a cave for two nights. Then the wet ground sucked at the horses' hooves, slowing their travel even more.

But at last, the lights of the citadel bloomed brightly ahead. Helen, Castor, and Pollux grinned at one another and picked up their pace. Helen's heart skipped a beat. *Home.* Sparta was in her bones. Sparta was her life.

And Sparta also meant Achilles. She yearned to see him. And with the ring and her new abilities, she had convinced herself that she would be able to marry him. She would *make* her father see reason.

The citadel walls came into view. Torches blazed on either side of the main gate. Helen glanced to the parapet, where guards always stood watch over the surrounding countryside. But there were no guards there now—the parapet was empty. No call of greeting sounded to welcome them home, and the gates did not open as they approached.

"Pollux?" Helen asked.

Pollux was already off his horse. He leaped high, his hands just reaching the top of the gate. He swung himself over and disappeared from view. A moment later, the gates opened. Helen and Castor dismounted and led their horses inside.

Helen could hear voices beyond in the training yard but the courtyard was empty and it was never empty. The hair on the back of Helen's neck rose. A figure rounded the side of the building and hurried toward them. The siblings had their swords drawn instantly, but quickly lowered them as they saw it was only Adorna.

She rushed towards them, her usual unflappable demeanor gone. "Thank the gods you've returned. You must come quickly." She hurried towards the front doors without waiting for a reply.

"What is it?" Helen asked, reaching her side.

Adorna looked at Helen with pity. "It's Achilles."

Before Helen could ask questions, a yell rang out from deeper inside the citadel. Pollux ran ahead and shoved open the doors—but instead of swinging wide, the doors crashed to the ground.

Pollux jumped back. "I didn't shove them hard enough for that."

Adorna plowed ahead. "No—Achilles did."

Achilles's voice echoed through the citadel. "Where is she?"

Helen gasped. Achilles sounded angry and in pain. She sprinted forward.

"Helen, wait!" Pollux yelled.

Helen ignored him—but she didn't make it far before a pain sharper than she'd ever felt rolled over her. With a gasp, she fell to her knees.

Castor was at her side immediately. "What is it?"

"The awareness—but it's greater than anything I've felt before."

"Helen!" Achilles yelled again.

Helen's head jerked up. She knew the feeling of awareness had come from him—but why was it so strong? She had always known Achilles was a Fallen, even without the ring; she'd seen him fight with Pollux. Was it the emotion between them that made the feeling so strong?

Regaining her feet, Helen ran down the hall turning to the door that led to the training grounds. Instead of a door, she was confronted by empty space.

The doors lay shattered on the ground beyond it. Shaken, Helen quickly crossed the destroyed entryway, stunned by the sight in front of her.

Achilles stood in the middle of the training yard, his chest heaving, his hair wild around his face, turning from one side to the other. Three arrows were embedded in his chest, and blood poured down his sides. Guards two deep surrounded the boundary of the yard, clearly keeping their distance. The ground in between them and Achilles was littered with broken bodies.

"Where is she? You are keeping her from me!" Achilles shouted. He lunged at a guard with astonishing speed and flung him through the air. Men scrambled to get out of the way as the guard flew across the yard and crashed into the wall of the citadel.

"Achilles!" Helen yelled.

Castor grabbed her arm before she could step forward. "Helen, stop."

Achilles blinked at her as if he thought she was a mirage. "Helen?"

"He will hurt you," Castor hissed.

"I am the only one he will not hurt." Shaking Castor off, she approached Achilles slowly, if she were approaching a wounded animal. Pollux and Castor followed right behind her.

"Helen?" Achilles asked again.

"It's me," Helen said. She shook her head at an archer taking aim.

Achilles's shoulders drooped. "You were gone for so long."

"I'm sorry. There was much to do." Helen stepped closer.

Achilles's words slurred. "I couldn't find you." He swayed on his feet.

Helen inched closer. What had happened here? Was he drunk? Had he truly gone mad? She tried to keep her voice calm while inside she whirled. "It's all right. I'm here now."

"It's all right," he echoed. Then he crashed to his knees.

With a cry, Helen ran forward. Her heart broke at the sight of Achilles like this.

He looked up at her with tears in his eyes. "I couldn't find you."

Helen dropped to her knees in front of him. Gently she wiped a tear from his cheek. "It's all right now. I'm here. Everything is all right."

Achilles nodded, then closed his eyes and pitched forward. Pollux grabbed him before he could land on Helen.

Castor took Achilles's other arm. "We'll take him."

"But—"

"We'll make sure he is taken care of and that he hurts no one else," Castor said.

Helen nodded numbly. She watched her brothers carry Achilles between them until they disappeared around the side of the stables.

Then she became aware of the silence around her. She looked around at the faces of the Spartan warriors who encircled the yard. The emotions on their faces ranged from anger to confusion to pity and fear. She looked at the ground—at Achilles's victims—and she understood why.

Then one of those victims began to stir. And the sight of him slammed the door on any plans she had made on the long ride home from Plataea. It was someone she recognized well.

Her father shook his head and rolled to his knees.

As Helen watched him she knew that whatever fantasy she had concocted about her and Achilles had been destroyed as thoroughly as the doors she had walked over on her way in.

CHAPTER 16

SIX MONTHS LATER

The sound of people walking down the hall could be heard through the door. Helen had been listening to the footsteps since before dawn, guessing each time who it was and what they were up to. And when she didn't hear any footsteps, she listened for conveyances. At one point she heard what she thought might be some minstrels or acrobats, judging by the oohs and aahs of people below. But no matter what she heard, Helen did not get out of bed. She just lay there wishing she had more time.

A knock sounded at her door before it was pushed open. Adorna spied her in bed as she bustled in, a gown over her arm. "Ah, good, you're awake. It's an important day."

Helen groaned. "Don't remind me."

Adorna disappeared into the bathing chamber and then reappeared without the gown. She started straightening up the room, humming as she went. Adorna clearly did not fear disturbing the future queen. Helen wasn't sure Adorna feared anything.

"Most girls would be honored to have dozens of men fighting for her hand," Adorna said.

Helen rolled her eyes. "Yes, because they all fell madly in love with me before they even laid eyes on me."

"Is that self-pity I hear?"

Helen sat up and swung her legs over the side of the bed. "No, simply an observation."

"Well, observe your way to the bathing room."

"Yes, Adorna," Helen said sweetly, earning a laugh from Adorna.

But Helen's smile dropped as soon as she closed the door behind her. Today was when the first of the guests for the competition arrived, and Helen wanted nothing more than to hop on a horse and race as far away as she could. *But that is not what we Spartans do. We do not run from problems. We charge straight at them.*

She glanced at the long, yellow dress with disgust. *Then again, no one said I needed to rush.*

Helen took her time bathing trying to keep her mind blank but the images of Achilles seeped in. After the destruction in the training yard, the king had not listened to Helen's pleas or even Leda's. "He will never be king of Sparta," he had told Helen. "Never." And he had banished Achilles before Helen could even speak with him.

Helen had tried to find a way to explain Achilles's behavior. She knew something had been done to Achilles that night—for she had never seen him behave like that before or since. After he returned to his senses, he told Pollux that he had been drinking with a man named Claudius, but that he was sure he was not drunk—that in fact he'd had very little to drink. And suspiciously, Claudius, who had arrived only a week earlier, had disappeared that very night. Helen had dispatched men to track him down, but they had all returned empty-handed. And thus Helen's fate had been sealed.

So Achilles was gone, and she was to be married to someone

else. Duty trumped love. As a Spartan, she knew that better than most. So she had thrown herself into her training, honing her skills as a ring bearer. She had tracked down and killed both men and Fallen who were preying on innocents. She had even managed to drum up a rainstorm for nearby lands on the edge of drought—only to be chagrined the next day when the people loudly credited Zeus's compassion for the rains.

And while she worked and trained, she studiously avoided thinking of Achilles. She walled him up in a corner of her mind. Until last night, when he had slipped into her dreams. And now he plagued her waking thoughts.

Enough. He is gone. And this is your duty. Resigned, she stepped from the tub. She put on the flowing pale yellow gown that waited for her. Her legs could move freely enough, as long as she didn't have to run or fight. But she supposed with a sigh she would not have to do either today.

When she returned to the bedroom, Adorna, who was making the bed, stopped, her mouth falling open. "You look beautiful."

Helen looked at herself in the mirror, as Adorna walked over and placed her hands on Helen's shoulders. Adorna's brown hair had begun to gray, her skin had more wrinkles than just a year ago, and her shoulders had even begun to stoop, making Helen feel taller and more aware that time was passing quickly. But Adorna's brown eyes and no-nonsense approach to life hadn't changed.

And now Adorna looked at Helen with understanding—but also conviction. "I know it is not what you want. But it is the duty of the future Queen of Sparta."

Helen placed her hand over Adorna's and stared at their reflection. "I know. But it would be nice if I got to choose my husband for reasons other than his political connections."

Adorna smiled. "You mean for his broad shoulders?"

Helen sighed. "Might be better than the size of his holdings."

Adorna tugged Helen away from the mirror. "Come on. A good breakfast, and all will be right with the world."

Helen let herself be led outside. She tried to sound cheerful as she replied, "I'm sure you're right."

Straightening, she blew out a breath, imagining what her parents would say about her self-pity. *I am the future Queen of Sparta. I will do whatever is best for my people.* But a small corner of her mind still asked, *But wouldn't it be nice if I could choose what was best for me instead?*

CHAPTER 17

Leda stood on the balcony, overlooking the grounds. Their visitors had begun arriving three days ago, and tomorrow the contests would begin—contests of strength, dexterity, and cunning.

An arm slipped around her waist. Tyndareus smiled down at her. "It will be fine."

Leda clasped his arm. "I wish none of this were necessary. Achilles—"

Tyndareus's mouth tightened. "Enough. The matter is settled. He is no more than a raging beast. He is not worthy of the Spartan title, never mind worthy to be its king."

Leda shook her head. She knew Achilles had been drugged. Helen knew it as well. But Tyndareus would not accept it. And as he had been among those so easily defeated by Achilles, his pride had played no small part in his decision to ban Achilles. Tyndareus was a good man but he was a product of his time. And in this time and place, the preferences of women did not count against the preferences of men.

But Leda knew how much Achilles loved her daughter. And with all that was to come in Helen's life, she had wanted her to have a husband who would always be in her corner. Achilles, though, was gone and Helen was heartbroken, though she tried to hide it. The only good to come from the whole situation was that Helen had come up with some possible new solutions to the Fallen problem. She now had alchemists trying various poisons to see if any could incapacitate a Fallen for an extended period of time, and she was also developing an idea for a containment unit.

Oblivious to his wife's thoughts, Tyndareus gestured to the land in front of them. "I know Helen is hurt. But with her hand comes all of Sparta. And the rumors of her beauty and strength have stretched across the world. She is a prize."

Leda narrowed her eyes. "She is a woman, not a trophy. And I wonder how pleased these men will be when they realize just how powerful she truly is? No man wants to take on a wife who can beat him in a fight."

Tyndareus's hazel eyes twinkled. "I seem to recall one who did not mind."

Leda smiled. "Spartan men are more evolved. They have a strength of character others lack."

"So do Spartan women. She will be fine. She is your daughter, after all."

Leda's smile faltered, but she only squeezed her husband's hand. She turned her gaze to where the flags of the differing kingdoms who were fighting for Helen's hand were raised. *That is why I'm worried*, she thought. *I know what is to come.*

She pictured her beautiful, headstrong daughter. *I'm sorry, Helen. I wish I could do more.*

CHAPTER 18

Helen had been a dutiful host for three days, smiling at guests and speaking when required. But every chance she got, she left for a run or a hard ride on her horse. Castor or Pollux always found her—and he would stay with her until she knew she needed to return. But those little bursts of freedom were needed to keep the feelings of suffocation at bay.

Her mother knew she was disappearing, but she had said nothing to her father. In fact, she had covered for her. And Helen loved her all the more for it.

The competition was now set to begin in two days, and hundreds of guests had already arrived. But none of those arrivals had elicited the same anticipation and dread as the one she was waiting on now.

Her twin sister, Clytemnestra, was finally coming home.

It had been three long years since Helen had laid eyes on her, and all the doubts from their last conversation flew through her mind. Had Helen pushed too hard? Not hard enough? Should she have said nothing? But how could she in good conscience have allowed her sister, her twin, to marry Agamemnon without first voicing her concerns?

Trying to push away the memory of the scene, she closed her eyes, but that only brought it out in vivid detail.

The sisters stood in the room they had shared since they were babes. They were identical from toes to face, except for their hair—Clytemnestra's was darker than Helen's. And Helen had often thought that Clytemnestra had a softness Helen lacked. Sometimes that softness angered her—Spartans were not meant to be soft—but at other times, she envied it.

The Clytemnestra standing in front of her now, though, showed no sign of that softness. Her arms were crossed and her chin was held up defiantly. "I am marrying Agamemnon."

Helen was unable to believe her sister could agree to such a match. "You cannot be serious."

"I am serious. He is a strong man and a king. And I will be queen."

"Yes, but he is not a good man. I worry how he will treat you."

Clytemnestra waved away Helen's concerns. "You worry too much. And you don't know him. He was a child when he was here. I'm sure he's changed."

"People don't change—not who they truly are."

Clytemnestra narrowed her eyes. "Are you worried for me, or are you jealous?"

Helen reared back. "Jealous? Of what?"

"That I am getting married before you. That I too will be a queen."

"I—You know that's not it. I want you happy."

"No, you want me second. Hidden behind the most beautiful woman in the world."

"We are twins! If I am beautiful, then so are you."

"But people don't write odes to my beauty, do they? They don't talk of me in foreign lands as if I am a gift from the gods."

"That has nothing to do with me. If I weren't the heir, they would not even look at me."

Clytemnestra went still, her voice quiet. "The way they don't look at me?"

Helen's mouth fell open. "No. I didn't mean that. You know that."

Clytemnestra shook her head. "No. All I know is that I am happy. And I am to be married. And you are making this about you."

Helen reached out a hand, but Clytemnestra slipped out of her reach. "No. If you cannot be happy for me, then you cannot be there for me. You are not invited to my wedding. You are my sister no longer."

And she slipped from the room.

In the years since that day, Clytemnestra had birthed two children, with a third on the way, and still, Helen had not seen her. Helen had sent letters begging her sister to speak with her, but she never received a reply. She missed Clytemnestra so much. She loved her brothers, but there was something about Clytemnestra that filled a space that neither brother could touch.

But Clytemnestra was finally coming home. Helen didn't know if she should hope for a reconciliation or prepare herself to be treated coldly. The uncertainty was adding to her nervousness over this whole ridiculous affair. She anxiously paced the length of the balcony that ran across the front of their home. "Where is she?"

Castor grabbed her around the waist. "Wearing a hole in the floor will not make her appear any faster."

Helen reached down and grabbed one of his legs from between hers. He went down with a yell, and avoided smacking his head on the floor only thanks to Pollux's quick shove of a pillow underneath him. Pollux raised an eyebrow. "Really? Is that the behavior of a future queen?"

She smiled sweetly at him. "It is when the future queen has annoying brothers."

Adorna appeared in the doorway. "Your sister's carriage comes, if you three can quit behaving like barbarians long enough to greet her."

Helen ran to the edge of the balcony, leaning over to see the bend in the road. Sure enough, a caravan was headed toward them. It could only be Clytemnestra; very few of the guests were allowed to reside in the house, and all of them had already arrived..

Butterflies raced through Helen's stomach, and she gripped the bannister tightly.

Pollux stepped up next to her. "It will be all right."

"What if she hasn't forgiven me?" The fight with Clytemnestra played through her mind once again. "She said I am no longer her sister."

"She didn't mean it. She knows you only said those things out of love."

"Maybe I was wrong. Maybe he is not as bad as—"

Pollux took her hand. "We all know who Agamemnon is. Father never should have let her marry him. Just be there for her if she needs you."

Helen nodded, clasping her brother's hand.

"Let's go." Pollux tugged her back inside and down the stairs to the front door. Pollux had already run ahead. A guard opened the door for them.

Helen held her breath, searching inside the conveyance for any movement. Then a hand appeared on the edge of the door, and Clytemnestra's face appeared.

Helen gasped. Her sister was so thin, and she had dark circles under her eyes.

Helen was moving before her sister could climb completely out. But Pollux got there first. He ushered the servant away, taking Clytemnestra's hand and helping her from the carriage.

Clytemnestra smiled, tears shining in her eyes. "Pollux."

Helen hung back, not certain what to do or to say.

Pollux hugged her carefully, as if he too realized how fragile she was. Then Castor was elbowing Pollux aside. "Save some of that for me."

Clytemnestra laughed as Castor engulfed her in a hug.

The brothers stepped back, one on each side of Clytemnestra, giving Helen her first full look at her sister. Her heart ached. *She looks so alone.* She examined Clytemnestra's eyes for some sign of how she felt.

Clytemnestra gave her a tentative smile, but it quickly dimmed. "You were right, Helen," she said softly. "You were right." She let go of her brothers and held out her arms to Helen, who ran forward and pulled her sister to her.

Clytemnestra's shoulders shook. "I have missed you so much, sister."

Helen said nothing; tears clogged her throat. She just held Clytemnestra tighter.

They managed to get Clytemnestra up to Helen's room without her being seen by any of the other guests. It would not do for tales of Clytemnestra's crying to make their way back to Agamemnon. Helen put her brothers on guard outside the door, banning anyone from entering, then curled up with her sister in bed, like they had done so many times when they were growing up.

"Tell me," she said simply.

And Clytemnestra did. Helen's heart broke at the loneliness in her sister's voice as she spoke of her treatment at the hands of Agamemnon. And the longer her sister spoke, the more Helen's anger grew.

"Do not go back to him," Helen said when her sister was done. "Stay with me."

Clytemnestra shook her head. "I can't. He will take the boys from me. I will never see them again. He has already threatened to do so. I cannot leave my children unprotected against him. Think of the men they would become. No. I must go back."

"Is there anything good there? Anyone who looks out for you?"

"Menelaus does. Agamemnon does not treat me badly in front of him. It is peaceful when Menelaus is staying with us. And he is a good man. He asks after my comfort."

Helen said a little thanks for that small kindness. "But what can I do? There must be something."

"Be my sister. Be my friend."

Helen clasped her hand. "Always."

∽

EVENTUALLY, Clytemnestra fell asleep in Helen's room. She was obviously exhausted, and not just from the journey—her whole life seemed to be weighing her down. And Helen couldn't help but notice the bruises around Clytemnestra's wrists and along her arms.

Helen stayed with her as long as she dared, but she knew her absence would be noted soon. So with promises from her brothers that they would not leave Clytemnestra's side, she made her way down the hall.

But instead of turning right, toward the staircase that would lead her outside, she turned left and headed for the library. She needed a minute alone after hearing of the misery of Clytemnestra's life, and the library was off limits to guests. She hoped it would give her solitude.

She opened the door and breathed a sigh of relief at the sight of the empty room and a comfort at the familiarity of the space. Books lined all the walls and two long tables dominated the middle of the room. Dotting the space were also busts of Spartan ancestors on pedestals.

She moved to an open window, where she could spy on the events outside without being seen. In the distance, tents had been erected for the guests. The gates were open and people were coming and going. The smells from the kitchen were mouth-watering, and there was an excitement in the air.

But all she could think about was whether or not Clytemnestra's fate was to be hers as well. Would her future husband also try to make her a punching bag? *My whole life, everything I've done, all my learning, all my training—and I've been reduced to a prize. Like Clytemnestra, I'll be used as a tool to solidify an alliance.*

Helen tightened her fists. She had been raised to view herself as the master of her own fate—as a woman who made decisions and followed them through. Now her parents had taken that from her.

Above one of the tents she could see the flag from the house of Pelion. She shuddered at the idea of being tied to their eldest son, Helarchus. The man rarely bathed, and he ate like he would never see food again. Rumor was he liked his dogs more than any humans. And only chance would determine whether or not she ended up with someone like him.

She looked over the other tents, at the flags of all the houses flying high. Among them, there was no one that she could imagine sharing her life with, her bed with.

Unbidden, an image of Achilles appeared in her mind. Crushing her fist into her hand, she shut her eyes against the image, but it didn't help. She had not heard from him in the six months since he had been banished, nor was it likely she would ever hear from him again. She had thought that her heart would harden to him—had hoped it would—but the truth was, he would always have a place in her heart, no matter the outcome of this ridiculous competition.

She pulled on the chain around her neck, the one on which she kept her ring, hidden in the bodice of her dress. She was tempted to put the ring on her finger. She could call down a lightning strike or a ferocious rainstorm. Then she could claim the gods were against the idea of this competition.

But her mother would know. And besides, what good would it do? She could never marry Achilles, so did it really matter whom she married?

Behind her, the door to the library opened. Helen dropped the ring so it was hidden once again. She had hoped for a little longer on her own.

Agamemnon stepped into the room. His purple cape blew out

behind him as he strode toward her. "Enjoying the view? All these men running around trying to impress you?"

The bruises on Clytemnestra flashed through Helen's mind, along with a sincere dislike for the man in front of her. But Helen made sure to keep her face impassive. "My father decided on this approach, not me. Now if you'll excuse me."

Agamemnon put out a hand to stop her. "We need to speak."

Helen avoided his outstretched hand with a glare. "Do *not* touch me."

For a moment, the real Agamemnon glared back at her, but the angry expression was quickly covered with a polite facade. "Of course. I would never dream of touching a daughter of Sparta."

"Really? Then perhaps you could explain the bruises on my sister."

Agamemnon shrugged. "Your sister is extremely clumsy, especially when she is pregnant. It must be all the extra weight."

Remembering her sister's gaunt frame, Helen rolled her hands into fists. It required an extreme act of control to keep herself from hurting this man. "What do you want?"

"To discuss your future."

Helen raised an eyebrow. "And why is that a concern of yours?"

"We are linked by marriage. Of course it's of concern to me."

Helen scoffed. "Right. What do you *want*, Agamemnon?"

"I want you to marry Menelaus."

Helen stepped back in surprise. "Menelaus? He's not even here, is he?"

"No. He is fulfilling an obligation in Thrace."

Helen shook her head. "Then what are you talking about?"

"I will act in his stead."

Helen raised an eyebrow. "*You* are going to compete?" Agamemnon's fighting prowess had been legendary at one point, but she had not heard of him fighting in the last few years. And judging by the look of him, he hadn't spent much of that time training, either.

"Of course not," he growled. "I will have Ajax the Greater fight on Menelaus's behalf." There were two Ajaxes, the greater and the lesser. The Greater was an incredible fighter—and a Fallen. Helen knew he would easily win any challenge placed before him.

Helen studied Agamemnon. The man's desire for power had been stamped upon his frame from a young age. "You want my army," she said softly, realizing his angle. "It will never be yours. Spartans belong to no man, and certainly not to you." She started to walk past him.

Agamemnon reached out a hand. His fingers had barely touched her arm when she grabbed his wrist and twisted it ninety degrees. "I said, *do not touch me*," she spat through gritted teeth. She was shaking, she wanted to hurt him so badly. She shoved him away before she gave in to the impulse.

Agamemnon held his wrist and glared at her. Anger came off him in waves. "Enough with the hiding behind words. You *will* marry Menelaus."

Helen laughed. "You're insane."

"No. I am your sister's husband," he said softly.

Helen narrowed her eyes. "What does *that* mean?"

Agamemnon smiled. "Your sister is so fragile, isn't she? It's hard to believe she's Spartan. And this pregnancy, it has been difficult. Women often die in childbirth, you know. I wouldn't be surprised if she was one of them."

"You wouldn't dare."

Agamemnon met her gaze. "Try me."

The air between them was filled with anger and promises of violence—on both sides. Helen imagined punching this awful man in the face over and over again until he was a bloody mess. Only her fear of what would happen to Clytemnestra stayed her hand.

"I'll sweeten the pot," said Agamemnon. "If you agree to marry Menelaus, Clytemnestra can stay here for the remainder of her pregnancy. And she will be free to visit you as often as she likes. I have my boys; I don't need her anymore anyway."

Helen rolled her fists.

"And if you don't agree... well, accidents happen, don't they?"

Helen looked into Agamemnon's face. She knew he would kill Clytemnestra—and there would be nothing she could do about it. "Your man will still have to win," she said. "And there is also the matter of payment."

Agamemnon smiled. "I have brought a treasure worthy of the hand of a queen. And why not? When you marry Menelaus, that treasure will still be in the family. So, what do you say, Queen Helen?" He sneered. "Do we have a deal? Or do you prepare for a funeral along with your wedding?"

Helen sprang, and the back of her closed fist struck him across the face. He flew backward into a table.

He regained his balance and put his hand to his cheek. He glared at Helen. "How dare you."

Helen stormed toward him, but she stopped short of striking distance, not trusting herself to stop at one punch. "That was a reminder," she growled. "If I see one single bruise on my sister, I will come for you. By this bargain, I am guaranteeing her safety. Do *you* understand?"

Agamemnon straightened, keeping a wary eye on Helen. "You will regret this."

"I will regret *many* things about this bargain. Striking you is *not* one of them."

He narrowed his eyes. "It is agreed, then. You will marry Menelaus."

"I will think on it. You will have my answer by the end of the day. And my sister stays here with me until I decide."

"Fine." Agamemnon tilted his head. "If you'll step out of the way."

Helen backed up and gave a mocking bow. "Of course."

He narrowed his eyes. "You know, I asked for your hand

before Clytemnestra's. Your father didn't think our personalities would mesh. But if you had been my wife, I would have beaten that defiance out of you long ago."

"And I would have shown you what a true Spartan woman is."

Agamemnon smiled. "Funny, your sister said something similar that first year. She hasn't said anything like that in quite a while." He strode past her.

Helen watched the door close behind him. Then she kicked the pedestal next to her. It fell to the floor, and a bust of her great-grandfather smashed to pieces, but she felt no remorse for the destruction—only a desire to do more damage. She wished she could do the same to Agamemnon. But angry as she was, she knew she could not simply kill him, not without starting a war.

No, she had played it right. She had not given him an answer. Still, she knew what she was going to do. She just needed a little more time to accept her fate.

Or better yet, find a way around it.

CHAPTER 19

Helen's bedroom was quiet when she stepped inside hours later. She was done with the festivities for the day. It had been near impossible to focus on the guests, not with Agamemnon's words ringing in her head. She had let Castor and Pollux go, promising she would call them if they were needed.

Her sister still slept under the covers. Helen had just turned for the bathing room when Clytemnestra let out a cry. Helen was next to Clytemnestra in a flash. "Sh, sh," she said. "It's just me."

Clytemnestra's shoulders dropped, and she leaned back against Helen, her breathing shaky. "I'm sorry. I don't know when I became this person—weak, scared."

"You are *not* weak. Never let anyone tell you that you are."

Clytemnestra shook her head. "No, Helen, you are wrong." Her voice trembled. "I *am* weak. My time with Agamemnon has proven that over and over again."

Helen held her tighter, not sure what to say.

"I think it's a girl," Clytemnestra whispered, her hand on her stomach.

"That is wonderful."

"Yes, but I do not think Agamemnon will be pleased." She took a stuttering breath. "How will I protect her from him?"

"I will help you. You don't have to do it alone."

Clytemnestra grasped Helen's hand. "I've been so stupid. He fed on my jealousy, kept us apart. I never should have—"

"Sh, sh. None of that matters now. You are here. And here you will stay."

"He will not allow it."

"Yes, he will. I will make sure of it."

Clytemnestra nodded wearily.

"Are you hungry? Thirsty?"

Clytemnestra's eyes were already closing again. "No, just tired. Will you stay with me?"

"Always," Helen said. She lowered Clytemnestra to the bed and adjusted the sheet over her. She sat next to her sister until her breathing had evened out. Then she quietly made her way over to the lounge and watched her sister sleep. She was so pale.

Agamemnon's voice echoed in her mind. *Your sister is so fragile, isn't she?* Helen had to agree. When they had been younger, they had often been mistaken for one another. Their likeness was so similar, and they were both strong and full of life. But no one would have trouble telling them apart now. Clytemnestra looked thin, pale. Broken.

As children, a split had developed between the two sisters. All because Helen would one day be queen. Helen had felt that split widen every time her father spoke with her about strategy, or introduced her to visiting dignitaries, while Clytemnestra stood silently and watched. She had felt it every time their teachers praised Helen unnecessarily for simple tasks, wanting to get in good with the future queen. Each and every incident had widened the gulf between the two sisters.

She hoped that now that gulf was gone. Clytemnestra was all that mattered. Clytemnestra, and the little girl in her womb.

But can I do Agamemnon's bidding? Helen leaned her head back, forcing herself to ignore her hate for Agamemnon so she could look at the issue objectively. She could not marry Achilles, as much as her heart desperately wished she could. And there was no other man she was interested in. So what was stopping her?

Menelaus is not the same as his brother, whispered a voice in the back of her mind. When the two brothers had lived here, the differences between them had been obvious. There was no cruelty in Menelaus, no need to prove his manhood. He was comfortable in his skin. And more than one woman had swooned over that skin.

But can I marry him? Can I lie with him, have children with him?

She knew she would have to do so with someone. And Menelaus was a better choice than most. Her brothers respected him. Her mother as well. Truth be told, were he not the brother of Agamemnon, she could quite easily have seen his appeal.

But he is *Agamemnon's brother.*

Helen sighed. If she agreed to the deal, Agamemnon would be a fixture in her life from this day forward.

Her gaze strayed to the bed. But wouldn't he be anyway? And if she could get Menelaus on her side, she might have one more person to help protect Clytemnestra. Wasn't that worth a try?

Helen knew that Agamemnon was playing her. The only reason he had allowed Clytemnestra to join him on this visit was to show Helen how much Clytemnestra had suffered—and thus manipulate Helen into doing his bidding. Helen hated it. But how could she turn her back on her sister? And the babe in her womb?

She pulled her legs into her chest, resting her chin on them. Her sister had asked for her help. She could not—she would not—turn her back on her.

Helen let out a sigh. *Which means I am going to marry Menelaus.*

CHAPTER 20

While Clytemnestra still slept, Helen left her to find Agamemnon. She wanted to tell him as soon as possible; she needed the deal done so she could focus on her sister. But she had not left Clytemnestra alone: Castor sat with her now. Helen had decided that until Agamemnon left, one of them would be with Clytemnestra at all times.

As Helen walked through the crowds, people extended her greetings and jokingly asked whom she was rooting for. Helen smiled and took it all in stride, but inside she cringed at every comment. *How have I come to this?*

A hand wrapped around her waist and pulled her into the shadows of an alley. Helen would have screamed, but she knew his scent, the feel of these hands, and she wasn't frightened, though her emotions swirled madly. *How—?* She turned and looked up at him, her heart aching at the sight. His hair was longer and blonder. The sun had turned his skin a darker tone, which made his eyes stand out that much more.

"Achilles," she breathed.

He stared down at her as if he wasn't sure it was truly her. "It's only been a few months, yet you're even more beautiful now."

A servant passed the alley and dropped a tray of plates. The noise shattered the spell between them. She grabbed Achilles's hand, both loving and hating the feel of his warm skin against hers, and pulled him deeper into the alley. "What are you doing here?"

"How can you ask that? You are to be married off."

"I know. It is my duty."

"No. Come with me. Live with me. Leave all this behind."

Helen stared into Achilles's eyes, and for a moment she allowed herself to be lost in the glory of a future with the man she loved. A future that did not require duty. A future that allowed her to do as she wished, rather than what she must.

But even as she imagined it, she knew it was just a dream. There was no out for her. Not with Agamemnon waiting in the wings to rule Sparta. Not with Clytemnestra's life in the balance. And not with her duties as both the ring bearer and the future queen of Sparta. She shook her head. "I cannot."

"You can," Achilles insisted, pulling her close. "Leave with me now."

She gave herself a moment to enjoy the feel of him, to breathe in his scent, knowing the memory of this moment was going to have to last a lifetime. Then she pulled herself from him. "You would have me turn my back on my family? On Sparta?"

"I would have you follow your heart. I would have you choose a life of love over one of duty."

"I *will* have love," she responded fiercely, because the idea of anything less was too difficult to contemplate. "It will not be like this, but... I will love my children. I will love my brothers, my sister, my family. It will be enough."

"You would give up *our* love? You damn yourself to a life without passion."

Helen's voice was soft. She knew what choosing a life with

Achilles would bring. "Our love is like a roaring fire," she said. "But fire consumes everything in its path. It destroys everything that it touches. And that would be our fate. If I choose you now, like this, the ramifications would go far beyond you and I. They would ring out through Greece and the world. The fire we start will become an inferno."

"I would risk it. I would risk it all for you."

Helen took a step back, shaking her head. "But I cannot."

Achilles looked as if she had struck him. "You choose duty?"

Her heart breaking, she fought to keep her voice even. "I do."

Without another word, Achilles turned and walked away.

Helen watched him go. With each step he took, the impulse to run after him, to tell him she was wrong and that they should be together, grew stronger. But she smothered those thoughts. Duty had to come first. Not just to Sparta, but to her sister, and to the legacy of the ring bearers. Following her heart was not her path.

And when Achilles disappeared from view, she straightened her shoulders, ran her hands down her dress, and let out a breath. *Time to meet my future.*

CHAPTER 21

Agamemnon walked through the festivities, his wrist still smarting. A fire breather let out a burst of flame, causing the people around him to gasp and then laugh. A juggler kept four small sacks afloat. Women wandered through the crowd providing food and drinks.

The bitch hadn't changed, he thought, *except maybe to grow haughtier*. Still, he knew what her answer would be; she would stop at nothing to protect her sister. *Even letting me choose her husband.* Agamemnon smiled. It was why he had allowed Clytemnestra to finally come back to Sparta.

He scanned the crowd and spotted Tyndareus's dark head. Tyndareus was smiling and chatting—very unlike his usual stoic self. *Apparently marrying off this daughter agrees with him.*

Tyndareus had really outdone himself for this event. All of Greece seemed to be in attendance, yet there was room for all. Of course the greater families, such as Agamemnon's, were given preferential treatment and extra servants, but even the lesser houses had their comforts met. By bringing all these families together, Tyndareus had unified Greece, if for only a few days.

And Agamemnon knew that that type of political capital needed to be expanded, not diminished. *Now on to the next part of the plan.*

Tyndareus caught sight of him and smiled. "Agamemnon! Wonderful to see you."

Agamemnon shook the older man's hand, noting the king had lost a little strength since they'd last shook. Looking closer, he saw the slight gray cast to Tyndareus's skin. Something plagued the king. He was not long for this world. *Probably why he insisted on seeing Helen married.*

"I was hoping to bend your ear for a moment in private," Agamemnon said.

"Of course, of course. Excuse me," he said to the group he was with.

He and Agamemnon walked a short distance from the crowd. "It is good to have all my children here for this occasion," said Tyndareus.

For a moment Agamemnon wasn't sure what the king was referring to—then he realized he had meant Clytemnestra. "Yes, well, I hoped it would bring you joy."

"It has. You're a good man, Agamemnon, and a good match for my daughter."

"It is as a member of your family that I wished to speak with you."

"Is something wrong?"

"Not yet." Agamemnon gazed across the guests. "You have assembled all the families of Greece here. It is an honor to the kingdom of Sparta."

Tyndareus stood taller. "Helen is a worthy prize for any man. All of Greece knows of her virtue."

"Yes." Agamemnon drew out the word. "Her beauty is legendary. Which is why I think you may have a problem."

Tyndareus laughed. "How can a beautiful daughter be a problem? Now an ugly one, *that* is an issue."

"Yes, well, beauty brings its own problems. And Helen brings the kingdom of Sparta. Whoever takes her hand also takes control one day of a fierce fighting force."

"Making her all the more attractive."

"True. But there may be some who are unhappy with how this competition plays out. The winner will be happy, yes. But what of the losers? What if they decide Helen should rightly be theirs? This competition could lead to war among families."

"It would never come to that."

"Are you sure? Wars have been fought over less."

Tyndareus frowned. "I had not thought of that."

"Let me propose a simple solution. Before any of the games begin, have all competitors pledge that they and all their armies will support the winner and this marriage—and that if anyone, at any time, attempts to interfere with the marriage of Helen and her mate, they will defend that marriage against all."

Tyndareus looked away, his hand on his chin. "It is an interesting proposition. What made you think of it?"

"I am only thinking of the peace of Greece."

Tyndareus clapped him on the shoulder. "I knew I was wise to allow you to marry Clytemnestra."

Agamemnon felt the old resentment rise up inside. *But not Helen.* "Thank you. I am honored to be a member of the esteemed kingdom of Sparta."

"I will think on this. Now go enjoy the day."

"As you wish."

Agamemnon bowed before heading back to the festivities, leaving Tyndareus to think about his proposal. Agamemnon was sure the king would make sure everyone took the pledge. It was in his best interest to do so.

Agamemnon smiled at a serving girl and accepted a glass from her. He took a sip of the strawberry wine. He wasn't sure yet how the pledge would benefit him, but he knew it was a card that would be useful in his deck.

And one day, he would play that card to his great benefit.

CHAPTER 22

FIVE MONTHS LATER

Helen stood staring at her reflection as Leda and Adorna fussed over her red gown. Her hair had begun to grow out, as was the custom, and Helen was getting used to her hair being occasionally in her face. It was now held back by a wreath of flowers.

When the games ended months ago, Helen had been unsurprised that Ajax had beaten every opponent soundly. There was some grumbling about the fact that Menelaus had not been there to fight on his own behalf, but the truth was, Menelaus was well-liked and respected, and that went a long way to soothing bruised egos. The pledge each of the men had sworn at the beginning of the games helped as well. Helen was not sure where her father had come up with that idea, but it had been a stroke of genius.

It also helped that every family had been invited back for the wedding. And so it was that all the same players had now arrived to take advantage of Spartan hospitality once again.

Clytemnestra was seated on the lounge nearby, one hand on her belly. Her baby was due soon. Helen had worried

Clytemnestra would be unable to make the wedding, but Clytemnestra had insisted nothing would keep her from it. "You look beautiful, Helen," she said.

Helen grinned at her through the mirror. "As my twin, isn't that like complimenting yourself?"

Clytemnestra's smile dimmed. "No one would mistake us for twins these days."

Helen and Leda shared a concerned look before Leda walked over to Clytemnestra. "Both of my daughters are beautiful. And you, my dear Clytemnestra, glow with the beauty of that little girl in your belly."

Clytemnestra's smile reappeared as she rubbed her belly. "She will be wonderful."

Leda laid a hand on Clytemnestra's belly as well. "Yes, she will."

A knock sounded at the door, and Adorna hustled over to it. "That will be Pollux. He's early."

But when Adorna opened the door, it was not Pollux who stood there, but Menelaus.

He caught Helen's gaze in the mirror, and his jaw dropped. Helen looked back at him just as surprised. She had not seen him in years. Menelaus had not been at the competition, and he had been in Thrace ever since—until last night. When he had arrived in Sparta, Helen had not wanted to speak with him. She rationalized she had a lifetime to get to know him, and she wanted one more night of freedom.

But now as she looked at him, she saw that the years had been good to the boy she had known. They had put muscle on his frame, and a man's deep angles on his face. The dark blue of his tunic brought out the green in his hazel eyes.

Leda hurried forward. "Menelaus."

Menelaus tore his gaze from Helen and kissed Leda on the cheek. "Queen Leda, your beauty only grows over time."

Leda smiled. "Thank you, my dear."

"I was hoping I could have a word with Helen before the ceremony."

Leda glanced back at Helen, who nodded. Leda smiled at Menelaus. "Only a few minutes."

Menelaus bowed low. "Yes, my queen."

"I need to go check on the boys anyway," Clytemnestra said, struggling up from the chaise.

Menelaus strode across the room and helped her to her feet. "I did not see you there. You look lovely as well. How are you feeling?"

"Like an overstuffed turkey."

Menelaus laughed and placed his hand gently on her swollen belly. "And my niece?"

"Active."

"She will be a fine addition to our family." He held out his arm and escorted Clytemnestra to the door.

Helen watched the exchange in disbelief. How could two brothers be so different? The warmth in Menelaus's voice and eyes was undeniable.

Leda tucked a flower into Helen's hair and whispered in her ear, "He is a good man." Then she followed Adorna and Clytemnestra from the room.

When they were alone, Helen and Menelaus stared at one another. Helen felt the silence growing between them. Finally she gave a small bow. "It has been years, Menelaus."

He nodded, shifting from foot to foot. "I am sorry I could not be at the competition. I had already obligated myself in Thrace and could not break my word."

"A person's word must be upheld."

"Yes."

Silence fell again. Helen struggled for something to say. But her mind was blank.

Menelaus crossed the room and came to stop before her. "I am not good at flowery words or speaking in riddles. Would it be all right if we spoke plainly?"

Helen let out a sigh. "That would be wonderful."

Menelaus gave her a tentative smile. "I know this is not how you would have liked to have chosen your mate. And I know that someone else is in your heart."

Helen's eyes widened.

Menelaus shook his head. "I don't fault you for it. You and I—we do not get to marry for love. We marry for duty. But I do not think duty means love is not possible." He took a breath. "I would like to make one simple request of you."

Helen nodded slowly, nervous about what he would ask.

He held out his hand. "Do not close your heart to the possibility of love between us. Give us a chance to have a happy union."

Helen looked at the man before her. He was not Achilles. But he was a good man. And he was to be her husband. She had seen the marriages of people who had set themselves against one another from the first. She did not want that kind of marriage. So she pushed Achilles to the side of her heart and made room for the man who had spoken so tenderly to her sister. She grasped his hand. "I would like a happy union as well."

Menelaus smiled and squeezed her hand gently. "Then let it be so."

CHAPTER 23

ATHENS, GREECE

NINE YEARS LATER

Helen crouched low on the building, scanning the street below. It was late, and the heat was oppressive, with no breeze to stir the air. But Helen looked to the sky, and suddenly a light wind blew over her. She smiled in relief.

"I don't think that's what your powers were intended for," Pollux said next to her.

"Really? Because keeping me focused seems an excellent reason for them." Then her head whipped toward the end of the street as an electrical pulse raced through her.

"How many?" Pollux asked.

"Six. Two nephilim, one Fallen, three humans."

"I'm on it." Without a sound, Pollux leapt over the side of the building. Castor appeared from the shadows and joined him.

Helen stayed atop the building and ran toward the

approaching group. She leapt to the next building, rolling as she hit the lower roof. She sprinted along it and jumped to a still lower roof. Then she ran to the edge and jumped off the side, using the wind to cushion her fall as she landed directly in front of the group.

"Hello, fellas," she said. "Looking for someone?"

The man in front let out a yell and raised his sword.

Helen eyed the nephilim and Fallen. "Lie down on the ground. Now."

Three of the men dropped to the ground.

The other four men backed up, their eyes wide. One of them growled. "You're the witch."

Helen smiled. "Hey, you called me a witch. That's nice. Most people use a b instead of—"

The men surged forward. Helen kicked the first man in the chest, and he dropped to the ground with a scream. A second man approached her from the side, but she caught him in the ribs with a sidekick, then grabbed his shoulders, twisted him, and pushed him toward the third man, who was almost upon her.

"Behind you!" Pollux yelled.

Without looking, Helen kicked backward, catching the man in the groin. She spun around, grabbed his head, and brought her knee up into his nose, crushing it.

She saw her two brothers lounging against the wall. "You two *could* help," she said.

Castor waved her on. "Nah, you've got it."

As Helen stomped on the ankle of the man whose ribs she'd cracked, the man he'd fallen on managed to get to his feet. He pulled out a serrated blade.

Pollux let out a low whistle. "Oh, my friend, you really don't want to do that."

Raising the blade above his head, the man charged at Helen. She stayed where she was until the last second—then she smoothly stepped to the side. Her hands covered the man's and helped him bring the knife down—right into his own stomach. Eyes wide, he let out a puff of air and fell to the ground.

Helen stepped back and looked at her bloody hands. *Great.* She glared at her brothers. "*Now* do you think you could help?"

"Oh, sure thing." Pollux stepped forward. One by one he snapped the mortal men's necks, including those of the nephilim and Fallen. They couldn't leave any witnesses to report back to their leader.

But for the moment, he left one man untouched—the one Helen had kicked first. Castor grabbed that man by the shirt and yanked him up. The man screamed. Pollux looked over at Helen. "I think you broke his sternum."

She wiped her hand on one of the men's tunics. "I think I don't care."

Castor turned back to the man. "Who are you working for?"

The man groaned.

Castor shook him. "Who. Are. You. Working. For?"

There was fear in the man's eyes. "Zeus. Aeropus has offended Zeus. We have been ordered to make him and his kind pay."

Helen shook her head. She wasn't sure why she had expected to hear anything different. It was the same answer they'd gotten from every other man they had questioned over the last nine years. Someone was tracking down the Fallen and calling themselves Zeus. And although Helen and her brothers had been able to get ahead of some of the attacks, they had come no closer to finding this "Zeus" now than they were when she first got the ring.

"And how did 'Zeus' speak with you?" Pollux asked.

"He," the man groaned, "he appeared in my village to some of us who had gathered. He told us he needed our help to wipe out a great evil."

"Right. The all-powerful Zeus needed the help of a few mortals," Castor said.

"What does he look like?" Helen asked.

The man stared at the ground. "We never saw his face. No one dared to look upon the king of the gods."

Helen sighed. *Great. Yet another dead end.* "How do you know it was Zeus?"

"Because he said he was. And his men—the power they had. He was truly the king of the gods."

Castor and Helen exchanged a look.

"What do we do with him?" Pollux asked.

Helen looked at the man. "What will you do if we release you?"

"I am sworn to Zeus. If I fail, my family will pay. I will never stop trying to—"

Pollux snapped his neck.

Helen cringed, even though she knew it was a blessing. Years ago, when they had first started on this mission, Helen had insisted that they let the mortals go. But that had been no gift. "Zeus" found those men and killed them himself—and he killed not only the men, but their families. After that, Helen agreed that it was best to kill whoever they captured—if only to spare their innocent families.

"I hate this part," Helen grumbled. "These men are being duped."

"The mortals might be, but the Fallen aren't. Maybe this one will be able to tell us something about 'Zeus.'"

"Maybe," Helen said, though she didn't hold out hope. She was sure the Fallen knew more than the men did, but so far, none had ever been willing to talk.

Castor nodded down the road. "I'll get the coffins and tell Aeropus the village is safe."

Helen nodded, but she knew his words weren't entirely true. No one was truly safe as long as Zeus was planning something.

The lone Fallen stirred and glared up at Helen. "His time grows near. He will take control of this world and smash all those who oppose him. He will destroy you."

Another one talking about something coming, Helen thought. In the last few months, the Fallen had all suggested that Zeus was building toward something. And whatever it was would no doubt not be good for the world.

CHAPTER 24

It was almost dawn by the time they had the Fallen and nephilim in coffins, and loaded on a barge that would take them to Saqqara. Each of them had been drugged which should keep them out until they reached the necropolis. Helen watched the barge sail off, a frown on her face.

"What is it?" Castor asked.

"I don't know. These tales of Zeus and his sending people after other Fallen. Why? What is the point?"

"Someone wants to cleanse the world of them?" Pollux offered.

Helen shook her head. "No, because Fallen or nephilim—or both—are always part of Zeus's group. Something else is at work here."

"What?"

Helen blew out a breath. "That's the problem—I don't know. But something's building."

Castor put an arm around her. "We'll figure it out."

An eagle let out a cry, and Helen's gaze flew upward. The bird soared in a circle right above them. "Oh, no. Menelaus."

Without a word, Pollux lifted her into his arms and sprinted back toward Athens. Helen closed her eyes. To anyone watching, they would be no more than a burst of wind. But Helen knew from experience that keeping her eyes open during these runs meant she would be sick as soon as they stopped.

She and Menelaus were in Athens because Menelaus had been checking on their holdings here. Officially, Helen had offered to go along as a sort of second honeymoon, but in reality, she had wanted to go because Zeus had been stepping up his attacks in the area, and she had hoped to learn more about him.

"Almost there," Pollux breathed.

Helen nodded, feeling the flap of her tent. Pollux dropped her in her bed and threw the blankets over her before disappearing back through the tent flaps.

Helen kept her eyes shut and tried to calm her breathing, hoping Menelaus didn't climb into bed with her. She wasn't sure how she'd explain her clothes and sandals. *The ring.* She scrambled to yank it off her sweaty finger under the covers, but it was stuck. Then she heard the soft approach of her husband and went still.

Menelaus sat down on the edge of the bed and pushed a hair from Helen's face. Helen stirred, opening her eyes slowly. "Menelaus?"

He smiled. "Sorry. I didn't mean to wake you. But I wanted to see you."

She ran a hand along his arm. "I have missed you."

"I have missed you too."

"I hope you haven't been taxing yourself too much."

"Of course not. I spent the days with books and my brothers."

"Good. I will take a bath and then join you. Unless you wish to join me?"

"I will be along in a minute."

He leaned down and kissed her softly. "I will be waiting for you." He stood and left the tent.

Helen watched him go, her face softening. She loved him. Not the way she had loved Achilles, but that love... it was the love of young people. This love was the type that stood the test of time.

She sat up, throwing off the blankets. She reached for the water next to her bed, dunked her hand in, and pulled the ring off her finger. Then she held it up, watching the stones glimmer in the light. *I just wish I didn't have to keep who I am from him.*

CHAPTER 25

"Zeus" stormed into his study and picked up a vase he had found on a trip to China four years ago. It was a delicate, polished ceremonial object thousands of years old that he had plucked from the banks of the Yangtze River.

He hurled it across the room. It struck the wall and splintered into shards.

Gods be damned. The ring bearer had interfered again. Over the last ten years, she had continually thwarted his attempts to thin the ranks. And he still didn't even know who she was. In fact, all he knew was she was female.

The only saving grace was she did not know who he was either. But she had been trying to find his identity as well.

He spied a box and a scroll on his desk, a note beside them. Where had this come from? He picked up the note.

I believe your search is over.
—*Faenus*

. . .

Zeus smiled as he opened the box. A stone tablet, obviously ancient, lay inside. For a moment Zeus was silent, awe robbing him of his words. For years he'd been scouring the globe for this object; more recently, he'd taken to sending emissaries on his behalf. And now one of his best agents had succeeded.

His anger forgotten, he broke the seal on the scroll—a seal marked with two intertwined triangles—and unrolled it with trembling hands. His pulse ticked up with each word he read. He let the parchment drop to the desk and walked to the balcony, his hand to his mouth. After all this time...

His mind ticked through next steps. He ruled out two paths immediately. They would take too long.

Which left only one.

It would not be easy—but it was possible. With some thought, some planning, he could make it happen.

But first things first. He crossed the room and opened the door. The guard outside straightened his spine. "Find me Faenus."

"Yes, my lord." The guard bowed and hurried off.

"Zeus" poured himself a drink. It was a shame about Faenus. He was a good soldier. But loose ends were not acceptable.

CHAPTER 26

THEBES, GREECE

Paris, the prince of Troy, smiled as he stepped away from the fighting tent. The festival in Thebes was everything he had hoped it would be. Food, women, entertainment. *This is what I deserve.* His brother, Hector, had been right about this, at least.

He frowned. *And this is what I have been denied.* The bitterness of missing out on the privilege of his station in life was a constant companion. But he banished that thought. He was back with his family now, and he should enjoy it—not allow bitterness from the past to tarnish it.

He headed toward the avenue of merchants trying to sell their wares.

"A drink, good prince?" a woman called. She was clad in red and blue satin, marking her as a servant of the royal family. He had seen them all day, moving in and out of the crowds with food and drink.

Paris shook his head. "I am well."

"But good prince, this is a special blend. Only royalty have ever been allowed to let it pass their lips."

Paris raised an eyebrow. An exclusive drink. He smiled. "Well, I am royalty." He took the goblet and sipped. It was good, with a taste of cherries and other berries and a hint of something he could not quite recognize.

He walked away from the servant without a word, sipping from the goblet every few steps. It really was quite delicious. *No wonder it is reserved for those of superior birth.*

He stepped onto the path and squinted, his eyelids feeling heavy. His tongue felt dry as well. The goblet tumbled from his hand, and he stumbled, steadying himself against a tent pole.

"Good prince," a woman purred in his ear. "Let me help you."

He blinked at her. "Who are you?"

"Do you not recognize me, my love? I am Aphrodite."

Paris squinted. He could make out her long blond hair and shapely figure, but he couldn't quite make out her face. "Of course, your beauty is unparalleled."

Aphrodite put her arm around his waist. "Come with me, Prince. There is a task only you can fulfill."

Paris perked up even as his brain and vision stayed fuzzy. *The goddess calls on me. I am truly blessed.* He didn't question the goddess's interest in him; the gods had blessed him with incredible looks, and women had often beckoned him into their bed, even before they knew of his royal birth.

Aphrodite led him into a tent and lowered him onto a pile of colorful pillows. He reached for her, but she danced out of his way with a laugh. "Not quite, my prince."

The tent flap opened, and two more women entered. Both had long hair—one black, one brown. He couldn't see their faces, but he recognized them nonetheless.

"Hera and Athena," he said. "All of the goddesses have joined me. Lucky man."

"Yes," Aphrodite said. "We know, poor prince, that you have been treated so unfairly by your family. How could they turn you out when you are so rightly a prince? Why, you would make an even better king than Hector."

Paris nodded, knowing she spoke the truth. "But my brother is heir," he said. He had been going for humble, but even to his ears the words came out bitter.

"We are here to rectify this grave injustice," Hera said.

Paris grinned and tried to stand, but he fell onto his side and received a mouthful of pillow for his efforts. He pushed himself back up, but once up on his hands he couldn't remember what he was doing.

Gentle hands landed on his shoulders. "Let me help you, Prince." He was turned over, and pillows were piled behind his back and along his sides, keeping him upright.

Aphrodite stood in front of him, her hands on her hips. "Now, Prince. We have been fighting among ourselves over who is the most beautiful. We thought you could decide."

Paris blinked hard, but he still could not bring her face into focus. "You are all so beautiful, I could not choose among you."

Irritation crept into Aphrodite's voice. "But you must."

Paris's head tilted up, and a frown crossed his face.

"I mean," she said, her tone soothing again, "please allow us to each present our case, as well the reward you will receive if you pick us."

Paris perked up again. The reward of a goddess. That would truly be worth something. "Very well. Make your cases."

Hera stepped forward. "Handsome prince, you deserve much for the unfair treatment you have received at the hands of your family. If you choose me, I will make you the king of Europe and Asia."

"I can do better," Athena said. "I will give you wisdom and unrivaled skill in war."

But no riches, Paris thought sourly.

"But I," Aphrodite said, "will give you more than all of that. I will give you the world's most beautiful woman—Helen of Sparta.

Beauty, power, riches—Helen has it all. And it will all be yours. No man would dare turn up his nose at you with her at your side. No man would dare speak against you with her at your side. You will be the envy of the world. Your place in this world—your *rightful* place in this world—will be assured."

Paris nodded. She was right. Helen commanded the world's fiercest army. Everyone knew that no one could compete with the Spartans. And with that army, he could conquer the world.

But then he frowned. Something was wrong with Aphrodite's offer. "Isn't she married?"

"That does not matter. We have the backing of Zeus himself. Whichever of us you choose, Zeus will support. If it is Helen you choose, it is Helen you will receive."

"Then I choose Aphrodite as the most beautiful."

"Thank you, good prince."

A goblet was placed in Paris's hand, and Aphrodite said, "Now drink."

He took a long sip. It was a stronger wine than the one from before. He drained the cup and blinked. Black spots danced across his vision. The goblet was taken from his hand just before he tilted forward, asleep.

CHAPTER 27

When Paris awoke, he was in a seated position, his chin on his chest. But he could see nothing. He felt at his eyes, but there was nothing covering them. Where was he? What had happened?

Then he recalled the three goddesses. Had that been a dream?

"Awake, Prince," a voice boomed.

Paris's head jolted back and slammed into a rock wall behind him. He grimaced against the pain, his hand flying to the back of his head. "Who's there?" he called. "I am the prince of Troy. I will not—"

"I know who you are," the voice boomed back at him. "How dare you speak to me in such a tone?" The whole cave seemed to shake with the words.

Paris's eyes grew wide as he realized whom he had yelled at. "Zeus?"

For a moment the cave was silent. Then the voice spoke again. "You have ended a feud among three of my goddesses. That has been a great help to me. I find myself wanting to return the favor."

Paris's mouth fell open. *Zeus wants me to help him?* "I—I—"

"Aphrodite has promised you Helen of Sparta. You chose wisely. Helen is your way to riches beyond your imagining."

"But I have heard that Helen is happily married."

"She is. You must find a way to make her want to leave. If you do that, you will have all Aphrodite promised you and more. You will have tenfold the riches of Sparta. I promise you that."

Tenfold Sparta's wealth—that was beyond even Paris's imagining. "I will do it, sir. I will make her love me."

"Love is not necessary. Just be sure to take her from Sparta and bring her back to Troy. I have a plan in place to aid you in this endeavor."

Paris scoffed. "I need no plan. She is a woman. She will fall in love with me after only a glance."

Zeus scoffed. "Helen is not a girl whose head is easily turned. But possession of her *will* lead to untold power."

Paris stewed at the reprimand. "Yes, of course."

"Now listen close, for here is what is to happen…"

CHAPTER 28

SPARTA, GREECE

Giggles rang out through the courtyard, and Helen's heart lifted at the sound. Castor and Pollux had taken her two six-year-old boys, Davos and Theron, for training in the mountains. They had been gone for a month and would return in a few days. But Helen had eight-year-old Hermione all to herself, and she was loving it.

"Now, where could Hermione be?" Helen asked loudly as she walked toward the middle of the courtyard. In response, she heard more giggles.

Helen shook her head with a smile. She needed to teach her daughter how to hide more quietly. She had played this game with her since she was old enough to walk, and usually her daughter was good at it; it had taken Helen as long as an hour to find her on previous occasions. But Hermione's good mood today was making it difficult for her to stay silent.

Helen crept toward a small copse of trees. A branch rattled, and Helen frowned. *She needs to be better than this.* Although Helen had made it a game, it was also part of Hermione's training—

learning how to be unobserved by an enemy. For a child, being able to hide well was often more useful than being able to fight—although Hermione knew how to do that as well.

Helen moved toward the tree, scanning the limbs for any sign of her daughter. A small thump sounded behind her. Helen whirled around as Hermione rolled to her feet, running for the base with a laugh.

Good girl.

Helen took off after her. Hermione's strides ate up the ground, and Helen couldn't help but marvel at how fast she had gotten. Helen was almost upon her when Hermione reached out a hand and touched the side of the wall. "Safe!"

Helen put out her own hands to keep from running into the wall. "Well done."

Hermione beamed up at her. Helen saw Menelaus in her eyes, her mother in her cheekbones, and herself in the rest of her. She pulled Hermione into a hug. "You distracted me and sent me in the wrong direction. Excellent."

Hermione wrapped her arms around Helen and hugged her back.

Helen was content to stay there, with her chin on the top of Hermione's head, for as long as Hermione would let her. These moments were far too rare, and she had enjoyed this last month of being able to focus solely on her daughter.

"Excuse me, my queen." Darius had appeared in the doorway.

"Yes?"

"A ship in need of repairs has arrived. The owner insists on meeting with you to extend his thanks for allowing him the use of our docks."

A ship's owner thinking they were allowed to speak with her? That was unusual. She frowned. "Who is the owner?"

"Prince Paris of Troy."

Helen frowned. She knew of Paris, of course, but she'd never met him. He had been discovered by the royal family of Troy only a few years ago at the urging of a seer, and apparently he had been making up for lost time, embracing every privilege of being a royal. From what she'd heard, he eschewed war for bedroom activities.

Helen sighed. She really didn't feel like dealing with a spoiled royal right now, but decorum dictated she offer him food and lodging. "Very well. He may stay in the east wing until his ship is repaired. And tell the cook we'll have more at dinner."

"Yes, my queen." Darius bowed and took his leave.

"Mother?"

Helen looked down into Hermione's hazel eyes. "Yes?"

"Does that mean we cannot play anymore?"

Helen smiled and kissed her on the forehead. "Nope. But it does mean that it is my turn to hide." Helen took off at a run. Hermione's laughter trailed behind her.

Helen shoved the unexpected prince from her mind. He was simply an inconvenience. After all, how much trouble could a boy prince really be?

CHAPTER 29

That evening, Helen sat drumming her fingers on the long dining room table. "Enough. Tell Mariel we are ready to begin."

"We are not waiting for the prince?" Hermione asked.

"No, my dear. He is late. And *we* do not wait for people." Apparently the prince's thanks did not involve the courtesy of showing up for meals on time.

Two hours later, Helen and Hermione walked together in the courtyard again. Paris had never shown up for dinner, and Helen was quite glad for it. Hermione had become quite the storyteller, and Helen couldn't remember when she'd enjoyed a dinner more. But it had also been bittersweet, because she knew her mother would have loved to have seen the young woman Hermione was growing into. Hermione was adventurous, daring, smart, kind, and fair. Everything a future queen of Sparta should be. *I wish you were here, Mother.*

Hermione grinned up at her. "And then the princess scaled the side of the castle and slew the dragon. And all the town sang her praises in song and poem for years and years."

Helen clapped. "Well done."

"Yes, very well done," a male voice said.

Helen turned, her eyes narrowing as a man approached. He was undeniably beautiful. He had dark hair highlighted by the sun, skin similarly touched by the sun, and bright blue eyes. He wore a blue tunic, with a paler blue underneath, no doubt to bring out the color in his eyes. He was muscular, but not overly so. He was untouched by battle. All in all, he looked like the man-boy Helen had expected him to be.

Paris stopped in front of her and made a deep bow. "Queen Helen."

Helen tilted her head. "Prince Paris. We missed you at dinner."

"Yes. Time got away from me."

"I will have my staff prepare you and your men a plate," Helen said, taking in the four men that followed behind the prince. Unlike him, these men showed the scars of a few battles, although Helen still got a sense of weakness from them. Of course, they weren't Spartan, and Spartan-trained men were the only men she didn't sense weakness in.

Paris's eyes roamed over Helen. "The tales of your beauty have not been exaggerations. If anything, they have undersold the heavenly nature of your face."

Helen struggled not to roll her eyes. "Thank you. Now if you'll—"

"This must be your daughter. I see she will one day be as beautiful as her mother."

Helen narrowed her eyes as Paris's gaze traveled over Hermione in much the same way it had her. She stilled the urge to pull Hermione behind her, to block her from the man's view. Only her training kept her voice even. "I hope the repairs to your ship are going well."

Paris waved a hand. "Oh, we should be ready to set sail by the morning, noon at the latest."

Helen felt a sense of relief. She did not like this preening prince, and the sooner he was gone, the better. "Well, perhaps next time you will be able to stay for a longer visit. And I do hope you will be able to join us for a meal in the morning before you leave."

Paris gave another deep bow, one hand touching the floor. "It would be my greatest pleasure."

Oh gods, save me. Gently she took Hermione's arm and pulled her away. "Until tomorrow then."

"Yes, my queen," Paris replied.

As they walked away, Hermione glanced back at the prince and whispered, "He's still there. I do not like him."

"Me either. But as the rulers of Sparta, it is our duty to show hospitality to all our guests—even ones we do not like. Don't worry, he'll be gone by morning."

Hermione curled her arm more tightly around Helen's. "Good. Because then it will be just you and me again."

"Exactly as it should be." Helen patted her daughter's hand with a smile, but she was aware of Paris's gaze still on her. Before she had been married, she'd had to put up with such looks from men. But since she had gotten married, they had all almost disappeared. She was out of practice.

She sighed and banished him from her thoughts. Paris was just a boy playing at being a man. And he would be gone by tomorrow. The years with Hermione were moving too quickly, and she intended to enjoy every moment.

CHAPTER 30

A wind blew through the balcony doors, rustling the curtains and the sheets that draped Helen's bed. Helen breathed in deeply, looking for some peace, but she was having trouble finding it.

Her servants had reported to her that Paris had demanded a bath, and when the water wasn't hot enough, he had demanded they lug the buckets up again. Then he had sent back his dinner twice. Darius had also found Paris's men roaming the citadel. They claimed to be lost, but Darius had followed them quietly for a while, and concluded they were searching for something.

But most worrisome was what had been reported to her by the guard she had sent to the dock. He had informed her that Paris's ship was undamaged. Helen had not trusted Paris from the beginning, and now she knew she'd had good reason.

After receiving these reports, she had sent Hermione to the mountain house. She had not liked the way the spoiled prince had looked at Hermione, and she did not want him around her. Hermione had balked at first, but when Helen mentioned that one of the dogs had had puppies and that Hermione could pick one for herself, Hermione could not get moving fast enough. Helen would join her tomorrow after Paris had left.

Sleep, Helen. Sleep. Tomorrow the idiot will take his leave. She closed her eyes and tried to calm her breathing. She was just drifting off when footsteps on the stones outside her room alerted her. She jumped from the bed as the door flew open.

Four men stormed in, all wearing the royal colors of Troy. Paris sauntered in after them, arrogance splashed across his face. "Oh, no need to get out of bed. I was coming to join you."

"What is the meaning of this? I demand you leave my room at once," Helen said, even as her hand reached for the staff she kept leaning against the wall of her room.

Paris smiled. "Oh, I don't think so. I think you and I are going to have some fun."

Helen captured his gaze and smiled. "Oh, I think *one* of us is going to have some fun."

She twirled the staff in her hand, then swung it wide, catching one of Paris's guards in the face. A second guard lunged for her, but Helen stepped out of the way and slammed the staff on the back of his head, knocking him out cold. The third guard tried to grab her from behind, but got only a staff in the groin and then his face for his troubles.

The fourth was a little smarter than the other three. He held back, pulling a knife from the rope at his waist.

Helen smiled at the sight. "Tsk, tsk. Mine's bigger than yours."

The man lunged. Helen twirled out of the way and slammed her staff down on his outstretched arm, breaking his wrist. Then she swung the staff up into the man's neck, and when his eyes went wide and he grabbed for his throat, she brought the staff down on the back of his head. He fell to his knees and pitched forward.

Paris scrambled back for the door, but Helen wasn't about to let him escape. She swung the staff at his knees, sweeping his legs out from under him. He rolled onto his back, his hands up in surrender, and Helen pressed the end of her staff against his Adam's apple.

"How. Dare. You." She pushed the staff in further.

Paris gagged. "Wait, wait—if you kill me, you kill your daughter."

Helen stilled, her eyes narrowing. "What did you say?"

Paris slid along the floor so the staff was no longer at his neck. "Hermione—in the last few months, your household has been sprinkled with people who are just waiting for my command. Their first job will be to kill her, and then your sons."

Anger, pure and white, tore through Helen. She spoke through gritted teeth, stepping forward, the staff once again at his neck. "I will kill you."

Paris kept his hands raised. His voice was shaky when he spoke. "You kill me, and you kill all your children."

Helen wanted nothing more than to end this man's miserable, pathetic life. But she couldn't help but think of all the people who surrounded her children every day. She thought she could trust them, but… there was always a new face in her household, which meant there was always a new threat. The idea of her children being in danger enraged her until she was shaking.

But she knew she could not take a chance with her children's lives. She released the pressure on Paris's neck and stepped back.

Paris, his hands to his throat, glared at her as he climbed to his feet. "You will regret that."

"Letting you live? Yes, I'm sure I will."

"You Spartans, you always think you're tough. But one threat on your children and—"

Helen's staff came up lightning quick, stopping an inch from his cheek. All Paris had the time to do was widen his eyes. "And how do I know you're telling the truth?" Helen asked, tapping his cheek. "What's to say I shouldn't kill you right now and all of this goes away?"

"You kill me, they die."

Helen stepped forward menacingly.

Paris scrambled back, speaking quickly. "Your daughter—her favorite toy is a bunny Castor carved for her. Your boys love archery and playing in the wine cellar." Paris rattled off fact after fact about her children. And with each word that fell from his mouth, Helen's fear and anger increased. He was telling the truth. He had somehow placed people within her household.

The guards on the floor behind her groaned. Paris's gaze flicked toward them.

Helen's voice was steel. "They won't be able to protect you from me if I decide to kill you."

"But you can't kill me." Arrogance crept back into Paris's face. "Because you know I'm telling you the truth."

Choking back her anger, Helen spoke through gritted teeth. "What do you want?"

"I want you, Helen."

Disgust washed over Helen. "Lay a finger on me and I will make you a eunuch."

Paris's face grew red. "If I say—"

"What do you *want*, Paris? Because if it's to bed me, I assure you, you will not enjoy the encounter."

He narrowed his eyes. "Maybe not. But to the world, you will *look* like you want to bed me. So much so that you leave your family to join me in Troy."

Helen's mouth fell open. "Join you in Troy? Are you mad? That will start a war."

Paris smiled. "I know."

CHAPTER 31

Paris's throat hurt like hell, which only fed his anger. The haughty bitch thought she could win against him. Well she would learn. He had this planned out perfectly. She was under his control.

Still, doubt crept through him as she stood uncowed before him. He had pictured this whole night differently. In his mind, he'd seen his guards pull her from her bed. She had been frightened and unsure, begging him to spare her children.

But no, she had taken out all four of his guards—four!—in the time it had taken him to take three steps. Although he seethed with anger, he also felt fear. But he shoved that down. "You will act like the besotted fool, enamored of me."

"And my children?"

"Will remain safe so long as you do what I say."

Helen narrowed her eyes. "If anything happens to them—"

"If anything happens to *me*, you will be responsible for what happens to them. Remember that."

His guards were getting to their feet, and Helen positioned herself where she could keep an eye on them. Just like a soldier.

Just like he'd been warned.

His embarrassment made his voice sound harsh. "Two guards will be left with you to make sure you contact no one."

Helen raised an eyebrow at him and spoke in a bored tone. "And if I decide to simply kill the guards and send a note?"

"You will not!" Paris screamed. He took a breath. "I am in charge. You need to learn that."

She smiled sweetly. "And are you planning on teaching me?"

"No. But maybe I'll let one of my guards teach your children first."

Helen was across the room in a flash, a knife held to Paris's throat. Where had the knife even come from? The blue eyes that minstrels sang about and compared to a perfect sky stared into Paris's own eyes with the promise of death. "One hair on their head and I will end you—painfully."

He swallowed. Tears sprang to his eyes at the pain of her grip on his arm, and he knew she was not exaggerating. She would do it. "That—that's up to you—their safety. Do what I say and they will be unharmed."

Helen stared at him, and for a breath, he thought she was going to do it. She was going to kill him. Then, with a growl, she pushed him away. "Fine. I will go with you."

"And you will play the besotted fool."

She inspected him from foot to face, her lip curling. "As much as I am able."

Heat flooded his face. "We leave in the morning. And half of your treasury will accompany us."

"The treasury? You little—"

"*Half* the treasury. You will convince the staff that it is your choice to go with me. Is that clear?"

Helen glared. "Perfectly."

He waited, wanting to see fear in her face. But she gave him nothing.

"Is there anything else?" she asked.

"No." He nodded to two of his guards, who were giving the

queen a wary look. "You two stay with her." Then he turned and stormed from the room, the other two guards following him.

She would learn her place, he told himself. Once they were back in Troy, she would learn to fear him. After all, he had the gods on his side.

CHAPTER 32

Helen barely slept that night. Her mind was racing, trying to come up with a way to protect the children without having to go along with Paris. But she always came back to the same conclusion: with the children spread out, she could not guarantee their safety. And she would not risk their lives. So by the time dawn began to creep across the horizon, she had resigned herself to her fate.

She crawled from her bed, ignoring the hulking guards by the door. One gave her a smirk, and she turned to him. "Look at me like that again and I will remove your eyes. I may not be able to hurt your lord, but he won't risk whatever plan he's concocted over the body parts of a few guards."

The man glared, and Helen took a step toward him. The other guard grabbed the man's arm and shook his head. Both men then stared at the floor.

Helen took a seat at her desk and began to write notes, setting everything up for her departure. An hour later, she handed them to the guard. "These need to be delivered immediately."

The guard shook his head. "Prince Paris said—"

"Prince Paris intends to leave this morning with the queen of

Sparta and half the treasury of my home. That will not magically occur. Take the notes to Paris and have him read them, but then have them delivered so we can get this farce started."

The guard bowed. "Yes, ma'am."

He pulled open the door just as Adorna pushed it open from the other side. Adorna let out a shriek at the sight of the two men. The guard who was leaving nodded at her as he passed. The other continued to stare at the ground.

"Mistress?" Adorna asked.

Helen spoke wearily as she headed for her dressing room. "It's fine, Adorna. They're Paris's men. I will be joining him this morning when he sets sail."

"What? Why?"

Helen's voice was without an ounce of emotion. "I am in love, Adorna. And I cannot bear to be without my beloved."

Adorna went still, looking between Helen and the guard. "Yes, I see. Well, let me help you pack."

CHAPTER 33

It was early afternoon by the time the ship was ready to go, loaded with Helen's things and half the treasury. Helen felt sick. All day she had professed her love for Paris to all who could hear her. But she knew Menelaus didn't deserve this. *She didn't deserve this.* She stared at Paris as he walked down the dock toward his ship. *And that man certainly doesn't deserve this.*

She hadn't been left alone all day; the guards watched her every move and inspected each room after she left it. They were clearly making sure she could not leave a note telling her brothers or husband about what had happened to her, or warning them about the danger to the children. She desperately wanted to leave a message, and had composed notes over and over in her mind, but she could not chance one of Paris's guards finding it.

She had also been debating what to do with the ring. She couldn't leave it behind, because she did not know who would go through her things. But she was loath to bring it with her to Troy, where she knew she could trust no one. For now, it was tucked into a pocket sewn into her dress.

Adorna, who Helen felt was the only person on her staff she could trust, had decided she was going with her. Helen had tried to get her to stay, but Adorna would hear none of it. "I have been by your side since you were a babe. And if you are planning on going through with this idiocy, then I will be by your side for it as well."

"It is not idiocy. I am—"

"In love," Adorna said dryly. "Yes, you've mentioned it—repeatedly. And I don't buy it for one minute."

Helen's eyes went wide.

"I won't say anything. But remember—whatever I can do, I will do."

Helen nodded and let her facade drop for just a moment. "Thank you, Adorna."

Now Helen clutched Adorna's arm as they headed for Paris's ship. It was a floating palace, ostentatious and gaudy, just like its owner. And in that moment the gravity of what she was doing hit Helen like a wave. She was publicly breaking her vows to her husband. Privately, she was leaving her children in danger. Her knees buckled.

Adorna wrapped a strong arm around her waist. "I've got you, child."

Helen held on to her and steadied herself. Then she walked onto the ship and away from everything she loved.

CHAPTER 34

As soon as the treasure was loaded and everyone was aboard, Paris ordered them to set sail. But instead of setting a course directly for Troy, he sent them east. Grudgingly, Helen had to admit it was a smart move. Her brothers would undeniably take off after them as soon as they learned of her absence.

"A wise move, Prince," she said when the captain moved out of earshot.

Paris turned to her with a smug look on his face. "You'll find your husband and brothers are no match for my intellect."

Helen had to bite her tongue to keep from responding.

Paris waved his hand at her. "My men will escort you to your cabin. I'm sure you'll be much more comfortable there for the entire trip."

Adorna spluttered next to her. "Why, I never! How dare—"

Helen gripped Adorna's arm, silencing her. "Yes. A sea journey can be quite taxing."

Helen quietly followed the guards to her room. When the guards opened the door with a smirk, she braced herself. Stepping in, she looked around with a sigh.

A small bunk was bolted to one wall. A rough wooden table with two chairs sat in the center of the room. Three of her trunks had been tossed in the corner. One had cracked open, and its contents were spilled across the floor.

Helen blew out a breath, saying nothing. Adorna was less restrained. She whirled around to face the guards. "This is unacceptable. You tell Prince Paris—"

"Be quiet, woman," one of the guards snapped. "Or I'll show you what happens to mouthy women in Troy."

Helen was across the room in a second. A kick to the groin made the man double over. She grabbed him by his hair yanked him back, and twisted his arm behind his back. "And if you ever speak to her that way again I will break your bones one by one and show you what we women of Sparta do to disrespectful men." For emphasis she snapped the bone in his pinkie.

The man let out a howl. The other guard, who had momentarily been shocked into paralysis, now stepped forward. But Helen narrowed her eyes and twisted the wrist of the guard she held. "Try something. Please."

"No, no," yelled the man in Helen's grip. "Step back."

The other guard did so, though he did not stop glaring at Helen.

"Now apologize," Helen ordered.

"I'm sorry, I'm sorry."

"Not to me, you idiot. To her."

"I'm sorry, madam."

Helen shoved the man toward the door. "Now get out."

Cradling his hand, he backed away. The other guard stood where he was, his eyes locked on Helen.

Helen arched an eyebrow. "You wish to tangle as well?"

He didn't respond, but the first guard grabbed his companion and pulled him from the room.

Helen turned to find Adorna smiling at her. "Now that's the Helen I know."

Helen's own smile dimmed. "We should get this place cleaned up."

"Helen, what is going on? Why are you going along with this?"

Helen just shook her head. "I'm in love, Adorna. The happiest I have ever been."

Adorna brushed past Helen toward the bed and yanked the blanket from the bunk. "And I'm the daughter of a Sphinx."

Helen watched dust mites and rat droppings fly into the air. She couldn't help but feel jealous of the blanket, as it was now rid of the filth that had set up camp upon it.

Because it looked like the dung surrounding Helen would be here for a while.

CHAPTER 35

As Pollux pushed open the heavy wooden doors to the citadel, he was surprised that Helen and Hermione weren't waiting for them. Helen's boys raced past him, chasing one another. They'd been cooped up in the ship for days, and now they were letting that energy out. *Gods help them all.*

Pollux smiled as Darius approached. "Darius, where is the lady of the house? I have brought back her unruly sons."

Darius darted a glance at the boys, who were already running for the kitchen. "She—she is not here."

"Oh? Is she in the stables?" On the way in, Pollux had run into one of the stable boys, who'd told him a new foal had been born while he was away. He'd debated stopping there first, but the boys had been hungry.

"No. She—I don't know how to say this."

Warning bells went off in Pollux's head. "Just spit it out, man."

"She's gone to Troy with Paris."

Pollux frowned. "Troy? Why?"

"She says she's in love."

"With Troy?"

"No, sir, with Paris."

Pollux just stared at Darius, trying to figure out what the hell the man was talking about. "Paris? The son of Priam? The strutting peacock?"

Darius nodded.

"And Helen left with him?"

Darius nodded again.

"That makes no sense."

"She said she was in love with Paris and she was going to live with him in Troy. And she ordered us to load half the treasury onto his ships."

Pollux's eyes grew wide. "The treasury?"

Darius nodded, swallowing noticeably. "She ordered us, sir."

Castor came through the door behind Pollux. "Hey, what's—" He stopped short, looking between Darius and Castor. "What's going on here?"

"Our sister has apparently run away with Paris of Troy, whom she claims to love."

Castor laughed. "Right. If you're going to try to fool me, at least make it somewhat believable. Say Achilles or Odysseus or even a good-looking horse. Not Paris." He looked at his brother. "You *are* kidding, right?"

"No." Pollux turned back to Darius. "What about Hermione?"

"The queen sent her to the mountain house."

"Did she leave a note?" Pollux asked.

"No, sir. She just told me to send you all her love."

Pollux wasn't sure what to say or ask. Truth was, he didn't even know what to think. He'd seen the second son of Priam a year ago at a festival at Rhodes. It was the first and only time he had laid eyes on the prince, and he had not been impressed. The boy had been more concerned with chasing every skirt in town than any matters of state. And he had not a single battle scar to show for his years. Castor wasn't even sure the boy could grow a full beard yet. His sister would no more fall for him than she would a tree.

"This makes no sense," Pollux said. "When is Menelaus due home?"

"Not for a few days."

"Does he know?" Castor asked.

Darius shook his head. "I did not think it was my place to inform him."

"Did Helen leave *him* a note? Or one for their children?" Pollux asked.

Again Darius shook his head.

Castor looked at Pollux. "What the hell is going on?"

Pollux shook his head, equally bewildered. "I have no idea."

CHAPTER 36

THE AEGEAN SEA

Over the next few days, Helen spent almost all of her time in her cabin with Adorna. The guards stayed outside the door, and any time she tried to leave the cabin they dogged her steps, one in front and one behind. She decided she'd rather stay in the cabin than deal with their claustrophobic presence.

Five days into the trip, a storm hit. Thunder crashed, and the sea rolled. Adorna weaved her way across the cabin to Helen after tidying up their dinner. "The gods are angry tonight."

Helen just nodded rocking with the violent movement of the sea. She pictured the waves outside, crashing and bursting against one another. Helen knew storms like this could easily damage if not destroy a ship, and she wasn't sure if she should pray they were spared or that they were hit.

Had she done the right thing? Was there any way she could have kept the children safe and not gone with Paris? She had gone over and over it in her mind, but in her heart she knew there was no other option. The assassin, or assassins, could be anyone, anywhere—guarding the children, working in the kitchens, the yard. There were dozens of people in and out of her home each day. She could have released every last person from her employment, and she had considered it; but if Paris had found people to infiltrate her home once, he could do so again. She couldn't risk it.

Helen startled when another burst of thunder roared through the sky. Adorna sat down next to her, gently turned Helen's chin, and looked her in the eyes. "I think it's time you told me what's going on."

Helen shook her head and looked toward the door.

Adorna spoke in a low voice. "They cannot hear a thing above this storm. And I have watched you since we left—you are not eating. You are not moving. You just sit here. You are not in love with Paris. Even if you were, you would *never* turn your back on your family, on Sparta. So tell me, *what* is going on?"

Helen knew that if she was to survive, she would need one person who knew the truth—one person who could help her keep up this charade. She didn't know how she was going to convince anyone that she loved that snake in human skin. But she did not want to endanger Adorna. "I can't say."

Adorna put her lips together and crossed her arms over her chest. "He's holding something over you. What is it?"

Helen turned away.

"You sent Hermione away shortly after they arrived. You didn't want her around them."

The mention of Hermione tugged at Helen's heart. Her daughter would think she had abandoned her and her brothers. Hermione would think her mother did not care. A tear slipped past her lashes, and she took a shuttering breath.

"The children—you're doing this for the children. That bastard. Did he threaten them? I will kill him with my own—"

Helen grabbed Adorna's arm. "No. You can say nothing. As far as the world knows, I am a woman in love. And as long as I stay a woman in love, the children are safe."

"Oh, my child." Adorna pulled Helen into her arms.

Helen let herself release some of the emotions she had been holding back—some of the fear and stress of the last few days. But soon she pushed herself out of Adorna's arms. "Enough of that. I must stay strong for them."

Adorna wiped at her own eyes. "And I will stay strong for you as well. What can I do for you?"

Helen gripped her hand. "Just stay by my side. And help me when I start to falter."

"You will not falter. There is no stronger woman in the world. And Troy has no idea what it's in for."

Helen did not feel strong. She felt tired and scared and powerless—emotions she had no experience with and no interest in getting to know better. Outside the storm raged, and part of Helen wished the ship might be lost to the seas. Maybe then her children would be safe.

Adorna pushed Helen down into the bed. "Get some sleep. Tonight, let yourself feel the loss and the anger. And tomorrow, when this storm outside has passed, you will think of what to do."

Helen lay down, and Adorna pulled the blankets over her. "And if I don't?"

Adorna's voice held no doubt. "You will. You are Helen of Sparta. The blood of warriors runs through your veins. Paris is only a Trojan. He is no match for you."

Helen reached for Adorna's hand and gripped it tight. "I am glad you are here."

"I am too. Now sleep, my queen. For tomorrow you begin to fight."

CHAPTER 37

MYCENAE, GREECE

The gates to the citadel at Mycenae were thrown open as Agamemnon raced his horse toward them. The two giant lions carved into the gates roared silently at his arrival. He loved the beasts, and he knew he was a lion made human. Powerful, fearless, and to be feared.

He leapt off his horse, flicking the reins toward a waiting servant without a word. He strode up the stone steps, his guards opening the doors as he swept through into the large hall. A giant atrium stood in the middle, with three levels of rooms ringing it and a glass dome allowing the sun to light up the house. Acquisitions from his many travels, as well as gifts from his visitors, lined the walls. Agamemnon liked people to see how far his reach extended.

He glanced at his first servant, Cergen. "Where is Menelaus?"

"In your study sir." Cergen scurried alongside, trying to keep up with Agamemnon's long stride despite the painful limp he'd had since childhood.

"Are food and drink waiting?"

"Yes, sir. I had them brought in as soon as I was notified of your approach."

"Good. See that no one disturbs us."

"Yes, sir." Cergen hustled forward to open the door to the study ahead of Agamemnon, then closed it behind him.

Menelaus turned from the window with a smile. "You look like you have ridden hard, brother."

Agamemnon poured himself a goblet of wine and drank quickly before speaking. "There is much happening."

He studied his brother. Agamemnon had sworn all his people to secrecy to make sure he was the one who delivered the news. He had wanted to see for himself how his brother reacted. He knew his brother loved his wife. And by some miracle, it appeared that Helen loved him in return. Agamemnon would not have called that twist of fate in a million years.

Menelaus took a strawberry from the tray and took a bite. "So what is this news that has you rushing here?"

"There is troubling news from Sparta, brother. You need to prepare yourself."

Menelaus's whole body went rigid. "Has there been an attack? What of Helen and the children?"

"There is no attack. Your children are fine."

"And Helen?"

"She is... alive."

Menelaus frowned. "Why do you say it like that?"

"There is no easy way to say it, so I will say it plainly. Helen has left you for the prince of Troy."

"For Hector?"

"No. Paris."

Menelaus just stared. "He's a boy."

"Even so, she says she loves him, and she has left with him."

Menelaus shook his head and took a step back. "No. Helen

would never run. If she wanted to be with someone else, she would face me and tell me. Scurrying away to Troy? Leaving Sparta? Sparta is hers by right. She could claim the throne and oust me. No, something is at work here." Menelaus turned for the door.

"Wait."

"I must go."

Agamemnon hurried after him, placing a hand on his shoulder. "Even if Helen has been taken against her will, Troy will not merely hand her over. You will have to fight to get her back."

"Then I will fight."

"But not alone. All the families of Greece agreed that when Helen chose her mate, the rest of us would stand by that man and no one would be allowed to interfere. They swore to protect your union. We need to call on that promise and have them stand with us against Troy. Once the Trojans see our overwhelming numbers, they will back down."

Menelaus nodded slowly. "Yes. You are right."

"I will see that it is done. You go to Troy. Gather your soldiers. And we will fall on Troy like a wave and destroy everything in our wake. As your older brother, I will lead the men and make Troy pay for this grave insult."

Menelaus met Agamemnon's gaze. "Thank you, brother."

Agamemnon clasped him to his chest for a moment. "Of course. There is nothing I want more than to see Helen returned to you."

Menelaus gave Agamemnon a nod and strode down the hall.

Agamemnon watched him go before turning to Cergen. "Contact all the families of Greece. We go to war."

"Yes, sir. Right away, sir," Cergen said, before scurrying down the hall.

Agamemnon closed the door and headed back for the tray of food. He looked at the options before picking up the whole tray, taking a seat on his reclining chair, and balancing the tray on his stomach. He gnawed on a piece of chicken as his mind whirled through plans.

Then he smiled. *Well, this should be fun.*

CHAPTER 38

THE AEGEAN SEA

The storm passed during the night, but not before it had done its damage. The sail had been ripped and the tall mast broken. Adorna brought the news to Helen when she returned with breakfast.

Helen helped Adorna set up the table. "Will we be able to make Troy?"

Adorna shook her head. "No. In fact, the storm pushed us far off course. We are stopping at the island of Pharos for repairs."

Helen's head snapped up, and her eyes widened.

Adorna spoke carefully. "I've never been to Pharos. I hear it's beautiful."

"I have heard the same thing," Helen said, an idea forming in the back of her mind.

A quick knock sounded at the cabin door before it flew open. Two of Paris's guards walked in, followed by Paris and two more guards. Yet another two guards waited in the hall. Helen shook her head. If she wanted to hurt Paris, his guards would not be able to stop her. But a part of her took no small satisfaction in the fact that he needed so many guards to make him feel safe in her presence. And even with all the guards, he stood well away from Helen.

Paris waved his hand at Adorna. "Leave us."

Adorna glanced at Helen, who nodded. "It's all right."

Adorna bowed to Paris before taking her leave.

Paris waited until the door closed behind Adorna before he spoke.

"We will be making port in Pharos. I have sent a ship ahead to tell them of our arrival. They know you are with me and that you are my consort."

Helen flinched at the word, as well as at the idea of her name being associated with Paris's.

Paris noted her reaction. "And you *will* play your part. Or do I need to remind you what is at stake?"

Helen narrowed her eyes. "I am well aware."

"Then your performance had better be more convincing than it was in Sparta." He stepped forward. "Perhaps we should practice."

Helen smiled. "Perhaps you would like to limp for the rest of your days."

Paris glowered. "I am in charge here."

"So you keep telling me."

He pursed his lips, looking to Helen like a spoiled child, which no doubt he still was. She wouldn't have been surprised if at that moment he had stamped his foot and stuck out his tongue. "I expect you to look stunning when we arrive," he said.

She bowed low, fluttering her eyelashes. "Of course, my prince."

He nodded. "Very well."

His guards left with him, except for the one who, as usual, stood just inside Helen's door. She nodded to him. "You will need to leave while I change."

"Yes, Your Highness."

When the door had closed behind him, Helen turned to her wardrobe, looking for something that made her look "stunning." Anger and humiliation raged inside her at the thought of the upcoming farce. The only thing that kept her focused was imagining that when this ridiculousness was done, she could return to her family. She also imagined all the creative ways she was going to hurt Paris.

Over and over again.

CHAPTER 39

THE ISLAND OF PHAROS, OFF THE NORTHERN EGYPTIAN COAST

King Proteus had built a thriving kingdom by controlling the waters along the coast of Egypt. Helen had even heard him referred to as a sea god, as the tales of his control over the waters had been exaggerated in foreign lands. Helen went up on deck to watch as the island of Pharos came into view. It was beautiful. Long white beaches stretched along its outer rim, with tall palm trees beginning thirty feet from the water's edge. It looked raw and primitive—except for the large home that sat in its center, rising high above the trees.

Adorna stood by Helen's side. "It is stunning."

Helen nodded, wrapping Adorna's arm in hers. "It is."

"And you are as well. That blue sets off your eyes."

Helen's voice dripped with disdain. "Then my love should be pleased."

Adorna squeezed her hand. "You can do this. For your children, you can do anything."

Helen nodded. *Yes, I can.*

Too soon the ship was moored at the dock. Paris waved at the people who had lined the dock to watch them arrive. Then he turned to Helen with a smile, extending his hand. "They have heard that I bring with me the most beautiful woman in the world, and they have come to catch a glimpse of her."

Helen hid her revulsion behind a smile as she placed her hand in his and stepped to the edge of the gangplank. Cheers erupted from the crowd.

Paris tucked her hand in the crook of his arm. "Shall we, my dear?"

Helen graced him with a small smile. "Yes, of course."

Surprise flashed across Paris's face, and for a moment he leaned in close. "Very good. Just keep smiling at me like that."

Helen envisioned slamming his face into her knee and shoving her fingers through those beautiful eyes. "Of course, my prince."

Together they descended to the dock, Paris waving at the crowd, Helen quietly maintaining a demure smile.

A litter awaited them. Four men lined the poles at the front and another four stood at the back. A servant held open the door. "The king of Pharos bids you welcome. He awaits your arrival at his home and hopes you find the ride comfortable." Inside the conveyance, silk pillows in bold colors were strewn about, and red curtains could be pulled to allow privacy.

Paris smiled. "The king is most kind."

The servant bowed and ushered them inside.

Paris extended his hand to Helen. "My dear."

Helen smiled. "Thank you." She climbed in carefully.

Paris crawled in after her. As soon as they were settled, the servant gave the signal, and the conveyance was lifted.

Another cheer went up from the waiting crowd.

Paris waved to the crowds outside, not turning to Helen as he spoke. "Do not forget to wave, my dear. They are here for you."

Disgusted at how the prince preened at the attention, Helen

nonetheless moved to the window and waved and smiled. Soon though, the crowds were left behind, and silence descended in the carriage. Paris smiled to himself, but Helen cringed at the thought of word of this arrival making its way to Sparta.

The king's home sat at the highest point on the island, and they slowly weaved their way through the trees along the long road toward it. As they came closer, Helen could see the three levels of balconies that dominated the front. Marble gleamed in the sunlight, and bright flowers spilled from boxes at every window. The king had a larger home on the mainland, but everyone knew he preferred his island retreat.

"It is beautiful," Paris said.

For once, Helen agreed with him. She took some calming breaths, steeling herself for the performance to come.

At the gates, more people stood waving and cheering. Helen mustered a smile and waved as they passed.

Finally they entered the courtyard, from which the crowds were forbidden, and the conveyance was carefully lowered to the ground. The door beside Helen opened, and a hand was extended toward her. "Your Majesty." A tall, heavily muscled, dark-skinned man in an orange vest ringed in purple and matching pants stood waiting to help her out of the vehicle.

Barnabus, Helen thought, but she said nothing to indicate she knew him. Barnabus was the illegitimate son of King Proteus. Ignoring convention, Proteus had named him his heir.

She placed her hand in his with a regal nod. "Thank you."

Paris exited from his side of the vehicle and came around to join her.

Paris looked up at Barnabus with annoyance on his face. "Where is your king? Why is he not here to greet us?" From his tone, Helen realized that Paris believed Barnabus to be only a servant.

Apparently Barnabus was not going to correct that assumption. He bowed. "He is just inside, sir. He thought you would not like to be out in the hot sun any longer than is necessary."

"Fine," Paris said dismissively. "Lead on."

Paris took Helen's elbow as they climbed the steps behind Barnabus. They passed through a large entryway guarded by two huge guards. Paris glanced at them nervously, and Helen wondered if he'd just realized that by providing them the "honor" of his carriage, Proteus had successfully separated Paris from his own security.

Barnabus stopped at an open doorway to their right. "May I present Prince Paris of Troy and Queen Helen of Sparta."

Paris stood straighter as he stepped into the room.

The dark skinned man across the room from them was close to seven feet tall, with a large barrel chest and hair just beginning to gray. King Proteus's gaze raked Paris from head to toe, and his voice thundered across the space. "How dare you steal the queen of Sparta."

CHAPTER 40

Paris's heart leapt into his throat. "King Proteus, there is some mistake here. The queen of Sparta was not stolen. She is here by her own volition."

Proteus turned his attention to Helen, and for a moment his gaze softened. Paris looked between the two. Had they met before? Did Proteus know Helen?

Helen bowed deep before the king. "Good King Proteus, I realize our first meeting brings with it some unusual circumstances. But my love speaks the truth. I am here under my own volition. I have chosen Paris as my heart's true desire."

Proteus frowned. "You are married to Menelaus. An agreement was put in place to assure that no one took you from him."

Paris jumped in. "In truth, I should have been given Helen. Had my heritage been known, I no doubt would have triumphed at the competition for her hand."

Proteus scoffed. "You were a child when Helen was wed. You would have eaten your teeth in the first round if you had been a contestant."

Rage billowed up inside Paris, and he straightened his shoulders. "I have been promised Helen by none other than Zeus himself."

"Did 'Zeus' speak with you as well?" Proteus asked Helen. He didn't even glance at Paris as he spoke, and Paris bristled at the slight.

Helen kept her gaze downcast, every bit the submissive woman. "No, but my beloved would not lie."

At least she's playing her part well, Paris seethed.

Proteus's eyes narrowed as he turned to Paris. "And what right have you to the wealth of Sparta? Did *Zeus* promise you that as well?"

Paris's mouth fell open as he realized he had been tricked. The royal conveyance had not been an honor at all, but a way to slow their arrival to the king—giving the king's men time to search Paris's ships.

Paris fought his rising anger. "I took only what I would have been given had I received a dowry, as is my right."

Proteus's voice was filled with disdain. "The men who competed for Helen's hand *paid* for that honor. They did not need to be paid. Now you steal a man's wife and then argue you are entitled to his wealth as well? You assume much, Prince."

"I expect what is *my* right. I *am* a prince of Troy."

"And I expect you to leave both Helen and the treasure here. I will not let you take either. You may fix your ships and be on your way. But your ships and your men are *all* you may take with you."

Paris fumed. Red splotches appeared in the corner of his vision. How dare the king think he could tell Paris what was or was not his due? He gripped Helen's elbow and pushed her forward with a hiss. "Do something."

"Remove your hand," Proteus bellowed.

Paris snatched his hand back but glowered at the king, who stormed toward him.

Helen stepped in front of the king, her hands up. "Good King Proteus. I appreciate your anger and your sense of fairness. But

Prince Paris does speak truthfully. He should have been my husband, but he was not at the contest. Had he been, he would not only have been my heart's choice, but I'm sure he would have bested the other competitors. I'm sure my father would have agreed. Regardless, as queen of Sparta I choose him now. And that is *my* right."

Proteus stared down at her for a moment before stepping back with a bow of his head. "Of course, Queen Helen." He turned to Paris, his face hardening. "But you are not entitled to the wealth of Menelaus. So I will give you a choice. You may choose the queen or her fortune. You may not have both."

Paris glared. He had been promised riches. Wealth beyond his imagining. He wanted to throw the king's demand back in his face, but by some miracle, he was able to choke down his anger. Greater glory awaited him. And he would have his wealth. Not just half the wealth of one kingdom, but the entire wealth of many. Zeus had promised him that if he was successful he would have a treasure tenfold the value of Sparta.

He bowed his head. "Then I choose love, Your Highness. Helen is worth more than any amount of wealth."

Proteus looked between the two of them before stepping back. "Very well. Barnabus will see you to your rooms. Your *separate* rooms."

Helen initiated another deep curtsy. "Thank you."

Paris merely inclined his head before taking Helen's elbow and leading her from the room. Anger flowed through him and he squeezed Helen's arm tightly. He knew it was painful, but she did not look at him or even change her breathing. He dropped his hand in disgust. She never behaved the way a woman should.

Barnabus stepped forward. "If you would follow me."

"Fine. Go." Paris waved the man on, stomping after him and promising himself that one day he would repay King Proteus for his high-handedness. He would make the man grovel at his feet and turn his kingdom to dust.

CHAPTER 41

RHODES, GREECE

Battle-scarred, with red hair and muscles that seemed to strain against his skin, Dugal held up a goblet in the packed tavern. "And then the man looked up at me and said, 'Achilles? Why didn't you say so? Please choose from among my daughters.'"

The crowd roared their approval.

Dugal stepped down from the table and wound his way through the crowd to a table in the back where a huge warrior sat. The man towered over everyone in the tavern, in both height and brawn.

Dugal fell into the seat across from Achilles with a grin. "That story never fails."

"And you always fail to mention that the daughters were both about as attractive as a cow."

The woman on Achilles's lap laughed and whispered in his ear. He nodded as she stood up. "I'll be right there."

Dugal watched the woman walk toward the stairs, shaking his

head. "I get that you're the son of a god and all, but couldn't you share some of the wealth with the rest of us?"

Achilles stood with a grin. "Nope."

Dugal huffed out a grunt. Grabbing the bottle of wine off the table, he took a long swig.

Achilles slapped him on the shoulder. "Have a good night with your hand."

Dugal grunted. "I will, although I doubt it will be as good as yours."

Achilles laughed and made his way through the crowd. Men stopped to speak with him or compliment him every few feet. A few bought him a drink, and he could not turn them down. By the time he was halfway across the room he had half forgotten the woman he was supposed to be joining.

A man grabbed his arm. "Good Achilles, have you heard the news from Sparta?"

"Sparta?"

The man nodded, his eyes bright. "Their slut of a queen ran off with Paris from Troy. Guess Menelaus couldn't—"

Achilles grabbed the man by the throat, lifted him off the ground, and slammed him into the wall. "Have care what you say about the queen of Sparta."

The room went silent as all attention turned to Achilles and the man he held in his grasp.

Another man rushed to Achilles's side. "Forgive him, my lord. My brother has had too much to drink."

Patroclus, Achilles's older cousin, appeared at Achilles's other side. His resemblance to Achilles was undeniable. He was a few inches shorter and slightly less wide, but he had the same broad shoulders, the same sun-lightened hair and blue eyes. When Achilles had left Sparta he had spent two years drifting from place to place, before hearing his old teacher Chiron was in Thessalonikil. He had wanted a taste of the familiar, and when he had found Chiron, he had found Patroclus as well. The two had been by each other's sides since that moment.

Patroclus raised an eyebrow. "Problem, cousin?"

"This man," Achilles shook the man for emphasis, "spoke disrespectfully of the queen of Sparta when imparting his news."

Patroclus winced. "How unfortunate for him. But perhaps we could allow him to live at least long enough to tell us this news."

Achilles stared at the red-faced man he held. Then he dropped him to the floor without a word.

The man's brother helped him to his feet. "Thank you, Achilles. Thank you."

Achilles crossed his arms over his chest. "Now, what is this news of Sparta?"

The man Achilles had grabbed rubbed at his throat, not meeting Achilles's gaze. His brother spoke instead. "We heard it when we were boarding at our last port. The queen of Sparta has —" He paused. "Um, she left Sparta with the young prince of Troy, Paris. There are some who say she left willingly."

Achilles growled.

The man continued quickly. "And others say she was taken against her will. I, of course, believe the latter, and I will make it my life's work to make sure everyone I come across is told exactly that."

"When did this happen?" Patroclus asked.

"It's only been a few days, maybe a week."

Patroclus waved the men away. He spoke to Achilles, his voice low. "Menelaus will no doubt raise an army to go after her."

Achilles nodded.

"What do you want to do?"

Achilles shook his head. "Nothing. It is no matter to me."

CHAPTER 42

THE ISLAND OF PHAROS

Helen paced her room, ignoring the guard who watched her. Paris had wasted no time ordering his men to guard Helen's room, insisting one stay inside her room at all times. At least the room itself was on the opposite side of the palace as Paris's.

Adorna had arrived with the guards, and she had quickly set up the room and run Helen a bath—which Helen had greatly appreciated. Helen hadn't gotten more than a quick wash on the ship, but here she could relax, if only slightly. After her bath, she'd eaten dinner in her room, claiming an upset stomach. And now she paced—waiting. Darkness had descended a few moments ago, and she knew it would not be long.

The smallest of movements on the balcony drew her attention. She spotted Barnabus standing in the shadows.

Helen turned to Adorna. "Adorna, would you mind taking my clothes to the laundress? Gods know when we will next be able to have them laundered."

"Yes, mistress, of course."

As Adorna gathered the clothes from the bathing room and their satchels, Helen made a point of not looking out to the balcony. And when Adorna left, Helen moved far from the balcony doors. A few seconds later, the guard by her door slumped to the ground, a small dart sticking from his neck.

Barnabus stepped into the room.

Helen raised an eyebrow. "I take it he is just sleeping?"

Barnabus shrugged. "If I grabbed the correct dart, yes." He bowed deeply. "It is good to see you again, Your Highness." Then he opened his arms.

Helen ran across the room and hugged him tightly. "And you as well, old friend." After a moment, she pulled away from him. "Where is he?"

Barnabus nodded to the balcony. "Where else?"

Helen groaned good-naturedly. "He never makes things easy, does he?"

Barnabus smiled, his eyes twinkling. "No. Much like someone *else* I know."

With a sigh, she stepped away from Barnabus, pulled her ring from the pocket in her dress, and slipped it on. A tingle ran over her due to the man in front of her.

Barnabus looked at the ring. "I was wondering if you brought it."

"I couldn't leave it behind. But I cannot let anyone know I have it."

Barnabus nodded, understanding in his eyes.

Helen stepped onto the balcony. She glanced toward the roof and shook her head. "He is always so difficult," she muttered.

All the torches on this side of the palace had been darkened, no doubt at the command of Proteus, and a careful look around told Helen no one was nearby. Staring upward, she called on the wind. A strong gust pushed at her propelling her up and over the next balcony. As she guided the wind to take her toward the roof, a tingle ran over her skin—almost as strong as the one she felt near Achilles.

When she landed atop the palace, a shadow separated from the dark near a small glass structure. "I see you have gotten more graceful with your landings," Proteus said.

Helen smiled. "I have had a great deal of practice."

"So I have heard." Proteus smiled, his teeth bright in the moonlight.

"It is good to see you," Helen said.

Proteus bowed slightly. "And you as well, ring bearer. It has been too long."

"Yes." Helen thought of the last time she saw Proteus—at her mother's deathbed.

"She is missed," Proteus said softly.

"Yes, she is."

Proteus had been a close friend of her mother's—although even that did not express the depth of the relationship between the two of them. Her mother had called Proteus "brother," and he was viewed as part of their family. He and Barnabus had not only been constant visitors when Helen was a child, they had once stayed for two full years. And when Proteus left, Barnabus stayed on even longer, training with Helen and her brothers for another few years. Barnabus was another brother to Helen, a son to Leda.

And after Helen's mother died, Proteus had taken Helen under his wing and shown her what the ring would allow her to do. He was also gifted, although she could not command him to do her will.

He and Barnabus led the hunt for Zeus and his men in this part of the world. It was that hunt that had kept them from Sparta's lands since Helen's marriage—which was, no doubt, what kept Paris from learning of their closeness.

"Now, what is going on, Helen? You can't expect me to believe that ridiculousness you spoke downstairs."

Helen sighed. When she had heard they were heading to Pharos, she had felt both happy and anxious. She knew Proteus would either help her—or seal her children's fate. "There is much happening. But you must trust that what I do, I do because it is the right thing."

Proteus stepped forward, searching her face. "Perhaps the right thing for someone, but that someone is not you, is it?"

Helen said nothing.

"I do not understand how *Paris of Troy*, that sniveling child, could hold something so strongly against you that you would turn your back on your husband, your people."

"There are some things more important."

"There must be," Proteus said quietly. "Tell me Helen. You know I will keep your confidence."

Helen looked up at Proteus. She knew he would stay silent if she asked. And she needed someone else to run her thoughts off. She took a deep breath. "Paris stopped at Sparta, saying his ship was damaged." She told him the whole story, leaving nothing out.

"That letch," Proteus growled when Helen finished. "How dare he? I will rip him—"

"No, Proteus, no. Not until I can find a way to protect the children."

"Do your brothers know? Or Menelaus?"

"No, I could not leave a note."

"I will get word to them."

Helen shook her head. "No. If they knew, they would act rashly and I fear there is more going on here. We must wait."

Proteus sighed deeply looking up at the night sky before turning back to Helen. "We have been through much, you and I."

Helen nodded. "You have taught me much."

Proteus studied her closely. "If you are asking me to going along with this, I will. But if you need my help—"

Helen gave a bitter laugh. "I wish I could ask you for it. But I can't—not yet."

"I could have him and his men killed. We could make it look like they were lost at sea."

Helen shook her head. On board the ship, she had come to a sobering conclusion. "I wish it were that simple," she said. "Paris is simple. But what is surrounding me is not. Someone else is pulling his strings."

Proteus considered. "You have made a great deal of trouble for Zeus. Do you think he could be behind this?"

"That is my guess. But we still have no idea who he is. All we know is he is a Fallen and that he seems to be able to be in two places at once. Have you found out anything more about him?"

"No. I continue to search, as does Barnabus, but we have no solid leads."

"And I don't see how Zeus benefits by me being disgraced and Troy being at war."

"Perhaps he wants you sidelined."

"Then why not just kill me? It would be a more permanent solution." Helen sighed. "Maybe it's not Zeus. Maybe something else is at work. But until I learn what is behind all of this, I must go along with this farce. And if you care for me at all, you will do the same."

"You have had my trust since I first met you. You are your mother's daughter in every way. So if this is what you need of me, then I give it willingly. I only wish that you would ask more of me."

"I am glad you said that, because there is one thing more I need you to do." She slipped the ring off her finger. "Give this to Castor and Pollux. No one else, only them."

Proteus frowned. "But you are stronger with it."

"Yes, but I cannot wear it out in the open, and I cannot risk taking it to Troy. Give it to my brothers. They will know what to do."

Gently he took the ring from her hand. "You don't ask enough."

A lump formed in her throat. "One day I may have to ask more. But today, this is what I need."

"And it will be done. I will send it with Barnabus, and no one will know he has it."

Helen felt relief that the ring at least would be safe. "Thank you."

"You are welcome. But I think there may be one more thing you need." He held his arms wide.

Helen walked into them, her breath catching as Proteus's arms wrapped around her. Tears rolled down her cheeks and she felt the strength of her old mentor, knowing that, at least at this particular moment, she was safe and protected.

CHAPTER 43

THE ISLAND OF RHODES, GREECE

Having received word about Helen, Achilles could think of nothing else. Needing to escape the noise and heat, he stepped out of the tavern, but even the cool night air did not calm the racing of his mind.

He looked toward the peak of Attavyros in the distance, and before he knew it he was running flat out, blurring in the night air. Anyone who saw him would think he was nothing more than a wind. He reached the peak too soon. He stood on it and stared at the valley below. A few fires burned, letting him know people were there, but he could hear no sound. He looked up to the skies.

Ever since he was a child, Achilles had known he was different. He had always been larger, taller, stronger, faster, tougher than any of the children. His wounds had healed quickly. He could not be bested in a fight. It had made him unstoppable. And it had made him arrogant. Everything had been his for the taking. Everything he wanted, he received.

Until Helen.

She had denied him. But even as she did, he knew what was in her heart. He knew what she felt for him.

After that, he had thrown himself into battle after battle, trying to erase her from his mind. But thoughts of her only grew stronger. The only thing time was able to erase was his anger. And when his anger subsided, he realized he had been the fool. She had a duty, and he had asked her to turn her back on it.

He shook his head. That would be like her asking him to never fight again. To swear off fighting for the rest of his days. To turn his back on Patroclus. That was what he had asked of Helen—not understanding that duty was who she was. Who she would always be.

He had stayed away all these years in part to keep from torturing himself, but mostly out of respect for her choice.

And now that choice had been taken from her.

He knew, deep in his soul, that Helen had not gone to Troy willingly. She would never turn away from Sparta. She would never turn from her children.

Now the question was, what was Achilles going to do about it?

CHAPTER 44

A chilles spent the entire night debating whether to join the fight in Troy. In the end, he could not banish the image of Helen—Helen in trouble—from his mind. So when dawn broke, he had his men prepare for war.

It took three days to gather the supplies they would need. In that time, the memories of his time with Helen had haunted him. He had built a wall against her these long years, but learning she was in trouble had brought that wall down, and now the memories wouldn't be contained. They were painful, but they also brought him warmth. She had loved him; he did not doubt that.

By the fourth day they were ready to depart for Troy. Just before leaving, he received word that the Greek armies were mobilizing to advance on Troy as well. He'd been only slightly surprised to hear that it would be Agamemnon and not Menelaus leading the effort. Agamemnon—the king of men. But Achilles had met him before that. He had met him in Sparta, when he had nothing but a claim to a throne.

The king of men had not impressed him back then. He preyed on people's weaknesses. *Or at least tried to*, Achilles thought with a smile. He knew Agamemnon had asked for Helen's hand, in part to spite Achilles, but also to gain power. But Tyndareus had turned him down. Instead, he'd offered Clytemnestra.

Achilles shook his head with a sigh. If the rumors were true, that union had not turned out well for Clytemnestra.

The wind shifted and the smell of the horses drifted toward him, reminding him of when he first met her. She had been only twelve and he had been fourteen. The years slipped away as he revisited the moment that had changed his life forever.

∽

THE FAMILIAR SMELL *of the stable filled Achilles's nose, making him smile. He grabbed a bale of hay, carried it down to the last stall, and opened the door, the bale on one shoulder. "Careful, Midnight," he said to the black stallion.*

Midnight shook her head in response, and Achilles grinned at the haughtiness in the gesture. She was a beautiful horse and fast. She was entitled to her haughtiness.

He lowered the hay. "All right, enjoy," he said before stepping out, careful to lock the door behind him.

"Achilles," Chiron called from the opposite side of the stable.

Chiron, Achilles's teacher, was a master horseman, sought after by powerful men all over the globe. In fact, there were stories that he was part horse, his knowledge was so great. It was Chiron who had originally brought Achilles with him to Sparta, when King Tyndareus called for him to help with his new horses. It had been three months since they had arrived here, and Achilles now knew why Chiron had brought him. The Spartans fought with a passion he had never seen, and Achilles loved every minute he was allowed to train with the men.

Achilles walked over to Chiron, trying not to look reluctant. He was hoping Chiron didn't have more work for him, because Castor and Pollux had said he could join them in the training yard as soon as he finished up, and he had been looking forward to it. The very first time he met Castor, he'd known this was someone with the same abilities as himself. Their first fight had been exhilarating; he didn't even have to hold back. And neither did Castor. He grinned just thinking about it.

He wiped the grin off his face as he walked up to Chiron. "Yes?"

"Are all the stables cleaned out?"

"Yes."

"The horses fed and given fresh water?"

"Yes."

"And have you completed your lessons for the day?"

"Yes." Achilles tried not to smile in anticipation of his teacher's next words.

"Very well. You may go."

With a whoop, Achilles ran for the exit.

"Achilles." Chiron's voice was sharp, halting Achilles. Chiron walked to Achilles's side. "Do not let anyone see your abilities."

"I know."

Chiron looked down at him and raised an eyebrow. "Really? Then care to tell me why Sabian said that a strong wind came along and ripped his sword right out of his hand earlier this morning?"

Achilles grinned. "Like he said—it was a really strong wind."

Chiron sighed. "Achilles, your abilities are a gift from the gods. But they will mark you for trouble if you do not keep them hidden."

"Let trouble come. I am not afraid."

"You should be. Because the trouble that comes for you will come for anyone around you. You need to take care of them as well. And we are guests here. Do not bring any problems for King Tyndareus."

Achilles let out a deep sigh. "Fine."

Chiron shook his head. "Go on."

As Achilles headed out of the stable, his joy ebbed. Chiron was always warning him not to let anyone see his abilities. He could run faster, hit harder, and fight better than anyone he knew—even Castor—and he was supposed to hide all that? For now that was all right. But one day, he was sure, everyone would know his name.

Three boys a little older then Achilles came running from the opposite direction, jostling Achilles as they passed. "Hey!" Achilles yelled. But the boys ignored him, continuing around the side of the barn. "Get him!" one of the boys yelled.

Get whom? Curious, Achilles followed them. He hadn't seen them chasing anyone.

The boys were running toward some trees when Achilles heard the unmistakable yelp of a dog up ahead of them. His eyes narrowed, and he sprinted for the boys. "What are—"

But he was cut off as another boy, not with the group, appeared out of nowhere. This new boy flew at the group, landed a kick to one of the other boys' groins, and followed it with a knee to the face.

Only then did Achilles realize the new boy wasn't a boy at all, but a girl with short blond hair.

Tossing the first boy aside, the girl turned toward a second boy who was running at her, throwing a punch. She nimbly slipped the punch, slapping the underside of his elbow with her palm, and slammed her other hand down on the topside of his wrist. The boy's elbow broke, and even as he screamed, she kicked out his leg.

The third boy backed away from her with his hands up and eyes wide. "I—I didn't mean nothing," he stammered.

The girl turned to Achilles, her blue eyes on fire, her cheeks flush with color. "What about you?" she demanded.

Achilles put up his hands as well. "I'm not with them. I just came to see what they were doing."

"Terrorizing someone who should be left in peace," she said, turning away from him. She wasn't going after him, but she was trusting him enough to give him her back. She approached a bush just inside the trees, her attention on something underneath it.

The first boy, the one the girl had kneed in the groin, still lay on the ground, but he reached for a stick, his eyes full of hate. Achilles walked over and kicked the boy in the head before he could get to his feet. The boy was knocked out cold.

The girl looked up, and Achilles shrugged. "One of them passed out." He looked at the scared boy and the boy with the broken elbow. "You should get him some help."

The two boys, one holding his broken arm to his chest, managed to lift the unconscious boy between them and hurry him away. Achilles kept himself between the girl and the boys as they left.

Finally he turned to see what had the girl's attention.

An old dog, with spots of fur missing, lay underneath the bush, one paw held up. Achilles sucked in a breath. He hated to see animals in pain. A sudden anger at the boys washed over him, but he kept it contained. His anger could spill over at times, but Chiron had been helping him gain control.

The girl looked up at him. Eyes that had been full of passion were now filled with tears. "I think her paw is broken."

Achilles knelt down next to the poor animal. "What can we do?"

The girl wiped away a tear that slipped past her long dark lashes. "I can take her to Adorna. She'll help. I need to get something to carry her in."

"I can carry her." Careful not to jostle the injured leg, he lifted the dog into his arms.

The girl hovered next to him, biting her lower lip. "Is she too heavy?"

"She weighs nothing. Lead on. What is your name?"

"Helen."

Achilles blinked in surprise—the king's daughter? That was not the name he'd been expecting. He had heard that the princess and the queen had been on a trip with her mother and had arrived home just last night. And here she was, her royal highness fighting with rabble over a dog— and fighting very well at that.

"I'm Achilles," he said.

She looked into his eyes, and for a moment Achilles was lost in the beauty standing before him.

"Thank you, Achilles," she said softly. She began to walk, and Achilles followed her, knowing that somehow his whole life had just changed.

∼

THE MEMORY of that first meeting flowed through Achilles's mind as the wind tugged at his hair and his tunic. Helen had been a force of nature from the start. And the two of them together... he had thought they were unstoppable.

Until Helen stopped them.

He bit down on that old resentment. It had taken him years to understand why she had made the decision she had. He had been young, foolish, without duty or honor. Helen had had both. She'd had no choice in what was to come, but she had faced it. And she had made Sparta stronger because of it.

Now he was supposed to believe that Helen had walked away from all of that? No, he couldn't. Something was amiss. His Helen would never turn her back on duty.

She's not your Helen. Not anymore, a voice whispered in the back of his mind.

He knew the voice spoke the truth—and the same time, it didn't. Helen was queen of Sparta, and she belonged to Sparta and Menelaus. But part of her, he knew, would always be his—the same way he would always be hers. Time and distance didn't change that. Some facts were as immutable as the mountains.

And right now, his Helen needed him.

He turned his face toward the sun. This time he would not let her down.

CHAPTER 45

SPARTA, GREECE

The arrow let loose from the bow and hit the center of the target, but Pollux felt no sense of satisfaction. All he felt was more rage. None of the ships they had sent after Paris had caught sight of him, and none of the ports from Sparta to Troy had reported seeing the ship. The slippery bastard had disappeared.

Menelaus had sent people to Troy, but that was only a week ago, not time enough for anyone to make it there and back in time. Menelaus himself had left with the first of the troops to join up with Agamemnon on the coast before heading to Troy. Castor and Pollux were staying behind with hopes that some word of Helen reached them, but would follow with the rest of the Spartan troops in a few days. Castor could think of no reason why Helen would willingly go with Paris, save that she was averting a greater harm. But by the gods, he still had no idea what that could be.

Beside him, Castor let loose three arrows in a row. Each hit the center of the target.

"Nice job," Pollux said.

Castor just shrugged.

An electric tingle rolled over Pollux, and he immediately went on alert. "We have company."

Castor nocked another arrow. "Where?"

Pollux nodded toward the hilltop.

A man blurred down the hill and then slowed and came into focus. "Is that any way to greet an old friend?"

Pollux lowered his bow. "Barnabus?"

Barnabus chuckled and jogged over to them. Pollux extended his hand, and Barnabus shook it, wrapping his other arm around Pollux's shoulder.

"It is good to see you, brother," said Pollux.

"You as well," Barnabus said before embracing Castor. "Both of you."

"What brings you to Sparta?" Castor asked.

"I bring news from Helen."

The name shot fear, happiness, and surprise through Pollux. "Helen? Have you seen her?"

"Is she all right?" Castor asked at the same time.

"She is not harmed, but I would not say she is all right." He recounted Paris and Helen's arrival at Pharos, and Proteus's response.

"He let her go? How could he do that?" Pollux demanded.

"Helen asked him to."

"And she said she loved Paris?" Castor asked.

Barnabus's brow furrowed. "She said it with her words, but in every other way she indicated she did not. There is something wrong there."

"She did not confide in you?"

"No. But I believe she confided in my father. He trusts her course of action, although I'm not sure he agrees with it. He just asked me to trust him and asked that I get this to you two." Barnabus withdrew a small satchel and emptied Helen's ring, the source of her power, into his hand.

With a shaky hand, Pollux took it. "She sent this? Was there any message?"

Barnabus shook his head. "No. She simply said she loved you all and that I should bring this to you two and no one else, not even Menelaus."

Castor looked at Pollux. "Why would she send this? What does it mean?"

Pollux didn't know. Did it mean she was giving up the fight? No, that couldn't be it. Helen understood duty more than any of them. And she embraced her role. She reveled in it. "No. She must have sent it to us for safekeeping. She does not trust Paris."

"She doesn't trust us either," Castor grumbled.

"No," Pollux said. "She is protecting us, or someone else, by her silence."

"That is my thought as well," said Barnabus. "I have also brought Menelaus's treasure, by the way." He nodded toward the ring. "Does he not know she is the ring bearer?"

"No," replied Pollux. "She has wanted to tell him, but she worries about Agamemnon and what would happen should he find out." And Pollux agreed with that concern. Menelaus was a good man, but his brother… that was a different story altogether.

"Not an unfounded worry," Barnabus muttered.

"No. But Menelaus is a good man. His blind spot is his brother. He does not see the extent of his cruelty," Pollux said.

"How is he handling Helen's absence?" Barnabus asked.

"He is confused," Pollux said. "He is letting Agamemnon run the war. We set sail in a few days for Troy. Menelaus has already gone ahead."

"So it has come to that," Barnabus said quietly.

Castor nodded. "All of Helen's suitors have been pressed into service, along with all their armies."

Barnabus's eyes went wide. "That is all the armies of Greece."

"And a few from Africa, and even across the Aegean Sea," Castor said.

Barnabus shook his head. "Why would Paris do this? There is no way Troy can survive against that force."

"We have no idea," Pollux said.

"What about you?" Castor asked. "Do you have to leave right away?"

Barnabus smiled. "My father said I may stay as long as you need me. And it sounds as if you will."

"It will be good to have you here," Castor said.

"It will be good to be here," Barnabus said. "And I look forward to finding whoever is behind this—and destroying them."

Pollux smiled—his first real smile since this all began. "As do we all."

CHAPTER 46

PELION, GREECE

Clytemnestra held her cloak tightly around her. She was cold even though not a single wind stirred. *It's a sign. This whole undertaking is folly.*

She had accompanied Agamemnon to the coastal city of Pelion at his insistence. The rest of the Greek forces would join them within the next few days. Clytemnestra hated every moment of their time here. She had felt cold ever since she had received word of Helen's abduction and the breezes from the Aegean Sea made it even worse. Of course, the people who had told her about Helen's plight had not used that particular word. In their gleeful eyes and with their salacious words, she had known they were looking for her reaction. So she had coolly stared them down and said nothing.

Since Helen's wedding, she and her daughter, Iphigenia, had spent as much time in Sparta as possible. In fact, Iphigenia had been born there. But Clytemnestra still had to return to Mycenae from time to time to attend her duties, and each time she felt like she was being cast out of heaven and into hell.

Now as she stood on the edge of the dock, she looked over the forces her husband had marshaled in Helen's name. It looked as if all of Greece were here. As far as she could see in all directions stood the armies of Mycenae's neighboring kingdoms—thousands of men. She shivered at thoughts of the battle to come.

She had heard the men joking about Helen's fickle ways. But Clytemnestra knew Helen—and she knew her sister had not gone with Paris willingly, no matter how many people tried to convince her otherwise. Oh, it was true that Helen had always been headstrong, adventurous, and willful. But beyond all that, she was loyal. She would never abandon Menelaus. She would never willingly walk away from her children. And she would never walk away from Sparta. Sparta wasn't just her home, it was her blood—her life. She would no more walk away from it willingly than she would cut off her own arm on a whim.

"There you are. I have been looking for you." Agamemnon stopped next to her, a frown on his face.

Clytemnestra cringed, telling herself not to step away from him. He didn't like when she showed her fear of him—at least not in public. "I'm sorry, my lord. I did not know you were looking for me."

"You should have stayed where you were put."

"Yes, my lord."

Agamemnon looked around. A group of six men stood farther down the dock, but none were within earshot. "I hear you are telling people you do not believe Helen ran away. That you believe she was forced against her will."

Clytemnestra looked up into her husband's face and wondered how she had ever seen kindness in it. When she was a young girl, looking into those eyes, she had been so sure that it was love shining back at her. She hadn't seen the cruelty. She hadn't seen the calculation.

Helen had. Helen had warned her. She had begged her not to marry him. But Clytemnestra had thought she'd known better.

She hadn't trusted Helen's reasons for speaking the way she had, believing Agamemnon's false words over her sister's words spoken in love.

But she was no longer a young foolish girl. Now she heard the dishonesty in Agamemnon's proclamations of love. She saw the calculation in his eyes as he spoke of people and considered what they could do for him. Clytemnestra had spent years cowing to this man. But no more. She would not betray Helen.

"She would not run from Sparta," she said. "It is not possible."

Agamemnon took her arm and squeezed it tight. "*I* say she has. And you will agree with me. Do you understand?" His words were harsh, but to anyone looking his face showed only concern.

Clytemnestra swallowed. "No. I will not say that. I know it is not true."

"You know *nothing*! You *are* nothing. You live, you breathe, only by my mercy. Your sister is a harlot. And you will declare her as such."

Agamemnon's words shot a bolt of terror through Clytemnestra, but she shook it off. He could do what he wanted to her. He had already done so for years. But he could not make her do this. She would never publicly speak against her sister. "No."

Agamemnon pulled his hand back as if to strike, but then apparently remembered they were in public. He brought his hand down and caressed her cheek, a smile across his lips. "You are no longer scared of me. Or is that you just don't care what happens to you anymore?"

She looked at him but said nothing.

"The latter, I think. But there are some things you still care about, aren't there?" he murmured. "You will regret this little rebellion." He leaned in close and kissed her cheek before walking off.

As Clytemnestra watched him go, horror grew inside of her. What had he meant by that? What was he going to do?

What have I done?

CHAPTER 47

TROY, TURKEY

Paris closed the door to his bedroom and stepped into the long hallway. He and Helen had arrived just a short while ago. Helen had played her part on arrival, and he'd had her taken to her room. His family hadn't been there to greet them, for which Paris was grateful; he wasn't sure how they were going to take the news of Helen. But more importantly, he hoped they did not hear of his treatment in Pharos. He was a prince of Troy, and Proteus had treated him like a beggar.

But by the time Paris had returned to his rooms, taken a long bath, and changed his clothes, the focus of his anger had shifted from Proteus to Helen. That bitch. Helen had played her part, true, but each time she looked at him he could feel her contempt, her derision. No doubt Proteus had merely been responding to it.

But Paris had faith in Zeus. Zeus had assured him that Helen would fall in line. The god was all-powerful, and he had chosen Paris to be his agent on earth. He had promised him wealth, influence, and even the kingdom of Sparta, which he would crush under his boot. Three times now Zeus had contacted Paris through his great falcon, assuring him of his plans. He even told Paris when Menelaus would be gone from Sparta. But in each missive he made it very clear that Helen needed to be brought to Troy. Only through that act would Paris receive his grand reward. And Paris knew that of all the men on the Earth, no one deserved riches as much as he did. After scraping by for most of his life, he was back in his rightful place, as a prince of Troy.

Still, Helen was testing his resolve. Gods, the men of Sparta were insane to give their women so much freedom! They were the equals to men, speaking their mind on all sorts of topics. Even their royal lineage went through the women rather than the sons. Men were focused on fighting while women ran the kingdom. Paris shook his head. Blasphemy. It was against the natural order, and the result was a woman like Helen, who thought she could do whatever a man could.

But I showed her, he thought with a satisfied grin. *Threaten her children and she turns back into a mewling cow—like all women.*

"Paris!"

Paris cringed at the sound of his brother's yell. He had not been looking forward to this confrontation. But he turned, pasted a smile on his face, and opened his arms. "Hector. It is good to see you."

Hector wrapped Paris in a hug. Paris seethed as his face was pushed into Hector's muscular chest. His shorter stature was another slight against him. But as he pulled back, he smiled up at his brother, the heir to Troy.

Worry lined Hector's face. "Paris, what have you done?"

With a sigh, Paris stepped back. "You mean Helen?"

"'Helen'? She's not just Helen. She is the queen of Sparta. You have declared war on all of Greece by taking her."

"I did not *take* her. She came on her own. Spartan women can choose their mates, and she has chosen me."

"She is married to Menelaus. She is not *free* to choose."

"We are in love, brother."

Hector sighed. "When she was married, all the kingdoms swore an oath that they would not interfere in her marriage with Menelaus. If anyone did, the rest would be honor-bound to retrieve her. It is not just Sparta we go up against, brother, it is *all* the kingdoms. Do you realize the troubles you have brought to our shores?"

Paris waved away Hector's concerns. "No one has ever breached Troy's walls, and no one will."

Hector sighed again; the sound grated on Paris's nerves. "Paris, you do not understand the rigors of battle. If they have to, they will surround us and keep us locked inside until they starve us out. And if we wait to fight until then, we will be weakened from hunger. Which means we will need to end this before that point. People will die, Paris. Good men will lose their lives because of this choice of yours."

"And what of me? *I* should have been Helen's rightful husband. The gods are on my side."

"You? We had not even found you then. And besides, you were too young. You were not ready for—" Hector went quiet.

"For a woman like Helen?" Paris asked quietly. "You have never respected me as a man. And that is what I am."

"Then act like it! Return Helen and stop this madness before it goes any farther."

Paris narrowed his eyes. "Aren't you the great military commander? Can you not defeat our enemies? Can you not protect a kingdom that has never been breached, with the world's greatest army at your command?"

Hector's shoulders slumped. "Any good commander worth his salt knows battle is unpredictable. Avoiding it is always best. Menelaus will bring his heroes with him. He will bring Achilles and the Myrmidons."

A chill ran through Paris. "Achilles? Why would he bother himself with this? He was not part of the games. He is not loyal to Sparta."

"Achilles was *trained* in Sparta, alongside Castor, Pollux, and even Helen. There were even rumors that Achilles fell in love with her when he stayed there—and that he now fights with such ferocity because he is trying to forget her. He *will* come. And he will bring his men with him."

For the first time, Paris felt a lick of fear. The rumors of Achilles's fierce strength had traveled far and wide. He was said to be stronger than any man alive, able to fight in two places at once, and invulnerable to any weapon created by man. "They say he is the son of a god. That he cannot be harmed."

"No. Achilles is human enough. He bleeds like any man. But he is someone you want standing *next* to you in battle—not *across* from you."

Paris straightened, puffing out his chest. "If he is human, then he can be killed. I see no reason to fear him more than any other man."

"And that is why I fear you doom us," Hector said quietly. "You do not see what the rest of us see." He turned and walked down the hall, leaving Paris staring after him.

As his brother turned the corner, Paris seethed. How dare Hector lecture him on the merits of war? Paris had been in enough battles to know what was at stake. Why, in the last battle, he had even drawn his sword and defended himself. He knew what it meant to go to war.

He turned and strode in the opposite direction, no longer wanting to go and greet his father. He did not want to hear another lecture. Instead, he headed for the courtyard. He needed some air.

When he pushed through the door, a bright sun in a blue sky smiled down upon him. This weather was surely a sign that the gods were indeed on his side. His brother was worried over nothing. They would defeat whoever came to their shores, including the legendary Achilles. Because Hector was right: Achilles was just a man.

And he would die like any other man.

CHAPTER 48

PELION, GREECE

Clytemnestra finished re-packing her things. She was on her ship and waiting along with everyone else for wind to allow them to set sail. She needed something to do to keep her from going insane. As soon as Iphigenia arrived from Mycenae, the two of them would go to Sparta to stay with Helen's children while Agamemnon and Menelaus sailed to Troy. She glanced out at the water, which was as still as glass. *If we ever manage to get there.*

Agamemnon's threat had stayed in the back of her mind and haunted her dreams for this last week. It had her on edge and jumping at shadows. But she was beginning to think he had forgotten about it. He did sometimes; his threats were so common. Now she just needed to get on her ship and set sail for Sparta. But the wind had died down days ago and had refused to blow since. It felt like the calm before the storm.

The door to her cabin flew open. Clytemnestra whirled around her, her hand to her chest.

"Madam, you must come immediately." Her attendant,

Morcant, rushed in. Her dark eyes were wild, and her hair, usually neatly pulled back, lay in a mess upon her head.

"What is it?"

Morcant grabbed her arm and pulled her from the cabin. "Iphigenia. She's here."

Clytemnestra frowned in confusion. "Iphigenia? But she isn't due until—"

"King Agamemnon sent for her yesterday. She arrived only a few moments ago."

You will regret this little rebellion. Clytemnestra's heart began to pound. "Why did he send for her?"

"He said—" Morcant's words were cut off by a cheer from outside. It sounded like dozens of men. Morcant's eyes grew wider, and Clytemnestra's trembling increased. Morcant pulled her out of the cabin and up onto the deck of the ship. It was filled with people staring at the docks.

"Hurry, ma'am, hurry," Morcant begged, pushing through the men.

Clytemnestra was shaking now, but she hurried along in Morcant's wake.

And then the men quieted as one man's voice carried above all the others—Agamemnon's.

"I have angered the god Artemis," his voice boomed. "I mistakenly killed a deer in her sacred grove. I did not know the animal was sacred to her. That is why the gods have refused to provide us with wind to begin our journey."

Morcant broke through the crowd and reached the gangplank, pulling Clytemnestra after her. Clytemnestra saw Agamemnon standing on a platform addressing his men—and she also saw who stood next to him. *Oh gods, no.*

"Artemis has given me a way to apologize to her. I begged her to allow me another method, but she would not be swayed. She demanded the sacrifice of my only daughter, Iphigenia."

Clytemnestra was shaking so hard, she could barely see.

Passing Morcant, she barreled through the gathered crowd, not caring whom she knocked into. When the men realized who she was, they made a path for her. Clytemnestra kept her gaze on Iphigenia, memorizing her light brown hair and her blue eyes. *I love you. I love you*, she thought over and over as she sprinted desperately toward her daughter.

Agamemnon grabbed hold of Iphigenia's hair and yanked her toward him. Iphigenia struggled, tears running down her face, but he held her tight. He pulled a long knife from the sheath at his belt.

"No!" Clytemnestra yelled.

Iphigenia's eyes locked onto Clytemnestra's, with both fear and hope in her gaze. "Mother!"

Agamemnon looked into Clytemnestra's eyes as well—and then ran the blade across Iphigenia's throat. The girl's eyes bulged, and she fell back into Agamemnon's arms.

"*No!*"

Clytemnestra's world slowed down and sped up at the same time. She scrambled up the stairs, sprinted across the platform, and fell to her knees, pulling Iphigenia from Agamemnon's grasp.

Agamemnon put an arm around Clytemnestra, looking to all the world like he was consoling her. He whispered into her ear. "I told you that you would regret denying me."

Then he stood and faced the crowd. "The gods have been appeased. We will sail in the morning."

The men let out a cheer.

But all Clytemnestra saw was her beautiful daughter's face, staring now at nothing. With a shaky hand, she pushed her daughter's hair back and ran a hand over her face as her tears fell on her daughter's cheeks. *I am sorry. I should have been stronger for you. I should have protected you.* She closed the eyes she knew so well one last time. *Sleep, my beautiful girl, and may the gods take you to their bosom.*

Agamemnon looked down at her, a small smile playing on his

lips. Clytemnestra looked back at him and felt only hate. *I will destroy you.* Inside her, any allegiance she had felt to Agamemnon snapped—and in its place, a burning anger took hold.

But she lowered her eyes, feigning submission. She pulled her daughter close and let sorrow overtake her. Tears cascaded down her cheeks, and she sobbed for the daughter she had lost.

I am sorry, my beautiful girl. So very, very sorry.

CHAPTER 49

TROY, TURKEY

Standing on the balcony, eyes closed, her head raised to the sky, Helen took a deep breath. She hated feeling powerless. As if she was just a piece of driftwood being pushed along by the current. She gripped the railing, but the inner calm she was searching for eluded her grasp.

She had been in Troy for three days now, and in those three days she had not once left her room. So far Adorna had been able to claim she was unwell, but Helen knew that lie would not last much longer. Soon she would have to go out and mingle with the ruling family of Troy.

And try to not kill Paris.

She knew that Menelaus would be gathering his army to come and get her back. And because of the agreement her father had elicited from her suitors, she also knew that Menelaus would not be coming alone. What had Paris been thinking? Everyone knew that anyone who intervened in Helen's marriage would face the wrath of the other suitors. Paris had to have known his action would result in war. So why did he do it?

Regardless of what Paris proclaimed—or what he forced her to proclaim—she knew his actions were not driven by love, nor lust, nor even like. So what did he hope to gain—other than his own death? There had to be an easier way to commit suicide.

And Helen could think of no way to stop it. When she left Sparta, she thought there would be an opening, a clue that would allow her to regain the upper hand.

But none had materialized. Her children remained in danger. And she remained here—the personification of a damsel in distress. It was sickening.

A knock sounded at the door, and Helen smiled. Now it was time for this damsel to get some answers. She had been waiting for this. She walked back into the bedroom. "Come in."

A small woman entered and bowed. "Queen Helen, Prince Paris would like you to join him in the courtyard."

"Please tell Prince Paris I would like to speak with him privately first."

The woman faltered. "I believe he is expecting—"

The smile on Helen's face did not waver. "I need to speak with the prince. I will not be leaving my rooms until I do."

The woman looked like a cornered mouse. "Um, yes, Your Highness." She bowed so deeply that for a moment Helen worried she might tip over. Then she hurried from the room, nearly colliding with Adorna as she left.

Adorna looked at Helen. "Terrorizing the help, are we?"

"Hardly. That woman is afraid of her own shadow. What have you learned?"

"The royal family is well liked, I'd even say loved. They take care of their people. The king and queen even remember all their servants' names and ask after their families. Hector, the eldest son, is also revered by all. Paris, however, is… shall we say, less well liked. His demands can at times be rather extreme or petty."

Helen snorted. "Well, that fits. Wasn't there also a daughter?"

"Ah, yes, poor Cassandra. They say she is mad. She claims to have visions, but all agree her mind is simply broken."

Helen wondered about that. She had found that sometimes those whose mind teetered on the brink saw more than those with both feet firmly planted on the ground. "And what do the people think about me?"

"There's some confusion. But no one doubts that you came for love."

Helen blanched. "Wonderful."

Adorna continued. "But they can't quite understand why you would fall for Paris. Hector they could understand, but Paris? He's not viewed as being particularly masculine or strong. And as the queen of Sparta, they feel that's who you would go for."

"They're not wrong about that part," Helen murmured.

"Still, they are happy for Paris to have found such a strong woman."

"Even one who is already married, who left her children behind to follow her lover?"

Adorna shrugged. "No one has mentioned that."

An impatient knock sounded at the door. Adorna looked at Helen. "Are you expecting someone?"

Helen took a seat and straightened her skirts. Adorna had found her some new clothes, but it was taking her some time to get used to these bulky skirts that weighed her down. She missed her Spartan clothes that allowed her to move. *No wonder women here just sit around. Just walking is a trial in this ridiculous dress.* "That would be Paris," she said. "You may want to make yourself scarce while we chat."

"What are you chatting about?"

"It's time to get some answers."

The knocking came again, this time harsher.

Helen waved toward the door. "Please let my beloved in."

Adorna moved toward the door. "I almost feel sorry for the man."

CHAPTER 50

Paris stood impatiently outside Helen's door. The woman did not understand her place. Well, he was going to remind her. He raised his hand to knock yet again when the door opened and he was caught with his fist in the air.

Helen's servant stepped back with a bow. "I bid you please enter, Prince."

Paris passed her without acknowledgement. Helen sat on the other side of the room, and Paris paused in mid-step. She was wearing a blue gown that almost matched her eyes. Her lips were plump as if begging to be kissed. And her skin was so smooth, it invited a man to run a hand over it. She was stunning, a true daughter of the gods.

He was barely aware of the door closing behind him as the servant left them alone.

Helen crossed her arms over her chest and raised an eyebrow. "Prince," she said, derision dripping from her lips.

For Paris, that voice brought everything back into focus. Yes, she was stunning, until she opened that damned mouth of hers. He narrowed his eyes. "You have not been upholding your end of the bargain."

Helen shrugged. "I have been unwell."

"You look fine now."

"I have indeed recovered."

Paris exploded across the room in three angry strides, his hand rising to strike. "Then what is this nonsense? I told you to meet me in the courtyard. How dare you—"

Helen leapt to her feet. "You touch me and it will be the last thing you do," she said quietly.

Paris looked into her eyes. He had no doubt she would do exactly that. By the gods, why would the Spartans raise women like this? Who wanted to fight with a woman over every small thing?

He took a step back, trying to act like he was the one in charge, even as he was overcome by the sinking feeling that Helen was no one's pawn. "So you have changed your mind? You wish your children to die?"

A knife appeared at his eye in a moment, and another below his waist. "If you continue to dangle that threat in front of me," Helen snarled, "I will remove anything that dangles from you. Are we clear?"

Sweat broke out along Paris's brow. "You doom them with your actions."

Helen took a breath and a step back. "We need to make some rules here, you and I. I have agreed to this ridiculous farce only because of my children. But if you continue to provoke me, I cannot guarantee your safety. So I would suggest you stop."

"I own you. You need to remember that."

Helen's eyes narrowed. "I am *owned* by no man. *You* need to remember that."

Paris felt fear snaking through him. It was not supposed to be this hard. By the gods, what had he gotten himself into? Zeus had better keep his part of the bargain.

Helen broke the staring contest first, taking yet another step back. She put up her hands. "I suggest we call a truce. For all our sakes."

Paris gave an abrupt nod.

"All right," Helen said. "I think you and I have some things to discuss before I meet with your family. They will assume we've spoken at length and know about each other's lives. It seems wise not to meet with them until we have covered some basic details."

Paris could have kicked himself. She was right. They did need to talk. "Fine. What do you need to know?"

"According to your story, we fell in love when you came to Sparta."

"Yes. And?"

"Well, why did you come to Sparta? You knew Menelaus was not there."

"We had trouble with the ship and we needed safe harbor to make repairs."

Helen's eyes bored into him as if they could strip away the falsehoods and find the truth. But Paris held firm. "What else?"

Helen sat back down. "You did not grow up in Troy. You only arrived here when you were approaching manhood. Where were you raised?"

Paris glared. He hated this topic. His ignoble upbringing was something he never wished to dwell upon. "Why does it matter?"

"Because you are my beloved, and I should know."

"I was raised by a shepherd."

"So the tales are true."

Paris nodded. Before his birth, a seer had warned his family that he would lead to their destruction. His parents had been told to kill him as soon as he was born. But neither of them could bring themselves to do the deed. Instead they handed him over to a man named Agelaus, with the instruction that *he* should kill him.

But yet again, Paris was spared; Agelaus could not bring himself to kill the babe either—at least, not with his own hands. He left him on Mount Ida for the animals. But three days later, he returned to find that Paris was still alive. Agelaus took it as a sign, and he took the boy home and raised him as his own.

Being cast out from his family as a baby was why he had never had the benefit of the military training Hector had. And it was why he threw himself into all the adventures he could find. He was *owed* the luxuries he had been denied as a child. And when Zeus offered him the world in return for this farce with Helen, he grabbed it with both hands. It was his due.

"How were you found?" Helen asked.

"Cassandra, my sister. She claimed that I was their son—and for once she was right."

Surprise flashed across Helen's face. "They believed her?"

Paris straightened. "Once they saw me, it was obvious I was from the royal line. It did not take any more than one glance." It was true—he looked too much like Hector for the relationship to be denied. And so his parents, Priam and Hecuba, opened their arms to him. *After ordering my death*, he thought bitterly.

"Hm," Helen said.

"What does that mean?"

"Nothing. It's just I thought Cassandra was merely mad—but apparently she is not. She does have the sight."

Paris scoffed. "Please. She was right one time—that does not make her a seer. She rambles around here making proclamations about this and that, comporting herself like a crazy woman rather than a princess of Troy. I do not know how she knew of me, but she is nothing more than an insane person. Father should have locked her away years ago."

Helen raised an eyebrow. "Then you never would have been found."

Paris puffed up. "*I am a prince of Troy*. I would have made my way home. After all, the gods watch out for me."

"What do you mean, the gods watch out for you? Are you—are you blessed?" Helen asked. For once, she looked scared. Paris smiled. Even the mighty Helen of Sparta feared the gods.

"I am," Paris said. "The gods have visited me." He looked down his nose at Helen, feeling the return of the pride he'd felt when he'd realized the king of the gods himself had chosen him for this mission. "They even gave me you."

"I don't understand."

"You were my gift. They told me I was your rightful husband, and that if I followed their instructions I would have treasure beyond my wildest imaginings."

Helen traced a shape in her dress. "Which gods promised you? It couldn't have been anyone of import. Maybe Eros or Dionysus—"

"It was Zeus himself. So you see, the king of the gods supports me. Which means you need to be more careful with how you treat me."

Helen looked up, and the fear Paris thought he'd seen before was now nowhere in evidence. She stood. "Of course, my prince. Shall we go?"

Paris stared at her for a moment, unsure what had just happened. But Helen brushed past him and opened the door. "Are you coming?"

Paris found himself hurrying toward her, then slowed his pace. He gave her a nod as he swept by her out the door. "I'm glad you're finally realizing your place."

"But of course, my prince," she murmured behind him. The words were right, but the tone sent chills down his spine.

CHAPTER 51

Helen held Paris's arm lightly as they walked toward the courtyard. The home of the royal family was beautiful. The walls were stone but draped with rich tapestries, providing color. And wildflowers were in every room, their scent wafting through the rooms and out into the corridor.

Ahead, the doors stood open, and beyond them was the courtyard. The sun beat down on trees and colorful flowers. A small yellow bird flew by the door, and at the sight of it, Helen ached to get outside. She missed being able to feel the grass between her toes and run for miles without seeing another soul. Of course, that wouldn't be an option here.

When at last they stepped outside, Helen couldn't help but gasp. Dozens of flowering trees dotted the courtyard, and roses bloomed along its outer edge. In the center stood a giant willow tree with a swing attached to one of the lower branches. There was even a small creek, running beneath the tree and disappearing under the citadel's walls.

"It's beautiful," she said.

Paris looked around the courtyard and shrugged. "It's fine. I prefer indoors."

Of course you do, you pathetic man, Helen thought

Beneath the tree stood a man and a woman. The man had obviously once been tall, but was now stooped with age. The woman had long white hair and a royal bearing. Both turned as Helen and Paris approached.

The woman smiled. "Paris, dear." She kissed him on both cheeks.

Paris turned to Helen. "May I present my mother, Queen Hecuba of Troy."

Helen curtsied. "Your Highness."

"Oh, none of that," Hecuba admonished with a smile. She placed her hands on Helen's shoulders and pulled her in for a hug. "You are the woman who has won my son's heart."

When she released Helen and stepped back, King Priam stepped forward. Helen gave another curtsy. "King Priam."

"Queen Helen." He inclined his head with a small smile on his face.

"Paris!"

Helen turned to see a taller, more masculine version of Paris striding across the courtyard. He was well-built and battle-scarred, and wore a serious expression. He bowed to his father and kissed his mother on the cheek before turning to Helen. "Queen Helen," he said.

She curtsied again, though inside she cussed the stupid requirement. She felt like a bird bobbing its head. "Prince Hector."

Hector acknowledged her with a nod before turning to Paris. "You were supposed to be at the training field an hour ago."

Paris took Helen's hand, and she struggled not to yank it away. "I have been so caught up with Helen that I lost all sense of time."

Hecuba sighed happily, and Helen tried not to gag. Who said such things?

Hector gave Helen a small smile. "Yes, Queen Helen's legend only underplayed her beauty. But we need to prepare."

"How are the preparations going?" Priam asked.

Hector's gaze flicked to Helen before returning to his father. "We'll be ready, Father."

Helen knew he meant they were preparing for war. Her stomach clutched at the thought of all the men who would die. Zeus had put this all into play. But why? It obviously wasn't to make a match between her and Paris. What was Zeus's plan? What did he hope to gain?

"Have we heard," Priam glanced at Helen, "anything from across the Aegean?"

"They have mobilized. They are on their way here."

Helen felt a chill run through her. It had already begun. *Gods help us all.*

Paris sighed dramatically, kissing Helen's hand. "I'm afraid that duty calls, my dear. I will see you later?"

Helen bowed her head. "I look forward to it," she said breathlessly, while forcing herself to not wipe his kiss off her hand.

Both sons kissed their mother, bowed to their father, and headed out of the courtyard, leaving Helen with the king and queen. Hecuba linked arms with Helen. "My dear, you must tell me all about how you and Paris met."

"Yes of course," Helen said, watching Hector and Paris disappear from the courtyard. All she could think about was the war that was coming. The war she was in the middle of for some reason. She wanted to scream in frustration.

"It will be all right, my dear," King Priam said. Helen realized that he, too, was worried about what was coming to Troy's shores. That he understood what Paris's actions meant for all of Troy. He understood that death was coming. "We will be ready. And the gods' will shall be done." With a small bow, Priam turned and strode off.

But Helen knew he was wrong. Whoever had set all of this into motion was no god. It was someone else's will that drove them all toward a battlefield filled with senseless death.

CHAPTER 52

What a strange day, Helen thought as she returned to her room that evening. She had spent almost all of it with the king and queen. She had met Hector's wife and children. And all the members of Paris's family had extended her a warm welcome, as if she were indeed his beloved and not a woman who had been stolen from her home—or a woman already married.

Helen was having a tough time understanding it. Maybe it was because she was Spartan, but in her world, any child who brought the wrath of another family down upon their own family—never mind kingdom upon kingdom—would not be so lightly indulged.

She realized, though, that they were trying to make up for Paris's lost childhood. For abandoning him out of fear of the prediction made at his birth. None of them realized that that prediction was about to come true: Paris would be the destruction of them all.

And since he had returned to them, Paris had been happy to take advantage of their guilt—ensuring his every whim was indulged. It was why he thought nothing was amiss when the gods promised him wealth beyond his imagining. Because in Paris's own mind, that was his due.

But who were these "gods"? Helen held no illusions—she knew the gods were not real, at least not the ones that spoke to Paris. Whoever was behind her abduction was no god—but he *was* powerful. He had money and connections. And the ability to hide his tracks.

But she could not for the life of her figure out why. Who stood to benefit when the world went to war? Death benefited no one. And Troy was not even one of the wealthier kingdoms; why focus on Troy?

Helen stripped off the ridiculous gown and pulled on her tunic. She flopped down on the bed and let out a breath. It had been difficult seeing Hector's children today. He had a daughter almost the same age as Hermione, and seeing her caused Helen both comfort and pain.

And then there was this stupid ruse. It could not go on forever. Whatever Paris wanted, he would one day get it if all Helen did was play along. And then what would happen to her children?

No. She needed to figure out what Paris was up to, and she needed to get her children away from his forces. She stared at the unfamiliar ceiling. *But how will I do that from here?*

She had overheard Priam speaking with Hector just after dinner. The Greek ships had been spotted; they would land in a few days. A chill ran over her.

And then the dying will begin.

CHAPTER 53

PELION, GREECE

The wind had returned the next morning—just as Agamemnon had promised it would—and the fleet had finally been able to depart for Troy. Agamemnon made a public show of telling Clytemnestra that she should stay behind to mourn for their beloved girl. Clytemnestra barely heard him. She was too busy trying to breathe through her grief.

Now, two days later, all she wanted to do was sleep—which was all she had been doing since Iphigenia's murder. She had awoken briefly this morning, only long enough to eat something, and then had turned back over and drifted off to sleep. In sleep, there was nothing. There was a blankness there, a blankness that Clytemnestra craved. No, *needed*.

So she closed her eyes and prayed to the gods to continue keeping her dreams empty.

But this time they didn't listen.

CLYTEMNESTRA WATCHED Iphigenia gather flowers in the garden. The girl was only six years old. "Mother, come see the butterfly."

Clytemnestra smiled and walked over to her daughter.

"It's there." Iphigenia pointed to a blue and green butterfly. "Isn't it beautiful?"

Clytemnestra ran a hand over Iphigenia's hair. "It is. Just like you, my beautiful daughter."

Iphigenia wrapped her arms around Clytemnestra's waist. "I love you, Mommy."

Tears sprang to Clytemnestra's eyes. She had been loved by her mother, by her brothers and sister, and she had loved them in return. But her love for her children—it eclipsed everything she had ever known. Even her sons, whom Agamemnon had turned against her, she loved. But Iphigenia—there was a special place in Clytemnestra's heart reserved just for her. "I love you too, my dear."

"It's not your fault. It's his."

Clytemnestra stilled as the sun disappeared behind the clouds and the wind picked up. She looked down at her daughter. "What did you say?"

Iphigenia stepped away, aging before Clytemnestra's eyes. Now she stood at almost eye level with her. "It was not your fault. Father is to blame."

The vision of Iphigenia's death played in Clytemnestra's mind. "I should have stood up to him sooner. Or never married him at all."

"But then we never would have been. And we needed to be with you."

Clytemnestra's chest heaved. "But I failed you."

"You never failed us. He did. But now you must fight. You must help Helen."

"How? I am not as strong as she is. I am not as brave."

"You are. You are the same. You always have been."

"I don't know what to do. I don't know how to help Helen. I have no army. I am not the fighter she is."

"You are a daughter of Sparta. You have just forgotten." Iphigenia glanced over her shoulder, and Clytemnestra saw shadowy figures behind her, although she sensed no menace from them. "I need to go."

Clytemnestra reached out her hand. "I cannot bear to let you go."

Iphigenia kissed her cheek. "I am never gone from you, Mother. I am always by your side." She began to walk backward toward the shadows, her smile never wavering. "Remember that. I will always be with you."

∽

Clytemnestra's eyes snapped open. "Iphigenia!" She sat upright, her hands reaching for her daughter. And the loss hit her all over again.

Morcant was at her side in a flash. "Shh, child. It's all right. Morcant is here."

Tears rolled down Clytemnestra's cheeks. She ached for her daughter. A wind blew through the window, making the curtains billow, and for just a moment Clytemnestra thought she caught a glimpse of a girl in their shape.

I am never gone from you, Mother. I am always by your side.

The weight on Clytemnestra's chest lifted enough for her to wipe away the tears.

"Clytemnestra?" Morcant asked, her voice anxious.

Clytemnestra gripped her hand. "Fetch me a bath, Morcant. There are things we must do."

"What things, my lady?"

Clytemnestra shook her head. "I'm not sure, to be honest. Find Aegisthus. Tell him I need to speak with him." Aegisthus was one of her most trusted servants and an accomplished sailor. Clytemnestra's father had given him leave from his Spartan duty to be available for Clytemnestra.

"Aegisthus? Why do you need him?"

"Because we need to sail to Sparta to bury my daughter—and to help Helen."

CHAPTER 54

TROY, TURKEY

The ships had begun arriving at Troy a week ago. Pollux surveyed the tents that had popped up around his own. There had been a hundred when he first arrived with Castor and Barnabus, and now there were easily five times that number—with more men still arriving.

He looked toward Troy. The city was well fortified; its thick, tall stone walls were said to have been built by the gods Apollo and Poseidon themselves. No one had ever been able to get through them. *But we'll get to her.*

He was tempted to ignore everything else and just run past Troy's defenses himself. But he knew there were Fallen roaming the perimeter. He'd be detected immediately, and that would not help Helen. No, first he needed to find out exactly where she was being held. He had spies in the encampment already—a few Trojans looking to make some extra money. Now he just needed to wait.

A tingle ran over his skin, and he spotted Barnabus walking through the crowd toward him. He did not look happy.

Pollux met him halfway down the line of tents. "What is it?"

"Agamemnon has arrived."

"Good. His men can set up—"

Barnabus placed his hand on Pollux's arm. "I have news."

A feeling of dread crawled over Pollux. "What is it?"

Barnabus met Pollux's gaze. "Agamemnon could not set sail for days. There was no wind. So a sacrifice was made."

Pollux nodded. It was not an unusual occurrence to sacrifice an animal prior to a launch. "So?"

"It was... Iphigenia."

"What was Iphigenia?"

"The sacrifice."

Pollux went still. *Iphigenia?*

He had known her well—she had spent half her young life in Sparta. She had always been a shy, quiet girl, but along the way, something had happened to make her even more shy. When she had last come to see them, she had hidden behind Clytemnestra's skirts for the whole first day. Pollux had known Agamemnon was somehow responsible for her behavior, but Clytemnestra had begged him to leave it alone. So Pollux had shown Iphigenia the pups that had been born down in the stable just before they arrived. The girl's face had lit up. She had spent the whole next week with him down in the stables, taking care of them. He had seen a softness to her then—a softness he loved and wanted to protect. This world could be cruel to those with a kind heart.

Her smile and laugh played through his mind. "Who?" Pollux asked quietly. "Who killed her?"

"Agamemnon."

Cold fury stole over Pollux. Without a word he turned on his heel and headed for the beach.

Barnabus hurried to keep up with him. "Pollux, be careful what you do next. He is a king and—"

Pollux cut him off, furious. "And she was my sister's daughter—and she was *good*."

Castor appeared between the tents and fell in step with Pollux. With one look at Castor's face, Pollux knew he had heard the news as well. "*I get to kill him,*" Pollux said.

Castor nodded. "Fine. But don't kill him too quickly."

"Fine."

"Gentlemen," Barnabus tried again, "perhaps we should take some time to think through the ramifications of this action."

"Agamemnon!" Pollux yelled, catching sight of his brother-in-law up ahead.

"Or we can just skip that and get right to the fighting," Barnabus muttered.

Agamemnon turned to face the approaching brothers with a smile. "Castor, Pollux, good to see—"

Pollux slammed his fist into Agamemnon's face. Agamemnon flew backward. A dozen of his men rushed to his defense, taking positions between Agamemnon and Pollux.

Pollux ducked a spear aimed at his head, shoved the weapon aside, and kicked the man in the ribs. From the corner of his eye, he saw Barnabus give a weary sigh before clotheslining a man attempting to attack Pollux from the side. After that, Pollux had no time to think—only to react.

He, Castor, and Barnabus stood back to back as Agamemnon's men rushed them. Fists, swords, spears came in a flurry of attacks. But Pollux's fury was so great that he did not care. All he could see was Iphigenia. And his need to punish Agamemnon overrode everything else.

As he kicked a man in the ribs, sending him into three others, he saw a disturbance at the back of the group of men, as if someone was fighting toward him. Hoping it was Agamemnon, he fought harder to reach him.

But it was not Agamemnon. It was a large man who almost effortlessly flung Agamemnon's soldier aside. He let out a yell that rang through the camp and into the mountains themselves. "*Enough!*"

Everyone went still

The large man extended his arm to Pollux. "I see you and Pollux are still as charming as ever."

Pollux clasped the offered arm. "Achilles."

Achilles gestured to the men littering the beach around them. "Care to tell me why I just beat up a good dozen men?"

Pollux looked around for Agamemnon, but the coward was gone. "My niece was sacrificed by Agamemnon."

Achilles winced. "I am sorry, my friend."

Pollux grabbed a sword from the ground. "Thank you for the help. But I'm not quite done."

Achilles threw an arm around Pollux and steered him back toward the tents, leaning down so he could not be overheard. "It is not the time for this."

"He killed—"

"I know. But Helen is still at risk. And human waste though he is, we need Agamemnon. And more importantly, his men."

Pollux shook his head. "No—he dies."

"Fine. But how about we do it *after* we get Helen back? I'll even hold him down if you wish."

"I don't need—"

Achilles pulled Pollux to a stop. "Let us drink to your niece. Let us remember her and honor her."

Grief washed over Pollux. "She was just a child, Achilles."

"This world can be cruel to the innocent. Let us drink to her and immortalize her in stories."

Pollux caught Castor's eyes and the world of grief in them. He knew his own eyes had the same pained look. He was not thinking clearly. "All right."

Achilles clapped him on the shoulder and nodded to Barnabus with a grin. "It looks like the old gang is getting back together. Let us take a moment to enjoy it before we begin this bloody business."

Pollux could not believe it was Achilles who was talking him down. Achilles, who as a teenager would start a fight if someone merely looked at him wrong. And from reports, Achilles had not mellowed in the time since he had left Sparta; he had grown even more reckless, more angry. But this man walking next to Pollux was an older, wiser Achilles.

Still, Pollux remembered the power of Achilles's rage on that last night before he was banished. He was glad to have his powerful friend at his side. Because even with the gods themselves helping Paris, he did not think the boy prince would fare well against a wrathful Achilles.

CHAPTER 55

Within two days of Agamemnon's arrival, the remainder of their force had arrived. Now all that remained was for the order to be given by Agamemnon.

Agamemnon's men created a path through the throngs of waiting men. He could feel their energy, their rage, their eagerness to fight, and he reveled in all that power being at his fingertips. Ahead, the wooden platform he'd had his men erect stood waiting for him. It was positioned to allow him to see almost all of the battlefield without getting too close. Anticipation and excitement rolled through him. This was the moment when all his carefully laid plans would begin to bear fruit. He climbed the steps to the platform, careful to keep his expression serious.

A somber Menelaus walked behind him. His brother had thrown all his focus into war preparations, poring over every map and plan, inspecting the troops, and gathering information on their strengths and weaknesses. All that information he then conveyed to Agamemnon.

Castor and Pollux flanked Menelaus. Agamemnon ignored them, although his eye still bore the signs of Pollux's greeting.

Helen's brothers were known for their incredible loyalty to Helen, and they apparently extended that loyalty to Iphigenia as well. He had not considered that. But it was no matter. Castor and Pollux were incredible fighters, and they would help the Greeks succeed. And once he succeeded, Agamemnon would make sure he repaid both Castor and Pollux for their insult.

A small twinge of jealousy reared up inside him when he saw Castor pat Menelaus on the shoulder, but Agamemnon shoved it away. Menelaus was loyal to Agamemnon above all others; Agamemnon had spent his life cultivating that loyalty. There was nothing that would change it.

Dismissing the three men from his thoughts, he turned to the sea of soldiers staring at him. All the houses of Greece stood before him—a sea of battle-hardened men ready to fight to the death at Agamemnon's command.

Even among this majestic fighting force, one group stood out: Achilles and his Myrmidon. In size they eclipsed every other group. There were rumors that no man was considered for their ranks until he could wrestle a bear and fill a citadel doorway. Most discounted the tales, but seeing them standing together, legs braced, arms crossed over their powerful chests, even Agamemnon wondered if there might be a hint of truth in the tales.

Achilles stood at their front, stone-faced. He looked like he could take on the gods himself. Some said he *was* a god. However, Agamemnon knew that Achilles had a fatal flaw: his love for Helen. *Fool.* Achilles could end this all in a moment with his abilities, but fear of what Helen would say or do stayed his hand. One woman had enraptured an entire world of men. All who gazed upon her seemed to fall under her sway.

But that ability of hers was what had allowed all of this to happen. It was going to allow Agamemnon to go down in history as one of the world's greatest military commanders. *So thank you, Helen.*

Agamemnon raised his arms. "Brothers, we have been brought together to right a grave injustice. Many of us were there when Menelaus was chosen as Helen's rightful husband. All of us pledged to honor that choice."

He curled his lip. "But the prince of Troy has no such honor. He has stolen Helen from her rightful place. And his act is not against Sparta or Menelaus alone. He insults us all with his actions. Does he think so little of the power of the Greeks that he throws our pledge in our faces? Does he think so little of our ability that he thinks walls of stone can keep him safe?"

"No!" the men roared back at him.

"How dare he take a woman of Greece. And not just any woman—the queen of Sparta! She is beloved by the entirety of our people. She is the glory of Greece. And he dares to remove her from our land?"

More yells answered him.

"This injustice will not go unpunished. This insult will not go unanswered. Paris, and all of Troy, will pay for this violation. Helen will be returned to her rightful place. And Paris will be sent to his—under the heel of our sandals!"

The men banged their spears and swords against their shields and yelled, "Helen! Helen!"

Agamemnon smiled at their enthusiasm, feeling the bloodlust in the air. "Now go and retrieve our queen!" he yelled.

The men turned and marched toward the walls of Troy. Agamemnon watched with satisfaction—a human wave of violence. *Yes, go get the whore.*

CHAPTER 56

The dream of Iphigenia had stayed with Clytemnestra throughout the long journey to Sparta. But as the shoreline came into view, she had begun to doubt. If Agamemnon had taught her anything these long years, it was how truly powerless she was. How could she possibly do anything to help Helen?

So she had gently pushed the dream aside and focused on the business at hand: saying goodbye to her beloved daughter. Morcant had suggested interring Iphigenia in Mycenae, but Clytemnestra would not hear of it. The only place her daughter would rest easy was in Sparta.

Now Clytemnestra climbed the same hill where she had said goodbye to both her father and mother. The entire household was present to pay their respects.

Darius gently laid Iphigenia's body on the pyre. Hermione clasped Clytemnestra's hand, tears rolling down her cheeks. Her grief was raw and palpable. Iphigenia had been her older sister, her best friend, her confidante. In a strange way, the depth of Hermione's grief was a comfort to Clytemnestra—it helped to know that someone loved her daughter as much as she did.

Clytemnestra gently detached her hand from Hermione's and, with a trembling breath, lit the pyre on fire. Then she stepped back and watched the flames consume her daughter. One by one the other mourners left, until only Hermione and Clytemnestra remained. The two of them stood together, holding on to one another, as Iphigenia's body slowly turned to ash. They stayed until the last flicker had died away. *Goodbye, my love.*

∽

EARLY THE NEXT MORNING, Hermione and her brothers left for training with the guards. Without their company and distraction Clytemnestra felt lost. She spent the days wandering aimlessly around the citadel, looking for some sign of what Iphigenia had wanted her to do. But there was nothing. Just reminders of Helen and Iphigenia's absence.

Clytemnestra had finally decided she would leave for Troy. Perhaps there she would find a way to help Helen. But fate had other plans as her door was flung open before dawn the next morning.

Boudica, trainer of the guards, pulled back the drapes. "Still in bed, I see."

Clytemnestra blinked against the light. "Boudica? What are you doing?"

Boudica marched to the bed. Her tall, muscular frame towered over Clytemnestra. As a child, she had terrified Clytemnestra, and the years had only given the formidable woman an even harder edge. "What am I doing? What are *you* doing, daughter of Sparta? You walk around here like a ghost, or a mewling cow from Athens."

"How dare you! I mourn for the—"

"You should be seeking *revenge* on those who took her. You can mourn when you, too, are dead. Or do you think *this* is how you honor Iphigenia?"

Clytemnestra flung herself from the bed. "Do not *ever* speak of my daughter."

A smile slowly spread across Boudica's face. "Ah, there is the Clytemnestra I trained. I thought Mycenae had gotten rid of her for good."

"Almost," she muttered.

For just a moment, compassion flashed across Boudica's face. But then her scowl returned. "Well then, let's see what else you remember. Training starts at first light, which means you're almost late." She started toward the door. "Don't eat much, because you'll probably be seeing it again before lunch."

Clytemnestra gaped as Boudica disappeared out the door. How dare she! And train? She hadn't picked up a weapon since she had married Agamemnon. She couldn't possibly train with the warriors again.

But the idea of training, of losing herself in something physical, lit a spark inside her. She grabbed her tunic and quickly dressed. She'd need to get to the yard fast, because Boudica's punishments for being late were legendary.

CHAPTER 57

Two months passed quickly. The news from Troy was not good. The Greek army was winning the skirmishes, but still had been unable to pass the walls of Troy. Clytemnestra knew she should grieve for the men who were losing their lives, but she could not work up the compassion. To be honest, she was enjoying the peace of having no one to answer to—save for Boudica during training hours. Her muscles had protested at first, but soon she longed for the aches and exhaustion. They always led to a dreamless sleep. And always, she kept watch for some sign to show her how she could help Helen.

Then one day Hermione came into the training yard. She had been away the entire time Clytemnestra had been in training. She had just returned before noon but Clytemnestra had yet to see her. When she caught sight of Clytemnestra, she let out a cry. "Mother!"

She sprinted across the yard, nearly getting killed more than once as she dodged between sparring matches. Soldiers yanked their weapons back to keep from striking the young girl. Oblivious, Hermione sprinted forward and flung herself at Clytemnestra's legs.

Clytemnestra went still. Hermione's arms around her felt so much like Iphigenia's that for a moment her heart stopped and her breath caught. But then she got hold of herself and laid a gentle hand on Hermione's hair. "Hermione, it's me. It's Clytemnestra."

Hermione looked up, tears in her hazel eyes, confusion on her face. "Clytemnestra?"

Clytemnestra nodded.

"But—but, you look like Mother. You move just like her."

"We are twins. We look alike."

Hermione shook her head. "I've never confused you before."

"I know. You miss her. You are seeing her everywhere."

Hermione nodded, wiping the tears on her cheek, her shoulders slumping.

"Why don't you go to the kitchens? Cook made a cake this morning. She could be talked into an early taste for you, I'm sure."

"Okay." She started to leave, then turned around quickly, her eyes still wet with tears. "Will you come?"

"Yes. I will be along shortly."

"Okay." Hermione walked back across the training field, much more slowly this time. Clytemnestra's heart broke, as did the hearts of everyone else who watched her leave.

Boudica stepped up behind her. "She's right, you know."

Clytemnestra turned. "What do you mean?"

"You are the picture of Helen. It is like having her here. The only difference is your hair. I bet you could even fool the brothers."

Clytemnestra laughed. "That's—" Then she went still, her eyes snapping to Boudica's face and a smile spreading across her own. "That's perfect."

CHAPTER 58

Clytemnestra had wanted to leave for Troy right away, to put her plan into action, but it took three days for Aegisthus to prepare her ship—and besides, she was worried about Hermione. Boudica promised she would do her best to keep the girl distracted in Clytemnestra's absence; Clytemnestra felt a twinge of doubt as to what Boudica might think was a suitable distraction, but she also knew that Boudica, for all her gruffness, had a soft spot for children.

The voyage to Troy took five days. The winds were in their favor. They arrived south of Troy in a cove, and Clytemnestra and Aegisthus made their way across the land, careful to stay out of sight.

But when they reached the Greek camp, Clytemnestra grew uneasy. Back in Sparta, she had begun to feel at peace—but here, the reminders of Iphigenia's violent death were all around her, in every face she saw. And the confidence she had regained began to slip as well. In her mind, she could hear Agamemnon taunting her weaknesses. *No*, she thought, forcefully. *I am not that woman any longer.*

Despite her attempt to keep her doubts and insecurities at bay, though she felt raw and unbalanced. But she couldn't let her brothers see any of that. If they did, they would never help her.

Aegisthus went ahead and found the brothers' tent, then returned to Clytemnestra to lead her to them. Aegisthus stood guard outside the tent as Clytemnestra took a deep breath and ducked inside.

Castor turned to her with a frown. "Who—" And then he went still.

Clytemnestra saw the look of shock splashed across her brothers' faces.

"Helen?" Pollux asked.

Clytemnestra shook her head and lowered her hood. "Close."

"Clytemnestra? But your hair…" Pollux touched her golden locks.

"Easily changed. Did you really think I was Helen?"

Castor nodded, his eyes never leaving her face. "It's uncanny."

"Well, if I can fool you two, I can fool anyone."

Pollux frowned. "What does that mean?"

"It means I have a plan to get Helen out."

She explained what she had in mind. But before she was even finished, both brothers were shaking their heads.

"No," Pollux said. "It's too dangerous,"

"It's not," she insisted. "It's the only way. We need to know what's going on. And we all know Helen hasn't taken up with that idiot."

Pollux grinned. "You actually sounded like Helen just now."

Pollux slapped Castor on the arm. "Don't encourage her."

"Ouch." Castor rubbed his arm before he turned to Clytemnestra. "I agree with Pollux. It's too dangerous."

"As dangerous as it was for Iphigenia when I stayed out of it?" Clytemnestra took Castor's hand. "I have to do this. For Iphigenia."

Castor's face fell. "Oh, sister, I am so sorry. We never told you—"

She waved his words away, not wanting to give her grief an inch. "I know you loved her."

Castor nodded at Pollux. "He nearly killed your husband. Achilles stopped him before he could."

"A shame he held you back," she murmured.

"My thoughts too," Pollux said darkly.

Clytemnestra suffered a sudden image of Iphigenia staring at her, blood pooling along her neck. She gripped Castor's arm. "You *must* let me do this. I cannot sit back any longer and watch my family be destroyed. Helen needs us. Helen needs *me*. And I will find a way to help her, with or without you."

"No," Castor said. Next to him, Pollux nodded his agreement.

Clytemnestra looked between her brothers. She pictured the strong women in her life—her mother, Helen, Boudica, even Adorna. They had a way of making others do as they wished. And damn it, she wanted to be one of them.

Summoning her courage, she crossed her arms and narrowed her eyes. "Yes."

CHAPTER 59

TROY, TURKEY

Helen sat on the balcony, her back resting against the palace wall, her knees pulled into her chest. The war had been going on for two months now. She had listened to the cries of men losing their lives. Did she have the right to doom them to this war? All these men were someone's son, someone's father, someone's brother. Did she have the right to put her children before the lives of potentially thousands? But how could she sacrifice her children?

When the fighting had begun, Paris had gleefully told her that all the people she cared about would be destroyed. Helen knew his promise of death to all she loved was a young man's boast. But men *would* die. Men she cared for. And all because a stupid little boy was reaching for a treasure he did not deserve. He was a pawn.

And what are you, if not the same? If she was honest, the voice at the back of her mind was right. Paris had pulled the one string guaranteed to make her jump.

Helen rested her head on her knees and stared at the night sky.

Did Paris not realize how many would die? How many already had? And for what? Her alleged honor? An honor, according to the rest of the world, that she had already abandoned as soon as she had run off with Paris.

She had racked her brain trying to understand the motivation behind the events that had been set in motion. And she had done what research she could. King Priam had been kind enough to let her use his extensive library, and Helen had found a little-used section that addressed the Fallen. After re-reading the tale of their fall, she could come to only one answer: Samyaza and Zeus were gathering their forces.

But what was "Zeus" up to? She knew Zeus had been taking out Fallen who weren't interested in working with him, and she knew Zeus was behind Paris's move. But were those two actions connected? And why focus on Troy? Was Zeus on Troy's side? But even that made no sense. The battle was happening on Troy's doorstep. Even if Troy was victorious, they would gain nothing after having lost much.

Did that mean Zeus was on the side of the Greeks? But then why sacrifice so many of Greece's sons? And for what purpose? And if they won, Troy would be destroyed. There would be little treasure for the victor when split amongst all the houses who had waged the war.

Helen wanted to pull her hair out and scream in frustration. *This makes no sense.*

She was going around and around and getting nowhere. She needed to focus. And she was certain that the key to all of this was finding out who Zeus was. He had to be someone with power. Or at least someone *connected* to power. Samyaza was a master at working behind the scenes. Could he be the real mastermind?

The door to her room opened behind her. Adorna had gone to the kitchens to retrieve some dinner for Helen to eat in her room. After hearing the latest death toll, Helen couldn't bear to eat with Paris or his family. She didn't trust herself to not rip out Paris's throat—and she pitied his family, who had all been put in jeopardy because of their ridiculous son.

"I'm not hungry, Adorna. You go ahead," Helen called, not taking her gaze from the night sky.

Adorna stepped onto the balcony. "I've brought a guest for dinner."

Helen sighed. "Adorna, you know I'm in no—"

"I think this guest will be to your liking."

Shaking her head, Helen uncurled herself from the ledge and stepped into the room.

A woman stood by the door, her face covered in a veil. Helen had seen a few women around Troy dressed as such. Sometimes it was due to mourning, other times due to a strict husband or father who did not want their daughter's virtues seen by any men.

"Can I help you?" Helen asked.

The woman pulled back her veil. "Actually, I think it is I who can help you."

Helen stared at the woman in disbelief. "Clytemnestra?"

Her sister smiled.

Helen could not believe that her sister was here in Troy, in her room. She also marveled at her sister's appearance. For once, they looked like the twins they were. Clytemnestra had turned her hair as blond as Helen's, and there was a color to her cheeks, as if she had spent time outdoors. Gods' truth, they'd be impossible to tell apart now, except among those who truly knew them.

"How did you get in?"

"Pollux brought me over the wall and quickly returned to the other side."

Helen gaped. That had been a huge risk. The Fallen constantly roamed the walls. In fact, she had been worried about Castor foolishly pursuing a misguided rescue attempt. But never had she imagined it would be Clytemnestra who came to her. "You never should have—"

Clytemnestra's smile dimmed, and her chin began to wobble. "I needed to see you."

Her obvious grief made Helen gasp. She sprinted across the space and hugged her sister to her tightly. "What has happened?"

Clytemnestra clung to her sister, her whole body shaking. "He killed Iphigenia."

Helen did not need to ask who, because she already knew. Anger hit deep and burned through her. It was joined by grief that went all the way to the bone. "Oh, sister, no."

Helen's words seemed to cut the strings holding Clytemnestra upright. Her knees buckled, and Helen had to hold her upright. Adorna hurried over, and the two women helped Clytemnestra to the bed.

Helen sat beside her sister, her arms wrapped around her. "Tell me everything."

And Clytemnestra did. She didn't stop talking for hours. Finally, she lay quiet, her head in Helen's lap as Helen stroked her hair.

"I should never have let you marry him," Helen said. "I should have—"

Clytemnestra wiped her eyes. "You tried to stop me, to warn me. You share no blame for this. The blame is mine."

"No," Helen said forcefully. "The blame is Agamemnon's. Don't you dare carry it for him."

Clytemnestra nodded wearily. "You are right."

They sat quietly. Helen marveled at all her sister had been through, and cursed herself up one side and down at the other for not stopping her sister all those years ago. She had known who Agamemnon was, even then. She should have tried harder, locked her sister away until she saw reason.

Finally Clytemnestra sat up, wiping her tears. "There will be time for grief later. Now we need to get you out of here."

Helen looked away. "I cannot. I have chosen Paris."

"You listen to me, Helen. You may say whatever you wish to

the rest of the world, but I know you. I *know* you. And I know you are lying. What does he hold over you?"

"Nothing. I—"

"Enough." Clytemnestra's gaze was unrelenting. "Tell me."

And then it was Helen who found herself talking for hours. She told Clytemnestra everything, starting with Paris's arrival and continuing all through her stay here at Troy. When she was done, she felt like a weight had been lifted, even though nothing had truly changed.

Clytemnestra gripped her hand. "I knew he had to have something on you. You would never turn your back on your family. Or on your duty."

"Not unless something more important was at risk."

"Tomorrow, we will get you out of here, and then—"

"No. Did you not hear what I said? Hermione, the boys—they are in danger. I cannot risk their lives."

"You won't have to, because you will remain here."

Helen frowned. "Then why did you say that I should go?"

Clytemnestra ran a hand through her hair. "Why do you think I am here? I will stay in your place. You will get your children to safety and then find out who is behind this. Because I agree—Paris is not smart enough to do this on his own."

"Clytemnestra, no—you can't. They'll know you're not me."

Clytemnestra stood up and put her hands on her hips. "Who do you think you are? *I* am Helen of Sparta. I can do anything I damn well please."

Helen's mouth fell open. "I don't sound like that." She turned to Adorna.

Adorna shrugged. "You kind of do."

Helen glared at her.

Adorna chuckled and put up her hands. "I'll help her, coach her. No one will know."

Helen looked between the two of them. "I cannot risk you as well, Clytemnestra. After Iphigenia—"

Clytemnestra took her hand. "Iphigenia is the one who sent me. She came to me in a dream and told me to come help you. Even if she hadn't, I think I would have made my way here eventually. I have been blind for too long. Now that my eyes have been opened, I cannot close them again. You need to leave so you can end this. You are the only one who can."

"Won't Agamemnon realize you are gone?"

"Even if he does, he can't take anything more from me. I am choosing to do this. Do not deny me my part to play."

Helen could feel her sister's conviction. "If something should happen to you…"

"It won't. I am a daughter of Sparta."

Helen nodded. "Yes, you are."

Clytemnestra pulled a small satchel from a pocket in her dress. "Castor sent this for you." She upended the bag into Helen's open palm, and Helen's ring fell out.

Helen clasped it to her with a breath of relief. She had missed it. She slipped it onto her finger, feeling stronger already. "Thank you."

For a moment Clytemnestra smiled, but then her smile dimmed, and sadness filled the room again. Helen grabbed a blanket from the bed and took Clytemnestra's hand. "Come."

She walked to the balcony, spread out the blanket, and took a seat. Clytemnestra sat next to her. Helen pulled up the sides of the blanket so it wrapped around them both.

"I am sorry for the loss of Iphigenia," she said. "She was a beautiful girl."

"Yes. She was."

"And she was also a daughter of Sparta. She deserves a warrior tribute." Helen nodded to the far cliff, hundreds of yards away, where a single tree stood reaching for the heavens. She wound her fingers through Clytemnestra's and squeezed. "My warrior niece will never be forgotten."

Focusing on the tree, she called on the powers in the skies. The wind blew and the clouds shifted. A single bolt of lightning tore from the sky and crashed into the tree. It burst into flame, even as some of it fell to the ground from the blast. Helen used the wind to push the blaze higher and stronger. "She was blood of our blood. A true daughter of Sparta. And she will be avenged."

"I will be the one who avenges her," said Clytemnestra quietly.

Helen turned to her sister and saw the resolution in her face. "Yes. Agamemnon is yours. But that is for tomorrow. For tonight, we remember her and love her and—" Helen swallowed, trying to speak past the tears in her throat. "And say goodbye."

Tears trailed down Clytemnestra's face as she laid her head on Helen's shoulder. Helen gently laid her own head on her sister's, staring at the memorial she had created. *Safe journey, my niece.*

The sisters sat quietly until the tree had burned to ash and the sun began its journey across the sky.

CHAPTER 60

At dawn, Helen crept from the room. She had borrowed Clytemnestra's veil and kept her head down. No one she passed gave her a second look.

She made her way to the rear wall of the castle. She had known it would be lightly guarded this early in the morning. It stood mere feet from a sheer cliff dropping down to the sea, making it an unlikely breach point. Sure enough, only two guards were on duty.

She ran a finger over her ring, loving the feel of the metal once again. She had grown used to it being there, warning her of danger, giving her the power to do what needed to be done. To be without it these past months had been more difficult than she had anticipated.

She called up a wind, which tore a tree at the far end of the wall from its perch. And as soon as the guards went to check it out, Helen, with the aid of the wind, was over the wall.

At the cliff's edge, she once again called on the wind. It lowered her gently below the edge of the cliff, then floated her alongside it, out of view of the guards. When she was far enough away from the guards, the wind lifted her back atop the cliff, and she sprinted for the trees. She slipped into them without any shouts from behind.

She quickly stripped off the long gown. Now clad in her tunic, she ran swiftly through the countryside toward the spot to which Clytemnestra had directed her. Her legs ate up the ground, and she felt a freedom in her chest that she could not deny she had missed.

Even with her speed, it took almost a full day to reach the site. But finally, she came upon the remains of the old prayer henge. It was long abandoned, used by an ancient cult of priests long forgotten to history, and only a few of the stones remained upright.

Helen kept her eyes peeled for any sign of trouble. She moved in the shadows cast by the dimming light. A light tingle ran over her skin.

Two figures moved about the ruins. "Where is she? She should have been here by now."

"Patience. She'll be here as soon as she can. She doesn't have your speed."

Helen smiled at their voices and then stepped into the circle of stones. "You two, always complaining."

Castor and Pollux whipped around. Looks of shock and then joy appeared on their faces.

Pollux reached her first, pulling her into a hug. "Thank the gods."

Castor pried Pollux's arms off her. "Right, let her go. My turn." Helen laughed as he pushed Pollux aside and pulled her into his own hug.

Helen closed her eyes, feeling as if she could let down her guard for the first time in months. *I feel safe*, she realized with a jolt. *But not everyone I love is.* So she pulled herself back. "It is good to see you two."

"Are you all right?" Castor demanded. "Did Paris do anything—"

Helen shook her head. "No. He didn't. And if I thought he would try anything, I would not have allowed Clytemnestra to trade places with me."

"Is she all right?" Pollux asked quietly.

"She is. She has a purpose, and I don't think she's had that in a long time. It's given her focus. But I think it won't be long before the horrors of Agamemnon catch up with her."

"We should have killed him," Pollux said.

"I'm surprised you didn't," Helen replied.

"We would have, but we were stopped."

Helen arched an eyebrow. "Who could have stopped you two?"

"Achilles."

The name was like a blow. "He's here?" She hadn't heard his name mentioned in the war talk. Although she knew everyone was trying to keep the details of the fighting from her; she heard only snatches of conversation here and there.

"Where else would he be when he heard you had been taken?" Castor asked.

"I never thought—" She shook her head. Achilles was here. He had come to try and defend her. Helen felt lightheaded. "But how —why would he come? He hates me for marrying Menelaus."

"No," Pollux said quietly. "He hates himself for letting you get away. It is not hate he feels for you."

"He is fighting like a man possessed," Castor said. "He is not even hiding his abilities well."

"Does he think it's true? That I ran off with Paris? Does everyone think so little of me?" Helen asked.

"He does not know what to think. He knows you—and he knows you turned him away for duty. He knows that Paris would not be the man who could turn your heart. Yet a small part of him worries that he did."

"Oh, save me from men and their egos," she grumbled.

"Hey, two men, right in front of you," Pollux said.

She smiled. "Present company excluded, of course."

"I should think so," Pollux grouched.

Helen leaned into him. "Sorry, big brother. You two are men among men."

Castor gave a tip of his head. "Nice of you to notice."

Helen smiled. "Right, well, if we're done with all the ego soothing, we still have to deal with what happens next."

"No." Pollux crossed his arms over his chest. "First I want to understand what is happening. Why did you come to Troy? You could have destroyed Paris and all his men. So what are you doing here?"

"Paris threatened the children," Helen said. "When he arrived, he already had men embedded near them—embedded in our own household. I had no choice. If something were to happen to Paris, or if I were to go to the children, or warn anyone about what was happening—those men had orders to kill."

Castor's face turned red, his lips though were a white line. "What? I'll—"

Helen put up her hand. "Trust me, any version of Paris's death you have come up with I have already thought of, and probably in more detail. But I could not risk their lives."

"And now?" Pollux asked.

"When I was girl, you two saved me from Theseus when no one else could. I am now placing my children's lives in your hands. When the time is right, get them to safety, and trust no one but yourselves. Once you've gotten them away, take them to Proteus and Barnabus. I know Paris has no allies there."

"What of Menelaus?" Castor asked.

Helen's heart lurched. "He cannot know."

"What?" Pollux exclaimed. "Helen—"

Helen's voice was firm. "No. Menelaus—he loves his children. But if he knew they were in danger, he would rush to their aid without thinking. His focus would be on them, and he would leave himself vulnerable."

"You think Paris would have him killed?" Castor asked.

"If he had a chance to, yes. So Menelaus cannot know. Promise me."

Reluctantly the brothers nodded.

"Well, we can take them to Proteus, but Barnabus is here," Castor said.

Helen felt relieved. "That is good news. Because I may need him for my part in this."

"What *is* your part? And why is any of this happening? The world is at war over you," Pollux said.

"No," Helen said. "Not over me. It is 'Zeus' who is behind this. He told Paris that if he took me, he would be a ruler in his own right, and he would own the riches of thousands of kingdoms."

"That's insane," Castor said.

"But Paris believes it."

"You think it's the same Zeus?" Pollux asked.

Helen nodded. "Yes. He's up to something. He wants the armies of the world focused on Troy. I just can't figure out why."

"So where *are* you going?" Castor asked.

"Do you remember the last thing Mother said? She told me where to go—with her very last breath."

∾

HELEN PACED the hall outside her mother's room. She had been inside until a few minutes ago, but when Menelaus arrived, he had suggested she go outside before she made everyone in the room a nervous wreck. With every sharp intake of her mother's breath, she had glared at the healer and his servants.

She heard the front door swing open with a bang, then the sound of running feet. Castor and Pollux sprinted down the hall, coming to a stop in front of her.

"What happened?" Castor asked.

"How bad is it?" Pollux demanded at the same time.

Helen took their hands. "It was a boar. It came out of nowhere while she was walking with Hermione. The blood—there was so much blood."

"By the gods," Castor murmured as he pulled Helen into a hug. "Is Hermione all right?"

"Yes. Mother kept Hermione behind her, even as—" Her words choked off. "Proteus got to them as quickly as he could. But the damage—it is not good."

The door to the room opened, and Menelaus stepped out, with the healer and his servants behind him. Through the door, Helen could see Proteus kneeling next to the bed speaking quietly with her mother. Proteus had been visiting for a week; he was the one who had carried Leda into the palace, and he had refused to leave her side ever since.

Helen gripped her brothers' hands tightly. "Well?"

Menelaus's voice was slow and measured. "The injuries are too severe. She has lost too much blood. It will not be long now."

Helen's knees went weak, and she could have sworn a tremor ran through all of Sparta. "No."

Menelaus pulled her to him. Helen clasped her arms around his neck, borrowing his strength while she felt her own leave her.

"I am sorry, my love," Menelaus whispered.

Castor and Pollux went into the room, leaving them alone. After only a few moments, Helen pulled back from her husband. If her mother didn't have much time, she would not spend it being weak. She would spend every moment with her.

"Do you want me with you?" Menelaus asked.

Helen nodded. "Yes. But Hermione needs you. She was with Mother. She saw what happened. Will you stay with her?"

Menelaus kissed her on the cheek. "Of course. But I will only be down the hall. If you need me, send for me."

Helen placed her hand on her husband's cheek. "You are a good man, Menelaus of Mycenae."

"And you are an incredible woman, Helen of Sparta," he said before heading down the hall.

Helen took a deep breath and entered her mother's room. Proteus had stepped back to make room for Castor and Pollux, who were now kneeling next to the bed. A sheet covered their mother, hiding her injuries, but her face was paler than normal, and her skin had a glassy sheen.

Helen hurried to her side. "Mother."

Leda's violet eyes turned to Helen, a smile struggling onto her face. "Good. I need to speak with you." She grimaced.

"It's all right, Mother. There's nothing that—"

"No," Leda breathed out quietly. "There is much coming for you, my child. I wish I could spare you it. But this is your responsibility. Much will be asked of you. Perhaps too much."

"I am Spartan, Mother. There is nothing I cannot handle."

"And she has us," Pollux said.

A smile ghosted across Leda's face. "She always has you. Stay by her side, but listen when she speaks. She is the one who must direct the action that is to come."

"Yes, Mother," Pollux said.

"Even if she sends us off a cliff," Castor added with a smile.

"I fear it may come to that," Leda said softly.

Helen frowned. "Mother?"

"You three, along with Clytemnestra, are my blessings. Take care of one another. A time of darkness is coming. You will need each other if you are to come through the other side."

The siblings looked at each other, unsure where this side of their mother had come from.

Leda gripped Helen's hand. "I thought I had more time to prepare you. You have more strength than you know. Trust in that. Trust in yourself, in your heart. It will see you through."

"Yes, Mother."

Leda looked to her dark-haired friend who stood silently in the corner. "Thank you, my friend. For being by my side."

"It has been my greatest privilege." Proteus stepped forward and placed a kiss on her hand.

Leda captured his gaze. "You will make sure none of my blood, not even a drop, is left."

"Not even a drop," he promised.

"And you must help Helen."

Proteus frowned. "My queen?"

"You must help her. You have a role to play. Do not follow me—not yet."

Proteus nodded. "As you wish."

Her shoulders relaxed. "Thank you."

Proteus stood, and Helen saw the slight tremble in his hands. "I will leave you to your children," he said. "Until we meet again."

Leda's gaze remained on Proteus until the door closed behind him. "Until we meet again," she said softly.

Then she turned to her children. "The world will experience a tumult like it has never before seen. You must be ready."

"We will be," Castor declared.

Leda looked at Helen. "When the world is on a cliff's edge, look to Crete for the answers. At that time, the ring bearer, you, must find the Omni. It will be your only hope."

Helen frowned. "The Omni? But—"

Leda's eyes grew wide, and her breath struggled. "You must go to Crete. Promise me."

"Of course, but—"

Leda's mouth opened wide, and her back arched.

Helen leaned forward, clutching her mother's hand. "Mother?"

But her mother was beyond responding now.

"No." Castor ran a hand over their mother's cheek.

Pollux put a hand on Castor's shoulder. "She is gone, brother."

Helen just stared at her mother. She had been such a force in her life. How could she be gone?

The world will experience a tumult like never before seen. You must be ready. Despite the heat, the room felt cold. Helen wrapped her arms around herself. Ready for what?

"When the world is on a cliff's edge, look to Crete for the answers," Pollux said quietly.

"And find the Omni," Helen added.

"And you think she meant this moment?" Castor asked.

"It feels like the world is on an edge, does it not? And I have no other ideas," Helen said.

"So you will go to Crete, and we will go get the children," Pollux said.

Helen shook her head, hating the words that were about to come out of her mouth. "No. I will go, but you will not. Not yet."

Castor's voice was incredulous. "Not yet? But the children! What are we waiting for?"

Helen had thought long and hard on this point. "We can't tip our hand."

"Something is happening. Zeus has been building toward this. Clytemnestra's ruse will keep them fooled for a while, and that will protect the children. If she is discovered, you must get her out and immediately get the children. But if she is *not* discovered, everything must stay as it is—until we find out what is going on. There is a reason we are all in Troy. And it has nothing to do with me."

Helen made sure she locked eyes with each of them. "Zeus wants the world to fight against Troy. Zeus wants the world to *defeat* Troy. Which means we need to make sure we lose. Or at least, we need to make sure we don't win. You two need to stay here to make sure that happens."

Castor and Pollux exchanged a look. "Um, that may prove a wee bit difficult," Castor said.

"Why? Just send fewer men—or hold the men back a little until I return."

"Yeah." Pollux drew out the word. "I don't think that's going to work."

"Why not?"

"Because Achilles fights like a man possessed, and the men follow his lead. As long as he continues to fight, they will fight as well," Pollux said.

"So just tell him to pull back. Or better yet, get him to sit out."

Castor laughed. "Sit out? Of a fight? Have you *met* Achilles?"

"Castor is not wrong," Pollux said. "Achilles will not back down from a fight. Unless... someone in particular were to ask him to."

Both brothers turned to Helen.

Helen stepped back, her hands up in front of her. "Oh, no. Absolutely not. No one is even supposed to know I'm out."

"He would never endanger Clytemnestra. He'd keep your secret," Castor said.

Helen crossed her arms over her chest and shook her head, even as butterflies danced through her stomach at the idea of seeing him again. "No. I'm not talking to him."

"Helen, you said we need to stall the war. You said it's important. Which means we *need* Achilles to sit out. You're the only one who can get him to do that," Pollux said.

"You don't know that."

Pollux pinned her with his gaze. "I do. He fights for *you*. It is written all over his face. He loves you, Helen. He always will."

Could it be? "I can't speak with him," she whispered.

"There is no other way," Pollux said.

Helen shifted her gaze between the two of them, but her mind was hundreds of miles and years away—in a time when her every breath was for Achilles, and his for her. She had married Menelaus, and she loved Menelaus—that was true enough. But Achilles... he had been right. Theirs was a fire that would burn forever. At least for her.

Still, she shook her head. Speaking with Achilles would open a whole other bag of troubles. She was not ready for that. "No," she said. "You need to convince him."

Pollux raised an eyebrow. "And if we can't?"

"*Then* I will speak with him." As she said the words, an image of Achilles slipped into her mind and she wasn't sure if the leap in her pulse was because she didn't want to see him again… or because she did.

CHAPTER 61

While Castor went to find Barnabus, Pollux stole into the camp to find Achilles. He was still trying to wrap his head around Helen's insistence that he and Pollux not go save the children. But he knew she was right. If word got back to Troy, Clytemnestra would be in danger. And if they saved Clytemnestra, the children would be in danger. Right now, difficult as it was to swallow, this was the safest course of action.

Now he was left with the task of convincing Achilles to stay out of the fight. *And then I'll walk on water and perhaps turn all the sand on the beach to gold.*

The impossibility of the task weighed on him. Helen might think he could convince Achilles, but Pollux knew better. He had seen the fear in Achilles's eyes—fear of something happening to Helen; fear of what would happen when he came face to face with her again. So instead he fought like the devil. *And I'm supposed to convince him to stand down.*

Ahead he saw the Myrmidons. They had two dozen tents set up at the back of the camp, and few of the other soldiers traveled this way without direct invitation. The Myrmidons had a fierce reputation for being the bravest and most ruthless fighters—and not just on the battlefield.

No one personified those traits more than their leader, Achilles. When he'd been at Sparta, Pollux had seen what Achilles was capable of. It wasn't just his strength that made Achilles formidable; on that dimension Pollux and he were evenly matched. But Achilles had an almost supernatural ability to tell where an opponent would strike. He was tuned to battle in a way Pollux had never been. It was what drew men to him. They wanted to witness his abilities, and most hoped that perhaps some might rub off on them.

Dugal caught sight of Pollux and stood up with a grin. "Who let the beggars in?"

Pollux grinned in return. "Your mother, Dugal, right after I got off of her."

The men laughed, and Dugal did as well before offering his hand. "It's good to see you, Pollux."

"You too, Dugal." With all that had been going on, Pollux had not seen much of the Myrmidons or Achilles. It was almost as if Agamemnon had been intentionally trying to keep them apart.

"A nasty business this, stealing a man's wife. But we'll get her back. Won't we, men?"

A cheer went up around the fire.

"Sparta thanks you," said Pollux. "And drinks are on me the next time you grace our shores." More cheering accompanied his announcement. Pollux nodded toward the tent in the back. "Achilles here?"

Dugal waved him toward it. "He's speaking with Patroclus. Go on."

With a nod, Pollux strode to Achilles's tent. He could hear Patroclus inside, speaking about troop movements.

"You going to stand out there all day, Pollux?" Achilles called.

Pollux smiled as he ducked into the tent. "Just checking to see if you still could sense when you were being snuck up on."

"It still works," Achilles said.

Pollux knew Achilles had the same abilities he did—speed, strength, healing, and the ability to sense others with abilities. And yet, strangely, Pollux had never been able to sense Achilles in that way. Barnabus, too, who could sense all the Fallen, got not even a whiff of a signal around Achilles. Which meant Achilles was something different than either Barnabus or Pollux, neither Fallen nor nephilim. He was something else, something greater.

Patroclus gave Pollux a warm smile. "Pollux. Good to see you."

"You too."

"Sorry I missed the fight right off the ship. The invitation still stands for you and Castor to join the Myrmidons. You two would fit right in."

"Not sure if that's a compliment or not. I will admit that though some days, there is nothing I would like more. But duty calls."

Patroclus stood. "Speaking of which, I need to get these to Agamemnon." He grabbed the papers from the table and slipped out of the tent.

Pollux turned to Achilles. "I need to speak with you."

Achilles raised an eyebrow. "You look serious."

"I am." Pollux was about to say more, when he noticed a young girl in the corner. She couldn't have been more than twelve. Her eyes were large, and she let out a small cry when Pollux looked at her. "Who's this?" he asked.

Achilles turned to the young girl, his voice soft. "It's all right. Pollux is an old friend. He won't hurt you."

The girl looked between the two of them, her fright obvious. Achilles stood. "Get some sleep, Briseis. I'll be back in a little while."

Achilles took Pollux's arm and led him from the tent. Pollux wasn't sure what to say. Achilles had shown such compassion for the young girl. He was obviously acting as her protector. "Who is she?" he asked again.

Achilles put his hand to his lips, leading Pollux away from the tent and toward a fire pit that was empty. "Briseis. She was taken as a spoil of war."

"*You* took a slave?"

Achilles's head whipped toward him, and there was a warning in his voice as he said, "Briseis is *not* my slave. She is under my protection. Once this is over, I will find a home for her."

"My apologies. I had forgotten how much you disliked slavery." It was a strange characteristic for a warrior. Achilles loved a good fight, but he did not take from those that could not defend themselves—and he believed strongly that no one should be owned by another.

Achilles took a seat on a log that had been pulled up to the fire. "Now, what did you need to speak about?"

Pollux looked around to make sure no one could overhear them. "I need you to not fight for a while."

Achilles snorted. "You mean with that idiot from Scythia? Because I assure you, the man had it coming."

Pollux shook his head. "I'm sure he did. No—I mean, I need you to not fight Troy for a while."

Achilles stared at Pollux like he had lost his mind. "Why on earth would I do that?"

"Because I asked nicely?"

Achilles snorted and crossed his arms over his chest. "You're going to have to do a lot better than that."

"There's not a lot I can tell you. For now, all I can say is that there's something going on, it involves Helen, and she wants you to stop fighting."

Achilles's gaze snapped to Pollux. "You spoke with Helen? Is she free?"

"Yes—no. It's complicated. But I assure you, she wants you to stop fighting."

Achilles stood, and Pollux once again realized how large his friend had grown in the years since he'd last seen him in Sparta. "What is going on, Pollux?"

Pollux sighed. He had known Helen would be the only one who would be able to get Achilles to listen. Achilles was just not the sort to follow a request that went against his nature. To be honest, Pollux wasn't even sure Achilles would obey even if it was Helen who asked. But it was their only chance. "I need you to speak with someone," he said, "and it must remain secret. You cannot even tell Patroclus."

"I don't like deceptions."

"I know. But I assure you this one is necessary. Please. You know I would never do anything that would endanger Helen. And it's on her behalf that I'm asking this of you."

As the silence grew between the two warriors, Pollux began to worry that Achilles would say no. That he would continue to fight and hasten the end of the war before Helen could uncover the reason behind it.

Then Achilles shrugged. "All right. I'll play along. Who am I meeting?"

"I can't tell you that."

Achilles raised an eyebrow.

Pollux put up his hands. "But I assure you they mean you no harm. I can take you to them."

Achilles stretched. "You know if anyone does try to harm me, I will rip your head off right after I take theirs."

Pollux grinned. "You can try."

Achilles slapped him on the shoulder. "As long as we understand each other."

CHAPTER 62

Pollux had told Helen he would either return to the prayer henge and tell her all was well, or he would send Achilles to speak with her. She was both anxious and excited as she waited, and she hated herself for hoping it was Achilles who appeared. Achilles was her past. He needed to stay there.

But the fact that he had come to save her meant something to her. *Or maybe he came to curse you,* she thought.

She had been only twelve years old when she had met Achilles, and after her abduction by Theseus, she did not trust men easily. Yet she had trusted Achilles almost immediately. And from the moment they met, they had spent every moment they could together. *And I was so sure we would spend the rest of our lives together.*

The image of him walking away from her on the day of the competition would be forever burned in her brain. She had found herself wondering over the years what would have happened if she had chosen differently. What if she had said yes that day? But every time she thought that, a vision of her children would pop into her mind. No, she would trade them for nothing. Not even Achilles.

A whistle sounded behind her, and Helen whirled around, her hand to her throat. It had been years, yet the idea of him could still make her lose her breath. She stepped closer to the fire, hoping that it would be blamed for what she was sure were her enflamed cheeks.

The night was silent. Then the feeling rolled over her, and her knees became weak. Her gaze never left the shadows across from her, even as her heart began to hammer and her mouth went dry.

And then Achilles stepped out of the darkness.

CHAPTER 63

Achilles stared at Helen, drinking in the sight of her. Somehow, in the last ten years she had become even more beautiful. Her figure had shifted from that of a girl to that of a woman. Her face held the strength of her burdens and the power of her throne. She stole his very breath away.

"How are you here?" he asked.

"Clytemnestra. She traded places with me."

He nodded, although he didn't understand. Why trade places? If she could get out, why not just end this? But he didn't ask those questions. Instead, time stood still as he stared at her.

He realized she was staring at him just as intently. He wondered what she saw. Did she see the man who had lost himself in battle after battle and bottle after bottle to rid himself of her, only to fail at every turn? Or did she see the warrior the rest of the world saw, unbreakable and untouchable?

Helen spoke first. "Are you just going to stare, or are you going to say hello?"

He grinned. "I was just thinking the same thing about you."

"Hello, Achilles."

"Hello, Helen."

They fell silent again.

"Are you all right?" Achilles asked.

Helen nodded. "I wasn't hurt."

He took a step toward her. "What happened? Why would you go with him?" He had to practically bite his lip to keep the real question he wanted to ask from escaping: *How could you go with him and not with me?*

"It's not what you think. It's not what anyone thinks. I didn't go willingly. He threatened my children. The threat still hangs above them. That is why Clytemnestra took my place."

Relief rushed through him. He had been right. She had not changed. Duty and love were still her two most important pillars. "I saw your sons in Athens once last spring. They will be fine warriors one day."

"So will Hermione."

Achilles smiled, picturing Helen when he'd first met her. "Her mother's daughter—what choice has she?"

Helen laughed. "True."

That laugh was like water to a dying man. It filled him up. "I have missed you, Helen." The words slipped out before he could stop them.

She took a step back. "I—I didn't come for that."

Inside he cringed at the vulnerability his words revealed. But all he gave Helen was a shrug as he slipped easily into his arrogance, a well-tested skin. "Perhaps, but it needed to be said. Now, what do you need of the great Achilles? A dragon to slay? An army to repel?"

She rolled her eyes, and for a moment he saw the girl in the queen. "Actually," Helen said, "I'm kind of hoping you would agree to not fight."

He reared back. "What is with you Spartans? First Pollux and now you. Tell me, have you all become pacifists since I left?"

Helen smiled. "Not quite. But there is much happening. I have a plan, but for it to work, I need time. And with you fighting for Greece, well… you're simply winning too quickly."

Achilles grinned. "I am pretty amazing."

She rolled her eyes again. "I see your modesty has not increased over the years."

"Why on earth would I become more modest when I have only become more amazing?"

She laughed out loud this time, her eyes shining. And Achilles would have given his life to keep that smile on her face. But too soon, she turned serious again. "Please, Achilles. I need your help."

Her eyes pulled him in, and he clasped his hands behind his back so as not to reach for her. "You need to give me more of a reason than that. You know if I stay out, Greeks will die. What is so important that you ask me to step aside? And if you are already out, Clytemnestra could be as well. We could end all of this."

Helen shook her head. "I wish that were true. This whole battle—it is not what it appears."

"Then explain it to me."

"As I said, he threatened my children. Months ago he put people in place inside my household. With one word from him, they will be killed."

Achilles sucked in a breath. "Bastard."

"Yes—that and more. But as reprehensible as he is, he is not the one who put all of this into motion. Someone is pulling his strings. Someone is using my 'abduction' as a reason to attack Troy."

"Do you know who?"

"Not exactly." She told him about Zeus attacking the Fallen over the last few years and Paris's claim that Zeus had promised him untold riches for his support.

Achilles scoffed. "There is no Zeus."

"No, not as most believe. This Zeus is not a god sitting on high. He is flesh and blood, and he's pushing us all around like his personal chess pieces. If I leave Troy, this won't end. He will simply approach his goal from a different angle—one we can't see. We have a chance here to end this—if we can figure out what he's after."

"That's a pretty big if. Is Zeus really such a threat?"

"I think so. His attacks—they're on peaceful Fallen, Fallen who are just living quiet lives. He's removing them from the playing field. And his men have let it slip that he's planning something. I do not think the world will benefit from his plans. We need to find out what his end goal is and end *him* once and for all."

Achilles studied her. She was clearly convinced of the truth of what she said. And if Paris held no love for her, then this ruse of a kidnapping must have some other underlying motive. "Where will you start?"

"Crete."

"Crete? Minos is not known for his hospitality."

"No, but it is where I need to begin." Helen told him about her mother's last words.

Achilles felt a pang of grief. He had liked Leda. More than that, he had respected her. There had been something about Helen's mother… something that hinted at a knowledge of the ages. If she was the one sending Helen, then Achilles had to believe it was not a fool's mission.

He nodded. "You have asked for my help, and you have it. But I do not think Agamemnon will simply believe I am not interested in fighting. We will need to give him something more believable than that."

"I'm sure you can come up with something. After all, you are the legendary Achilles. The tales of your deeds and your temper rival one another."

"My temper is much more leashed these days."

Helen looked into his eyes. "I have heard that as well," she said softly.

Achilles would have been content to spend days just standing there listening to her breathe. Seeing her, being near her, made him feel alive for the first time in a long, long time. But he knew that this small reprieve from reality had to end. "You're right—I'm sure I can come up with something. One thing we can count on is Agamemnon being a pompous ass. I'll just be sure to take great offense at his next act of stupidity."

Helen smiled. "I'm sure you won't have to wait long."

He returned her smile. "Undoubtedly. But be careful, Helen. If Zeus is behind this, he will not like you snooping."

She shrugged. "Life is dangerous whether you go searching for that danger or not."

A tingle ran over him, and Achilles lunged for Helen, pulling her behind him.

Barnabus stepped from the shadows. "It is just me, old friend."

"Barnabus," Achilles said. "I thought you had headed back to Egypt."

"I have been called into service. Whenever you are ready, my queen." He bowed to Helen and nodded at Achilles before stepping back into the shadows.

Helen's hand on Achilles's waist burned through his tunic. He couldn't help but note that even when Barnabus had stepped out, she had not let him go.

Helen looked up at him and then stepped back quickly, a flush in her cheeks. "I should go," she mumbled before following Barnabus.

"Helen?"

"Yes?"

"Be careful."

"You as well."

He gave her a lazy grin. "I will be very careful as I sit quietly in my tent."

She smiled and turned to leave. His whole body wanted to run after her and keep her from leaving. But he was no longer the boy who had demanded she give up everything she was for him. So he simply watched.

As she reached the edge of the circle of light created by the fire, she stopped and looked at him over her shoulder. "I have missed you too, Achilles." Then she hurried into the night.

Achilles strained to hear, listening to her footsteps until he could no longer sense any trace of her. His whole body slumped in response. But then he pictured her face, and her words played again through his mind. *I have missed you too, Achilles.*

You are mine and I am yours, he pledged silently before heading back to the camp.

CHAPTER 64

Helen hurried down the path, her mind filled with the man she was all but running from. Achilles had grown into a man in the years since she had seen him last, only making him more handsome. His shoulders seemed broader, the angles in his face more severe. He was a god brought to life, just as the songs said. She picked up her pace, knowing she needed to put distance between herself and Achilles lest she be tempted to run back to him. Even now she could feel the heat of his body on her hand.

How could she still feel this way after so many years? She had banished him from her thoughts. But every now and then someone would mention one of his deeds, and it was as if the years in between them meant nothing.

I am yours and you are mine. The words floated through her mind. She pressed her eyes shut as if that would somehow make the words or the feelings behind them go away. Tremors ran through her body, and she ached for him in a way she had never ached for Menelaus.

And yet again she felt guilty at that betrayal. But she couldn't be blamed for that, could she? Her body, her mind, *they* were betraying *her*. She had done everything in her power to keep Achilles from her heart. But nothing had worked.

He would forever own part of her. He had been her world well before she had married Menelaus, and there was nothing she could do about that. And if she was being honest with herself, she could admit she wasn't sure she *wanted* to do anything about that. Her life was duty and responsibility—and she embraced that. She did not begrudge her role in this world. But Achilles... he was *hers*. He made her feel alive in a way nothing else did. He had loved her not because she was a queen, but in spite of it. He was the secret she took out sometimes to remind herself that she was more than just a queen, more than just a duty. He was the secret in her heart that reminded her she was a woman first.

And she loved him even more for that.

A tingle ran over her skin, and Barnabus appeared at her side. "Is everything all right, Your Highness?"

She gave him a side glance. "'Your Highness'? What happened to 'Helen'?"

Barnabus's white teeth shone in the moonlight. "We are not kids any longer."

She stopped and looked into his eyes. "Are you trying to tell me something?"

Barnabus looked back toward the prayer henge. "All of us have duties that keep us from what we really want and deserve."

"Yes. All of us do," she said quietly.

"The ship should be ready. I could run you there."

Helen shook her head. "No. I think I'd like the walk. Would you like to join me?"

"I would be honored, old friend." He extended his arm.

Helen smiled as she took his arm. "Old friend—I like that much better."

CHAPTER 65

Achilles felt no rush, no urgency, as he walked back to the camp. Helen was safe. Safe, and on her way to save the world. Always putting others first—she hadn't changed.

For the entire walk, he tortured himself with memories of her. They had been children, but there had been nothing childish about how they loved each other. His world had revolved around her, and when he left Sparta it was as if he had been thrown into a world of darkness. Only Patroclus's appearance had kept him from forever wallowing in despair.

And now he had been given a second chance—a chance to give Helen what she needed. To be there for her in a way that he hadn't been able to all these years.

He would not let her down.

Most of the camp was still asleep when he returned. Patroclus stepped from their tent almost as soon as Achilles spied it. He looked around, and his shoulders slumped in relief when he saw Achilles. He jogged over. "I was worried when I didn't see you."

"I just felt the need to stretch my legs."

Patroclus was quiet for a moment. "We'll get her back."

Achilles glanced over at him in surprise. He had not met Patroclus until after he had left Sparta—left Helen. He had never mentioned how much they had meant to one another. As far as he knew, he had never mentioned her at all.

"Of course we will. That's why we're here," he said lightly as he entered the tent—but then he cursed his words as he remembered what he had told Helen. He needed to act as if he did not want to fight. How was he supposed to do that?

He looked around and frowned. "Where is Briseis?"

"Agamemnon took her."

Achilles whipped around, his eyes narrowing. "What? When?"

"A short while ago. That's why I was up. I was looking for you."

"*Why* did Agamemnon take her?"

"Because Chryseis was returned to her father." Chryseis and Briseis had both been taken from the same village in a raid as spoils of war. Achilles had protected Briseis, but Agamemnon had claimed Chryseis as his own.

Achilles felt anger burn low in his gut. "And I'm sure it was done out of the goodness of his heart."

"He said the gods demanded her return in exchange for ending the sickness that has plagued some of the men."

Achilles shook his head. The men who had gotten sick had eaten spoiled meat. He'd seen it himself and had warned them to stay away from it. But they'd been too drunk and too stupid to listen. Which meant that money had somehow changed hands. Agamemnon would never willingly give up anything. He had no doubt benefited in some way from returning the girl.

Achilles turned and stormed from the tent, picturing Briseis's small face.

Patroclus hustled after him. "Achilles, be smart."

"Oh, I'll be smart."

"I mean, maybe attacking Agamemnon is not the smartest move."

Achilles growled. "To the contrary. I think it's very smart."

CHAPTER 66

Agamemnon's tent stood out among the others. While some of the stronger fighters, like Achilles, had larger tents, they tended to share them with their men. Agamemnon did not. He had the largest tent, and yet he shared it with no one. Carpets were laid inside, purple cloth was draped everywhere, and Agamemnon slept in a full bed complete with a wooden frame. It was his own personal palace. He didn't even eat with his men; water and food were brought to him by his servants.

Speaking of which, Achilles spied a familiar form shuffling toward Agamemnon's tent with chains around her ankles, making the walk difficult.

Achilles let out a roar of rage. "Agamemnon!"

Briseis whirled around, nearly tripping over the chains. Her eyes went wide and she started to tremble.

Her reaction only increased Achilles's fury. He had finally gotten her to trust him. He had finally gotten her to not be scared of her own shadow—and in one fell swoop Agamemnon had destroyed all of that.

Achilles reached Briseis's side. "Are you all right?"

She looked up at him with tears in her eyes.

He leaned down and, not caring who was looking, snapped the chains at her feet. "You do not deserve these," he growled.

"How dare you," Agamemnon bellowed from behind him.

Achilles whirled around. Agamemnon stood defiantly, his men surrounding him. "I dare because she belongs to me," Achilles growled.

Agamemnon strode closer, but Achilles noticed he kept out of striking distance. Or at least a normal man's striking distance. "And *I* dare because as leader of the Achaean army the spoils of war first go to *me*."

"You returned your 'spoil,'" Achilles sneered. "This one is mine."

"The gods demanded the return of mine—which means you forfeit yours."

Achilles stepped forward. He did not miss the widening in Agamemnon's eyes nor the slight tremor in his chin. "I do not accept that."

"If you accept my rule, then you accept your role." Agamemnon gestured to one of his men. "Re-chain her."

"Touch her, and it will be the last thing you do," Achilles warned.

The man looked between Achilles and Agamemnon, swallowing visibly.

Patroclus laid a hand on Achilles's shoulder and spoke so only Achilles could hear. "Be careful, Achilles. You are stronger, but Agamemnon is sneaky. He will punch back at you in a way you do not see coming."

Achilles then saw that they had been surrounded by yet more of Agamemnon's men. A few were archers, and they were not looking only at Achilles. Their focus shifted between Briseis and Patroclus—waiting for Agamemnon's signal.

Achilles rolled his fingers into a tight fist. *Bastard.*

He glared at Agamemnon. "She is not to be chained. Do you understand?"

Agamemnon opened his mouth, then seemed to think better of it and nodded briefly.

Achilles gently took Briseis's arm and addressed the gathered men. "If anyone harms this girl, anyone at all, they will answer to me. Is that understood?"

The men looked around uncomfortably.

"*Is that understood?*" Achilles bellowed.

"Yes, Achilles," the men responded.

He bent down to whisper in Briseis's ear. "I will see you free. You can count on that." Then he once again faced Agamemnon. "I have decided I do not feel like fighting today. And I do not think I will feel like fighting tomorrow either."

Agamemnon narrowed his eyes. "Is that so?"

"Yes, that is so. You are such an incredible leader—as you have told us time and time again. *You* lead the men." He turned on his heel and strode back toward his tent.

But he had to force himself to not look back at Briseis. She did not deserve to be caught in the middle of this. She was an innocent.

Patroclus ran to catch up with him. "You're not going to fight?"

"No."

"But Helen—we traveled all this way to free her."

Achilles pictured Helen's face in the firelight, and his stomach tightened. He did not like the idea of Clytemnestra being locked inside Troy with Paris, but he preferred it to Helen. And he had promised. "I will not fight until Briseis is returned. Some things are more important."

He walked into his tent, leaving a stupefied Patroclus staring after him.

CHAPTER 67

Agamemnon was looking at the plans for the attack, but he wasn't really seeing them. All he saw was Achilles's arrogant face. The challenge in Achilles's eyes, in his whole body... power was stamped all over the man's frame. How dare Achilles challenge *him*? And in front of his own men?

But even Agamemnon was not powerful enough to go against Achilles. No man would survive a one-on-one fight with that... thing. Not for the first time, Agamemnon wondered exactly what Achilles was. He was certainly more than a man. *And something far more powerful than me.* Agamemnon slammed his fists into the table, making everything on it jump. *For I am merely a man.*

"King Agamemnon?" a voice called quietly.

Agamemnon turned. Claudius, one of his spies, was standing by the door, shifting from one foot to the other. He was a slip of a man; he looked like a strong wind could blow him over. Although he had reached his thirtieth year, he looked as if he was barely into manhood. But his slight frame and young appearance belied a devious mind. Claudius had slipped in and out of camps and cities, gathering knowledge without drawing the slightest notice from those who he watched. He was one of Agamemnon's favorite spies and one of his most trusted. At least, as far as Agamemnon trusted. His only concern about Claudius was his greed. So Agamemnon simply paid him enough such that greed was never an issue.

"What is it, Claudius?"

"Begging your pardon, my lord, but I have some news that might be of interest."

"What is it?"

"A ship, sir. It's moored in a cove north of Smyrna."

Agamemnon frowned. "Is it one of ours?"

"Yes, sir. It's the *Queen Leda*."

"Clytemnestra's ship?" Agamemnon's mind whirled. What on earth was it doing here? He immediately dismissed the idea of Clytemnestra herself having sailed for Troy. She was too devastated by Iphigenia's death—and besides, she was so broken and terrified she would never dare. But perhaps she had granted the use of her ship to someone else. Her servant, the sailor Aegisthus, perhaps? He was Spartan. But why would he not just moor the ship with the others?

"I took the liberty of joining the crew," said Claudius. "It seems they had an opening—one of their fellow crewmembers disappeared right after I found the ship."

Agamemnon smiled. "Disappeared, huh?"

Claudius smiled in return. "The world is a dangerous place, sire. I have to get back. I told them I needed to tell my family I would be gone. Assuming you wish for me to continue?"

This was probably nothing, but Agamemnon did not trust Helen's brothers or any of the Spartans for that matter. And if they were planning something… "Continue. If there's anything worthwhile, report it to me immediately."

Claudius smiled, showing off the two cracked teeth he'd received as a child. "Yes, sir. Thank you, sir." He bowed and turned to leave.

"Claudius?"

Claudius turned back.

"If someone is plotting against me or our mission here, they need not return."

Claudius smiled. "Yes, sir." And he disappeared through the tent flap.

Humming, Agamemnon rearranged a troop formation on the table before him. *There is nothing like ordering a death to turn a day around.*

CHAPTER 68

THE ISLAND OF CRETE, GREECE

Helen and Barnabus set sail aboard the same ship Clytemnestra had brought here—the *Queen Leda*. The crew was known to Helen—all except one, and the captain, Aegisthus, assured her he would keep an eye on him—and all the men were sworn to secrecy. But Helen couldn't help but wonder if Zeus had gotten to any of them. Just in case, none of the crew would be allowed off the ship until Helen's mission was complete. It was the only way to be sure.

She knew there was danger ahead, but she couldn't help but feel a sense of satisfaction as the journey began. After weeks of waiting around, she was finally doing something to help her children. Unfortunately, the trip to Crete was plagued by bad weather. It took three weeks to arrive, double the amount of time she had expected. Helen hoped it was not a sign of the difficulty they would face at the island.

Now Barnabus rowed himself and Helen to shore in the predawn dark. She was having a hard time shaking a feeling of foreboding.

"We can go ashore there." Barnabus nodded toward a piece of empty beach. "You've heard the stories of Minos, haven't you?"

Helen nodded. Crete had been a closed kingdom ever since its inception, but the current king—King Minos, he called himself, as he claimed he was the literal reincarnation of the original King Minos—had taken that predilection to an even more drastic level, completely cutting the island off from all visitors and barring any of his people from leaving. But a few brave souls had managed to escape, and they had brought with them tales of the king's cruelty. Helen hoped those tales were exaggerations.

Pink streaks were just appearing in the sky as Helen and Barnabus stepped onto the shore. It was not exactly an ideal time to arrive; Helen would have preferred the cover of darkness.

"What do we know about the layout of the island?" Helen asked.

"Very little. But that is Minos's home there." Barnabus pointed to the top of Mount Ida in the center of the island, where tall walls surrounded an even taller building. From the parapet, the king could no doubt see every inch of the island and the sea surrounding it. Which meant Minos's men may have seen their arrival.

"Let's hope the darkness kept our arrival quiet," Barnabus said, as if reading Helen's thoughts.

There were no homes near the beach, but two seven-foot-tall statues marked the entrance to a path that led toward the center of the island. Each statue depicted an extremely muscular beast with the head and legs of a bull and the torso of a man.

Barnabus examined the statues. "Minos does not receive guests often and has little interaction with outsiders—but the few that do make it off all speak of one thing."

"The maze and the minotaur."

"Exactly."

Helen put little stock in those types of tales—most were just exaggerations made greater by time. But as they moved down the path, she was beginning to doubt that. All along the path were more symbols of the minotaur—carvings, etchings in trees, smaller statues.

"Minos wants to make sure no one forgets the minotaur," Barnabus said.

"Or that no one forgets to fear him," Helen said as they passed some hovels that looked as if a slight breeze could knock them down. A small, naked child no more than two years old stood holding onto the post of one. His eyes were vacant.

"So how do we think Minos will receive us?" Helen asked quietly, not wanting to wake any of the villagers, even as she wondered how they had not been noticed yet.

Barnabus shrugged. "He could embrace us with open arms or kill us on sight."

Helen gave him a sidelong glance. "I had forgotten how comforting you can be, Barnabus."

He smiled. "It *is* one of my charms."

Helen laughed.

They were halfway to the center of the island before they encountered anyone other than the little boy. A man came down the path toward them, a basket of fish lures in his hands. Barnabus raised his hand in greeting. "Good morning, sir. Would you perhaps—"

The man shook his head violently, then turned and sprinted up the path away from them.

"Well, that was odd," Helen said.

As they climbed the path, they began to run into more citizens of Minos, but each of them had the same sort of reaction as the man did. Doors were closed, blinds were pulled. More than one person had sprinted away in fear.

"I have never heard of people reacting like this," Helen said after a fearful woman yanked her child into her hut.

"Me either. Perhaps we should head back to the ship and figure out—"

"Too late," Helen mumbled.

A group of guards, all wearing the uniform of Minos—a white tunic rimmed in gold thread with the minotaur depicted in black in the center of their chest—stormed down the path toward them. "Halt!"

Barnabus pulled his sword.

Helen grabbed his arm. "The trees," she whispered.

Barnabus narrowed his eyes at the two archers there. "We can take them," he said.

"Yes, we could. But we need to speak with Minos, and I don't think killing his guards will make him more talkative. So let's play it his way for now." She made a show of raising her hands.

With a growl, Barnabus re-sheathed his sword and put his hands in the air as well.

The guards surrounded them.

Helen gave the men a wide smile. "I believe a mistake has been made."

CHAPTER 69

The guards did not seem to agree with Helen. They wrapped their visitors' wrists in ropes and marched them to Minos's home.

"Are we *still* going along with Minos?" Barnabus asked Helen quietly.

The ropes chafed at Helen's skin. "Yes."

Barnabus sighed. "Just checking."

At Minos's home, the guards led Helen and Barnabus through an outer courtyard decorated with several small fish ponds, through the front doors, and into a hallway with marble floors. Servants gaped at the new arrivals and then quickly shifted their gaze away. *At least they do not run*, Helen thought. They continued on through several turns until they approached an open doorway that looked as if it led to an inner courtyard. Sounds emanated from the doorway that Helen couldn't quite place. "Is that a lion?" she asked.

Barnabus frowned. "I think so."

They stepped through the doorway into a lush, green space dotted with palm trees. There were tables, chairs, and even a giant bed draped in red linens. But the overly sumptuous landscaping did nothing to detract from the courtyard's greatest attraction—the animals in cages that lined the perimeter. Zebras, giraffes, a nadir, a giant bear, and in the middle, two lions.

A whip cracked, and one of the lions roared.

The king of Crete laughed as he pulled the whip back and let it fly again. The king was a small man, with pockmarked olive skin and small dark eyes under a heavy brow. He had incredibly slim arms, yet somehow managed to have a belly that strained against his tunic. *That's what a life of indulgence and no hard work will do for you.*

The king handed the whip to one of his servants before turning to the young boy standing next to him. "You see, my son, even the king of the animals is under our control."

The boy nodded. "Yes, Father."

Minos caught sight of Helen and Barnabus and frowned. He pushed his son toward a servant before striding over. With only a glance he disregarded Barnabus and turned his full attention to Helen. He bowed. "Your Highness, it is a pleasure to see you again."

Helen frowned. "I'm afraid you have me at a loss, as I do not recall our first meeting."

"I was at your wedding. It was quite an affair." His gaze flicked to Barnabus. "Although he was not your groom. I have heard you like to swap husbands."

Barnabus stiffened, but Helen spoke before Barnabus could snap the ropes around his wrists. "You have heard wrong, good king. I am loyal to my one husband: King Menelaus." She held up her bound hands. "But I must admit, your hospitality leaves much to be desired."

The sun glinted off her ring, and Minos' eyes went wide. His mouth fell open as he stepped back. "You're the ring bearer?"

CHAPTER 70

So—Minos knew who she was. She had thought she would have to explain about the ring bearer before she could request his aid in finding whatever her mother had sent her here for. But it looked like as if things might be a little easier than she had feared. "Yes. I'm the ring bearer."

Minos's face went from shock to anger to calculation in seconds. "Untie them," he said to his guards. "How dare you treat our distinguished guests in such a way?"

The guards quickly cut off the ropes. Helen rubbed her wrists; angry red marks showed where the ropes had been bound too tightly. Next to her Barnabus did the same, although Helen had no doubt his arms had already healed.

"Excuse me for a moment." Minos inclined his head to Helen before motioning two of his guards off to the side.

Helen moved closer to Barnabus. "What are they saying?" she whispered.

Barnabus kept his voice low. "Minos is ordering that his archers surround the courtyard and all of his guards be brought up."

Helen sighed. "Apparently I was too optimistic."

"Plan?"

"It remains the same. We need Minos. So we play along until we no longer do."

Now it was Barnabus's turn to sigh. "As you wish."

Minos returned to them. Helen noted that archers were already stepping into the balconies that rimmed the courtyard.

"What can I do for you, Queen Helen? Or should I call you the chosen one?" Minos asked.

"Something was left here for me a long time ago," Helen said. "Answers that I need. I have come to learn them."

King Minos's eyes narrowed, his anger evident. "And what makes you think you deserve them?"

Helen straightened her spine. "Do you know where the Omni is?"

Minos scoffed. "You know nothing. You don't even know what you are looking for. But *I* know what you are here seeking. It's my sacred duty to watch over it until the one *worthy* of it appears to retrieve it."

Despite his tone, Helen felt relieved. He knew about the Omni and what she was supposed to find, which obviously was an object. She had worried that she and Barnabus would waste all their time searching. Now they should be done with this quickly. She raised an eyebrow. "Well, here I am."

Minos smiled without warmth. "Which proves nothing. You must prove to *me* that you are in fact the ring bearer. You must pass my test. You must retrieve the box with the scroll that will lead you to the Omni. If you can do that, then you are truly the ring bearer."

Helen narrowed her eyes. Something was off here. The king looked entirely too pleased with himself.

"My queen?" Barnabus asked quietly.

Helen knew he was asking if she wanted him to *make* the king tell them where the scroll was. She shook her head at him.

"Very well, King Minos," she said. "Lead me to your test."

Minos placed his hands on his waist. "It is fortuitous timing, your arriving now. Almost as if the gods had planned it themselves. And perhaps they did. We are about to begin our celebration. You can join our other guests."

Minos's guards opened a set of doors to his left, and a group of children was dragged in. A single rope tied them together, wound around the wrists of each child. There were fourteen in all—seven boys and seven girls. The oldest was no more than eight, and the youngest looked closer to three. Tears trailed through the dirt on more than one little face.

Helen whipped her head toward the king. "What is the meaning of this?"

Minos stretched his arms wide. "It is the first night of our celebration. The gods must be appeased—as must their pet. With their sacrifice, these children bring honor to their families, as well as to our great nation."

Helen's mouth fell open. She had heard that when the first King Minos began his rule, he sacrificed fourteen children to the minotaur every two years. Apparently the "reincarnated" King Minos had adopted more than the first Minos's name.

Helen took a step toward the king, and Minos raised an arm. The archers took aim—but not at either her or Barnabus. No, the archers had aimed their arrows at the children. Helen narrowed her eyes. "What are you doing?"

Minos smiled. "I have a heard a great deal about you, Queen Helen. I know the premium you place on the lives of the innocent. Tell me: if you were to use your powers, how many innocents do you think you could save before my men cut them down? Here and throughout the island? Exactly *how* powerful are you? I'm guessing not powerful enough to save them all. But if you pass my test, I will give you what you are looking for, and no one will be harmed. It is your choice."

Beside her she could feel the anger burning off Barnabus. She didn't turn toward him though because she was having a tough enough time keeping a lid on her own anger.

"Besides," the king continued, "the key to finding the Omni is in the maze. Without it, I cannot help you. You will enter the maze with these children." He shrugged. "Perhaps you will even save a few of them."

"When does this *celebration* begin?" Helen asked through gritted teeth.

Minos smiled. "Now."

CHAPTER 71

The trail leading to the maze entrance wound around the backside of Mount Ida. No homes were built on this side of the island; it seemed to be used mainly for livestock and grazing. Long rolling hills with shepherds and sheep could be seen in the distance. The citizens of Crete lined the path, although none of them cheered or even smiled. They wore dirty, tattered clothes on their skinny frames, and the looks on their faces were haunted, as if they had long ago learned that fighting was useless. Worst of all were the heartbroken looks they gave the children as they passed.

King Minos led the procession in his ornate litter, carried by eight incredibly muscular men. "Obviously Minos is saving the food for himself and his personal guard," Barnabus muttered.

Helen nodded, her anger at the man growing.

Barnabus leaned toward her. "I overheard some of the guards talking. He does this every two years. The maze is a natural cave system, and there is some sort of beast inside. The king feeds the beast fourteen children. It's his way of keeping control of the populace. It seems anyone who disagrees with him has his or her child chosen."

"Do any of the children survive?"

"No."

Helen had not needed to hear that. She balled her hands into fists. "What is this beast?"

"Most say it is the minotaur, that he has survived since the rule of Minos the First. At night, they say he howls at the moon, and sometimes shepherds find some of their flock missing. It is alleged that he walks like a man but has the head of a bull."

Helen snorted. "Right. What's *really* in the cave?"

"No one knows. No one has survived to tell."

"Great."

They arrived at the entrance to the caves. The opening was huge, but was barred with an equally huge wooden door. As Helen approached, she realized the door was made from entire trunks of trees, doubled up and nailed together, with a giant metal bar holding it all in place. Whatever was behind that door, the people of Crete definitely did not want it to get out.

"Whatever happens," Helen said quietly, "we protect the children first."

"Agreed," Barnabus murmured. "But are you sure we don't want to kill Minos and get this over with?"

"We still need to find whatever is in the maze, and I do not trust Minos. If we force Minos's hand, he will make these children pay—and probably others as well. So for now, we follow through with this stupid test."

Barnabus sighed. "As you wish."

The procession stopped, and Minos's litter bearers lowered him gently. And it was Helen's turn to sigh. She was hoping a few might stumble, dumping the tyrant to the ground.

The children huddled together, terror in their eyes, looking around wildly. Helen's heart constricted. This world was too cruel a place for children, she thought thinking of the dangers her own children were in as well.

A woman broke free from the crowd and ran for the children,

but a guard stepped in front of her and slammed the end of his staff into her face. Her feet flew out from under her and she landed hard on her back.

"Mama!" cried a little girl with dark eyes and hair, the smallest in the group. She tried to run to her mother, but an older boy grabbed her and held her back. His eyes were too similar to the girl's and his gaze too heartbroken as he looked at the woman on the ground, to be anything but her brother.

Helen grabbed Barnabus's arm before he could step forward. "No. There are too many, and the children would be the first ones hurt. Minos will order them slaughtered if anyone steps out of line. He is not new to this. He's done it before."

"He is the monster."

"Don't worry about him. I have no intention of leaving Minos unscathed when we take our leave of this island," Helen said. She watched the king, who was busy stuffing his face with a pastry as he stepped from the litter with the help of one of his litter bearers. Red jam slid down his chin. "As soon as we have what we need, we will make sure these people are free of him."

Seeming completely oblivious to the emotions of his people, Minos held up his hands with a giant smile on his face. "My good people, it is the time again when we honor the gods with our sacrifice. We thank the gods for the bravery of these children and the willingness of their families to protect our blessed kingdom."

Not a single person in the crowd smiled or cheered.

"But tonight," Minos continued, "we have an even greater gift for the gods. Two members of royal families far from our shores have agreed to sacrifice themselves as well."

Helen glared at him. *Bastard*. But she said nothing. Her actions would disprove his words soon enough.

One of the guards unbolted the door. Another guard joined him, and together they pulled open the giant door. A third guard leaned in with a torch and set ablaze a line of oil high on the wall.

Other guards shoved the children forward roughly. Most

moved forward obediently, but one boy was petrified with fear. When the guards pushed him, he merely fell to his knees.

Barnabus rushed forward and reached out his hand to the boy. "It's all right, child. I won't let any harm come to you."

Filled with tears, the boy's big brown eyes stared up at Barnabus. Barnabus gently pulled him up. "Let us go together then."

Helen peered into the cave. The oil fire cast shadows along the walls, but she could sense nothing moving beyond that. "Well," she said to Barnabus, "let's get started."

Helen stepped into the cave. It was dry, which was at least one small blessing. And it was more tunnel than cave, about ten feet wide and bending out of sight about fifty feet in. She moved forward, casting about for any sign of danger. She sensed nothing near, but there was a vague presence somewhere in the distance. She could not tell if it was friend or foe.

Barnabus then entered with the children. As soon as they were all inside, the door slammed shut behind them, and some of the children cried out.

Helen turned. Careful to keep her voice calm, she said "Sh, sh. It's all right. We are about to have an adventure. So before we begin, let's start with some names. I am Helen, and my tall friend here is Barnabus, the strongest man in all of Pharos and one of the greatest warriors I have ever met."

All the children's eyes turned to Barnabus. Barnabus smiled. "Queen Helen speaks true. But she forgot to mention that *she* is the greatest warrior that *I* have ever met."

The children looked between the two of them, and Helen saw one small smile on an equally small face. It was a start.

"Now, why don't you all tell me your names?" She pointed at the oldest boy, who still held the hand of his younger sister. "You first," she said.

"Samuel." He nodded to his sister. "This is Kyrael."

"It is pleasure to meet you both."

Helen continued pointing at the children until they had all given their names. Then she broke them up into pairs, one older and one younger. "All right, does everyone have their partner?"

The kids nodded.

"Good. All right, troops, let's move out."

Helen peered into the dark cave. *We can do this.*

An animal screamed somewhere deep in the cave. The sound echoed and was distorted by the acoustics of the cave, making it impossible to identify—but Helen knew misery when she heard it. More than one child let out a cry of fear, and Helen had to hold back the shiver that tried to creep down her spine.

There is no such thing as a minotaur, she thought as she started forward. But a smaller part of her brain whispered, *Are you sure?*

CHAPTER 72

The fire trench along the wall gave them enough flickering light to see by, but the dancing shadows made it appear as if the walls and path were alive. The effect was chilling and caused Helen to jump at more than one shadow. The effect on the children was even more pronounced.

More concerning, Helen could feel animals just out of her view. Her animal sense had been honed over the years, and while she had been in Minos's courtyard, she had briefly spoken with the animals there. She had learned that when an animal got old or sick, it disappeared. She now had a feeling she knew where those animals had disappeared to.

She had a feeling the animals would be more difficult to reach down here. The darkness, the terror—it would have that effect on anyone. And if these were indeed the animals from Minos's zoo, they'd suffered a lifetime of abuse and pain as well. Animals in pain were always difficult to connect with.

We mean you no harm and we could use your help. She sent the message out over and over again. But she received no response.

After reaching the bend in the path, they entered a large cavern with three other tunnels leading away from it. Helen chose one on the left. Marking the tunnel with a rock, she turned back to make sure all of the children were still with her. Kyrael caught her gaze.

Helen said, "It will be all right."

The girl's big dark eyes, full of trust, looked into Helen's—and Helen prayed she would not let the girl down.

They walked in silence. Occasionally a smaller tunnel branched off to one side, but Helen stayed the course. Too soon, they came to another cavern with three choices. Helen stayed left again, figuring it was best to stay consistent. Again she marked her way with a rock.

Doubt began to trickle through her. Even without the danger offered by the animals down here, they could wander around here for days and days without ever coming across the key. The children were not in the best shape to begin with; after a few days without food or water, many of them would be unable to continue. They needed to find the key quickly.

If we have no luck today, maybe I can leave Barnabus with the children while I go on alone.

Just then, she felt an animal presence again—and a feeling of protection. But it slipped from her mind before she could get a firm grasp on it. She couldn't even tell what direction the thought had come from. But she felt no threat. She thought of telling Barnabus, but there was nothing really to say, so she just continued on.

After what felt like hours, she stepped into a new tunnel off another large cavern. They had made turn after turn, and Helen worried about being able to backtrack. She had used a rock to mark each turn, but still it would be difficult.

Then she stumbled over something, catching herself on the wall before she could fall. She looked down to see what she'd stumbled over—and she went still. The hair on the back of her neck rose.

The tunnel was littered with bones.

Her breath caught as she saw one skull that could only have belonged to an infant. Behind her, several children let out a cry as they, too, saw what filled the path ahead.

Barnabus grabbed the children and started pulling them back. Helen assisted, ushering the children back out of the passage and into the cavern, against a wall, her breathing a little faster than she would like. "All right, stay here for a moment while we go see, okay?"

The children held on to one another, staring to the tunnel. But Samuel nodded back at her. "I'll look after them."

"You will make a fine soldier one day," Barnabus said, clapping the boy lightly on the shoulder.

A look of pride crossed Samuel's face, but then he shook his head. "I will never fight for this king."

Helen had no reply to that, and neither did Barnabus. So in silence the two of them ducked back into the tunnel of bones.

Helen knelt down and picked up a bone—a femur. She walked closer to the flames to get a better look, and what she saw did nothing to slow her racing heart.

"What is it?" Barnabus asked.

Helen handed him the femur. Keeping her voice low, she said, "Teeth marks. Something has gnawed on these bones."

Barnabus cast a critical gaze around. "What do you think it was?"

"I'm guessing it's one of the animals that have been trapped down here."

"So this is what has happened to all the children Minos has sent down here," Barnabus said softly.

Helen nodded. A vision of her own children trapped in here, eaten by animals, assaulted her mind. She slammed her eyes shut and rolled her hands into fists. *No.*

A roar sounded from ahead, bouncing off the walls. Helen's eyes flew open. Behind them, the children let out a cry of fear.

The shadows shifted ahead. Something approached.

"Barnabus, get to the kids."

Barnabus hustled back down the passage in a blur. Helen heard a grinding of rock, then Barnabus rejoined her.

"What are you doing?" she hissed. "I told you to guard the children."

"I blocked them in an alcove. They're fine. You I am not so sure about."

The shadow grew closer. Helen could now make out its shape.

A beast with three heads.

"Cerberus," Barnabus whispered.

But Helen shook her head. Her mother had told her there was no such thing. But even as she clung to that belief, the shadow belied her mother's teachings.

Helen grabbed a long bone, as did Barnabus. They were the only weapons they had.

The creature finally came close enough to be visible in the flickering light. And it was not Cerberus. But that did nothing to relieve Helen.

Because standing in front of them was a huge male lion.

CHAPTER 73

Helen and Barnabus backed into the cavern where they had left the kids. Helen saw that the children were indeed well protected in an alcove blocked by a massive rock. *They're safe from the lion—but they'll never be able to get out of there if we don't survive.* Helen pushed the thought away.

The lion stalked toward them slowly, letting out a roar. The beast's coat was riddled with mange, and his bones poked through his skin.

"We mean you no harm," Helen said softly, sending feelings of love and peace toward him.

But from the lion all she felt was fear—fear and pain. And the feelings of fear weren't directed at her, but at Barnabus.

"You need to step back," she said. "You're scaring him."

"*I'm* scaring *him?*" Barnabus asked.

"Yes. He is old, Barnabus. And in pain. He does not have much control." Helen's own fear was turning to pity. "Please."

Barnabus backed up three steps. "This is as far as I go."

Helen called on the power of the ring. "Do not interfere," she ordered Barnabus.

Barnabus's eyes grew wide, and he struggled to move. "Damn it, Helen."

The lion let out a roar, and Helen felt his anger. Before she could try to calm him, he charged.

"Helen!" Barnabus yelled. The children screamed from their hiding spot.

From one of the other tunnels, a giant she-bear burst forth. With one of its massive paws, it took a great swipe at the lion. The lion screamed in pain.

"Stop!" Helen yelled. Both animals froze.

The bear was on its hind legs, standing at least seven feet tall. Helen recognized her thoughts from earlier. She was the animal Helen had felt when they first entered the cave—the animal who had given Helen a sense of protection.

Thank you, Helen thought to the bear, *but he is old and in pain. Let him have peace.*

The bear paused for a moment, then dropped down onto her front paws and backed away.

Helen looked at the lion. The charge had apparently taken all his energy, and his side now bled from the bear's swipe. He offered no threat now. Suddenly, Helen felt all the lion's pain and suffering, now and throughout his life. It assaulted her mind, and she choked back a sob. The lion was just looking for peace.

Helen sat down against the wall of the cavern and patted the ground next to her. "Come, my friend."

After a moment's hesitation, the lion moved forward a limp in his step. With a weary sigh he sat tentatively next to Helen.

"It's all right," she said.

The lion rolled onto his side and placed his head in Helen's lap. Helen ran her hand through the cat's mane. *It's all right, old boy. It's all right.*

A cavalcade of images drifted through Helen's mind as the lion showed her his life. He had been taken from his parents as a cub. His mother had been killed in front of him. He had been kept in a crate for over a year before he arrived at Minos's castle. And then the real torture began. Helen felt all of it, all the pain, as strongly as she felt the pain the lion was in right now—the result of a lifetime of injuries.

Tears dripped down Helen's cheeks and onto the lion's fur. "I am so sorry," she said. She gently ran one finger from the top of his skull to the base of his nose. "Sleep, my friend."

She felt the lion let go. She felt the peace that came with being freed from this life.

"Helen?" Barnabus asked softly.

She took a stuttering breath. "I'm all right." She ran her hand again through the lion's fur before gently disentangling herself from the beast and wiping her eyes. "He was in so much pain. He had a hard life. He was stolen from his family when he was young. Then he was abused by Minos, and when he grew too old, he was sent down here to be a snack for the beast."

"There *is* a beast?"

"The minotaur is real." She glanced down at the lion. "But it showed him kindness. The first time in his life he'd ever been shown it."

"The lion did not extend that kindness to us," Barnabus said.

"No. He fears humans. After what he's been through, I do not blame him."

Helen turned to the bear. "Thank you, my friend."

The bear huffed at her, and Helen sat back in surprise.

"What is it?" Barnabus asked.

"She has a cub. It's why she helped. She needs food for the cub. She was pregnant when she was sent here. They mistook it for illness." *It's all right.*

"Helen? Barnabus?" Samuel's voice called out.

"We're all right. I'll be right there," Barnabus called. He slid the large rock out of the way, releasing the children from the alcove.

Helen met the bear's gaze. *We are taking care of children too. We need to find something.* Helen flashed on an image of a box sitting on a tall column of rock.

The bear huffed again, and Helen smiled. "She's seen the box. She'll lead us there."

The children peered out from behind Barnabus. He nodded to the bear. "Will she be a problem?"

Helen shook her head. She felt a kinship with the bear. "No. In fact, she's agreed to help us. And she's just trying to do right by her child." *Just like me.*

CHAPTER 74

TROY, TURKEY

Clytemnestra was surprised by how much she enjoyed her time in Troy. Back in Mycenae, Agamemnon had always switched her servants so she could never grow too close to any of them—except Morcant—and he had encouraged her sons to defy her. Iphigenia had been her one bright spot. But here, she was made to feel a part of the family. In fact, if she was being honest, she felt more at home here than she did in Mycenae. Paris stayed away from her, no doubt because Helen had scared the life out of him, but the rest of the family, even Hector, treated her as a guest rather than a captive. After all, they believed she and Paris had fallen in love at first sight.

It was not, however, a carefree existence. The deaths were mounting on both sides, with neither side seeming to gain any true ground. She had heard nothing from her brothers or Helen, and each day she worried for them all.

Clytemnestra walked around the courtyard, her arm wrapped around Hecuba's. She found comfort in the older woman's presence. Hecuba reminded her of her own mother.

"My dear, your sewing is beautiful," Hecuba said. The two of them had been working on a tapestry this morning. "I did not realize Spartan women were so skilled in the domestic arts."

Clytemnestra hid her smile. She tried to imagine Helen sitting down with a needlepoint. Helen would have been less likely to put her needle through the fabric and more likely to put her needle through the eye of whichever person suggested she try it. But Clytemnestra found peace in the quiet work; it allowed her to take her mind off other troubling aspects of her life.

"You will find Spartans are very diverse in our skills sets," she said.

"Perhaps one day I will be able to visit."

Not sure how that is going to happen, Clytemnestra thought, but out loud she said, "That would be lovely."

"Ah, this garden always has the most beautiful flowers," King Priam said as he stepped from an alcove into the garden. He walked over and kissed Hecuba on the cheek. Despite their years together, she still blushed.

Clytemnestra watched the exchange with more than a little envy. The king and queen's marriage had been an arranged one, like all other royal matches—yet it was obvious that this one had resulted in a true loving union.

Priam nodded toward Clytemnestra with a smile. "And how are you today, my dear? You have some color in your cheeks. That is good."

"I am well, my lord. The fresh air is wonderful."

"Yes. This garden—"

A screech cut off King Priam's words. All three of them turned as a woman strode across the garden, her arm outstretched, pointing at Clytemnestra. Long, dark, unkempt hair swirled around her. Her dark blue dress was shredded at the ends and stained across the bodice. Clytemnestra would have thought she was a beggar or even a witch if not for the quality of the material of the dress—and if not for the woman's face. She was a younger version of Hecuba, but with darker hair and King Priam's blue eyes.

"Impostor!" the woman yelled.

Clytemnestra's heart began to race, and she took a step back. Hecuba patted her arm. "It's all right, dear."

Priam stepped in front of the two women. "Cassandra, what is the meaning of this?"

Clytemnestra started. *Cassandra, the daughter of Priam and Hecuba.* In all her time here, she had not met Cassandra yet. She'd thought she had been sent away before the fighting began. But rumors of Priam and Hecuba's youngest daughter had reached the kingdom of Mycenae. Cassandra claimed to have the sight, but no one believed her. According to the gossips, the woman was simply insane. But because she was of royal blood, she was allowed freedom within the castle, not locked up like other families would do with their afflicted.

Cassandra pointed again at Clytemnestra. "Father, she is an impostor. She is not Helen."

Hecuba gave a weary sigh—one filled with disappointment and frustration.

"I warned you," Cassandra said. "I warned you she would lead to Troy's destruction. Why didn't you listen to me? Why do you never listen to me? I found Paris for you. I told you he would bring the witch back." Cassandra turned to Clytemnestra. "And now this one stands in for her, and you still cannot see. How can you not see?" she wailed.

Priam spoke sternly. "Cassandra, Helen is our guest, and she will be treated as such."

"She is not Helen," Cassandra insisted, her eyes begging her father to believe her. Clytemnestra couldn't help but feel compassion for the woman. She was obviously desperate for her father's approval.

King Priam sighed deeply. "My dear, you are tired." He waved to two guards. "My men will help you back to your room so you can sleep."

The men grabbed Cassandra's arms, and Clytemnestra winced at how they gripped her.

"Go on, my dear," Priam said.

"She's the ruin of us all," Cassandra said. "All of us. She has deceived you. You are all doomed. I can hear the hoofbeats of our destruction." She dragged her feet as the guards pulled her away. Priam turned his back as she continued to rant.

"I am sorry you had to see that," Hecuba said softly.

"She is—" Priam hesitated. "Troubled."

"She has the sight?" Clytemnestra asked.

Priam shook his head. "No. It's just senseless rambling. Pay her no mind. Now, how about if we head to the stables? One of my prized horses has given birth, and I have great hopes for this foal."

Clytemnestra nodded absentmindedly as she followed them. But she couldn't help but glance back to where the guards had disappeared with Cassandra. The girl had been so distraught. Years of her family ignoring her visions had taken their toll.

But Clytemnestra knew that Cassandra truly did see. *They really should start listening to her.*

CHAPTER 75

CRETE, GREECE

The maze was extensive, and Helen sensed that even the bear was getting confused. They had gone down a few wrong tunnels and had to double back, but the bear always seemed to get back on track.

She was a large brown bear, and at first the children had been scared of her. But after she stopped off to pick up her cub—which now rode on her back—the children had warmed to her. Hours later, though, that curiosity and interest had shifted to indifference as trudged forward.

Helen wondered if she should call a stop and let the children rest. She had to admit she wouldn't mind sitting down for a minute herself. But just before she was about to say something, the bear let out a roar and stood on her hind feet. The cub scampered off her back.

Oh, no. "Children, duck into that last tunnel," Helen ordered without turning around.

"What is it?" Barnabus asked.

Helen's body was on full alert, all traces of exhaustion gone. "The minotaur."

She still had no direct sense of the minotaur—she'd had no sense of him in all their walking. If not for the lion's memories, she might have believed he was simply made up. But she could feel the bear's fear, and the bear was certain.

The bear roared, and the sound was amplified by the walls of the narrow tunnel. Helen peered into the darkness ahead, where the shadows danced with the firelight.

Then the shadows joined together and moved toward her.

Helen backed up a step as the beast stepped into view. It was indeed the minotaur. It stood at least six feet tall on two muscular human legs. Dark hair hung half way down its chest where it was then bare. Its head which was that of a bull with horns on either side made it look like a demon.

Helen's pulse raced, but she strove for calmness as she projected her thoughts to the beast. *It's all right. We are not here to hurt you. It's all right. We are not here to hurt you.*

But the beast continued forward, growling low in its throat.

"Helen?" Barnabus asked.

She frowned. "It's not working. I can't get through to him."

Barnabus gripped his bone weapon tightly. "Let me."

"No," Helen held out a hand. "Let me try again."

The bear fell in line with her as she stepped forward. *It's all right. We will not hurt you. There is no need to hurt us.* But no matter how hard she tried, she could not get inside the creature's head. She had no sense of it. Her fear skyrocketed. What had Minos done? What had he created?

The beast lumbered forward, dragging a giant club. Light glinted off its dark, matted fur. Then, with a scream, it lunged for her.

Helen stumbled back. *Protect!* she screamed in her mind, toward the bear.

The bear leapt in front of her with a roar, swinging at the

beast. Her nails carved deep into its flesh, and the minotaur fell to the ground with a cry.

Helen went still—because that was no animal cry. *Stop!* she ordered.

The bear growled, but backed away.

Barnabus grabbed for her arm. "Helen…"

"It's not what you think," she said quietly, her heart hammering as she shook off his hand. "Keep the children back. Don't let them see."

She walked slowly toward the creature. It lay still on the ground and released another piteous cry. Blood poured from the creature's chest. It was not long for this world.

As Helen approached, she saw that the minotaur's muscular arms and legs were hairless. Its giant bull head was thick with matted hair that hung down over its shoulders, but that hair stopped halfway down its chest.

She knelt down beside its head. Gently, she pulled the head off.

"By the gods," Barnabus whispered.

Underneath the bull head was the face of a man. He had gray hair, but his face was that of an child—a scared child. There was a simplicity in his gaze that told her he was not a monster born, but raised. He blinked, then pulled back.

Helen reached out a hand, and a cry erupted from the man's throat. "It's all right," she said. "I won't hurt you."

"What is he?" Barnabus asked quietly from behind her.

Pity threatened to swallow Helen whole. "A human. One who has been trapped down here to play the part of the minotaur."

From the look on the man's face, she knew his mind was slow. No doubt that was why Minos had banished him here, thinking he would die. But he had lived—and had taken on the role of the monster.

The man's blood flow was slowing. Then he wheezed—and went still. His eyes stared straight ahead, seeing nothing.

Helen reached forward and closed the man's lids.

"So there never was a minotaur?" Barnabus asked.

Helen sat back, suddenly exhausted. "I don't know. Maybe at one point. But I'm guessing Minos used this cave to deal with family members who did not live up to his expectations."

"You think he's part of the royal family?"

"Look at him, Barnabus. He is connected to Minos." The man's eyes had been an exact duplicate of Minos's—minus the cruelty.

"How has he survived all these years? I mean, children are only sent in every two years."

"The cattle that have gone missing—I'm betting that was him. He must have found a way out."

"If he could escape, why did he return to the cave?"

"Maybe he thought of the dark as his home."

"It is a sad existence." Barnabus gently pulled Helen to her feet. "But we are not done yet. We still need to find the key. And now we have no obstacles in our way."

Helen sighed. "Of course. We should go."

"It's not your fault, you know. His death."

The horror of this damnable cave washed over Helen. The bear and the lion, banished here to live out their days in darkness. The children, left to die. And this poor man, who had turned into a monster. Anger, pure and bright, burned through her.

"No, his death is not my fault. That blame lies at the feet of Minos."

CHAPTER 76

Helen and Barnabus covered the man's body in rocks, as they had done for the lion earlier. One day and two graves. The deaths were weighing Helen down, but she knew they could not stop. So they continued on. The maze seemed to run the expanse of the whole island. The bear had no sense of time or distance, so Helen could not tell if they were close or hours away.

Helen's feet were starting to ache, and she was pretty sure the kids were doing even worse. She wasn't sure if she should call a halt for the night or continue on.

Then the bear let out a roar. Helen's head jerked up. *Finally.*

She jogged to where the bear stood. They were on the edge of a cliff; there was no way to move forward. Helen looked down—and wished she hadn't. The drop appeared endless.

But across the expanse, fifty feet away, just visible in the flickering light, was a tiny ledge. And on that ledge, standing tall and proud, was the stalagmite from the bear's memory. Engraved on its side were two entwined triangles, and resting on top of it was the box.

Barnabus walked up and gave the bear a wary look. But the

bear merely sat on her haunches and licked her paws. Her cub curled up next to her and closed her eyes.

"So. We are here," Barnabus said.

"I guess so."

"Are you going over there?"

Helen stared at the ledge. It did not look as if it would support a person's weight, much less the impact from a jump. "Somehow, I didn't think it's going to be as simple as that."

"Ideas?" Barnabus asked.

Helen let out a breath, rubbing her ring. "This challenge is meant for a ring bearer—which means the box can be retrieved using an ability only I have."

She closed her eyes and called on the wind. She felt it stirring and created a funnel next to the stalagmite. Carefully she sent a second wind behind the box, blowing it into the funnel.

"Careful, Helen," Barnabus warned.

Helen gritted her teeth. Sweat rolled down her back as she drew the funnel toward her. "Barnabus?" she said.

As soon as the box was within his reach, he snatched it from the funnel.

Helen released the wind. Her shoulders slumping, she leaned against the bear for support.

Barnabus grinned at her. "See? A piece of cake."

"It's beautiful," Helen whispered, running a hand over the top of the wooden box. It was eighteen inches long and about ten inches wide. The lid had two intertwined triangles carved into its center, and ornate drawings rimmed its outer edge: someone falling from the sky; a group standing on a mountaintop; other signs of nature—wind, rain, animals. *All things I can control.*

Helen ran her fingers over the drawing of a woman, her hands held up.

"Is that you?" Barnabus asked.

Helen shook her head. "No. I think that's my mother."

"Well, let's see what all the fuss is about." Barnabus extended the box toward her.

Helen took a breath, and with a trembling hand, she opened it.

"Son of whore," Barnabus muttered.

The box was empty.

CHAPTER 77

"Empty?" Helen ripped out the fabric that lined the box, but there was absolutely nothing inside, and the fabric itself was just a piece of burlap.

"Do you think Minos has it?" Barnabus asked.

"Oh, I'm sure he does. I would bet anything that is why the first King Minos cut Crete off from the world—to keep it protected. To keep it for himself."

Barnabus's face darkened. "So what is the plan now?"

Helen's eyes flashed. "Now we are going to *chat* with Minos."

Barnabus grinned. "About time."

Helen turned and strode down the tunnel, the bear and cub at her side. She stopped short in front of the children. Their faces were covered in dirt, and exhaustion weighed down their frames. A few looked as if they were seconds from falling asleep on their feet.

Her anger was replaced with concern. "I think we could all use a little rest," she said. "What do you think?"

The children nodded.

"I was about to say the same thing." Barnabus turned to the children. "All right, children, let's get some sleep before we continue on." He led them all back down the tunnel to one of the larger caverns they had passed. It had multiple exits, which would make it harder to defend if needed, but it also had a rock shelf large enough for all the children to lie down on.

Helen watched the children climb onto the shelf and lay down their heads. Many of them fell asleep immediately. Images of her own children swam in her mind. She missed them so much. But until this was done, she could not even go near them without endangering them. Just as Minos was endangering these children. What was it with powerful men who felt no compunction about destroying innocent lives in their quest for more power? How did they sleep at night?

"Helen?" Barnabus called softly.

She turned to him.

"Are there any threats nearby?"

She shook her head. "No," she said softly, "all the threats are gone. Now it's just the maze. Get some sleep."

Barnabus leaned against the wall near the children and closed his eyes.

Helen turned to the bears. *Rest, my friends. And keep the children safe.*

The bears lumbered over to the ledge where the children slept and curled up in front of it.

Helen sat down and leaned her back against the cave wall. She struggled to keep her eyes open, then gave up the fight. The bears would warn them of danger, and besides, she had spoken truthfully to Barnabus—she sensed no other threats.

No threats—and no information. She grabbed hold of the anger trying to bubble through her and shoved it down. She needed to sleep before she dealt with Minos.

Sleep well, King, for tomorrow you will have a reckoning.

CHAPTER 78

Helen walked along the Eurotas River in Sparta. Its crystal-clear water sparkled in the bright sun. A family of six was seated for a meal by the river's edge, and asked Helen to join them. With a smile Helen shook her head, explaining that she had somewhere to be.

She continued her walk, each step bringing her more peace. She closed her eyes and tilted her head back as a wind blew. The scents of Sparta rolled over her. She smiled. There was no place in the world she loved more.

"Helen."

She turned and saw her mother walking toward her with a smile. Her red hair shone brightly in the sunlight. Helen knew immediately she was in a dream, but she would take any time she could get with her mother, dream or not.

She wrapped her mother in a hug. "Mother, I have missed you."

Leda put her hands on Helen's cheeks. "I am always with you. No matter where you go."

"But I didn't go anywhere. You did."

"Just because you can't see me does not mean I am gone." Leda linked her arm in Helen's, and the two began to walk along the shore of the lake. Helen felt the sun on her face and breathed deep, a sense of contentment rolling through her.

"You're almost there," Leda said.

Helen frowned, looking around. There was nothing as far as the eye could see. "Almost where?"

"At the end of this part of your journey. When you leave the cave, you will still have a long fight ahead of you. It will test all that you are."

"People will die," Helen said softly. The clouds moved to block the sun.

"They always do. But you must stop Zeus. No matter the cost. The world cannot survive his control. Thousands more will be killed."

Helen knew it was true. "Mother, I—"

A strong wind blew, and Leda's head whipped to the side. "Danger is coming."

Helen squeezed her mother's arm. "Don't tease. We are perfectly safe. Look around. There is nothing to fear."

Her mother's grip tightened painfully. "No Helen. It's coming. It's coming for you."

CHAPTER 79

The bear let out a roar, and Helen's eyes popped open to see an arrow embedded in the bear's side.

"Barnabus!" Helen yelled, but he was already moving. Helen rolled to her side just in time to avoid an arrow engulfed in flame. She looked to find its source, and saw a man standing just inside one of the cavern's side tunnels. He wore the attire of Minos's guard.

Wind, Helen ordered and a wind blew through the cave. It struck the line of fire that illuminated the cave, fanning the flames and blowing them onto the shooter. The man let out a yell as his hair and tunic burst into flame.

"Barnabus, get the children out of here! Go!"

Helen focused on the tunnel where the man still burned, searching for any sense of more men. But she didn't need any special abilities to know there were more men coming; an arrow sailed past her, cutting her cheek. With a grunt, she blasted the tunnel with wind. She heard a scream, and sprinted down the side tunnel toward it.

"Helen!" Barnabus yelled.

"Take care of the children until I get back!"

A man leapt at her with a kick, but Helen grabbed his leg, moved in a half circle, and slammed her elbow into the man's knee. Keeping hold of his leg, she spun around and slammed her other elbow into his face. The man screamed. Helen swept the leg he balanced on, and he fell backward into the wall and slid down it, remaining still.

The burning man also now lay still, and two more men lay underneath rocks that must have been dislodged by her wind. But farther down the tunnel she could see someone alive and running. Helen sprinted after him.

She followed him around two turns, both of them narrow side tunnels. Then, to her surprise, she turned a corner to see him scrambling up the side of the tunnel and through a hole that let in daylight.

That's how the minotaur escaped, Helen thought.

She reached up to climb after the man, but a soldier with a bow appeared above her. She leapt to the side just in time to avoid taking an arrow. Then, with a rumble, a large rock fell down onto the hole above, blocking out the daylight, and she could hear more rocks tumbling on top of it.

"No!" Helen yelled. She pushed against the rock, but it didn't even budge.

She slumped down to the ground. *Damn it.* The minotaur's escape route was now closed.

Helen looked around the empty tunnel, her anger at Minos growing. Apparently the king hadn't even been willing to wait for the cave to end them. *Coward.*

Helen narrowed her eyes. *I am going to destroy him.*

CHAPTER 80

Helen retraced her steps to the cavern where they had rested. Barnabus and the children were gone, but the mama bear still lay in front of the rock ledge, the arrow in her side. Her cub was pawing at her, trying to get her to move.

Oh, little one, she does not have the strength.

The mama bear let out a huff when she saw Helen. Helen knelt down next to her. "Thank you, my friend," she said. "For helping us. For protecting us. May the gods speed you on to your next journey, and may they give you peace."

As the bear looked up at her, Helen saw the soul in her eyes. Her mother had told her about the souls of animals, and about how each animal was here for a purpose—just like humans.

Helen laid a hand on the bear's paw. "It's all right. Your job here is done. I will take care of your little one."

The bear watched her for a moment longer. Then her eyes closed and her chest went still. The cub let out a cry, and Helen felt her pain and her loneliness.

For a while, Helen just sat quietly, letting the cub mourn her mother. Finally the cub curled up next to Helen, and Helen laid a hand on her head. *I am sorry, young one. Your mother was very brave.*

She heard shuffling from one of the side tunnels, and then Barnabus and the children appeared. A quick count told her they were all there. Barnabus let out a relieved sigh when he saw her. "I took the children to a more defensible location," Barnabus said. "Are you all right? And please tell me you killed them all."

"I'm all right," Helen said. "And the men are no longer a threat. One escaped. Four did not."

He nodded. "Not bad."

"Are all the children well?"

"They're scared, and a few fell, but they suffered only scratches."

"Good." Helen lowered her voice. "I found the minotaur's escape route."

Barnabus grinned. "That is excellent—"

"The men covered it with an avalanche of rocks."

Barnabus's face fell. "That is not so excellent."

"No, it's not. We'll just have to return to the entrance." She looked at the children. The rest had done them good; she hoped they could handle another long walk.

"But there is no way to open the door from the inside," Barnabus said.

"Oh, there's a way."

∼

AFTER COVERING the mama bear with rocks, and coaxing the cub to leave her, they set off through the maze, back the way they had come. Helen was worried about getting lost, but the rocks they had used to mark their path did their job, and they avoided taking any wrong turns. It was still a long journey, and Helen's muscles ached, but she was driven forward by her impatience to deal with

Minos. She felt such anger toward the man. Here she was, trying to stop a war, and what was he doing? Playing games.

Finally, they came around the final bend. The door to the entrance was just up ahead, still bolted shut. "Stop here," Helen said. "Keep the children back. I'll go open the door."

Barnabus looked down the path at the immense door. "Open it? How?"

She shook her head, realizing Barnabus didn't know the extent of her abilities. She waved her ring finger. "With a little help from the gods. Keep everyone back." She moved forward a few feet to another alcove so she could focus. She closed her eyes and brought forth a memory of what the door looked like from the outside. She couldn't have taken this approach to open the minotaur's escape route, because she couldn't picture what the outside world looked like at that location. But the door—that she could picture.

In her mind, she made clouds roll across the sky. A wind shrieked. Helen took in a deep breath, and as she exhaled, she called on the power of the sky. Four blasts of lightning, one right after the next, shrieked through the sky and struck the door, blasting it to bits.

Helen waved her hand at the resulting dust. She let the clouds depart, and down the tunnel, sunlight shone through the opening.

Barnabus gaped at her. "You—how—"

She patted his arm. "Sometimes it's best to not ask questions. Now, how about we get out of here?"

Barnabus nodded. "I am in complete agreement."

They led the children toward the opening. All of them blinked in the sudden brightness. "I'll go first," Helen said, wanting to make sure it was safe.

Barnabus shook his head. "You are lucky I am a confident male."

Helen snorted. "I have never known one more confident," she

teased—then she thought of Achilles and Menelaus. *Well, perhaps two.*

She reached out with her senses but could not feel anyone or anything outside—at least, no one with abilities. Stepping cautiously through the door, blinking against the bright light, she looked down the path and at the trees. She saw no threats.

But she did see two women. They were huddled together just down the path, staring in awe at the shattered door. Their eyes were red, as if they had been crying. Helen recognized one of them as the one who had been attacked without mercy when she'd tried to run to her children.

Helen smiled. "It's all right."

The women scrambled to their feet, still clutching one another.

"Helen?" Barnabus called.

"Come on out. We're good."

Barnabus sent the children out ahead of him, protecting the rear. Kyrael and Samuel appeared at the entrance first, and one of the women let out a cry of joy. The young boy and his sister ran for their mother, tears streaming down their faces. The rest of the children followed, and three of them ran for the other woman, who fell to her knees to embrace them.

Barnabus kept the rest of the children with him. After a time, one of the women broke away from her children, ran to Barnabus, and hugged him tight, thanking him over and over again.

Helen rescued Barnabus from the woman and pulled him aside. "We need to keep the children hidden until Minos is taken care of."

"All right, I'll have the women watch over—"

"No. You need to stay with them. Keep them hidden."

Barnabus narrowed his eyes. "You're going to face Minos alone?"

Helen held up her hand with the ring. "I'm the ring bearer—

I'm never alone. I bring the power of the gods with me. And Minos is now going to learn exactly what that means."

CHAPTER 81

Helen wanted to get to Minos's castle as quickly as possible—and that meant taking to the air. But not wanting to frighten the children, she jogged down the path until she was out of view before summoning a wind to lift her skyward.

Dark, gray clouds rolled behind her as she swooped down toward Minos's castle. She landed in a storm of dust on the path in the outer courtyard. Four guards at the door saw her land, but they were apparently too stunned to react—they just looked at her with wide eyes.

Helen directed a wind toward two of them. It blew them off their feet. The other two guards finally shook off their shock and braced their spears. But when a second gust of wind tore open the door behind them, they looked at each other, dropped their spears, and took off at a run.

Helen stormed through the doors. Servants scurried out of the way, and no more guards appeared. She strode forward, knowing she needed to get control of her anger—but she was so truly sick of all these stupid games. People were losing their lives.

The animals went silent as Helen stepped into the inner courtyard; the sight of them only pushed her temper hotter. A long table had been set up in the center of the space, and thirty people dined—with Minos at the head. Helen stormed toward the table. "Where is it?" she demanded.

Minos looked up in surprise. Then he sat back, wiped his mouth on his sleeve, and held up a hand, waving off his guards. "So you live. Tell me, did you listen to the children scream as they died? Did you let them die so you could survive?"

A strong gust of wind pushed over the pitchers on the table. "Where is it, Minos?" Helen demanded. "I am done with your games."

Minos smiled as archers appeared on the balconies rimming the courtyard. "But *I'm* not done yet."

Helen smiled back. Clouds rolled overhead and thunder crashed. "You really don't understand who I am, do you?"

"I really don't care." Minos raised his hand to signal his men to fire.

Anger the likes of which Helen had never felt boiled through her. She was trying to save the world, and this petty little tyrant was trying to gain power. She brought down lightning on the archers. Some were struck dead on the spot, while others stumbled back in horror. She summoned a gust of wind and used it to lift the long table and fling it against a wall. She rained down hail the size of fists.

Minos's guests scattered, screaming. Minos himself fell backward, his chair tipping over.

But the wind never touched Helen, and the hail created a clear path that led her straight to Minos. When he scrambled to his feet and ran for the door, a bolt a lightning crashed down in front of him. He fell back, screaming.

Helen lifted him by his tunic and slammed him into the wall. "Where are the contents of the box?"

"I—I—"

Helen slammed him into the wall again. It cracked, and pieces of plaster fell around him. "My patience is at an end," she growled.

"It's—it's—it's in my bedroom."

She shoved him toward the doorway. "Show me."

CHAPTER 82

Minos stumbled in front of Helen, his whole body shaking with fear. Wind slammed doors shut as they passed, destroying priceless works of art. Each time they passed an open window, thunder boomed and lightning struck.

By the time they reached Mino's bedchamber, he was a shell of a man. He fumbled with the door handle but Helen simply blew the door off its hinges, sending it flying across the room. A servant who had been making the bed let out a shriek and backed against the wall, her eyes wide. Minos let out a screech himself.

Helen grabbed him by the back of his tunic and pushed him inside. "The contents."

Minos fell to his knees and crawled to the opposite wall. He pushed past books and other treasures on his shelves before pulling out a box. It was an exact replica of the one from the cave, except this one was made of ivory. With trembling hands, he offered it to Helen.

"On the table," she ordered. He obediently set the box on the marble table to his right. "You bastard."

He scrambled back against the wall, and she saw that his tunic was now soaked in his own urine.

Helen lifted the lid of the box. Inside lay a scroll, obviously ancient, with a seal affixed to it—two triangles overlapping. *It's still here.* But the seal had been broken. She snapped the box shut, and Minos jumped. "You *opened* it?"

"No, no, of course not."

Helen glared. She didn't believe him, but it didn't matter. She had what she needed. But all the difficulties she had gone through to get to this point raced through her mind. All the pain the pitiful man in front of her had caused for his own amusement. She set the box back down on the table. "In the cave, the minotaur was a man," she said. "He was about your age."

The king looked away.

"You know who he was. Who?"

Minos shook his head. "I don't—"

"*Who?*" Helen demanded.

"My brother," Minos cried. He took a breath. "My brother. He was older than me, but not right. My parents sent him to the cave when he was eight."

Helen felt sick. What kind of family was this? "You knew he was alive?"

"I—I had food delivered to him every month, ever since I learned he had survived."

Helen paused. Minos had taken pity on his brother. "That action saved your life."

She grabbed the box and headed for the door. But as she glanced once more over her shoulder, she saw that Minos had straightened, and the arrogance had crept back into his face.

Then Helen heard a cry. She paused, tilting her head. It came again. "What is that?"

"Nothing. Nothing, my queen."

Helen narrowed her eyes. A wind blew through the room,

rustling all the curtains. Behind one, she saw a door. She walked over to it.

Minos scurried after her. "There's nothing in there. Nothing important."

Helen tried the handle. It was locked. "The key."

"I don't seem to—"

Helen kicked the door open.

The door led to a small, dark room. Three boys were chained to the walls, their arms and legs held tightly in place. They wore only loincloths. Helen guessed they were only about seven years old.

Helen turned to Minos. "Why are they here?" she asked quietly.

"They—their families could not control them. They begged me to take them. They are evil—possessed by evil spirits."

Helen glanced at the serving woman, who shook her head slightly.

"Don't move," Helen ordered Minos. Placing the box on the ground, she grabbed a key that hung just inside the door and used it to unlock the shackles around the boys' wrists and ankles. The first two boys just slumped to the ground. The third, his eyes big, tears streaming down his face, fell to Helen's feet and croaked, "Thank you. Thank you, mistress."

Helen gently pulled him to his feet. "What is your name?"

"Orestes."

"We'll get you to your family, Orestes."

"I have no family," he said.

"Why?"

"They were killed when I was taken. My father spoke against the king. These are my cousins. We are all that is left."

Helen whirled on Minos, who was trying to sneak away. "Is this true?"

"No, they lie. They would say anything to—"

"Be *quiet*."

Helen knelt down and picked up one of the other two boys. He was barely conscious. "Orestes, have you enough strength to lift your other cousin?"

"Yes." Orestes quickly wrapped his arms around the other boy.

Helen walked over to the serving woman and placed the boy in her arms. "See that they are fed, clothed, bathed, and taken care of. They are under my protection now. Is that understood?"

The woman glanced quickly toward Minos. "He—what he does to them is not natural."

Helen went still. She saw Orestes look down, shame in his eyes. She turned to him and spoke softly. "Look at me, Orestes." She waited until he complied. "What he did—that is his shame, not yours."

"But I—"

Helen held his gaze. "Did nothing wrong. Do you understand?"

Orestes nodded. But Helen knew it would be a long road for him to truly accept that fact. After Theseus, it had taken her a long time as well. "Go on. You are safe now."

"Are you sure?"

"Yes, I am sure."

"Thank you, mistress."

Orestes and the serving woman walked slowly from the bedchamber, carrying the other two boys.

"You—you will be leaving now?" Minos asked hopefully.

Helen tried to keep a lid on her anger. "In a few days. I have a long list of things I need to do before I go."

"Is there anything I can do to speed your departure?" he asked.

Helen grabbed the box from the table. Thunder rumbled. "Actually, there is."

Half a dozen bolts of lightning shot through the window and struck Minos. The force flung him across the room into the wall, his skull cracking. He fell to the floor in a smoking, smoldering heap.

Well, that's one thing off the list.

CHAPTER 83

Helen wanted to leave immediately, but in good conscience she could not. Crete was without a leader, and she knew all too well how evil people could step into a power vacuum and create a situation much more dire than the one these people had just escaped. So she and Barnabus spent two days in Crete searching for a new leader who would restore the freedoms of the people.

They first considered Minos's son, but he was far too young to take the mantle. Minos also had a few cousins, but after speaking with them Helen was convinced they would be any better than the deceased king. But then she came across Gaelous. He was the next adult in line for the throne, but in order to protect his family from Minos, he had renounced his claim to the throne fifteen years ago. Ever since, he led a quiet life as a blacksmith. Yet word was that he was well liked by the people of Crete—he was known as a good man who cared for others.

So Helen summoned him to the palace. And after a long conversation knew she had found the right one. Now she just needed to convince him.

"A lightning bolt? The great King Minos was killed by a storm?" Gaelous asked.

"Apparently the gods were unhappy with his rule." Helen paused. "A reminder to all of us that the gods watch us. We are not without accountability."

"Yes," Gaelous said, casting his gaze to the heavens. "A wise reminder. And the maze? How did you escape the minotaur?"

"He—" Helen paused, picturing the poor man's face.

"Helen is a warrior of no equal," Barnabus cut in. "She has yet to meet a foe she could not vanquish."

"Yes." Gaelous bowed. "We are most honored and humbled by your service to us."

"It is I who am humbled," Helen said. "You will be a wise king."

Gaelous shook his head. "I will be the king's consort. And I will raise my nephew to be a good king. When he is old enough, I will hand over power to him."

"A pity you will not agree to be the king. I think Crete would do well under you."

"I have no interest in ruling. But I will do what duty asks of me. I will take on the responsibility for now."

After Gaelous left, Helen turned to Barnabus. "What have you figured out about the parchment?" She had taken one look at the paper from the box and knew it was not a language she was familiar with. She had put Barnabus in charge of deciphering it.

"I've ruled out many languages until I am left with only one —Sanskrit."

"I don't suppose you can read Sanskrit?"

He grinned. "I can only read some of it. But Reyansh from our ship is formerly from India. I sent for him, but I did not want him to read it until you were ready to hear it. I can retrieve him now— with your permission?"

Helen nodded. "Get him."

Barnabus returned a few moments later with a small, thin man. Reyansh bowed deeply. "Queen Helen."

"Please rise, Reyansh. We are in need of your help. Can you read this?" She nodded to Barnabus, who handed him the parchment.

Reyansh took it with shaking hands. "It has been a long time since I have seen the writing of my people. I was captured before I had reached manhood."

"I am sorry," Helen said.

Reyansh shrugged. "You and your brothers freed me and my family. I am very grateful. I will do my best to translate."

He sat on the ground cross-legged and studied the paper. As Helen waited, she imagined the horror of being a slave. It was a reality of their world, but it was a practice she did not believe in. All her "slaves" were paid, and anyone who mistreated a slave received the same mistreatment in return. That rule had not eliminated the abuse, but at least it had limited it. Sadly, even as a queen, there was only so much one could do.

Reyansh looked up. "I think I understand most of it."

"Go ahead," she said.

"*The great ones arrived in a hail of fire and light. The world rejoiced and was amazed by their skill and strength. A time of peace ensued. But then they wanted more than they were given. They demanded it. The world fought back and won, but only because they were able to bring the great ones to their level. Since that time, we, the brothers of Dwarka, have guarded this weapon of the people, keeping it safe, praying it would not be needed again, but preparing in case it was.*"

"Dwarka?" Helen asked. Dwarka was a legendary city of India favored by the Hindu god Krishna. It was a city of beauty and incredible magic. And one day, it sank beneath the waves. In the east, there was no doubt in people's minds that the city had once existed—but farther west, Dwarka was viewed as just a legend.

Helen felt a chill crawl over her. "Please continue."

The small man nodded. "*They came again when our city was at its greatest heights. We had to destroy them and our beloved home to keep the world safe once again.*" Reyansh frowned. "There's another line, but it's difficult to make out. The ink has faded. I think it says they moved to... yes. *The island of the two gods.*"

Recognition flashed across Barnabus's face, but Helen shook her head before he could speak. To Reyansh she said, "Thank you. You have been most helpful. Please do not speak of this to anyone."

"I am glad to have been of service." Reyansh stood and bowed before leaving the room.

"The island of the two gods," Barnabus murmured.

Helen nodded. The mysterious island in the southern part of the Ionian Sea. It would take weeks to get there. But the distance was the least of their problems.

"Helen, you know the legends of this island, don't you?"

"That it is haunted by the ghosts of sailors who attempted to land there? And this is what accounts for the screams that come from the island?"

Barnabus shook his head. "I was thinking more of the rumors that say no one has ever safely landed on the island."

Helen had heard those rumors as well. "Well, there's a first time for everything, right?"

CHAPTER 84

Helen walked toward the docks. She had tried to see all the rescued children this morning, saying her farewells, but there was one child she had not been able to find. She searched the docks but saw nothing. She let out a sigh.

All the children from the cave were safe and secure with their families. But the same was not true of the boys she had rescued from Minos's room. She had been checking on them for the last two days, but despite receiving the best medical care, Orestes's cousins had only grown weaker, and this morning they had both passed away. She had hurried through her task this morning, but she had not been there when they passed. And by the time she had arrived, Orestes had run off.

"We'll find him before we leave," Barnabus said.

"I hope so."

A bamboo crate sat by itself on the dock. Helen frowned. "I wonder why it's not on board yet."

"I'll check." Barnabus went over to speak to Aegisthus. Helen couldn't hear what was said, but the captain shook his head.

When Barnabus returned, she asked, "What happened?"

"His men are scared. They won't go near the crate."

"Did you tell them it's safe?"

"I did, but he does not believe me."

"Oh, for goodness' sake." Helen strode over to the crate and began to unwind the rope that held it shut.

Aegisthus ran over to her, his eyes wide. "My queen, what are you doing?"

"Showing you there is nothing to fear." She let the crate door drop to the ground. Aegisthus jumped back as a furry head appeared.

Helen smiled. *It's all right. Come on out.*

The cub stepped out of the crate and went to Helen's side, licking her hand. Helen ran a hand through his fur. *Come, little one.* She walked up the gangplank, and the cub trotted behind her. Behind her, she heard Barnabus order two men to carry the empty crate on board.

As Helen stepped onto the ship, the sailors already on board stopped what they were doing, their eyes locked on the bear. *Have a seat, little one.* After a moment's hesitation he sat next to her. The men didn't look reassured. Helen considered. *How about waving?* She raised her hand, and the little cub imitated her. That made the sailors smile.

"It's all right," she called to them. "He won't hurt you."

The cub leaned into Helen, and two men set the crate down on the deck beside them. Helen knelt down to look into the cub's eyes. *You need to go back in, but just for a little while—until the men are not scared of you. Okay?*

The cub licked her cheek and walked into the crate. Helen gestured for the men to lock it up.

"He listens to you."

Helen turned at the small voice. "Orestes. I've been looking for you."

The boy was too thin, too pale, and Helen could see the trails of tears through the dirt on his face. And yet all she felt at the sight of him was relief.

He kept his gaze focused on his feet. "I—I was here. I—" His voice cracked. "I didn't know where else to go."

Helen's heart broke for the young boy. He was alone in the world. "I am sorry for your loss."

Orestes swiped at a tear that rolled down his cheek. "I don't have anyone left."

"I've been thinking about that." She patted the deck next to her. "Sit with me."

Orestes obeyed, but he wouldn't meet her eyes.

"Have you been on a ship before?" Helen asked.

Orestes shook his head.

"Well, this one has been to Egypt and Sparta, and now we are heading to the Ionian Sea."

"So far?" Orestes said. He looked on the verge of tears.

"Yes. There are some people there I need to speak with. It is a long journey. And a ship like this always needs a few extra hands." Helen paused. "Say, you wouldn't like to come with us, would you?"

Orestes's head popped up, and Helen saw hope in his eyes. "Really?"

"It won't be easy. You'll have work to do. And you are years behind in training. So you will have to train very hard with me and Barnabus for the entire journey."

His eyes grew even larger. "Train? You will teach me to fight?"

"If you wish. And Barnabus has offered to take you to Egypt with him to live."

"Really?"

"You don't need to decide now. We have much time."

"But you want me to go with you?"

Helen smiled. "We both do."

Orestes turned away, but not before Helen saw a new sheen of tears in his eyes. She pretended she didn't. He would need to learn to hide those emotions. Best to start now.

"There is one additional responsibility, however, that you will need to be in charge of for the journey."

"What?" Orestes asked.

Helen nodded to the cub, who could be seen through the bars of the bamboo crate, contentedly chewing on a bone. "He will need to be fed and walked and played with. I would like you to do that."

Orestes's eyes grew huge. "You want me to play with a *bear*?"

"Yes. He has lost all those close to him as well. Will you look after him for me?"

Helen could see the fear in the boy's eyes, but he nodded. "Yes."

"Excellent." She stood up. "Let us go make introductions." She held out her hand to him, and he grasped it. And for a moment, it wasn't Orestes standing next to her but one of her own children. She swallowed down the emotions that bubbled up and cleared her throat. "All right, I have not named him yet. You will have to do that as well."

"I can name him anything?"

"Anything you like."

The boy paused, his face showing how seriously he took the task. Finally he said, "Achilles."

Helen nearly tripped over her own feet. "Achilles?"

Orestes's eyes widened. "Have you heard of him? He is the greatest warrior that has ever lived. He is the son of Zeus."

Zeus really seems to have gotten around. "Yes, I am familiar with Achilles."

Barnabus joined them. "Achilles?"

"Yes," Helen said dryly, "Orestes has decided to name the cub Achilles in honor of the great warrior."

Barnabus laughed, but he quickly turned it into a cough at Helen's glare. "Do you know that Queen Helen and I know Achilles very well?" he asked.

"You do?"

Barnabus smiled. "Come. Walk with me and I will tell you stories you would not believe."

Helen smiled at the sight of the two of them walking off together.

The captain approached. "We are ready to sail whenever you are, my queen."

"Then let's begin. It's time for the next leg of this adventure."

"As you wish." The captain bowed and departed.

Helen moved to the railing. The scroll had said that the island would have the weapon of the people. Helen had no idea what that referred to, but she prayed that the scroll was correct— because good men were losing their lives while she chased it down. At the same time, she couldn't imagine what kind of weapon could possibly change the entire course of a war.

And she prayed she wasn't on a fool's errand.

CHAPTER 85

TROY, TURKEY

The tent flap flew open and Patroclus stormed in. Achilles blinked, trying to bring him into focus, but after a few seconds he gave up and let his head fall back on his cot. He held up the bottle he was holding. "Patroclus. Come join me."

Patroclus stood with his arms crossed. "I think you've had enough."

"Nonsense. There is no such thing as too much wine—or too many women." Achilles took a swig to accentuate the point. Truth was, he barely tasted it, he was so numb from all the alcohol he'd already drunk. For alcohol to have any effect on him, he needed to drink it continuously, and so that was exactly what he had been doing since his confrontation with Agamemnon. It was the only way he could drown out the sounds of battle—the sounds of men falling when he could have saved them.

"How long do you plan to continue like this?" Patroclus demanded.

Patroclus was the only one who dared to speak to Achilles that way. Everyone else worried about how the mighty Achilles would react. But Patroclus, he never worried. He never backed down. And Achilles loved him all the more for it.

He had longed for a brother for years. When in Sparta, he had seen the closeness of Castor and Pollux—how they would die for one another without hesitation—and he had been jealous. He wanted that bond with someone. And then, as if the gods had heard his prayers, he found Patroclus. His presence had soothed the ache of leaving Sparta. And Achilles had learned from him about duty and commitment. He was as devoted to Patroclus as Patroclus was to him.

As Helen is to Sparta. The thought appeared unbidden in his mind, but he could not deny the truth of it. Her family and duty to Sparta would always come first to her.

Achilles shrugged. "It seems to be working so far."

"Men are dying! You could save them. Yet you sit here and *let* them die."

"I am not responsible for their deaths," Achilles growled. "Agamemnon is in charge."

"But they look to *you*! They look to the great Achilles to lead them forward, to show them how to win. Agamemnon—he barely steps onto the battlefield. He sends men into battle and then hightails it back to his tent to strategize. They need you, not a fat old man playing at soldier."

Achilles gripped the bottle, his knuckles turning white. "Has Agamemnon released Briseis?"

"No."

Achilles's spirits dropped. He had hoped Patroclus would say yes, allowing him to join the battle, to work off some of the guilt eating at him. A day or two would not change the course of the war. Then he could find another reason to sit out. He closed his eyes, not wanting to see the look of disappointment on Patroclus's face. "Then here I will stay."

"Achilles, just come to the battlefield. Your presence alone will bolster the men. They are beginning to lose heart. They are beginning to think they cannot win. Hector will be leading the Trojan forces this morning. Your men need you."

"They are not my men. They are Agamemnon's. He should be the one to bolster their spirits."

"He cannot, and you know that. Those men will die because you would rather sit here and feed your ego than help them win."

"I have given Agamemnon my terms. I will not break them."

Patroclus shook his head. "You disappoint me, Achilles. I thought you were more than this."

Patroclus's words cut through the fog of drink surrounding Achilles. Not for the first time, he wanted to tell Patroclus the true reason why he was sitting out this fight. But he had promised Helen, and he knew the stakes—Zeus needed to be stopped.

If Helen had truly known what she was asking of me, she would not have asked.

But she had. And he had promised. He would abide by that promise. Even if it meant sitting here while he burned to fight. He waved at Patroclus. "Tell the men we are not fighting."

Patroclus opened his mouth, then shut it. "Very well."

Achilles closed his eyes, feeling the pull of sleep. He heard Patroclus rummaging through their tent, but he paid it no heed. *When Helen returns, I will tell Patroclus all. He will understand,* Achilles thought as Patroclus disappeared from the tent and Achilles drifted off to sleep.

CHAPTER 86

Agamemnon paced his tent. He had left the battlefield as soon as Hector had stepped from the gates, his soldiers arranged behind him. He knew the men whispered about his absence, but he made sure they understood that only he and he alone could develop the strategies that would win them this war.

Of course, without Achilles, those strategies were turning out to be more and more complicated.

The tent flap opened, and Briseis walked in and set a flask of wine on the table. Agamemnon narrowed his eyes. She was the cause of all this. But he did not raise his hand to strike her. There was still a small chance of getting Achilles back in the fight, but Agamemnon knew that chance would vanish if the girl were harmed.

Agamemnon waved toward his bed. "See to my clothes." The girl quickly gathered his clothes from the floor and disappeared from the tent.

A roar went up from the battlefield, and then the men started to chant. Agamemnon tilted his head, trying to make out what it was they were yelling.

Cergen burst into the tent, gulping air. "Achilles. Sir—Achilles." The man bent at the waist trying to catch his breath.

"What is going on? Why are the men yelling?" Agamemnon demanded.

"It's Achilles—he has joined the fight with his Myrmidon."

Agamemnon felt satisfaction roll through him. He had known it would only be a matter of time before Achilles rejoined the fight. He had never met a man more crafted for battle than Achilles. "Well, let's go see how he's doing, shall we?"

He strode forward, and Cergen bowed as he held open the tent flap.

Agamemnon blinked at the bright sunlight but did not pause as he headed for his platform overlooking the battlefield. Now he could make out the chants of his men. "Achilles! Achilles! Achilles!"

Agamemnon disliked the raw energy Achilles's appearance had elicited, but he shrugged it off. It was he, Agamemnon, who held the real power, who held armies under his sway. Achilles was merely a weapon, a dog trained to fight. Of course the men cheered for him. Everyone loved a good dog fight.

Agamemnon climbed the wooden platform and looked toward the gates of Troy. Achilles's Myrmidon were easy to spot in their black armor and red leather skirts, and Achilles's armor was even more conspicuous. The gold eagle displayed on Achilles's chest sparkled in the sunlight as he flipped a man over his shoulder and stabbed another that had tried to sneak up on him from the side.

Agamemnon smiled. The man was ruthless in battle.

Not far from where Achilles stood, Hector fought just as ruthlessly. He slammed the hilt of his sword into one man's face, kicked the chest of another, and then ran his sword through both.

Soon, nothing separated Achilles and Hector. Warrior stood facing warrior. Agamemnon smiled, smelling the blood in the air. *This will be good.*

Hector and Achilles circled each other. As if by some unspoken agreement, all the men near them stopped their own battles to watch.

Hector struck first. Achilles easily sidestepped the move and brought his own sword up to retaliate. But Hector had only been bluffing. He kicked Achilles in the ribs, sending him sprawling.

The Trojans began to chant the name of their king to be. "Hector! Hector! Hector!" Agamemnon frowned. He'd never seen Achilles stumble in a battle.

The two men circled each other once again. This time Achilles moved first. He lunged at Hector again and again, forcing the man to retreat under a merciless onslaught. But then Hector parried and held, stopping Achilles's forward momentum. Hector grabbed Achilles' sword hand and slammed the hilt of his sword into Achilles's face. Achilles's head snapped back.

Hector wasted no time bringing his sword around and catching Achilles just under his armor.

The field went silent as blood poured from the wound in Achilles's side. He lunged at Hector, but Hector neatly sidestepped the attack and swung again, catching Achilles at the base of his neck. Achilles fell to his knees and toppled forward.

For a moment, not a sound could be heard. The Greeks stood silent as if in shock. Even the Trojans could not believe what they had witnessed. Then Hector raised his sword in the air, and the Trojans let out a scream of victory.

"Enough blood has been spilled this day," Hector yelled. "We leave you to collect your dead." Then he turned, and with his men chanting his name and following behind him, he jogged for the gates of Troy.

The Greek army didn't even move. They could only stare at the fallen Achilles. Even Agamemnon was in shock. He had never thought the mighty Achilles would be bested in battle. *Certainly not by a mortal.*

Agamemnon turned his gaze to the walls of Troy. *We are well and truly lost now.*

CHAPTER 87

His head fuzzy and his mouth dry, Achilles raised his head from his cot. "Patroclus?" he called. He swallowed, trying to get more moisture into his mouth. "Patroclus?"

He reached below his cot for his wine bottle. He pulled it up to his lips and frowned. He turned it upside down, and a single drop hit the ground. Sighing, he dropped it back to the floor. He stared at the tent ceiling, reliving the argument with Patroclus. It wasn't right. He needed to tell him why he would not fight. Patroclus would understand.

He sat up, and soon the effects of the wine disappeared. He'd never been very good at getting drunk. He felt the effects all right, but they never lasted as they did with other men. It was a blessing at times, but there had been many a time when he had wished for the oblivion that other men seemed to find at the bottom of a bottle.

He walked over to the basin and threw some water over his face. He wiped his face with a rough cloth and dropped it next to the basin. His stomach growled. *A little food and all will be well.*

He stepped out of the tent and blinked at the bright sun,

shading his eyes with his hand. A fire with a kettle of soup over it sat not far away. He walked toward it, the smell making his stomach growl even more.

It took him a minute to notice the silence and shocked stares of the men he passed. He stopped short of the fire and looked around. A man near him backed away, almost tripping over his own feet.

Dugal approached from the opposite side of the fire. "Achilles?"

Achilles smiled. "I realize I've been in my tent for a while, but I don't think seeing me walk around should result in this response."

Dugal's mouth hung open.

"Dugal?"

Dugal shook himself. "You're dead."

Achilles laughed. "Dead? Dead drunk, perhaps, earlier, but I assure you I now—"

Dugal hurried toward him. "You don't understand. You were felled in battle. I watched you die."

Achilles went still. "What are you talking about? I have not set foot on the field in weeks."

Dugal stared at him before yet again getting ahold of himself. "Something is gravely wrong here. Come with me."

Achilles wanted to demand the man explain himself, but he was not sure he wanted the answers.

Dugal led him through the camp. Every man they passed did a double take. Mouths dropped open. Murmurs reached his ears.

"Achilles is alive."

"The gods have brought him back."

Dugal stopped at a tent on the outskirts of the camp. Achilles's Myrmidon stood guarding it, and they looked just as stunned as everyone else at Achilles's approach.

One of the Myrmidon opened his mouth to speak, but Dugal shook his head. He turned to Achilles. "Inside, Achilles, we will find our answers."

Trepidation running through him, Achilles stepped into the tent.

Torches blazed, casting shadows across the body of a man lying on a table. The man was almost the same height and width as Achilles, and he wore Achilles's armor. Achilles could see how, from a distance, the mistake could be made.

His knees began to tremble and his stomach rolled. He stared at the face that he knew as well as his own. "Patroclus," he whispered, and Dugal startled next to him.

Patroclus stared straight ahead, seeing nothing. Blood had splashed across his face, helping disguise his identity from those too shocked to look closely. More blood soaked the bottom of his chest, staining the armor.

Shock rooted Achilles in place. "Who?" he whispered.

"It was Hector."

Hector. Achilles wanted to feel anger, but right now all he felt was loss—as if a hole had been carved out of his chest. Patroclus was the only family he had in this world—the one person who tied him to this planet in blood. "Tonight," he said, "we honor Patroclus."

"Yes, Achilles."

Achilles forced his mind to thoughts of Hector. The Trojan prince was a worthy fighter and from all reports an honorable man.

Achilles did not care. "And tomorrow, I will kill Hector."

CHAPTER 88

Achilles had never felt grief like this. Raw and unending, it flourished inside him. He wanted to rip his own heart from his chest to make it stop. His skin felt like it was holding him in, when all he wanted was to be free.

He had spent the night honoring Patroclus. When the time came, he had been the one to light his cousin's pyre. And as Patroclus's body turned to ash, Achilles's last shred of restraint snapped. Anger boiled inside him, blinding him to everything but his need to exact revenge. He would kill Hector—and he would drag his body through the land.

He stormed into his tent, Dugal at his heels. "Bring me my armor."

"Yes, sir. I will clean it of—"

"No." Achilles bit out the word, picturing his armor smeared with his cousin's blood. He would wear it as it was—to keep his cousin with him as he destroyed Hector. "Bring it as it is."

Dugal nodded, his eyes wide. "Yes, Achilles." He ducked out of the tent.

Achilles knew his men were worried about him. He could tell they were even scared of him. And they had every reason to be.

Because if anyone, anyone at all, tried to get in his way, he would destroy them—like he was going to destroy Hector.

Dugal returned with Achilles's armor and silently helped him into it. Then Achilles grabbed his sword and stormed out. Dugal ran to catch up with him. The rest of his Myrmidon fell in line behind him.

Achilles did not say a word as he made the long march to the gates of Troy. He did not slow, either, and some of his men had to jog to match his pace. All remained silent.

Finally, the gates of Troy stood in front of him. Tall, massive gates that had never been breached. It took all of Achilles's restraint not to simply bash them open. Instead, he looked up at them and yelled.

"Hector!"

CHAPTER 89

The news of Achilles's death had invigorated everyone in Troy—everyone except Clytemnestra. She had liked Achilles. He had never paid her much attention, not when Helen was near, but he'd always at least had a smile for her. For a few months, he had even met her early in the morning to help her with her fighting. Boudica had been amazed at her progress, and Clytemnestra had said nothing of her secret lessons. She did not think Achilles had told anyone of them either.

But Clytemnestra was more upset for her sister's sake than for her own. She knew Achilles's death would bring pain to Helen. She prayed her sister did not hear of it any time soon.

The family was in the morning room, finishing up breakfast, when they heard shouts from the hall. "Hector! Hector!"

A soldier sprinted into the room, his face ashen. Clytemnestra recognized him as Hector's right-hand man. Before now, she had never seen the man look anything but confident.

Hector frowned, handing his son to his wife, Andromache. "What is it?"

The man's breaths came out in pants. "It is Achilles. He makes his way to the gates."

Priam moved to stand beside Hector. "Achilles is dead."

The man shook his head. "No. It was not Achilles that fell yesterday. It was his cousin, Patroclus."

Hector paled, as did almost everyone else at the table. Clytemnestra forced herself to look down at her plate in case anyone saw the relief in her eyes.

Paris scoffed. "So? Achilles, Patroclus, it makes no difference. You killed one. You will kill the other."

Clytemnestra had no doubt they all knew how foolish Paris's words were, but Hector ignored his brother. "Prepare my armor and tell the men to be ready," he told his soldier. To his father he added, "I must prepare."

"Yes, my son. Make us proud."

Paris shook his head, looking around the table. "Achilles—he is just a man. Hector will beat him. I don't see why—"

"Be quiet, Paris," Priam snapped before softening his voice. "Achilles is no mere man. You should go help your brother."

Paris gave his father a stiff bow. "Very well, Father."

Hector walked around the table to his mother. He leaned down and kissed her on the cheek. "All will be well, Mother."

Hecuba touched his cheek. "Be brave, son."

With a smile for his mother and a nod for Clytemnestra, Hector left, Priam and Paris following.

Clytemnestra watched them go, knowing she would not see Hector again and feeling the loss. Hector was a good man—and there were so few of them in this world. Clytemnestra was glad Achilles was alive, but the idea of Hector facing him... no that did not bring her any joy.

"My dear," Hecuba said to Clytemnestra, her voice shaky, "I am going to the parapet. Would you mind accompanying me?"

Clytemnestra did not want to go—she had no interest in seeing Hector killed. But she knew how Hecuba felt. She had felt the same way as she had run through the crowd to be with Iphigenia. When you bring a child into this world, there is a cord that ties you to them, that makes you want to be with them at every moment, even the most painful. Especially the most painful. To make sure they know that they are loved."

Clytemnestra stood. "Yes, ma'am."

Hecuba took Clytemnestra's arm, and together they made their way up the long staircase to the battlement. As they stepped out, the guards looked over at them. More than one had regret in their eyes. They cared for their queen; they did not want her to see this. But none tried to stop her.

Hecuba leaned heavily on Clytemnestra as they made their way across the parapet. The whole of the Achaean army stood arrayed before them—but one man stood out. It wasn't his size or his armor, which was already covered in blood, that distinguished him from every other man on the battlefield.

No—it was his rage.

Hecuba let out a gasp. Her knees buckled and she began to tremble. Clytemnestra placed an arm around her waist; she did not know how the woman was still standing. If her own child were to face someone like Achilles, she could not bear it.

No, that wasn't true. She *would* bear it. She would have no choice. As a mother, she would never turn her back on her child. A child comes into this world through a mother's pain. That pain changes form as a child grows, with a mother feeling every hurt of her child. But no matter the hurt, she will stand by him to let him know he is not alone. And so it was that Hecuba stood by her son, tears already pooling in her eyes, her body trembling.

And then the gates of Troy opened, and Hector stepped out.

Hecuba clutched Clytemnestra. "He will survive, won't he?" she asked.

Clytemnestra knew Achilles. She had seen him fight on many occasions. But the passion he held now—the same passion he had loved Helen with—was overwhelming.

So she just held Hecuba closer. Because she could not bring herself to say out loud the answer that echoed through her mind.

No. Hector will die.

CHAPTER 90

His legs braced, Achilles waited for Hector to appear. Death was a part of war—he knew that better than most. But Patroclus was Achilles's *home*. And for someone to have taken his home from him—that was not just war. That was *personal*. And as such, Achilles would settle this debt himself.

The great doors of Troy opened, and Hector stepped out. His armor had been cleaned, and Achilles seethed at the sight of it. As if Patroclus's death was something the prince could wash his hands of so easily.

Hector walked forward to face Achilles. "It was a good death, Achilles. Patroclus fought bravely."

The sound of Patroclus's name on Hector's lips broke what little semblance of control Achilles had. He leaped forward, not even drawing his sword, and slammed his fist into Hector's shield.

With a yell, Hector fell back, but he managed to stay on his feet. His shield now bore a giant indentation where his fist had hit.

Hector drew his sword. "So be it. Patroclus's death brought me no pleasure. Yours will bring me none as well."

"But yours will pleasure me greatly." Achilles stepped forward, and Hector swung. But Achilles was already on the other side of Hector and shoving him with two hands. Hector stumbled, but again he did not fall.

He whirled toward Achilles. "Will you not draw your sword? Will you not fight me with honor?"

Achilles recalled a conversation he had once had with Patroclus about honor and duty. It had been a turning point in his life. He growled. "There was no honor in his death. There will be no honor in yours."

Hector swiped at Achilles's legs. Achilles brought one foot down on Hector's sword, pinning it to the ground, and kicked Hector in the chest with his other foot. This time Hector fell back, grunting. He got to his knees slowly, cradling his wrist to his chest. "I yield, Achilles. I yield."

In a blur, Achilles slammed his fist into Hector's nose. Blood sprayed. Achilles grabbed Hector by the collar and dragged him to a chariot waiting on the side of the field. "Out!" he growled to the men in the chariot. They stumbled over one another in their haste to follow Achilles's order.

Achilles grabbed a rope and tied it around Hector's neck. He tied the other end around the back of the chariot.

Dugal grabbed Achilles's arm. "Do not do this. Hector does not deserve this insult."

Achilles shoved him away. Hector struggled to his feet.

Achilles leapt into the chariot. Taking the reins, he set the horses to a run.

Hector was yanked off his feet. But the sight of Hector's body being dragged did nothing to dampen the fire burning inside Achilles. He urged the horses to go faster.

CHAPTER 91

Achilles wound around the walls of Troy yet again. He had not stopped for food or water. All that accompanied him were the memories of his time with Patroclus and the deep hole in his chest reminding him that he was now alone.

For a time, his men had implored him to stop and let Hector be buried. But Achilles drove faster, and soon they gave up. Now they stood silently, some watching, some turning their heads away in shame. Part of Achilles's mind acknowledged he was committing an atrocity but the larger part of him could not work past his grief to care.

Achilles wound around the side of the wall heading back to the front gate. His men still stood watch, but now a man stood at the gates, in the path Achilles had worn around the walls. His posture was stooped and his frame gaunt. As Achilles approached, the man put up a hand.

Curiosity had him slowing the horses before he could think better of it. Priam, the king of Troy, nodded. "Thank you for stopping to speak with me," he said. His voice shook, and his eyes shifted to where his son lay.

Achilles looked back as well and realized the prince was no longer recognizable as such.

Priam took a breath and straightened his shoulders even as tears shone in his eyes. "I am sorry for your loss, good Achilles. I have heard tales of you and Patroclus. And I recognize that besides being a fine warrior, he was a true companion."

Achilles looked away from the compassion in the man's eyes.

"I ask—" Priam put hand to his mouth, fighting back emotion. "I humbly ask you extend some compassion to me and my wife. We have lost our son today, a most beloved son, father, and husband. He, too, was a good man—one who was loved. We would like to give him the respect of a good burial."

And then he waited. He did not demand Achilles return the body of his son. He did not use his status as that of a king to order Achilles. He asked Achilles man to man, heart broken father to heart broken man.

Achilles felt shame burn deep next to his grief. Patroclus would never approve of what he had done. He did not honor Patroclus with his actions. He dishonored him.

He saw the pure grief in the old man's eyes. A grief he shared. With a shuddering breath, he stepped from the chariot and bowed to the king of Troy. "He is yours."

His Myrmidon fell into formation around him, offering him their companionship, their loyalty, even though through his actions since Patroclus's death he deserved none of it. And although he walked with his men to his tent where he was surrounded by thousands of more soldiers, he had never felt more alone in his life.

CHAPTER 92

The island of the two gods was located to the west of Greece, in the southern reaches of the Ionian Sea. The winds favored Helen and Barnabus's voyage there, and when they did not, Helen helped them along. Even so, it took them two weeks to reach the enigmatic island.

It looked impenetrable. Sheer cliffs towered a hundred feet above them, and waves crashed against them, sending up huge plumes of water. Jagged rocks jutted from the sea, suggesting a labyrinth of obstacles underneath the waves. It was said that no ship had ever been able to find a safe harbor, and more than one had been destroyed in an attempt to land. No man had ever set foot on the island and lived to tell the tale.

"Achilles!" Orestes called.

Helen turned to see the bear lumbering after the boy. The two had become inseparable. At first Orestes had been cautious around the cub, but soon he was sneaking out of his bunk at night, and in the morning she would find him curled up next to the crate, the cub pushed up against the side, as close together as they could get. The two orphans seemed to be offering each other some comfort. Finally, Helen had given up and just made up a bed for Orestes next to the crate.

When he wasn't playing with the cub, Orestes had proven a dedicated student. He was years behind Spartan youth of his age, but he was picking up fighting techniques quickly. It was good for him—he was gaining weight. He was also losing some of the haunted look around his eyes, though that was due more to Achilles than to training.

Achilles. Every time Orestes called the bear by name, though, Helen thought of *her* Achilles. He seemed to slip into her every thought now, no matter how mundane. A boar stew reminded her of the time she and he had hunted one down. A light wind reminded her of his breath on her neck. The laugh of a sailor reminded her of the laugh he'd shown rarely with others but regularly with her. After years of banishing him from her thoughts, it was as if the floodgates had been opened, and she was drowning in memories.

And she hoped they continued. Until she had seen Achilles again, she had not truly realized just how much of her self she had closed off. He made her feel alive by his mere presence. Even now, her skin tingled with life. *How can one man have such an effect?*

Aegisthus joined her by the ship railing, facing the cliffs. "Are you sure you want to do this, my queen? This island is not a safe place." Helen and Barnabus had decided to take the rowboat to the island, leaving the crew with the ship. The ship itself was much too large to risk an approach through the rocks—and besides, if anyone on board was not loyal to them, Helen did not want them learning anything about the island.

"It will be all right," Helen said. "But if we should not return, you will take Orestes and Achilles to King Proteus."

"Yes, my queen." Aegisthus shot another worried glance at the cliffs.

"Do not worry, Aegisthus. Barnabus and I have this well in hand."

Barnabus grunted as he joined them.

Helen raised an eyebrow. "Do you disagree, Barnabus?"

Barnabus put his hand to his chest. "Me? Disagree with the queen of Sparta about our ability to safely land on an island that no one has ever been able to land on without being killed? Of course not."

Helen clapped him on the shoulder. "That's the spirit."

CHAPTER 93

The island of the two gods lay dark, and Helen wondered if the scroll had been mistaken. Or if whatever had been hidden there had long since disappeared. Waves broke along the island's cliffs, tossing spray hundreds of feet into the air. Only desperation—or madness—would drive anyone to even attempt a landing.

I hope we fall into the former category, Helen thought as she and Barnabus rowed around the rocks dotting the sea. Wind whipped, tossing water into their faces.

"Not that I do not have complete faith in your abilities, Helen," Barnabus said, his muscles straining as he rowed, "but are you sure you have this?"

Helen looked at the cliffs. "Of course." But even she heard the uncertainty in her voice.

"Oh, good," Barnabus murmured.

Helen gripped the sides of the boat as it rolled down one wave and up the next. She looked behind her, but could no longer see their ship. She turned back to the cliffs. *I guess now is as good a time as any.*

She focused on the sky. The wind around them went quiet and the sea silenced. In moments, the water was as flat as glass.

Barnabus rowed faster now. As they neared the cliff face, Helen called on the wind again. Barnabus let out a yelp as a huge wave built behind them, raising them a hundred feet in the air—and carrying them right toward the cliff.

Sweat poured down Helen's face from the strain of controlling the elements. But still, the top of the cliff was another twenty feet above them. Focusing on the wind, she used it to push the water even higher. With a burst, they sailed over the top of the cliff and landed with a thud. As the water rushed back off the edge of the cliff, Barnabus jumped out, grabbed the side of the boat, and dug his heels in, keeping it from being pulled back to the sea below.

Helen hunched over, exhausted. She had never called on so much power before.

"Helen?" Barnabus asked.

"I'm all right. That was just a bit much."

Barnabus grinned. "Remind me to never doubt your abilities again." He offered her his arm as she stepped from the boat.

Once her legs were steady, Helen looked around. The area near the edge of the cliff was barren, but a forest blocked their way just fifty feet inland. She could make out fruit trees among them.

"Shall we?" Barnabus asked.

Helen nodded. "I wonder how long—"

"Helen." Barnabus's smile dropped, and he nudged his chin toward the trees.

A group of men stepped out from the trees. None of the men appeared younger than four decades, and all wore long tunics, threadbare but clean. And their arms... Helen squinted, thinking it was a trick of the light. But as they approached she realized it was not. Their arms were stained blue.

Helen counted twelve men and noted the absence of any weapons.

The man in front put up a hand, and the rest went still. Nothing about their posture suggested aggression, but Helen was still too keyed up to let down her guard. From the corner of her eye she saw Barnabus move farther to her left, giving them each more room to maneuver.

The leader stopped ten feet in front of Helen and bowed his head. Some strands of his long gray hair had been worked into braids. Necklaces of different colored beads hung over his chest. His skin had been wrinkled by the sun. But it was clear to Helen that he was not an original inhabitant from the area. His skin tone was too deep. His features were too fine.

Helen's heart began to race. He looked like the men she had seen on a trip to India.

All the men behind him had the same coloring—save one. And that was the one Helen sensed. He was a Fallen. Seeing Helen staring at him, he gave her a small nod, his long blond hair falling forward.

The group's leader smiled widely, showing off a mouth missing four teeth. "We have been expecting you, ring bearer."

CHAPTER 94

Helen scanned the group but got no sense of a threat, even from the one Fallen. "How do you know who I am?"

"Our seer told us of your arrival. And we watched you arrive. No one else could breach these cliffs in such a way. We have been waiting a long time. My name is Ajeet. I am the leader of our group, such as it is."

The man continued to smile. He seemed content to wait for her to speak.

"And your group," Helen said. "Do you have a name?"

"We are the priests of Dwarka and the guardians of the ancient wisdom. But I believe you know that already."

Helen gaped. *The priests of Dwarka? But that means...*

"We are the last descendants of the priests who escaped the destruction. We have spent our lives guarding Dwarka's most sacred weapon—and waiting for you."

Helen took in the dozen men in front of her.

Ajeet nodded. "We have lost many from our numbers. When Dwarka was destroyed, we numbered in the thousands. Now the twelve you see before you, and the few left back at our camp, are all that are left. Had you taken much longer, I'm not sure we would have still been here." He nodded toward Barnabus. "I know you both have many questions. But it is our custom to share a meal to show our goodwill toward one another and forge the beginnings of trust. We invite you to dine with us."

Helen glanced at Barnabus, who shrugged. "I could eat," he said.

Helen nodded. "All right, let's eat."

Helen and Barnabus followed Ajeet and his men back to their home—although "home" seemed too formal a word. They lived in a destroyed temple that overlooked the Ionian Sea. Simple huts, more tents than actual houses, had been constructed outside the temple, with a fire pit in the center.

A few men around the fire stood when Helen and Barnabus appeared. Helen wondered where the women were. How were they going to continue on without any children?

Ajeet walked to the edge of the cliff and looked down. "The city of Dwarka dwells beneath the water now. Thousands of years ago, when we escaped, some of our brothers and sisters arrived here and set up this temple to honor our loved ones."

Helen looked at what was left of the temple. Half the roof was gone, and only two and a half walls still stood. Columns had toppled over, and trees had grown through some spots in the floor. "What a horrible twist of fate," she said. "Mother Nature can be cruel."

Ajeet's head snapped up. "It was not Mother Nature who caused the destruction. I would have thought *your* mother would have told you the tale."

"*My* mother? You knew her?"

"Of course. We have known of the Great Mother since the beginning of our order. How is she?"

Helen's mouth fell open. She didn't know what to say. Ajeet knew of her mother? "She—she died. She told me there was much she still needed to tell me, but there was no time."

"For her, there is always time."

Helen frowned. "What do you mean?"

"The Great Mother—she always exists. Always lives. Her location changes, but she is the great constant." Ajeet smiled. "Now, let us eat."

She always lives? Was it possible? Did her mother live again? Helen and her mother had discussed how people returned, but she had never suggested that *she* would return. Helen wanted to press Ajeet for more information, but she feared that if she started asking questions it would distract her from the mission she was on. She needed to stay the path.

The meal was simple but fulfilling. As they ate, Helen explained how she and Barnabus had come to the island. When all were finished eating, Helen thanked Ajeet for the food.

"You are most welcome, ring bearer. And you have been most patient. Now come, both of you." Ajeet stood with the fluid movement of a much younger man.

He led Helen and Barnabus into the ruins of the temple. Half the circular roof had collapsed, but the other half showed the remnants of a mosaic. A few statues of intricate beauty remained intact beneath what was left of the roof. One depicted the god Krishna in his four-armed Vishnu form, and Helen stopped at its base. Towering above her, Krishna carried his four weapons: the conch, disc, club, and lotus. But despite his weapons, on his face was peace. *Who were you?* Helen wondered.

"Helen, you should see this," Barnabus said. He stood in front of another statue, its back to Helen. All she could tell from her vantage point was that it was a female.

Helen rounded the statue to stand next to him. "Who is—"

Her words cut off as she got a look at the statue's face. Her hand rose to her mouth. "Mother." The statue was so lifelike, Helen expected her mother to smile down at her, her violet eyes shining.

Ajeet came to stand next to her. "The Great Mother. We are honored to have her likeness here."

Helen was content to just stand and stare at her mother. "What do you know about her?" she asked.

"She is the world's moral center. She shows us the path."

Helen felt tears spring to the back of her eyes. She missed her mother so much. Her guidance, her wisdom—she would know what to do about Zeus. "I wish she was here," Helen said softly.

Ajeet shook his head. "This is *your* path. She has given you the tools. Now it is up to you to walk it."

She recalled her concerns about Zeus's foray into far-off lands. She knew in her soul that there was so much more going on than she knew. "What if I'm not up to the task?"

"You are. You just have more to learn. Let me help you with that." Ajeet gestured for them to follow him. He stopped at one of the still-standing walls of the temple, although only half of the wall remained. Copper scrolls adorned it, each one carefully engraved with images.

Barnabus ran his fingers lightly over the engravings. "Whoever did this was very skilled."

Helen walked along the panels, stopping at one that depicted a giant wave about to crash down on Dwarka. A shudder ran through her as she realized how terrified its inhabitants must have been. She imagined a giant wall of water rushing toward her and breaking over all the people she loved. But she shoved the image away. It was too painful to dwell on.

"Your people had no warning?" Barnabus asked.

"Some of us were able to escape, but no, it happened quickly. We needed to destroy Dwarka."

"*You* needed to destroy it?" Helen asked.

Ajeet's voice was filled with sadness as he reached up a hand and touched the image of people running from the wave. "We called it to us. There was no other way."

"How is that possible?" Helen asked.

"Dwarka was a city well ahead of its time. Even today, it is beyond our imagining. We have lost much to time."

Helen recalled her mother saying almost the exact same words.

"Dwarka was a place of learning, a sacred place."

Barnabus studied the panel showing the destruction of Dwarka. "But why destroy it? And how? Everyone knows Dwarka was destroyed when the sea rose up and reclaimed it. Did your brothers have power over the sea?"

Ajeet shook his head slowly. "The weapons and machines we have now are nothing compared to what our ancient brothers and sisters had. One of those was a stone of immense power and energy. It was used to light homes, to let craft fly through the air, to communicate over long distances."

"These things are not possible," Barnabus said.

Ajeet shrugged. "Today, yes, it sounds like magic. But I assure you, it was very real."

Helen said nothing. Her mother had told her about the incredible civilizations in the past, about technology that she could barely imagine. But Leda had spoken with such conviction and detail, Helen knew it was true. Her mother had had a knowledge of the world that rivaled any scribe's. So Helen knew that what Ajeet said was not only possible, but likely.

She also knew how the city had been destroyed.

"The Belial Stone," Helen said softly. "It was turned against the city."

Ajeet nodded. "We called it the tuari stone. Its power can lift up humanity or drag it into its depths. On that day, they unleashed its destructive power. The earth itself was torn apart, and Dwarka was swallowed by the sea."

"But why?" Barnabus asked, incredulous.

"To protect Dwarka's greatest discovery. Our greatest weapon." He paused. "And to prepare for this moment. The world has reached a dangerous point, ring bearer. When our ancestors knew the time of Dwarka was coming to an end, they sent three groups out into the world."

Three. Helen ran her thumb over the face of her ring, tracing one of the triangles.

Ajeet noticed the movement. "Yes, three's a critical number. Three groups were sent to different parts of the world. Each of those groups split again and then once more. One would test the ring bearer should she find them. The second would provide the history of the weapon and the directions to its final resting places. And the third would hide the weapon itself."

"That's nine separate groups. Why make it so complicated? Why not just one group?" Barnabus asked.

"No one could know where the ring bearer will be called, and the Great Mother knew it could be thousands of years before the weapon was needed. The world can change a great deal in that time. With three groups, there was a greater chance for the ring bearer to find one of them."

"And a greater chance someone else could find them," Helen said.

"That is true as well," Ajeet said softly. "But the risk was thought to be worth it. And there is one other safeguard in place to assure that the fallout should anyone but the ring bearer find the weapon was contained. Now come." He led them to a series of panels on the opposite wall.

Helen inspected them. "These look newer."

"These show why our numbers are so small," Ajeet said quietly.

Helen looked at him in surprise. "I thought it was due to time, or illness."

"No. When I was born we numbered two hundred. But then one of the evil ones arrived."

"Someone else scaled the cliffs?" Barnabus asked.

"Yes. Only the most determined have ever been able to do so. This man—he was determined. He demanded a tuari stone."

Helen started. "*You* have one?"

Ajeet shook his head. "No. But he knew some had escaped the destruction. When he learned of our existence, he thought we must have had one here."

"This man that came to you, he was a Fallen?" Helen asked.

"Fallen have sought us out over our history." Ajeet nodded at Helen. "Our order has met many of you throughout time—sometimes a man, sometimes a woman. But your job has always remained the same: to keep the Fallen in check. To protect those of us without power from those who would abuse theirs."

Helen looked at the panels. In the first one, a man arrived alone, confronting the priests. "This man—he abused his powers?"

"Oh, yes," Ajeet said softly. "He killed over half of us."

"By his sword?" Barnabus asked.

Helen could feel Ajeet's sadness. "No. He used trickery. When he arrived, we knew he was a Fallen, but we did not know if he was good or evil. Some Fallen have been born into our ranks. Some have joined us and helped us, staying on the side of the light."

Helen glanced back toward the fire pit. "Like the man with blond hair."

Ajeet smiled. "I thought you recognized him. But the evil one, he initially acted as a friend. He stayed with us for days. We thought he wanted to join us. Too late, we realized he was only trying to learn our ways and search for the stone. Then one night, he poisoned our food. We lost half our numbers to the poison. They died in their sleep. He slaughtered the ones who survived."

"How did you survive?"

"Our greatest weapon—we deployed it against him. I had been on watch when I heard the screams. My father was with me, and he knew immediately what had happened, without even seeing the camp. He had the gift. He ran to help, after instructing me to run for the weapon as quickly as I could." Ajeet took a shaky breath. "I did, along with these men. But I was not fast enough.

When we returned, we were all that was left." Ajeet looked away, but not before Helen caught the look of horror in his eyes.

After a moment Ajeet continued, his voice subdued. "The evil one was waiting for us at the camp. He smiled as we approached. I remember his words as if they were yesterday. *So you have finally brought the stone.*"

"I pulled the satchel from my belt. He snatched it from my hands and emptied four smooth stones into his palm. I sliced my knife across his forearm. He leaped back and sneered. *You cannot kill me.*"

Ajeet smiled, although there was little victory in it. "I said, 'Before you were right, but now, I can. Look at your arm. You are not healing.'

"The evil one looked down, and the blood continued to flow. He backed up, but I stalked him now. 'You think you are a god, but your powers are gone. You are mortal. And you will die like one.' I raised my knife to finish him off, but he escaped. I gave chase, but he slipped into the night."

"He was too fast?" Barnabus asked.

"No. He ran like a normal man. But I stopped chasing him when I saw our temple and all my brothers and sisters lying dead." The horror of that moment was etched across Ajeet's face.

The image stayed in Helen's mind but so too did what it meant. "The greatest weapon of Dwarka—he believed it was a tuari stone but it's not. It's something even more powerful in its way."

"Yes," Ajeet said softly.

"I don't understand," Barnabus said.

Helen looked from Barnabus to Ajeet as the full impact of Ajeet's words hit her. She felt as if the earth had shifted under her feet. "The Fallen—you figured out how to make them mortal. That's what the weapon does."

CHAPTER 95

Helen stepped back. The ancient priests of Dwarka had found a way to remove the Fallen's abilities. They could make them human. They could level the playing field. "It's a potion," Helen said. "You dipped the knife you sliced the evil one with in it."

Ajeet nodded.

"A potion that can remove powers? That's not possible," Barnabus said.

"I assure you it is. It is why Dwarka was destroyed. Before the city was leveled, a group of twenty Fallen slipped into Dwarka. They wanted the weapon. We had Fallen on our side, but not enough. We could not fight them. But we needed to make sure that the weapon remained safe. So our brothers and sisters made the ultimate sacrifice and destroyed the entire city—with the Fallen inside."

"All to protect this weapon," Helen said.

"We call it the Omni." The Omni—her mother had mentioned that phrase before she died.

"And the stones in the satchel? What were they?"

"Nothing—just a distraction."

Helen's head spun. Zeus and his minions had been wreaking havoc across the land. But if she had a way to remove a Fallen's ability, she would easily be able to stop him and his men. She wouldn't even have to take all of their abilities—once she removed the abilities of a few, fear would keep the others at bay. And if she found Zeus and removed his . . . She turned to Barnabus. "Can you imagine?"

Barnabus looked a little pale. "For me, it is frightening. The idea that such a thing exists—if it were to fall in the wrong hands..."

Helen frowned at Barnabus's choice of words. Why *had* the Fallen attacked Dwarka for the weapon? They must have known it would take their powers. Why risk it? Unless . . . She turned to Ajeet. "As with all things in this world, there must be a balance. There's a way to return the Fallen's powers as well, isn't there?"

"Just as the Omni has the ability to take their powers, the same weapon can return their powers to them."

Helen studied Ajeet. "Return them? Or *create* them?"

"Create them."

Helen was dumbstruck. *By the gods.* "You can *create* abilities in someone?"

Ajeet nodded.

"Why would your people have created such a thing?" Barnabus asked.

"It was not our intent. My ancestors were looking for a way to remove the powers of the Fallen. Only by accident did we find that the same potion could also create them."

The idea of someone being able to create an army of Fallen, of *Zeus* being able to create an army of Fallen... *He will rule the world.*

"You used it on the evil one. So you have it here," Helen said.

Ajeet shook his head. "No. Each group was given only one dose. We used ours to protect ourselves."

"You said a third group from your original group hid the Omni. Do you know where?"

"Yes. We know where our group's hiding place and the two hiding spots as well. I fear two of the locations are buried too deep for you to reach it now. But one remains. " He paused and then spoke words Helen had the feeling he had memorized and repeated to himself time and time again over the years. "The weapon was hidden where man first split from the way of the righteous. But then the sands of time began to reclaim this ancient site, and it was moved to the kingdom whose walls were created by the gods. It resides there to this day."

Walls created by the gods. Helen recognized the description immediately and felt sick at the knowledge. Apollo and Poseidon had been rumored to have worked together to push this island from the sea floor. But this island was not their only creation. According to the legends, the two had also worked together to build a wall around a city that would never be breached.

Helen went cold. "Troy. The weapon is in Troy."

CHAPTER 96

The weapon was in Troy. Helen finally understood. It all made sense. The reason Zeus had arranged for her to be taken by Paris was so that the world would bring its might against the impenetrable city.

It was all so Zeus could get inside Troy.

She looked back at the panels on the wall. "The Fallen who came here. He was not just any Fallen, was he?"

"No." The old priest was quiet for a moment. "He was much more than that."

Helen felt a chill steal over her. It couldn't be. "Samyaza."

Ajeet nodded.

Samyaza had been the one searching for the tuari stone. Samyaza was the one who had lost his powers. From what she had read and what her mother had told her, she knew power was everything to Samyaza. He would stop at nothing to get his power back—even if it meant the death of thousands.

"His ambition knows no bounds. He led the men that infiltrated Dwarka before its destruction," Ajeet said.

Barnabus balked. "But that's not possible. Are you saying he is thousands of years old?"

"No. But he has been reborn time and time again. And in one of those lives, he was the leader of those Fallen in Dwarka. He died along with them."

Ajeet paused. "He does not remember the details of his past lives but his greed, his ambition remain constant throughout his lifetimes. Samyaza, no matter his form or when he is born, is always after the same thing—complete domination. And each time, it is the ring bearer's duty to push him back. He must be stopped. He must not be allowed to find the Omni. Our seer has seen what will happen if you do not stop him. The deaths of the war will be but a drop in the ocean of death should Samyaza succeed."

"The Fallen who came here. Samyaza. He's also the one claiming to be Zeus." Her mind whirled. But how could Zeus know the Omni was in Troy? "Ajeet, do you know where the other Omnis can be found?"

"Yes. We have all the locations." Ajeet walked to the edge of the ruined temple and beckoned to the Fallen among his people. The man joined them and pulled a stone tablet from the satchel he wore slung across his shoulders. He extended it to Helen.

Helen took it reverently, running her hand lightly over the engravings. One included the words Ajeet spoke moments ago. Two other locations were described as well. "All three groups have one of these?" she asked.

Ajeet nodded.

"What are you thinking?" Barnabus asked.

"Zeus must have found one of these, sometime after he left here. That is how he knows of Troy. Is that possible?" Helen asked Ajeet.

"We lost contact with the other two groups eons ago. It is possible they have not survived to the present day. We have barely survived. So yes, it is possible that the tablet of the Omni was unguarded and found."

"How would he have found it?" Barnabus asked.

"I don't know. But I would guess that after he came here, he knew about the weapon. And he went looking. It is the only thing that makes sense." Her gaze strayed back to the panels. "The evil one—what did he look like?"

"He looked like a white man with dark hair and dark eyes," Ajeet said. "He was only a youth then. But that was years ago."

Helen considered bringing Ajeet with her, on the chance he would recognize Samyaza. Or perhaps someone younger—having watched Ajeet squint at the panels, she feared his eyesight was failing.

"Do you think any of your men would recognize him?" she asked.

Ajeet shook his head. "It has been so long, and he has undeniably changed. We would never be able to be sure."

Helen knew he was right. Dark hair could be lightened by the sun. A strong youth could grow into a fat man. There were so many ways his appearance could change, especially if he wanted to disguise himself.

"I have something of his, though. Perhaps it will help you." Ajeet walked over to the wall that depicted the evil one's destruction. He removed one of the stones, reached behind it, and pulled out a bundle of fabric. Slowly he unwrapped it. It was a knife.

Shock made Helen's thoughts slow. "This was his?"

"You recognize it," Ajeet said. It was not a question.

Helen nodded. The need to return to Troy burned through her.

Barnabus looked dazed as he stared from the knife to Helen. "But that's— It can't be—"

On the pommel of the knife, the seal from the house of Mycenae was engraved.

"Agamemnon," Helen said. "He's Samyaza."

CHAPTER 97

Helen had known Agamemnon since she was a child, yet she had never even suspected anything remotely like this. At the same time, she had to admit—she wasn't as surprised as she should have been. Agamemnon was always on the edge of troublesome situations. And now, he was leading the charge in Troy.

"How is this possible? Agamemnon has never had powers," Barnabus said.

"People come into their powers at different times. He must have gained his after leaving Sparta and lost them before returning." Helen thought of all the tales her mother had told her of Samyaza—strong powerful, ambitious, and drawn to power. "If he believed a Belial stone was out there, he would have stopped at nothing to find it."

"Why would he risk his powers?" Barnabus asked.

"He couldn't have known about the Omni." Helen said. "He never would have chanced his powers. If he had known, he would have sent someone else. Remember, Agamemnon had just reclaimed his kingdom. The sting of having lost it was branded on him. For years he was adrift, an emperor without an empire. He would never have chanced being in that position again. But finding a stone that would grant him even greater power? Oh that would have enticed him."

As she thought about it, something else occurred to Helen, bolstering her conviction that she was right. When he was younger, Agamemnon had bested almost everyone in a fight. But then one day, he just stopped fighting; he let his reputation do his fighting for him. Helen always thought it was because it was the smart move—but what if it wasn't? What if he stopped fighting because he had lost his powers and could no longer fight the way he did before? What would happen to his reputation if he was bested?

And what will happen to the world if he gets his powers back?

Even without his powers, Agamemnon had marshaled all the armies of Greece and placed them under his command. His kingdom spread to all the habitable lands. If he regained his powers, he would be a god. And he would demand to be treated as such. All would suffer under his reign. This was a man who had sacrificed his own daughter out of spite. Helen didn't even want to imagine what he would do to the world.

"Is there anything else you can tell us?" she asked Ajeet.

"The hiding spot you will know by this symbol." He knelt on the ground and traced two intertwined triangles.

Of course. "You said there was one last safeguard."

"Yes. In the hiding spot, there is only a small supply of the Omni. But the instructions for how to create more will be with it. They however only be revealed to the one who bears the ring."

"Well, that's good news," Helen said. "Samyaza can't create an army of Fallen—he won't have enough of the Omni. But he can still get his own powers back, which is bad enough—plus perhaps create one or two more faithful Fallen followers."

"We need to get to Troy," Barnabus said.

"Immediately," Helen said. But she feared they might already be too late.

CHAPTER 98

Helen felt a sadness at leaving Ajeet and his men. Meeting with her, being guardians of the Omni—it had been the whole point of their existence. And now, their mission was complete. She had the tablet of the Omni and was on her way to retrieve it, hopefully before Samyaza was able to breach Troy's walls. "What will you do now?" she asked.

Ajeet smiled. "Perhaps I will find myself a wife. Besides, even though you have arrived, there may be need of us again. We will continue on as we have, slipping into the shadows until the world needs us again."

"I wish you peace, Ajeet."

"I wish I could offer you the same. Instead, I will wish you success. For all our sakes."

The voyage back to Troy was rough; barely a wind stirred, and it was up to Helen to urge it along as much as she dared. She did not want to risk burning out her abilities—she would surely need to be at full strength when they arrived—but the knowledge that Agamemnon was at the heart of all of this only added to her feeling of urgency. He had been so close this whole time—and so well hidden. He was within striking distance of those she loved.

Menelaus would never recognize his brother for who he was. And her brothers would never suspect Agamemnon.

Gods be damned. She knew the man was evil—even as a child she had not liked him. But she had never considered *this*. And her sister—how would she handle the news? Doubts, worries, and fears plagued Helen the entire journey.

But finally, after six weeks of travel, the coast of Turkey appeared in the distance. But this only brought to mind more doubts and fears. Who knew if the weapon was still there? What if she couldn't find it? What if she did? How would she stop the war? How would she convince anyone that this, all of this, was nothing but one man's thirst for power?

But all she could do as she watched the coast of Turkey draw closer was pray. *Please let us not be too late.*

CHAPTER 99

Once again, Helen and Barnabus departed the ship alone. If they did not contact Aegisthus within two days, he was to set sail and take Orestes and Achilles to Proteus.

Barnabus ran ahead. He would find Helen's brothers and Achilles and instruct them to meet at the prayer henge. Helen cursed her slowness as he left her to make her way to the prayer henge by herself. It was not the first time she'd wished for the Fallen's speed. It took her hours to make her way across the land. As she recognized the hill before the henge, a tingle ran over her. Barnabus' familiar figure jogged up to her.

"Well?" she asked.

"I found Castor. He is gathering Pollux and Achilles."

"Good. And the war?"

"The war continues. They have not breached the walls."

Even though this meant many more men had been dying, Helen felt relief. If Samyaza were to breach the wall and regained his powers, the deaths from this war would pale in comparison to the deaths to come.

They continued together in silence to the prayer henge. As

they drew near, another tingle ran over Helen's skin—her brothers. She picked up her pace.

As she and Barnabus stepped from behind one of the stone pillars, Pollux ran over and hugged her tight. "We were worried."

She returned the hug just as strongly. "There was nothing to worry about. Barnabus and I had everything well in hand."

Pollux released her and extended his hand to Barnabus. "Good to see you. I see you still have all your body parts."

Barnabus laughed. "Not for want of trying on your sister's part."

Castor, now taking his turn to hug Helen, looked down at her with a raised eyebrow. "I thought you said you had it well in hand?"

"We did," she said. "We are here, no worse for wear. How is Clytemnestra? Have you heard anything?"

"She is all right. According to reports, she has grown close to King Priam and Queen Hecuba. Even to Hector's family."

"And the war effort?"

"Achilles stayed out of the fight as long as he could. But then Patroclus was killed by Hector. It was a good death. But Achilles did not see it that way."

"What did he do?" Helen wasn't sure she wanted to know.

"He killed Hector himself, then dragged his body by chariot. Only when King Priam intervened did Achilles agree to release Hector's body."

"Since then he has fought little," Castor added, "but he has allowed the Myrmidons back into the fight."

Helen remembered the gentleness Hector had shown to his children and wife. He had not wanted to be part of this war, but he had been duty bound to fight. And then she thought of Achilles and how devastated the death of his cousin must have left him. *This war was nothing but devastation for the lives it touched.* "Where is he?"

"He could not get away immediately. Agamemnon called a meeting of his leaders right before we left."

"You were not asked to attend?" Barnabus asked.

Castor grimaced. "It seems we have fallen out of favor with Agamemnon. He keeps us as far from himself as possible."

"And Paris?" Barnabus asked.

Pollux spat. "He lives. He was to fight Menelaus to end this war, but he chickened out."

The mention of Menelaus hit Helen hard. She had not even asked about him yet. "How is Menelaus?"

"He is well. He misses you. We have not said anything of your escape."

Helen sighed. "Thank you. I know it has been hard. But we think we know why all this has happened."

Castor pointed to a satchel by the fire. "We brought food. How about we hear every detail while we eat?"

They sat together around the fire while Helen and Barnabus told the brothers about their travels. When they reached the part about the minotaur, Pollux cut in.

"Better not tell Theseus the minotaur is dead. He keeps bragging how he's going to be the first one to kill the beast."

Helen shook her head. "He was no monster. Just a man forced into a cruel life by a cruel father. Minos was the true monster. But that monster is also no longer."

Pollux raised an eyebrow. "Had a little chat with him, sister?"

"You could call it a chat." She continued her story, taking her brothers through the journey to the island of two gods, Ajeet's message, and Agamemnon's role.

"I should have killed the bastard the first time he touched Clytemnestra," Castor spat.

"We all have that regret," Helen said. "But now we need to deal with him, before this war is over."

A tingle ran over Helen's skin, stronger than any she felt when a nephilim or Fallen were near. A feeling of this intensity was reserved for only one man.

Achilles stepped out of the shadows. "Then you need to move quickly. Because Ulysses has come up with a way to end this war once and for all."

CHAPTER 100

Throughout their voyages, Claudius had kept his ears open, listening to Barnabus and Helen when he could, and to the other sailors when he couldn't. He hadn't learned as much as he had hoped, but he had picked up on one very, very juicy tidbit.

Queen Helen was the ring bearer.

He'd also overheard enough to know what that meant—he knew the basics of the conflict with the ring bearer and the Fallen. And he also knew that Agamemnon was somehow connected to that ancient conflict. So he was confident this little piece of information would be well received—and well rewarded.

In addition, yesterday he'd overheard Helen and Barnabus talking about the need to find the symbol of two interlocking triangles. He didn't know what that meant, but he could tell it was important. Claudius smiled. *Two critical pieces.* His instincts had served him well—again.

When they arrived at Troy, Helen and Barnabus departed the ship first. Claudius waited what he thought was an appropriate amount of time, then slipped over the side. He held a note in his hand—a note he had crafted just last night. He ran through the hills until he saw the small cave where one of Agamemnon's men was supposed to wait for him each day. The man came to attention.

Claudius thrust the note at him. "Quickly, send the bird."

The man tied the note to the falcon's leg and sent him into the air.

Claudius hoped the bird reached Agamemnon in time. And if it did, well... He smiled. *Agamemnon will pay well for this information.*

CHAPTER 101

With all the armies of Greece at his command, Agamemnon had expected to defeat the Trojans easily. But those damn walls! And thanks to the childish behavior of Achilles and his refusal to fight, this war was stretching on for months. Agamemnon had been growing increasingly impatient.

But now Ulysses had crafted a plan to end the war once and for all. It was daring and creative, Agamemnon had to admit—but it could also just as easily fail as succeed. If he were King Priam, he would burn the damn horse where it stood. He'd be surprised if the Trojans didn't do the same. And then what? He *needed* to get inside those damn walls. He needed to find the Omni.

He pulled the stone tablet from the chest where he stored it. Unwrapping the velvet, he looked at the engravings again. When Faenus had found the tablet, Agamemnon had begun to prepare for this moment.

Now he studied the tablet, looking for any clue that he might have missed even though over the years he had pored over it and knew every mark and blemish on it. But there was nothing on the tablet to indicate where inside Troy the Omni was. Many times he had considered trying one of the other two locations, but both were now deeply buried. He'd be an old man before they uncovered even one of the sites. No, Troy was his best hope—his only hope. He needed to be whole again. Wasting all these years in a weak body, remembering who he had been and the power he had wielded as a youth—it was beyond torture.

And now, he was so very close. And still so damn far.

The tent flap opened, and Cergen stepped in, bowing deeply. "My lord, a message."

Agamemnon waved him in. "Yes, yes."

Cergen placed a note on Agamemnon's open palm before stepping back and waiting by the exit.

Agamemnon unfurled the note and read it. Then he read it again. *Helen?* All this time it had been Helen! Anger roared through him as he imagined every slight, every insult, every look of veiled contempt the woman had thrown at him. How had he not seen it?

Did Menelaus know? No—if Menelaus had known, he would have confided in him. Which meant Helen had kept it from him. But Castor and Pollux—yes, they must be the other two members of the triad.

They had all been within his reach this whole time.

He gripped the tablet, and barely managed to keep himself from smashing it to the ground. He carefully placed it out of his reach as his temper rose higher and higher. But he could not let it rule him. He swallowed it down. He grabbed a sheet of paper and sat at his table. Thinking carefully, he wrote:

PRINCE PARIS,

You are so close to everything you have desired. Within days, if you are able to complete this one last task, you will have all the riches and power you deserve. Within the walls of Troy there is a symbol of two intertwined triangles. Find the symbol and report back to me. But do not touch it. That is for the hands of a god alone.

~Zeus

AGAMEMNON ROLLED up the paper and handed it to Cergen. "Send it to Troy."

Cergen didn't even blink. This was not the first time he had sent the falcon over the wall. "Yes, sir." He bowed and hustled out of the tent.

Agamemnon sat back, his mind whirling. If Paris was able to find it, he would figure out a way into the walls. If the horse failed, he'd find another solution. *Maybe I'll even offer my personal surrender. Priam would be honor bound to welcome me.*

Yes, one way or another, he was getting into Troy, and he was getting his powers back. And then he would repay Helen for all the trouble she had caused him.

But not too quickly. She needed to suffer. And the best way to make Helen suffer was by hurting the ones she loved.

CHAPTER 102

Helen drank in the sight of Achilles—and her heart broke at the sadness that clung to him. She clasped her hands behind her back to keep from running to him. "Achilles. I am sorry—for Patroclus. He was a good man."

He tipped his head. "He was the best of men."

"How much did you overhear?" Pollux asked.

"Enough. It sounds like you have been through quite a lot." Achilles's gaze roamed over Helen. "But you look to be in one piece."

"I've gotten pretty good at taking care of myself."

"That I do not doubt," he said.

Barnabus cleared his throat. "I am fine as well. In case you were worried."

Achilles grinned, breaking the spell between Helen and himself. He turned to Barnabus. "It would take an act of the gods themselves to harm you."

Barnabus clapped him on the shoulder. "You speak the truth, brother."

"Join us," Castor said, gesturing to the food and the fire.

Achilles's gaze flicked back to Helen.

She nodded. "Yes, join us. And tell us what Ulysses has come up with."

Achilles sat next to Castor, and Helen couldn't help but appreciate the smoothness of his movements, the way the muscles in his arms and legs rippled in the firelight. She had to tear her gaze from his arms as he reached for some bread. Butterflies danced in her stomach. Only he had ever elicited this reaction from her. Damn him.

Achilles told them of Ulysses's plan. They were to build a giant, wheeled, wooden horse and hide soldiers inside it. They would leave the wooden horse at the gates of Troy as a gift—and wait for the Trojans to take it inside their walls. Then, once the horse was safely inside, the soldiers would climb out of it and open the city's gates from within, allowing the Greek armies into Troy itself.

Pollux scoffed. "The Trojans won't fall for that."

"Agamemnon will have all the ships leave, making it appear that we have departed. The horse will be seen by the Trojans as a parting testament to their skill in battle. There will be no reason not to trust it is what it appears."

Helen's mind raced. If the Greeks succeeded, the war would end. "How long will it take them to construct this horse?"

"It is already done. The first of the ships have set sail."

Helen's mouth dropped. She had not imagined the war would end so quickly. She turned to her brothers and Barnabus. "I need you three to set sail immediately for Sparta."

"What?" Pollux shook his head. "No. We're not done—"

"I need my children *safe*. When Troy is defeated, and the men watching my children learn of it, they will kill them. I need you to get them to safety. There are no other men I trust with this. Please, I beg you."

Pollux looked away, but Castor took her hand. "We will get them to safety. No harm will come to them."

Barnabus nodded. "You have my word. We will leave immediately."

Helen felt some of her terror subside. "Thank you."

"You do not want me to go protect your children?" Achilles asked.

His tone was light, but Helen heard the hurt behind his question. "Your absence would be questioned too much. You are too visible. And besides—I need your help with something else."

CHAPTER 103

The creak of a door worked its way into Paris's dream, and he saw the goddesses filing into his bedroom one by one. "My prince, we are awaiting you."

Paris smiled. "My apologies. Let me make it up to you."

Aphrodite placed her hand on his shoulder. "Wake up, Prince."

He frowned. "What?"

She shook him. "Wake up."

Paris's eyes flew open, and he reached for his knife on the table next to his bed.

His manservant, Agaro, stepped back hastily.

Paris stood, his eyes flashing, even as the room spun around him. He had spent the day drinking with some of the soldiers, celebrating the departure of the Trojan ships. Early the day before, they had begun to leave. Now, there were very few left on the beach. They had toasted to their success and Paris had fallen asleep just after lunch. "How dare you intrude into my sleeping quarters. You have woken me from my sleep."

Agaro dropped to his knees, his hands up. "Forgive me, Prince. But you instructed me to bring you any correspondence immediately."

"What is it? It better be good, or you will spend the week in the stocks."

Agaro pulled a crumpled note from his pocket. His eyes were downcast as he extended it above his head. "This—this came for you."

Paris snatched it from the man's hand with a growl. But when he read the note, his eyes went wide, his headache forgotten. "Who gave you this?"

"A falcon just arrived with it. I saw it had your mark on it."

"You can read?"

"No, sir, no. But I know your mark, sir."

Paris smiled slowly. "Very good. Tell the cook I said to give you and your family extra rations."

Agaro's jaw dropped, but he nodded. "Thank you, Prince. Thank you."

Paris waved him away. "Yes, yes. And tell no one about this."

The man got to his feet, still nodding. "Yes, Prince Paris. Of course."

The prince eyed the man. "Actually, on second thought—" He grabbed the back of Agaro's head and sliced the front of his throat. Blood sprayed on Paris's face. He let the man's body drop.

He set down the knife and washed off the blood in the basin. Then he strode to the door and yanked it open. "Guards! Guards!"

Two men in Trojan uniforms ran down the hall. "Yes, Prince Paris?"

Paris stepped back, sweeping his hand toward the body in his room. "The Greeks must have paid him to kill me. See to the body."

"Yes, Prince Paris."

The two guards picked up the body and carried him out. Paris shut the door behind them. *And now, Zeus, let us see what it is you want so badly.*

CHAPTER 104

Helen had to wait until it was dark to re-enter Troy. It was easier to escape Troy then to enter it, especially with the Fallen roaming throughout it. Achilles was to meet her when he had sent his Myrmidon to their hiding spots. Then they would go in when the festivities were under way and the Trojans guard was down. Until then, she would just have to wait.

Helen made her way to the back of the citadel. The cliffs behind it were supposed to be unassailable, but with the aid of her ring, she made her way to the bottom of the hill that ran along the eastern part of the wall. Here there were small outlets that would allow her to hide. Achilles was to meet her here after he had sent his Myrmidons to their hiding spots. When the festivities were under way and the Trojans' guard was down, they would enter.

As darkness fell, the horn of victory rang out. *The last of the ships have left. They think they've won.* Music and laughter filtered over the wall, along with cheers. Happy sounds, peaceful sounds, as if from another world.

She settled in to wait. She would allow the celebration to go on and then she would slip in when the Fallen were distracted. Her eyelids grew heavy. She kept yanking them back open, but after a time she gave up the fight. She had slept little on the voyage here, and she had taxed her powers to keep the wind blowing. Sleep would serve her well in the battle yet to come. Pulling her cloak close around her, she let her eyes close.

CHAPTER 105

Achilles blurred along the walls of Troy, keeping to the shadows. The sentries still stood along the parapet, but even they had joined the celebration, passing a bottle among themselves and paying more attention to what was happening inside the gates than what was happening outside.

He made his way around the side of the citadel. He felt the Fallen inside but he knew they could not sense him although he still did not know why. He slowed as he approached the back wall. Where was she? He scanned the shadows and spotted her gray cloak in a hollow. He snuck quietly toward her, glancing up at the city walls, but no one looked out in this direction.

Helen lay curled up against a rock. Her face was peaceful in sleep—all the worry and responsibility gone. He knew he should wake her. They should head inside. But instead he sat down next to her. When she stirred and shivered, a frown crossing her face, he gently pulled her into his lap and wrapped his arms around her. The frown disappeared from her face and a sigh escaped her lips.

He had kept himself from her for ten long years. It had been right. But he knew as she did, that time had done nothing to lessen the feelings between them. And for this moment, there was nothing between them. So he would let himself have this moment where he could imagine what could have been. He would let himself hold her for a little longer, let her rest for a little longer, let the world continue to turn without both of them for just a little longer.

CHAPTER 106

Helen awoke, feeling warm. She snuggled in deeper and felt the heartbeat underneath her. She opened her eyes to see Achilles's face mere inches from hers.

For a moment, time stopped, and she simply stared at him. Never in her life had she seen a man more beautiful. She thought back to that horrible day when all her hopes for a future with Achilles had been crushed. His anger had destroyed so much. And her father had been unrelenting. But had she chosen correctly? Menelaus—he was a good man. He was a good father. And she did love him. But Achilles was the air she breathed. She came to life when he appeared. And now that she had seen him again, how could she go back to a life that was only half-lived?

She suspected now that Agamemnon was behind that horrible day. That man Claudius who had drugged Achilles had been in his employ. She could not prove it but in her heart she knew it. Agamemnon had destroyed her chance at a life with the man she loved, all so he could gain more power. She stared at Achilles's face and wondered what it would have been like to have awoken to this sight every morning for the last decade. Her heart ached at the thought.

She reached up and placed her hand along Achilles's cheek, all the love she had felt for him causing her to tremble. And slowly he opened his eyes.

Helen gasped and tried to pull her hand away, but he placed his hand over hers. They stared at each other, neither one moving.

The clash of swords and the sound of yells inside the walls broke the spell.

"It's begun," Achilles said.

"Yes." Helen gave herself one more moment, then pulled her hand from underneath Achilles's and stood. What could have been is a dream. This was their reality. "We need to get to Clytemnestra."

Achilles stood as well, opening his arms. "I am at your service, my queen."

Helen hesitated for only a moment before stepping into them. "Then let us go."

CHAPTER 107

The sounds of fighting grew closer, and Clytemnestra sprang to her feet. She grabbed the staff that Adorna had smuggled into the room and went to the maid's cot in the corner. She shook Adorna's shoulder. "Adorna, it's time. Wake up."

Groggily, Adorna opened her eyes. "Helen?"

"Close enough." She helped Adorna up. "You need to go to the bathing chamber and wait."

"But—"

"No buts, Adorna. Go."

Adorna studied her for a long moment, then nodded. Clytemnestra stood facing the door, knowing the moment would come soon.

It wasn't long before she heard running footsteps. When they stopped outside the door, Clytemnestra adjusted her grip on the staff.

The door burst open, and three Trojan guards ran in. Clytemnestra recognized them—they were members of Paris's royal guard.

"What is the meaning of this?" she demanded.

"Prince Paris is done with you," one of the men said with a leer, his words slurring together. "He said we could have you."

"Oh, I don't think so," Clytemnestra replied. She kept her voice steady even though fear tore through her. *They think you are Helen. So be like Helen.*

The man lunged for her, and she stepped to the side, slamming the end of the staff into his face and then the back of his head, pitching him forward. He hit the ground and didn't move. She didn't even wait for the other two to attack. She whirled the staff back around, hitting one man hard in the stomach and the other just under the chin. Both fell to their knees, the latter grabbing for his throat.

The first man reached for her again, but a sudden gust of wind from the doorway sent him crashing into the wall.

Clytemnestra gaped as Helen and Achilles ran in. Helen grabbed her by the arms. "Clytemnestra! Are you all right?"

Clytemnestra looked between her sister and Achilles, who was now holding the guard who'd first attacked her by the throat. "How—?"

Helen kicked one of the other men in the head when he attempted to stand. "We know what's going on. It's been Agamemnon this whole time. He's Zeus. He's after a weapon hidden here in Troy."

Clytemnestra's jaw dropped. "But, that's not possible. He doesn't have powers."

"I know, but he did once." Helen quickly explained what she had learned, and with each word Clytemnestra felt sicker. She had children with that man, had turned her back on her family for him.

Helen grabbed her arm. "Clytemnestra?"

Clytemnestra cleared her head with a shake. "It's just—how did I not see it?"

"None of us did. Where is Adorna?"

"I'm here." Adorna stepped out of the bathing room, and Helen hurried over and pulled her into a hug. "You're all right?"

Adorna took Helen's face in her hands. "Yes. And it looks as if you are as well. Hello, Achilles."

Achilles inclined his head with a smile. "Adorna." He tossed the man he held into the wall.

"Achilles will take you two out of here while I find the Omni," Helen said.

Clytemnestra shook her head. "No. I'll—"

Helen squeezed her arm. "It's my duty. Go with Achilles. But first, have you seen this symbol?" She pointed to the two triangles on the face of her ring.

Clytemnestra shook her head. "No."

Adorna cut in. "I have. The old chapel on the third floor. It's quiet. No one goes there. That symbol is engraved on a brick near the back wall, on the right-hand side."

Helen's relief was obvious. "Thank you, Adorna." And with those words she ran out the door.

"Helen, no!" Clytemnestra moved to follow her, but Achilles stepped in the way. "I'm taking you two to safety."

Clytemnestra pushed against his chest. "How can you let her go alone?"

"I am not *letting* her do anything. I promised her that I would get you out, and as soon as I have, I will come back for her." He threw Adorna over his shoulder and wrapped an arm around Clytemnestra's waist, lifting her. "Hold on."

Everything blurred, so Clytemnestra squeezed her eyes shut. She could hear fighting, but she wasn't worried about her safety. She knew Achilles would not let her or Adorna be harmed.

She just wished he would move faster so he could return to Helen. *Be careful, sister.*

CHAPTER 108

Helen hurried down the hall, clutching her sword tightly. If she was lucky, she wouldn't run into a soul. This was the old part of the castle, where no one lived and very few of the rooms were ever used.

The sounds of the battle grew louder as she passed the main stairwell. Apparently Ulysses's plan had worked. The Trojans would not survive for long with the Greeks inside the wall.

She found the chapel at the end of the hall. The door creaked loudly as she opened it, and she winced at the noise. She slipped inside and shut the door behind her.

Clytemnestra had said the marked brick was near the back wall along the right-hand side, but the shadows made it difficult to make out anything. She walked slowly along the wall, squinting at the bricks, looking for the mark.

Her heart was pounding and her muscles tense. *Where is it?*

Then she spotted it, four feet from the corner. Relief washed over her. *Thank you.*

She tried pulling the brick but nothing happened. But when she pushed directly on the interlocked triangles, she heard a click, and a small drawer popped open beneath the brick. Inside lay an ivory box—the same design as the one in Crete. *Thank the gods.*

With trembling arms she withdrew the box. She walked over to a table at the end of a pew and set it down. Taking a breath, she opened the lid.

It cannot be.

The box was empty.

CHAPTER 109

Helen wanted to scream. Twice—twice!—she had been deceived. *Gods be damned.*

A tingle rolled over her. Before she could even react, a figure dropped down from the rafters and yanked off her ring, pulling the box from her hands as well. Helen struck out with her fist, but all she hit was air.

"Tut, tut. You really should learn to be more aware." Agamemnon smiled from the other side of the room. "Looking for something?"

Fear tried to choke Helen's throat. "You already found it."

Agamemnon smiled again. "Not me. Your love, Paris. So accommodating for a prince."

"Is he dead yet?"

"Not by my hand. But it's doubtful the man will survive the day. His fighting skills leave a little to be desired. I must say, Helen, you've been a little slow on the uptake. I expected more of the ring bearer." Agamemnon unfurled his fingers, displaying the ring in the palm of his hand. "Or should I say the *former* ring bearer?"

"What do you want?"

"Nothing. Now that I have this," he held up the ring, "I have everything I need."

A chill washed over Helen as Ajeet's words came back to her. *The instructions for how to create more will be with it. They however only be revealed to the one who bears the ring.* And now Agamemnon had it. But she shoved that fear aside, ring or no ring, she could not let him leave here. "You did all of this just to get your powers back? There wasn't another way? A way that didn't result in thousands of deaths?"

Agamemnon shrugged. "Perhaps. But this way I was guaranteed to find what I needed. Do you realize what power I hold now? I can make an army—an army of Fallen loyal to just me."

"Why? You have power. You've beaten Troy—"

Agamemnon laughed. "Troy? Troy is nothing. I have a *world* to conquer. And I will."

"You know I can stop you."

"Not without this little ring of yours. I have to admit, when I first realized it was you, I kicked myself for not insisting your father let us marry. With you by my side, why, just think of what we could have accomplished."

"I would never have helped you."

"But you already have. Without you, I never would have found the Omni. In fact, you led me right to it. So thank you for your help, Helen. It is good to feel strong again."

Helen pulled her sword from its sheath. "Let me rid you of that feeling."

But before she could move, Agamemnon had blurred out of the room.

Helen sprinted out the door after him. "Come back, you coward!"

Then she came to a sudden stop. Agamemnon was long gone, but the hallway, which had been empty just a few moments earlier, was now filled with mercenaries.

Helen raised an eyebrow. "I don't suppose you're here to rescue me, are you?"

The mercenary closest to her grinned, showing off a half dozen brown teeth. Then he charged.

CHAPTER 110

His head was still fuzzy from all the ale he'd drunk, Paris hurried down the hall, constantly checking behind him, a cold sweat covering his body. The staff had long since disappeared. Most had fled. Some had fought and died. He, like everyone else, had been celebrating Troy's victory when the first Greek soldier had crawled from the belly of the horse. Paris had seen the man himself, but he'd thought he was imagining things. Not until the first scream of death did reality come crashing down. He had stumbled away from the fighting, demanding his guards protect him as the next king of Troy.

Then he had run.

How had it gone so wrong? Zeus had promised him they would be victorious.

Or was it really Zeus? Ever since that last missive, he'd wondered. Zeus needed *him* to find a symbol within the walls of Troy. But shouldn't the almighty Zeus be able to find it himself?

The doubts had begun to creep in. What if it was *never* Zeus?

He shoved that thought aside. All of this was Helen's fault. All of this was because of that bitch. Thinking she was the equal of men! No, not the equal—the better. But he'd teach her, once and for all.

He climbed the stairwell to his room and threw open the door. "Agaro?"

Silence answered. *Oh right, I killed him. What is the new guy's name?* "Manservant?"

Still no answer. He growled. His new manservant was supposed to wait for him, but like everyone else, he had probably run away—or died. *He had better be dead.* His room hadn't even been tidied since this morning.

He stomped over to the shelves lining the wall and pulled down a box. He set it down carefully on the table and lifted the lid. Twelve vials sat carefully in velvet—his own personal collection of poisons. Just yesterday there had been only eleven. He pulled out a vial marked with two intertwined triangles. *But then I found you.*

The vial had been in the ancient box, along with another. He had left one for Zeus, but he had kept this one. He knew power when he saw it.

Paris held the vial of strange blue liquid aloft. He'd heard the tales—they had been handed down from father to son for generations—of a powerful weapon hidden inside the walls of Troy. He'd given those tales no credence—until Zeus had asked him to find the symbol. But if the stories were correct, the contents of this vial would be the death of a god.

Or just the daughter of a god, he thought, picturing Helen.

He retrieved his quiver from the corner, removed an arrow, and dipped the tip into the vial. Then his gaze drifted over the other vials. *It never hurts to be prepared.* But which one to choose? Nothing too quick. She needed to suffer.

He reached for a dark liquid—winter rose. *A pretty name for a nasty death.* He'd seen someone die of it once. It caused its victims to suffocate, their throat and mouth swelling. He imagined Helen gasping for air, clawing at her throat. Perfect.

He carefully stood the vial on the table and uncorked it. He dipped another arrow, then, after a pause, dipped two more. He carefully closed the box and hesitated before tucking it under his arm. He might need more later, but he had a feeling four would be more than enough to deal with one troublesome woman.

CHAPTER 111

After depositing Clytemnestra and Adorna back at the camp, guarded by six men he trusted, Achilles headed back to the walls of Troy. Clytemnestra and Adorna would be safe. Now it was his job to protect Helen.

Inside the gates, which were now flung open, he paused to take stock. Greek and Trojans clashed in battle, but the Trojans were not up for the fight. The few left standing were sluggish.

When a Trojan roared and sprinted toward him, Achilles slammed his fist into the man's face. The man flipped a complete circle in the air before landing with a thump. Achilles didn't even glance at him. He had no time for this.

Dugal gave a yell. "Achilles!"

Ignoring the call, Achilles raced through the throngs of men. He could see that he was not needed by his men. What he needed was to get to Helen. True, she was a warrior, and a skilled one. She would fight. But he could not rest until he knew she was safe.

He was only a blur to the people he passed, but he willed himself to go even faster. He vaulted up the stairs and turned down the hall that led to the chapel.

Then his heart all but stopped. The hallway was littered with bodies.

Achilles slowed his pace, scanning the bodies as he passed. None of them were Helen. And when he reached the chapel, he saw that it was empty.

But she had been here. A tiny drawer lay open in the wall.

Fear poured through him. How did the mortals handle this feeling? How did Helen? Achilles had always relied on his strength, his speed, and they had been all he had needed. But for the first time in his life, he found himself praying to the gods. *Please keep her safe.*

He ran back out into the hall. At the far end, the doors to a balcony stood open, letting in the sounds of a fight in the courtyard. The sounds of Helen.

Achilles sprinted down the hall and threw himself off the third-floor balcony, rolling as he hit the ground two stories beneath him.

Helen was fighting with two men. One swiped at her with a blade. She circled into him as he swung, her back to his chest. Wrapping her arm around his knife hand and continuing the arc of his movement, she yanked him off his feet. As the man took flight, Helen kept hold of his arm, breaking his shoulder. The man screamed in pain.

The second man came at her with his knife high above his head, bringing it down at Helen's heart. Helen stepped to the side easily, put her two hands over the man's, and helped his downward swipe continue right into his own gut. She Helen yanked the knife upward several inches before pulling it out. She stepped back, and the man fell to the ground, dead.

Achilles felt the blood rush back into his body.

Helen gave him a frown. "Achilles?"

He forced himself not to snatch her into his arms. "You handled that well."

She ran up to him. "Are you all right?"

Achilles laughed. "I rushed in here to rescue you. You seem to be really struggling without me."

She smiled. "My hero. I would be lost without you." Then her smile faded. "But I did lose my ring. Agamemnon surprised me."

"We'll get it back—" A movement in the corner of Achilles's eye caused him to turn just in time to see the arrow fly. He pushed Helen to the ground, covering her with his body.

The arrow pierced his calf just above his ankle. Three more struck his back.

"Achilles!"

"I'm all right," he said, even as pain lanced through his back. He pushed himself to his side, and Helen rolled from underneath him.

He saw fear on her features as she saw the arrows in him. "I'll get help."

"It will be all right. They didn't go in very deep. I'll heal."

Dugal and four Myrmidons appeared at the entrance of the courtyard.

"Dugal!" Helen shouted. "Achilles has been hurt."

The men rushed across the grass. The Myrmidons took up position around Achilles and Helen as Dugal dropped to his knees beside Achilles.

"Who did this?" Dugal demanded.

"Paris," Helen said, her voice cold.

"Paris?" Achilles asked.

"I saw him just before you pushed me to the ground." She pushed hair off Achilles's forehead. "Just before you saved me."

He smiled. "See? You do need me."

"Always," she whispered. She placed a kiss on his cheek. "Take care of him, Dugal."

"Where are you going?" Achilles asked as she stood.

"To find Paris." Helen said. And she took off at a run.

Achilles reached out to stop her, but his movements were too slow. He wanted to tell her that it was too dangerous. But he was so tired all of a sudden. So very, very tired.

CHAPTER 112

Helen pounded down the stairs. At first she had feared she wouldn't be able to find Paris, but she had followed the sound of running footsteps, then spotted him darting into this stairwell.

She slowed as she neared the bottom. Her heart pounded, but not out of fear. No, fear was not one of the emotions coursing through her right now. Anger, disgust, and hatred were the top three when she thought of Paris.

He had shot Achilles in the back but Helen had no doubt those arrows had been meant for her. If Achilles hadn't been there, she would be dead. He had saved her.

And Achilles would be fine—she knew that. The arrows had not gone in too deep. He would heal. But seeing him injured, it had frightened her, jarred her. She had always thought of him as invulnerable; he thought of *himself* as invulnerable. She shook her fear off. *Achilles will survive, but Paris will not.*

She reached the bottom of the stairs. A noise had come from farther down the hall. As Helen stepped onto the dirt floor at the bottom of the stairs, a sword swung at her head. She dove for the ground and rolled to her feet, bringing her own sword up in front of her.

Paris smiled. "You think you can beat me? You? A woman? All of this is because—"

"You talk too much."

Helen feinted for his chest, then swiped low. Her blade raked across his thigh, and he let out a scream. But Helen was beyond caring about this man's pain. This man had brought a world to the edge of disaster. He was nothing but a boy stomping his foot and demanding someone pay attention to him.

Helen was a blur of movement as she attacked. She sliced again and again, opening a new wound on Paris each time her blade whirled through the air. But by her design, none of the wounds were fatal.

Paris retreated, trying to get his blade in front of him to defend himself and failing. "Stop it! Stop it!" he shrieked. Finally, he crashed into a wall. There was nowhere else for him to run.

Helen's blade was at his throat. "Goodbye, Prince."

"Achilles," Paris panted out. "Don't you want to know about Achilles?"

Helen pressed the blade into his throat. Blood dotted his neck. "You shot him."

Paris shook his head. "No. It's more than that."

Helen wanted nothing more than to run him through with her sword. But the look in his eye—a look of victory—stayed her hand. Burning with anger, she hissed, "What have you done?"

"I've killed the great Achilles."

Helen laughed. "You can't kill Achilles with an arrow. The arrows barely broke his skin."

"They were dipped in poison. The first was designed to kill even a god."

Helen went cold.

Paris smiled. "It was meant for you. But I think Achilles's death might be even more painful for you than your own. Especially knowing it should be you and not him."

Helen's eyes flashed. "No."

Footsteps pounded down the stairs. Two Trojan soldiers appeared. "Prince Paris!"

Paris shoved Helen away. With a growl, Helen swung her sword. It sliced his neck, and he dropped to the ground. She then whirled to meet the advancing guards. She kicked the first man in the ribs as he tried to rush her from the side, while the other advanced from the front.

"Enough." Helen sidestepped the second man's lunge, stabbing the first man through the chest as she did. Her quick move caused the second guard to stumble forward, off balance, and she brought her sword down on the back of his unguarded neck. He fell to the floor, unmoving.

Helen then turned back to Paris, to make sure she had finished him off.

The hallway was empty.

Damn it.

She followed his trail of blood to a heavy wooden door. But it was locked. She pushed at it but it wouldn't budge. She slammed her shoulder into it and then kicked it with all her might. It had no effect.

Paris had escaped.

Gods be damned. She turned and ran back to the stairs, then stopped suddenly. Just beneath the stairs, in the shadows—no doubt where Paris had been hiding before he ambushed her—lay a small box. *You don't belong here.*

Helen knelt and opened it. Twelve vials lay on velvet. She ran her hand along them. Then her breath caught. Two intertwined triangles were engraved on a small piece of metal adhered to the glass of one of the vials.

The Omni.

She slammed the box shut, tucked it under her arm, and sprinted up the stairs, her heart pounding. *The arrows. Achilles.*

CHAPTER 113

They were dipped in poison. The first was designed to kill even a god. Paris's words ran through Helen's mind as she sprinted through the halls of the castle. When at last she reached the opening to the courtyard, she flew through it.

It seemed that all of Achilles's Myrmidons were here now, and they had set up a protective circle around him. Some of them raised bows toward Helen before recognizing her. Surprise flashed on their faces, but they stepped aside to allow Helen through.

Dugal stood at Achilles's side. The arrows had been removed from Achilles's flesh, and two men were placing him on a stretcher. "He's not healing," Dugal said.

Helen dropped to her knees and placed her hand on Achilles's forehead. It burned. "He's been poisoned."

"Do you know what poison?"

"No. But it's one of the poisons in this box." She knelt down next to Achilles and opened the box, pulling out the Omni.

Dugal grabbed her arm. "What are you doing?"

"Hopefully, saving him. Tilt back his head."

Dugal stared into her eyes before doing as she instructed.

Helen uncorked the Omni and emptied the contents into his mouth. *This will work. This has to work.* He swallowed it and Helen let out a breath. It would be all right. He would be all right.

She corked the Omni and slipped it into her pocket. Only a small amount was left but she would not let it out of her possession. Then she handed the box to Dugal. "Give this to the healer. Perhaps it will help her figure out which poison was used."

Dugal handed the box to one of his men, who took off at a run. Then he turned to the Myrmidons. "Let's find a more comfortable spot for him to rest."

The Myrmidons picked up the stretcher and set off. Helen walked along next to them, not wanting to let Achilles out of her sight. He was too still. She could not recall him ever lying so still. She gripped his hand. *Do not leave me again.*

"Queen Helen." Dugal's voice was low.

She looked up at the warning in his tone. Standing in the open doorway ahead of them was a man with his legs braced, his armor stained red with blood. Helen met his gaze, her hand slipping from Achilles's grasp.

"Menelaus."

CHAPTER 114

Menelaus stepped aside to allow Dugal and his men through. They all tipped their heads to Menelaus in passing. Helen stayed behind with her husband.

Together, Menelaus and Helen watched the men carry Achilles out of view. Then Menelaus turned to her. "I did not think Achilles could be harmed."

"Neither did I," she said softly.

Silence descended between them before Menelaus broke it. "You are all right?"

Helen nodded. She had not seen Menelaus since before her abduction. He looked so strong, so confident. *He looks like home,* she realized. His hair was the same color as Hermione's, and she could see their boys in his strong build and clear eyes. In that moment, she loved him so much she ached. She wanted to throw her arms around him, forgetting this whole nightmare.

But she held herself back. "I did not go willingly with Paris."

Surprise flashed across Menelaus's face. "I know that. I never doubted that."

The truth of his words was in the timbre of his voice and the look in his eyes. She loved him all the more for that trust. And she felt guilty that she could not completely give him her heart, or even her full attention, at this moment. Because Paris's words and the thought of Achilles's injuries played on a loop in her mind.

"There is more going on than I know, isn't there?"

"Yes."

Menelaus sighed looking away before turning back to Helen. "Is Agamemnon part of it?"

Stunned by the question, Helen nodded. "Yes. You knew?"

"No, I—I don't know. Maybe I knew. Maybe I suspected. I know you think I don't see him. And it's true, I have been blind. But I've seen enough."

"I'm sorry." Helen wasn't sure what she was apologizing for: the pain of realizing who Agamemnon was, the pain she had caused him... or the pain she was going to cause him now.

He took her hand in his and turned her toward him. "Go to him."

She looked into his eyes. "What?"

"He loves you. I know how that feels. And from the look of him, he doesn't have much time."

"But you're my husband."

"Yes. But it doesn't stop the heart."

Helen's chest heaved. "I love you."

"I know. But you love him too. I knew when I married Helen of Sparta that I married a woman of exceptional strength, character, and love. You love him, yes. But it doesn't place a shadow on *our* love." He leaned down and kissed her gently on the lips. Helen nearly shattered right then and there. "He loves you as I do. And I know I want your face to be the last thing I see in this world; I'm sure he feels no differently. Go."

Helen placed her hand on his cheek. "I do not deserve you."

"You deserve the world, Helen. Now go."

She stared into his eyes for one more moment. Then she turned and walked away from the man who held her heart—and toward the man who held her soul.

CHAPTER 115

Helen found the Myrmidons gathered outside one of the guest bedrooms. One man stepped forward as she approached.

"How is he?" she asked.

"He—" He shook his head. "The healer knows it was the winter rose poison. But there is no cure for it."

"But, he was given a potion that should have healed him."

"I am sorry, Queen Helen. But it had no effect. The healer believes the poison had already worked its way too deeply into his system. He— I'm sorry, my queen. He will not last long."

Helen reached out a hand for the wall to steady herself. Achilles was dying. She hadn't saved him. The whole way here she'd told herself Paris was wrong. Achilles would be fine. He was *Achilles*, after all. No one could take him down—and certainly not someone like Paris of Troy. But now that false hope had been ripped from her. "Is there nothing they can do?"

The man shook his head. "No, my queen."

For the first time, Helen really looked at the gathered Myrmidons. These fearsome men, men who had terrified both sides of the Aegean Sea, now looked shattered. Achilles was their heart—

she could see it in their eyes. Among these men, Achilles had finally found the home he'd always wanted.

She moved toward the door, taking deep breaths to help control her emotions. A Myrmidon opened the door for her, and she stepped inside. The drapes had been drawn on the windows nearest the bed. Dugal sat vigil. When Helen approached, he stood.

"How is he?" she asked.

"The poison, it—" Dugal wiped at his eyes. "I cannot believe this has happened."

"It hasn't happened yet," Achilles grouched from the bed, his breathing labored. "So quit moping."

Dugal laughed. "Who's moping? I'm crying with joy at the thought of all the women I will now have when you are gone."

"That's more like it." Achilles smiled, but even in the dim light Helen could see the sweat on his face, the paleness of his skin. He looked at Helen but spoke to Dugal. "Give us a moment, would you?"

"Of course." Dugal bowed to Helen and left the room, shutting the door behind him.

Achilles reached for the water on the side table but missed, his hand falling short. Helen rushed forward. "Let me." She poured the water and held the cup to his lips, pretending not to notice how much effort it took him to just lift his head.

When he had taken a few sips, he fell back against the pillows. "How goes the battle?" he asked.

"It is done. There are a few soldiers still fighting, but Troy is defeated."

"So we won."

"Yes." Although Helen didn't know what they had gained. The only one who had won anything was Agamemnon, who had regained his powers.

"Did Agamemnon get the Omni?"

"Yes. He restored his powers." And he had her ring, which

meant whatever that last safeguard was involving the instructions was no longer in his way. *I have failed.* But Helen shoved those thoughts aside. She would figure something out. Right now, Achilles needed to be her focus.

Achilles spoke again, but his words were mumbled, and Helen had to lean in to hear. "Will you go after him?"

Helen ran her thumb along her empty ring finger. "Yes. He has something of mine. And I intend to get it back."

"You will defeat him. There is no one stronger in all the world."

"I am only strong because of the people I have surrounding me."

"I am the same, you know. I'm not sure my Myrmidons ever knew that. They gave me strength." He closed his eyes. His breathing was slow. His heart was failing. Helen held her breath until he opened his eyes again and continued. "But you, Helen—you are the one who has always been in my mind through every battle. I remember every moment, every conversation, every touch."

Helen took his hand. Tears wanted to burst forth, but she forced them back. "I remember as well. You have been with me every step of the way." Her chest felt tight as she tried to memorize every detail of his face. "You should have let the arrows hit me. They were meant for me. And without my ring, the Omni would have given me powers so the poison would have—"

"No—you don't know that. You have abilities, too. Who can say how the Omni would have worked on you? You could still have died—from the poison, or even from the arrows alone. And I could not have lived with that."

"But I am to live with your death?"

"Yes, you are to live. You are to be the queen Sparta needs, the mother your children need, and the ring bearer the world needs. Your life is more important than mine."

Helen gripped his hand tightly. One tear finally escaped and slid down her cheek. "No. It is not."

He gently wiped the tear away. "Yes. It always has been. So live, Helen. For me."

Helen's heart ached. She wanted to scream and rail. *This cannot be happening.* "Don't leave me, Achilles. Not when I have just found you again."

He smiled. She could see the effort it took. He took a stuttering breath and closed his eyes, swallowing hard. His words came out slowly. "But this... is the best death... I could ask for. By... your side. Feeling your... love. I want nothing more than... this moment. Better... to die in your arms... than live without... you by my side."

Helen's tears dripped onto Achilles's chest, which had slowed its movement even more. Helen knew only his pure force of will was keeping him here. She gently kissed his lips, sending him all her love, all her emotion. "I do love you."

"And I love you. In this lifetime... and every one yet to come." His hand squeezed her hand one last time—and then went limp.

Helen gasped. She willed his chest to move. But it did not.

"Achilles? Achilles?" She shook his shoulders. Tears rolled down her cheeks, and her chest felt as if someone had cleaved a hole in it. "No, no."

She laid her head on his chest, wrapping her arms around him as if somehow she could bring him back. *I love you, too. In this lifetime, and every one yet to come.*

CHAPTER 116

Helen informed the Myrmidon of Achilles's death and then left them to pay their respects. More than a few of the incredibly powerful men had tears in their eyes.

Helen walked down the hall with no destination in mind, feeling disconnected from everything around her. *Achilles is dead.*

It wasn't real. It couldn't be. Achilles—he was life itself. He walked into a room and it came to life. His presence could not be stamped out. It was not possible.

But then she pictured his face, his hand going limp in hers, his life draining from him. *By the gods.* Her stomach clenched and her knees went weak. "Achilles." Tears sprang to her eyes.

She stumbled down the hall, her hand on the wall the only thing keeping her upright. Soon even that wasn't enough and she crumpled to the floor. *Achilles.*

Every moment she had spent with him flashed through her mind. All those times she had yearned for him over the years. She had survived their separation only because she knew that at least he lived, that he was somewhere in the world—that he was loving her as much as she was loving him. And that knowledge meant that her dream of them being together, the dream she harbored secretly, could live on. She had clung to that spark of love. It had kept her warm on cold nights.

And now that little light of hope had been snuffed out. She felt empty and lost.

Arms wrapped around her, and through her tears, Helen saw her own face. "He—he is gone," she stammered.

Clytemnestra held her close. "I know."

"How can he be gone? It's not possible."

"I am sorry, sister. But know he loved you. With his every breath, even with his last, you were the one he loved more than any other."

Clytemnestra's words broke the last of Helen's restraint; sobs burst forth from deep in her chest. Her whole body shook, and she felt as if she was going to break in two.

Clytemnestra continued to hold her tight. "Cry, sister. I am right here. I have you."

Helen cried for the love that had broken her heart and mended it time and time again. She cried for the man she had always loved and had never been able to banish from her heart.

She cried for her Achilles.

CHAPTER 117

The light chirp of birds was the first sound Helen heard the next morning. Her eyelids felt heavy. Her chest felt hollow. Achilles's face swam into her mind before she was even fully awake, and the pain of his loss crashed over her again. She took a stuttering breath and slowly opened her eyes, squinting against the bright light.

Clytemnestra rubbed her back. "It's all right, Helen."

Helen realized they were in the room Paris had given her when he'd brought her here. "How did we get here?" she asked.

"Menelaus found us. He carried you."

A new pain bloomed in her chest, this one created by guilt. "I do not remember that."

"You were beyond remembering anything at that point."

"How is he? Menelaus?"

"I think it is difficult for him to see how hard you are taking Achilles's death. But he knew how much you loved Achilles when you were first married. And he knows you love him as well."

Helen's eyes teared up at the idea that she was causing Menelaus pain. She had never wanted that. He was a good man.

But she could not stop herself from loving Achilles. She had never been able to. Perhaps it was too much to expect.

"How long have I slept?"

"Two days."

Helen sat up. "Two days?"

"You needed to rest. You have been through a great deal in the last few months."

"Have you heard any word from our brothers? Or Barnabus?"

"It's too soon. But you know them—they will get to the children before any harm can come to them."

Helen fell back against the headboard. "I know." Her gaze caught site of the vial on the bedside table. She reached out and pulled the Omni toward her. It didn't work on Achilles. Perhaps it was because she was too late administering it, the poison having already worked its way through his system.

Or maybe it is because he is not a Fallen. The thought whispered through her mind. The signal she felt when Achilles was near was far greater than for any other Fallen. And the Fallen could not sense him. Was he something else? Was that why it didn't work? *No, it had robbed him of his powers. It should have been able to return them. I was just too late.* The failure weighed on her and she closed her eyes against the pain of it.

"I'm afraid there is some other bad news," Clytemnestra said.

Helen opened her eyes taking in her sister's concerned face. "What?"

"Agamemnon has already sailed for home."

Exhaustion weighed Helen down. "It's worse than that. Agamemnon has regained his powers."

"How?"

"I was too late. And he's got my ring as well."

Clytemnestra shook her head. "No."

"What of Paris?"

"He was found not far outside the walls. He had died from a wound on his neck."

Paris's death brought Helen no happiness. Not with the failure of the last few days pressing down on her. Agamemnon's power restored. The ring gone. And Achilles... A fresh wave of grief rolled through her.

None of that changes what I must do. "I will have to follow him. Figure out a way to recover my ring. And I have not forgotten my promise to you. I will kill Agamemnon—somehow."

"No," Clytemnestra said.

"No?"

"You have done enough for now. Besides, you cannot kill Agamemnon while he has both his power and the ring. It would be suicide."

"It doesn't matter. It's my duty, ring or no ring. I will get the ring back, and *then* I will take care of him."

Clytemnestra shook her head. "He will never let you near him now that he knows who you are."

"I will find a way. I made you a promise. I intend to keep it."

Clytemnestra squeezed her hand. "It is a promise I never should have asked of you."

"He deserves to die. For all he has done."

"Yes. But it will be by my hand."

"Clytemnestra—"

She held up her hand. "No. I have relied on others for too long. Perhaps if I had been stronger, I would have realized who Agamemnon was before things had gone this far. Perhaps I could have saved Iphigenia."

"Do not take that guilt on yourself. That is his burden to shoulder, not yours."

"I know. But from this point on, I will not allow him to control me. I need to do this myself. I will find your ring. Besides, you are in no shape for the fight to come. You need to hold your children in your arms and breathe in their scent."

Tears pricked at the back of Helen's eyes as she thought of it.

THE BELIAL WARRIOR

"And you need to mourn Achilles. I know what he meant to you. Do not deny yourself the chance to say good-bye."

Helen looked up into her sister's knowing eyes and realized that she had changed through this whole experience. She had regained her strength. And it gave Helen a small measure of comfort. Whatever happened from this point on, Clytemnestra could handle it.

"Can you trust me with this?" Clytemnestra asked.

"I trust you. But you do not need to do this alone."

"I am not alone. You go with me, I know that now. I will contact you when I find the ring. Then we will finish this together."

Helen hugged Clytemnestra close. "Be careful, sister. We have already lost too many to Agamemnon's machinations. I could not handle losing you as well."

"You will not. This time it is Agamemnon who needs to fear me."

Helen studied her sister, seeing the determination in her face. She was right. It was her time to step forward. "Be safe sister."

Clytemnestra hugged her tight, whispering in her ear. "Heal, sister."

CHAPTER 118

FOUR MONTHS LATER

MYCENAE, GREECE

She walked slowly down the hall, a basket in her hand, keeping her head bowed. Two of Agamemnon's soldiers lounged in the hall leading to his rooms. Neither of them bowed to her or showed her any respect. Agamemnon had long ago shown them they did not need to respect his wife. Everyone knew Clytemnestra was a beaten woman.

She passed Agamemnon's bedroom, where he often took other women to his bed. His latest trophy was Cassandra, Priam's daughter, whom he had taken as a spoil of war. But Cassandra was not the only addition to the household since the war. Agamemnon had doubled his guard, and he kept his men around him at all times. He was taking no chances. He knew Helen would come for him, and regardless of what he said, he feared her.

Helen may have been the only one he feared. All others bowed to his will, even the nobility from neighboring kingdoms. And if they didn't, if they acted against him or even slighted him inadvertently, they would soon turn up dead, their throats slit while sleeping. The nobility were growing worried. *As they should be.* Agamemnon was clearing a path, making sure there was no one to stop him.

When he wasn't bedding his women or silencing his critics, Agamemnon spent hours in his study, poring over maps and the box he'd brought from Troy. Those long hours only seemed to anger him more. It wasn't until just the other day that she found out why: it was because he couldn't find the instructions to create the Omni. Even with Helen's ring, he was still unable to create more of the Omni. His failure caused his agitation and paranoia to grow with each day that passed.

She stopped beside the door to Agamemnon's bathing chamber. She could hear the slosh of water from inside. She took a breath. He had been so paranoid, he had not even let her near him for the first few months he was home. Not that he knew anything of her activities during the war—he thought she had been in Sparta the whole time. No, he worried about anyone getting near him and finding the instructions themselves. It had taken her weeks for her to be allowed near him without his guards. But she knew how to play the vulnerable wife. She kept her head down, demanded nothing, and eventually he forgot she was even in the room.

She gripped the basket in her hand, its towels and oils visible. She thought of Iphigenia, Hector, Achilles, and all the others who had lost their lives because of the man beyond the door. And she had no doubt—Agamemnon needed to die.

She opened the door.

Agamemnon, soaking in his bath, scowled at her. "Clytemnestra! What are you doing in here?"

"I—I thought I would wash your back for you." She held up the basket. "I have brought some oils."

Agamemnon grunted. "Good. You've finally come to your

senses. You are weak, Clytemnestra. Like Iphigenia. It is better she died than lived to embarrass us."

Adrenaline coursed through her veins when Iphigenia's name passed Agamemnon's lips. But she kept her head bowed. "Yes, my lord."

She placed the basket on the floor and began placing the oils on the ledge of the bath behind Agamemnon's head. He barely paid her any attention.

"And your sister—she is weaker than she believes. I will make her pay for what she has done. She will beg for death. Oh, I have plans for her." He paused. "Clytemnestra, are you listening?"

She snatched the knife from the bottom of the basket and held it to his throat. She leaned down and put her lips beside his ear. "I am not Clytemnestra." Helen ran the knife across Agamemnon's neck. Blood poured from the wound, mixing with the water and turning his chest red.

Agamemnon jerked away from her, but he laughed even as blood seeped through the fingers he pressed to his neck. "Stupid woman. You cannot kill me."

He went to backhand her. But she raised her palm blocking his strike. His eyes went wide. "But—"

She smiled. "What? You thought I'd fly across the room?"

Helen sliced him again, across his chest this time, and he fell back into the tub with a shout. And Helen smiled. They had not been sure if the small amount of Omni left from Troy would do the trick. But apparently, it did not require much.

Helen leaned down close to Agamemnon and whispered in his ear. "Your powers are gone. Your little puppet, Paris, kept some of your precious Omni—then left it behind in his futile attempt to escape. It courses through your system, stripping every ounce of your ability from you."

Agamemnon had both hands pressed to his neck now, but blood continued to seep through his fingers. Helen slashed at him again, cutting his fingers. He struggled to get out of the water, to escape.

Behind Helen, the door opened. Clytemnestra strode in, flanked by Castor and Pollux.

Pollux looked at Agamemnon and smiled with satisfaction. "The wounds are not healing."

"No, they are not," Helen said. "The Omni worked."

She smiled at Clytemnestra. Helen may have made the first cut, but it was her sister—her strong, resilient sister—who was responsible for this moment. For the last four months, Clytemnestra had played the role of the dutiful wife. That time had taken a toll on her. Her skin had paled, her hair had darkened, and dark circles had appeared under her eyes. But it had paid off. Agamemnon had finally let her near him, and Clytemnestra had learned where Agamemnon had hidden Helen's ring. Then she had contacted Helen and her brothers, so they could help her finish the job.

Helen yanked the necklace from around Agamemnon's neck. Her ring hung on the chain, just as her sister had promised it would. She wrapped her hand around it and released a breath. *Finally.*

Agamemnon gurgled. Helen turned away from him and extended the knife handle toward her sister. "He is yours," she said. "I promised you that honor. But if you wish, I can—"

"No." Clytemnestra took the knife from Helen's hand. Her eyes were already wet with tears as she stepped toward her husband and stabbed him in the chest. "This is for Iphigenia. This is for what you have done to my sons. This is for what you have done to me." With each statement she plunged the knife once more into her husband. Soon she was sobbing. Helen watched her in agony, wanting to intervene, but knowing Clytemnestra needed this after all she had suffered at this man's hands.

Finally, when water and blood covered both the floor and her sister, Helen wrapped her arms around Clytemnestra and pulled her back. "Shh, shh. That's enough."

Clytemnestra shook her head. "No—not until it's done."

"It is done. Look."

Clytemnestra looked. Agamemnon lay sprawled in the bloody water, his head tilted to the side, his eyes seeing nothing.

Whatever force was holding Clytemnestra together vanished. She sagged in Helen's arms.

Helen held her tightly, keeping her from falling. "This time I've got you, sister."

CHAPTER 119

The halls were empty as Helen made her way to Agamemnon's study. All the guards were out searching for Agamemnon's killer. Clytemnestra had run from his room, crying that a man had attacked the king and disappeared back out through the window. The guards had given chase immediately, believing the same killer who had struck down the nobility across Greece had finally turned his attentions to Mycenae.

Helen stopped at the door to Agamemnon's study and glanced around but the hall remained empty. She opened the door and a chill ran over her skin. *Is that you, Agamemnon?* she thought only half-jokingly.

She ignored the cluttered desk, heading straight for the long table under the window where a map was unfurled. Marks had been made along both sides of the Aegean Sea and spread out from there. Agamemnon had been putting his men in place, getting ready to take control.

She rolled up the map. *But not anymore.*

Also sitting on the table sat the box from Troy. Clytemnestra had said that Agamemnon had studied it, looking for the instructions on how to create the Omni. Now Helen pulled the box over to herself, wondering if somehow the instructions had become lost over time.

She ran a hand over the lid. It felt strangely warm.

She was about to open it when her ring finger began to tingle. The stones on the ring's face began to glow—and the box grew even warmer.

Carefully, Helen opened the lid. And there, on the inside of the lid, in a glowing script, were the instructions. *The instructions require the ring bearer.* "I guess you were right, Ajeet," she whispered.

A tingle of recognition ran over her. She closed the box's lid before turning to the doorway. "Hello, Barnabus."

"I can never sneak up on you," he said.

"Not as long as I wear this." Helen held up the ring.

"It is good to see it back on your finger, where it belongs."

Helen's hand felt heavier, but she did not disagree. Clytemnestra had come through for them. Helen had hated letting her come back here, but she had recognized that Clytemnestra had needed to do this, for her own sake—she had needed to help. And Helen knew she herself could not play the hero *every* time. This time it had been Clytemnestra's turn.

Besides, Clytemnestra was right—Helen had needed time to grieve Achilles. And to hold her children again.

Helen looked out the window, where the sun was dropping below the horizon. She slipped her ring off her finger. "Thank you, Barnabus. For all your help."

He tilted his head toward her. "No thanks is necessary."

"Yes, it is. You could have chosen to sit out. Or even to side with Agamemnon. But you chose to help me. I will always be grateful for your friendship."

"And you will always have that friendship. Even if you weren't the ring bearer." He paused. "Have you made any decisions about what Ajeet told you? Will you go after the other sites? Find all of the hiding places for the Omni?"

Helen had been asking herself the same question. They had used the last of Paris's vial to make Agamemnon mortal. And the idea of burying herself in a challenge right now, something that would distract her from her grief and guilt—that would distract her from her *life*—was more than a little appealing. Somewhere out there was a way to make Fallen mortal and to make mortals with the power of the Fallen. It could be an invaluable weapon.

But Samyaza was dead. The threat was gone. And the rest of the Fallen would not band together without their leader. She shook her head. "No."

"Why not?"

"The Omni is too powerful. Yes, it can remove a Fallen's ability, but it can also *grant* abilities. Can you imagine if it were to fall into the wrong hands? No. The immediate crisis has passed. The weapon is not needed, and I won't bring it out into the world."

"Were you able to find the instructions?"

Helen didn't hesitate. The instructions, the temptation to use them, it needed to stay with her. "No. But others exist out there."

"So what is to become of that box?"

She handed it to Barnabus. "I will give it to a friend to hide and not tell me where it is."

"Me? Why?"

"Only I can create the Omni—which means I should not know where the boxes are hidden. I can avoid that temptation today, but one day, perhaps I will be unable to. You will keep me honest. Hide it well, Barnabus."

His hands wrapped around the box. "Yes, my queen."

CHAPTER 120

Helen lived well into old age. She saw her children grow and have children of their own. And she saw her share of sadness. Menelaus stood by her side, and she by his. He passed on years before she did, but her last few years were full of grandchildren and quiet walks. After a lifetime of adventure, she was content.

Hermione had watched her mother and father and knew they loved one another. But she also saw the look in her mother's eye when she thought no one was watching—the look of loss. When Hermione grew old enough, her father had told her all her mother had done during the war to save not only her children, but the world itself. Hermione had been astounded. She had known her mother was strong, she had known she was a hero, but she couldn't help but feel humbled by all her mother accomplished.

Finally her mother's time was at an end. A procession of those she loved came to her to say goodbye, tears dripping down their cheeks. When the procession had passed, there was only Hermione to keep her company.

Hermione was amazed at how fragile her indomitable mother now seemed. Something was ravaging her body from the inside, and there was nothing anyone could do. Hermione gently squeezed her mother's hand, noting the absence of her ring. Two years ago, as her mother's health had begun to fail, Hermione had traveled with her to Egypt to hide the ring. When they arrived in Egypt, her mother had disappeared for four days before reappearing without it. Hermione did not know where it was. A long chapter of her mother's life had closed at that point, and the closing had only hastened her mother's decline.

Helen had now been in and out of consciousness for days, with pain her constant companion. The healer had given her medicine, but all it did was make her sleep. The queen of Sparta deserved more than this. She deserved peace.

Hermione adjusted the blanket over her mother, a tear sliding down her cheek. With a tremor in her voice, she said, "It's all right to go, Mother. You have done enough. It's time for you to rest."

Helen let out a rattling breath. Hermione smoothed back her mother's gray hair. "It's okay. They're all waiting for you—Father, Castor, Pollux, Clytemnestra, Barnabus. It's time to go see them."

Helen smiled, and Hermione knew that she had taken one step over to the other side. "I love you, Mother. Now go."

Her mother whispered something that Hermione could not make out. She leaned closer. "Mother?"

Helen gripped Hermione's hand and gave one last sigh. "Achilles."

CHAPTER 121

HALFWAY BETWEEN PRUDHOE BAY AND BARROW, ALASKA

PRESENT DAY

Laney opened her eyes and sucked in a breath. She still felt the ache of losing her brothers, the pain of losing Achilles, the heartache over the scope of Agamemnon's destruction. But more than anything, she longed to see her children. She could still feel Hermione's hand in hers. All the love, all the anguish of the world's most famous and misunderstood queen—Laney saw it with perfect clarity.

And she knew why she had needed to remember Helen's life. *There's a way to strip the Fallen of their powers. We could actually win.*

But she wondered about the other lessons from Helen's life. The people she had cared about had been used as pawns to control her. Was there a warning there? A message telling her to keep those she loved far from this fight? And how if she wanted to could she even manage that? And who could want that—to live a life without love?

"You're awake."

Laney turned to the man slumped in a chair by the side of the bed, his blue eyes watching her intently. A beard had started to develop along his chiseled jaw, and from the condition of his clothes, she knew he had not left that spot in hours, if not days.

But it was the shock of recognition when she stared into his eyes that threatened to steal her sanity. She felt Achilles's arms around her, saw his still form lying on the bed. Her stomach hollowed out, and tears sprang to her eyes. One rolled down her cheek. "Achilles."

Drake leaned forward and gently wiped the tear away. Never pulling his gaze from hers, he spoke the word that sent her spiraling.

"Yes."

CHAPTER 122

Achilles left to get her a drink of water. Laney shook her head. *No, not Achilles—Drake.* But that wasn't true either. It wasn't one or the other. It was both. *He is both. Just like I'm Helen.*

Laney sat back against the headboard, her knees pulled in to her chest. She thought of Hermione, Castor, Pollux, Barnabus, Menelaus. She ached at their absence. *No. Keep it together.*

Then Drake returned. His eyes were so familiar that it stole her breath. He sat down on the side of the bed and handed her a glass of water. "Are you all right?"

Laney took the glass with shaking hands. "Yes. I think so."

She focused on nothing but the cold water sliding down her throat. She closed her eyes and leaned her head back on the headboard. "How?"

Drake didn't need to ask what she meant. "I had spent thousands of years on earth—both as guardian of the tree and among man. Yet I had never truly lived *as* a human. I wanted to see and feel what you did. I was given one lifetime to do so."

Laney wasn't sure what to say. "Why as Achilles?"

"I don't know. I was placed in that moment in time for a reason. I think because of you."

Laney wasn't ready to go there. "No, I can't—" She flashed on their first meeting in Vegas. "You said we had never met before."

"What should I have said? That in a past lifetime I lived for you? That you were my all? It seemed a bit much when you didn't remember me at all."

She felt the pain of that ignorance. How horrible to have loved someone so deeply—and have them not even remember you. "I'm sorry."

Surprise crossed his face. "No need. It was a long time ago."

Now a new pain joined the other. And she didn't want to take too close a look at it. She took a couple of deep breaths, trying to calm her racing heart. The modern furnishings of the room felt wrong. The snow outside the window felt foreign. She expected dry lands, olive trees, and the sea in the distance. Two worlds were colliding in her head, and the one from the past seemed so much more real than the one she now found herself in.

"It will be all right, Laney. Just give yourself a moment to adjust."

Her heart lurched. "You sent me back there."

"Not exactly. I just sent you into your own mind. I helped you remember who you used to be. What you're capable of."

"It felt real."

"It *was* real—at one point in time. But that was a long time ago."

She wondered if he was trying to tell her something more than the obvious. "You were there. You never mentioned being an archangel."

"I didn't know."

"How is that possible?"

He gave her a small smile. "I had watched humanity from the sidelines for a long time. Yet I didn't truly understand it. You all love and hate with equal passion. You take joy in small things, and yet some have everything and can find nothing to smile about. I wanted to understand. I wanted to experience being human."

"So you were?"

"In a way. I was born. I died. I experienced childhood, adulthood, love. I didn't know my true nature beyond what Pollux and the other Fallen knew. I thought I was like them."

"And when you died?"

"I returned to being the archangel you see before you."

Laney tried to wrap her head around an archangel playing at being human. "Was it worth it? Experiencing humanity?"

"It was the greatest joy and the greatest pain of my long life. The friendships, the sense of belonging, the love—I would trade it for nothing."

The air between them was filled with tension, unasked questions, and unspoken words. Laney felt a tremor running through her. Achilles, *her* Achilles, sat before her. But his recklessness was gone. Even the arrogance of Drake was gone.

She wanted to ask him what he thought of their time together. What he thought of her. But she wasn't sure she was ready for the answer. And besides, there were other matters that needed her attention.

"You remember how to defeat them, don't you?" Drake asked quietly.

"Yes. They can be made mortal. I just need to find where the Omni was hidden."

A shadow crossed Drake's face.

"What is it?"

"Your friends. They've been under siege."

Her present reality snapped to the forefront of her mind. "Are they are all right? What's Samyaza done?"

"Quite a lot."

Something outside the window caught her eye. It was… grass. Though the snow was still there, it had started to melt at the edges. How could that be? When she had fallen asleep, the winter's snow had just begun.

She turned her gaze back to Drake. "Drake, how long have I been out?"

He met her gaze, unblinking. "Six months."

CHAPTER 123

Six months? The words rang in Laney's mind. She had been asleep for six months. Patrick, Henry, Jake, Dom, Danny, Jen—what had happened to them? Oh god, Cleo—what would she think about Laney being gone so long?

"Are they all right? What's happened?"

"I think it would be easier to show you." Drake stood and extended his hand to her.

She placed her hand in his and let him pull her up. He released her as soon as she was steady on her feet, and Laney tried to ignore the feeling of loss at the removal of the warmth of his skin against hers.

He walked into the living room, and Laney was once again shaken by the unfamiliar sights. The TV seemed so futuristic. The phone, the kitchen. She put a hand to her head and swayed.

"Laney?" Drake's arm appeared at her waist, holding her steady.

"I'm okay. Just a little dizzy."

Drake's forehead furrowed in concern, then he swept her into his arms. She gasped, and he winked. "Don't worry, I have that effect on all the girls."

Laney laughed, preferring this old, familiar Drake persona. He was easier to deal with, easier to keep at an arm's length.

He deposited her gently on the couch, but then his head whipped up. A tingle ran over Laney's skin, and she jumped to her feet.

Drake put up his hands. "It's okay. They don't mean you any harm. In fact, I'm pretty sure you'll be pretty happy to see them. He insisted you'd wake up today, so they went to stock up the kitchen."

Laney frowned. "Who?"

But Drake just smiled.

The door opened, and a tall man with long dark hair, carrying two grocery bags, stepped through. But it was the boy that stepped out from behind him that made Laney's heart nearly burst. "Max?"

"Laney!" Max sprinted across the room and flung his arms around her. Laney hugged him tight, tears running down her face. "Max, I've missed you so much."

"I missed you too. So does Mommy."

"Is she here?"

"No," said Maddox, setting down the grocery bags. "If we need to move quickly, it'll be easier if it's just me and Max."

"Is everything all right?" Laney asked. "Did something happen?"

"We're fine," Maddox assured her. "But Max insisted we come."

Laney realized Max had grown a few inches since she'd last seen him. A lump appeared in her throat at the thought of how much of his life she was missing. But she pushed it aside. Because Max was no normal little boy. He could see beyond what most people could see.

"What's going on, Max?"

The boyish enthusiasm on Max's little face was replaced by a serious look, showing the old soul that lived beneath his skin. "You can't go looking for the weapon. Not yet."

Laney looked to Drake, who shook his head. "I didn't tell him anything. They just showed up a few days ago and insisted they stay until you woke up. We'll let you guys talk."

Maddox and Drake walked into the kitchen and started unpacking the groceries.

Laney focused on Max. "Okay, so tell me what's going on."

"Life's changing, Laney. You have two paths, and you need to take both of them. But you can't. You have to choose."

"Max, the weapon—it can help us defeat the Fallen once and for all. It can remove their powers."

"I know. But it's not important. Not right now."

"Why not?"

"Because you need to help Victoria."

Laney went still. "Honey, Victoria's gone. She died."

"She's never gone. You know that, Laney. She's back, and she's in trouble. And you need to help her—help all of them. Before it's too late."

∽

DELANEY MCPHEARSON's journey continues in The Belial Plan. Now available on Amazon

FACT OR FICTION?

Thank you for reading *The Belial Warrior*. I hoped you enjoyed it. I enjoyed writing it. I first started thinking about writing Helen of Sparta's story back when I was first figuring out *The Belial Library*. But I wasn't sure how exactly to make it happen or when. I didn't want to just tell Helen's story. It had to somehow relate to the modern plight of Laney and her friends.

Once we put Laney through hell in *The Belial Guard*, I knew it was time. So I decided to get started and see where we ended up. And I have to admit it has been fun!

So what's fact and what's fiction in *The Belial Warrior*? That's a little tough. For this novel, it was more a matter of what is consistent with Homer and other individuals writing about the Trojan War. It must be kept in mind, of course, that as Uncle Patrick explained, Homer wrote *The Iliad* at least five hundred years after the Trojan War allegedly took place. So that's what I had in mind when I was developing the story line—how stories tend to change over time depending on who's doing the telling. So here we go!

Geography. Most of the smaller Greek town names mentioned in *The Belial Warrior* are fictional. For the sake of understanding, the modern names of countries and some cities were used. This was done to allow the reader an easier time in understanding where scenes were taking place. But at the time of the Trojan War, there is debate amongst scholars as to whether there was any sort of country level identification.

The Trojan War. For hundreds of years, the Trojan War was believed to be a work of fiction. And then the city of Troy was found opening the door to the possibility that perhaps the war had indeed occurred. But it is still a matter of debate. Another matter of debate is when the Trojan War occurred. Most say the Bronze Age although that extends any where from 3000 BC to 700 BC. I chose to begin our story in 1450 BC in part due to a volcano that was said to have destroyed Crete in 1550 BC and would have therefore made it rather too difficult to have Helen and Barnabus visit Crete. But also because we know the ruins of Troy existed at that point.

Crete and the Minotaur. The minotaur was also written off as another fable from ancient times and then of course, a maze was found on the island of Crete. In fact, the symbol of the maze was found throughout the ancient world. King Minos of Crete was alleged to have sacrificed seven boys and seven girls to the minotaur every nine years. As to how the children were chosen, I do not know.

The Characters. Almost all of the characters were taken from *The Iliad* and are true to how Homer described them. A few characters such as Barnabus were added. Anyone who has read *The Iliad* knows that it is rather long with dozens of characters. Obviously, I could not include all of the characters. But many did make some cameos, although I changed the origin story of many. According to *The Iliad*, Orestes was the son of Agamemnon and Clytemnestra. He would later go on to marry Hermione. Aegisthus was the lover of Clytemnestra who later helps her kill Agamemnon in his bathtub. And Theseus is the individual who was believed to have killed the minotaur.

Clytemnestra and Iphigenia. I hated writing Iphigenia's death scene. I sobbed through it. Honestly every time I read it, I feel a catch at the back of my throat and I have to take some breaths. But it was in *The Iliad* and in *The Belial Warrior* it is the catalyst for getting Clytemnestra involved.

The idea of Helen being replaced by Clytemnestra was also taken from other works on Helen of Troy. According to the play by Euripides, Helen was replaced by Hera and Aphrodite by a lookalike while she spent the war in Egypt.

Two Sets of Twins. The siblings of Helen, Clytemnestra, Pollux and Castor are interesting to say the least. Depending upon whom you read, each was a set of twins, although they were also said to have had different fathers. Helen and Pollux were alleged by some to be the offspring of Zeus while Castor and Clytemnestra were said to be the children of Tyndareus. Some even suggest the four siblings were quadruplets. While the exact genetic nature of the siblings remains in doubt, Pollux's extraordinary skills do not. All agree he was gifted.

Dwarka. Dwarka is a city in India. But for centuries, the people of the area spoke of the legendary city of Dwarka which sank beneath the waters eons ago. Western historians wrote the tales off as the imaginings of a simple people. And then as is often the case it seems, remnants from the fabled city of Dwarka were found in the Bay of Cambay, exactly where the ancient tales said the incredible city had once existed.

Achilles and Helen. The idea of Achilles and Helen being romantically involved was not my original creation. Pausanias a Greek geographer from the second century AD maintained that Achilles and Helen were married in the afterlife.

Connections between the Main Characters. As mentioned in *The Belial Warrior*, Agamemnon and Menelaus did come to live for a short while in Sparta while Helen was younger. Tyndareus in turn helped Agamemnon regain his throne.

The Discovery of Troy. Troy was discovered by Heinrich Schliemann in 1870. But as explained by Father Patrick, Frank Calvert

FACT OR FICTION?

actually discovered Troy prior to Schliemann although Schliemann never gave him any credit.

Timing. As mentioned, Homer's tale was written at least five hundred years after the war allegedly was fought. That being the case, I think if it did happen, like in a game of telephone, some things were exaggerated such as the length of the war. According to Homer, the war lasted ten long years. Yet, during the Bronze Age the average lifespan was only about thirty years. Which meant, the Trojan War would have lasted a full third of someone's life. For this reason, I shortened the duration of the war considerably.

Helen of Troy. Helen has received a great deal of attention through time. She has become the consummate example of a feckless woman acting without thinking of the consequences of her behavior or worse as a woman who took joy in the destruction her actions brought to others. Yet, at the same time, Helen was revered for hundreds of years throughout Greece. There were cults dedicated to Helen.

The problem of course is that the men tended to be the ones who wrote about Helen—men who never met her and were writing in a time when independent women were viewed with the same appreciation as a rabid wolf. So the quotes on Helen at the beginning of the book, are not reflections of Helen so much as reflections of the writers view of women.

But those types of commentary have of course helped shape the view until all she has become known as is the face that launched a thousand ships. No mention is made of her being the Queen of Sparta, a kingdom known for the strength of its fighters and the women who ruled it. No mention is made of the cults of warrior women dedicated to her throughout Greece. No, according to the modern take, Helen is merely a flighty woman who took up with a man who was not her husband and sent the world to war.

Whatever Helen's true story is, I do not think it is what Homer has suggested. I think there was much more to the queen of Sparta.

So now, the question is where do we go from here? Or perhaps, better yet, what has everyone else been up to while Laney relived her life as Helen. *The Belial Plan*, out this Winter, will tell the tale of Henry, Jake, Patrick, and Jen while Laney slept. But have no fear, Laney and Drake will be part of the story as well.

If you are interested in reading a sneak peek of *The Belial Plan*, keep reading.

ABOUT THE AUTHOR

R.D. Brady is an American writer who grew up on Long Island, NY but has made her home in both the South and Midwest before settling in upstate New York. On her way to becoming a full-time writer, R.D. received a Ph.D. in Criminology and taught for ten years at a small liberal arts college.

R.D. left the glamorous life of grading papers behind in 2013 with the publication of her first novel, the supernatural action adventure, *The Belial Stone*. Over ten novels later and hundreds of thousands of books sold, and she hasn't looked back. Her novels tap into her criminological background, her years spent studying martial arts, and the unexplained aspects of our history. Join her on her next adventure!

To learn about her upcoming publications, sign up for her newsletter here or her website (rdbradybooks.com).

BOOKS BY R.D. BRADY

The Belial Series (in order)
The Belial Stone
The Belial Library
The Belial Ring
Recruit: A Belial Series Novella
The Belial Children
The Belial Origins
The Belial Search
The Belial Guard
The Belial Warrior
The Belial Plan
The Belial Witches
The Belial War
The Belial Fall
The Belial Sacrifice

Stand-Alone Books
Runs Deep
Hominid

The A.L.I.V.E. Series
B.E.G.I.N.
A.L.I.V.E.
D.E.A.D.

The Unwelcome Series

Protect

Seek

Proxy

Be sure to sign up for R.D.'s mailing list to be the first to hear when she has a new release!

Printed in Great Britain
by Amazon